Gods
of
the Katar

Tobin Loshento

New Libri Press

This is a work of fiction. Nothing is in it that has not been imagined.

Copyright © 2015 by Tobin Loshento

Cover Art by Arron McArthur,
Cover Copyright © 2015 by New Libri Press

ISBN: 978-1-61469-051-1

Published in 2015 by New Libri Press
Seattle, WA 98103
www.newlibri.com

New Libri Press is a small independent press dedicated to publishing new authors and independent authors in both eBook and traditional formats.

Gods
of
the Katar

To my mother, an artist, who died recently.
One doesn't do art for money, one does it because
you have to..

Acknowledgments

As always I would like to acknowledge the patient family, my friend Michael for helping edit and pushing this out the door, and my writing group for putting up with random chapters over the years.

Chapter 1

Tyna wiped her forehead with her bare arm and glanced skyward. The two spring moons of Nakana were nearing the northern horizon, making it near midday. It was hot for this time of year. She tugged on the reigns, slowing the wagon. She was using Mara, the old draft mare, because they were low on horses. Between donating horses for the war and the workers using the remaining few for rounding up the winter cattle, they were in desperate need. Years before the war—before father died—they had let a small herd go wild on the ranch. "Nakana needs more wild horses," her father had said. "We'll let these go wild as an investment in the future."

She scanned the rolling hills. There, almost hidden by a dip in the hills and the tall grass, a stallion and five mares. No foals. Too bad, but not unexpected. Horses bred slowly on Nakana. Some said they were not native.

Lerence, almost asleep next to her, lifted his head and looked vacantly around. She regretted, again, that her step-brother had come along. She nudged him.

"Lerence," she said softly, "wake up. We found some."

"What?" he almost shouted. The stallion in the distance lifted his head, then reared to look around.

"Quiet, you idiot." Tyna clapped her hand over his mouth.

Lerence looked guilty, but stood to get a better view. In the process his foot hit the backboard and the old mare jump forward. Tyna's hands tightened on the reins and her mouth tightened into a straight line.

She knew that it was unfair to compare Lerence to their father, Cram. Cram Valence had taken his father's humble beginnings and built a huge, profitable, ranch covering an area that took two days of riding to cross. On the far northwestern Muglanth plains it was literally on the edge of civilization. In her mind there was nothing that Cram could not do. Or could have done. Tyna wiped her eyes with her left hand, tied the reins and set the wagon's brake.

She motioned that they proceed on foot. Lerence nodded and jumped down, again startling the mare. Tyna rolled her eyes and smoothly got down on her side.

"I wish we were mounted, instead of trying to do this on foot," she said.

"Why don't I unhitch Mara and ride her. Maybe drive them toward you."

Tyna hesitated. It wasn't a terrible idea. But, it was Lerence's idea.

"No, she's ok with a wagon, but she gets lame if she runs. We can't risk it."

Lerence nodded and reached in the back for rope, handing her one hank and keeping one for himself. She quickly inspected hers, loosened the tie that kept it from tangling. She formed a loop through the hondo and gave it a light twirl. The rope wasn't quite stiff enough, but it would have to do. She glanced at Lerence, who had managed to tangle his rope rather than prep the loop. She sighed, something she had been doing a lot of lately.

Tyna was a fair horsewoman, but this was her first time trying to catch wild horses. By the Sea, she wasn't going to let Lerence screw this up. They needed these horses. The ranch needed them. Not letting Lerence take the initiative, she led the way.

They approached the herd at an angle. The big bay stallion watched their every move, but didn't bolt. They got within fifty feet. The bay bent his head to graze, almost in disdain, but his ears stayed rotated in their direction. Tyna saw Lerence loosen his rope. Fool, was he going to try to throw this far? She tried to signal him to wait, but was afraid to be too noisy or move too fast. Lerence either didn't see her gestures, or ignored her. Grinning, he ran forward, swinging the big loop.

The horses bolted. What was unexpected was that they bolted *toward* Tyna and Lerence. She stood tall and waved her arms and yelling. The five mares veered to the left and galloped away, but the stallion kept coming. Lerence threw the rope and missed. The stallion laid his ears back, rolled his eyes into the back of his head, and charged Lerence with a whinny that sounded more like a battle cry than a frightened horse. Tyna could see its eyes rolled back and ears flat against its head. It chose Lerence.

Lerence dove to the side, rolled and tried to get back up. The horse spun and kicked back. The stallion's hooves connected with Lerence's head, making a sickening sound, like that of dogs crunching through turkey bones. She screamed. She bent down, picked up a fist sized rock, and threw it at the bay. It bounced off its shoulder.

The stallion rolled his mad eyes and wheeled toward her. She waved her coils of rope and screamed in anger. He snorted, let out a whinny and rotated his ears toward the sound of the mares running off. Tyna bent again and with a buck he ran off after the other horses.

Tyna let out a shuddering breath and realized she had to pee. Instead, she knelt by Lerence, not moving his head, but feeling for the damage. There was blood everywhere and to her fingers the skull near the base of the neck felt soft.

"Lerence?"

She was shaking her head back and forth as she stood and backed up a step. She thought of her father. What would her mother say? She forced herself back to a kneeling position next to him. She listened to his chest. Nothing.

Fighting the need to scream, she opened his mouth and checked for a clear airway. Years ago, father had forced everyone to learn Sorin's heart massage from the healers in town. "Not all miracles take a god, or a talisman," he'd told them. "Learn what they teach you and you might someday bring the dead back to life."

She breathed into his mouth, holding his nose closed, and then pushed on his chest rapidly. Ten times? Or was it fifteen? Those lessons had been so long ago.

Then two breaths.

No pulse.

Repeat.

Repeat.

Repeat.

She couldn't move any more. Her arms and hands were numb. How long had it been? She glanced at the moons and the sun. Another moon rising! She had been trying for over an hour. No miracle. No dead returning back to life. She summoned one last burst of strength and pounded on Lerence's chest with both her fists, sobbing.

"You bastard. How could you? The horse was too far. I hope your *ka* is lost in the River of Death." She stopped. What was she saying? That was a terrible curse. Such a thing would mean true death.

"Oh, Lerence. I didn't mean it."

She hesitated. She, like many who lived away from The Cities, didn't really pray to the gods. She didn't even have a prayer rod. Why give up part of your own *ka* to gods that rarely responded? But this was family. At least she should take back the curse.

"Pé, if you answer prayers, guide my brother's soul to the Sea of Souls."

She crumpled over onto Lerence's body and gave in to the hysteria that had been waiting patiently for an hour. As her sobbing subsided she sat up and banged his chest again in anger.

Lerence moaned.

* * *

He opened his eyes and stared unblinking at the woman bent over him. She was familiar: a strong face, not what some would call beautiful, but all would call attractive. She was maybe twenty-five. A worried wrinkle on her brow marred the almost sculpted visage. Her eyes were puffy. She ignored the strands of dark blood red hair falling over her green eyes and smiled at his gaze. The smile transformed her from simply attractive to a radiant splendor.

He smiled back.

"Lerence! I was terrified. That horse. I think you have a brain injury. A … concussion. That's what the healers call it. Lay back and wait. Recover a bit." She had her hand on his chest and tears were running down her face as she smiled and cried simultaneously.

His sister. Tyna. Why had it taken him so long to recognize her?

"A horse? No horse has ever gotten the better of me."

Tyna looked at him strangely, the furrow deepened, and she patted his chest gently and reassuringly. Dark skin. Coffee with milk color. They must be in the northern part of the Muglanth Plains. Northerners had dark skin. He held up his own hand. Deep brown, almost as dark as hers. Why did he have to puzzle this out? Things that he should not even have to think about were buried deep in his memory. Maybe he did have a concussion. Loss of memory was a symptom, wasn't it? Yet, his head didn't hurt. Nothing hurt. He felt great.

"You stay there and rest a moment. I'll get some water and then we'll see if you can stand."

She stood. He admired her legs, visible due to the shorts she was wearing. Combined with her height, they seemed even more exposed. She was over six feet. Her hair draped over her back, loosely tied, as if a barely restrained animal were dangling its bushy tail back there. Strange that she wasn't married yet. When she was out of sight, he sat up and rubbed his head. Sticky. He looked at the drying thick blood on his hands. He must have been out for a while. Not even slightly sore though. He was not surprised, but gradually some small part of him realized he should be.

He stood cautiously. No dizziness. Everything was fine. He reached back over his shoulder for his sword. Nothing. Oh, he didn't wear a sword. He glanced at his left hand. Bare. No rings. Why was that important? He rubbed his head some more, the drying blood drifting to the ground in a flurry of dark flakes.

He wished for a mirror. We generally don't have an accurate picture of ourselves. How often does one memorize the reflection in a mirror? He rubbed his face, trying to recall his own image. Nothing. It troubled him, both that he couldn't remember and that he had this strong desire to know what he looked like.

Where was he? He looked for the omnipresent mountain range, the Web of the Gods. There. The massive mountain range was behind him. Near. That must be east. A sense of security washed over him. At least that felt right.

He stretched and felt the tightness in his muscles. Muscles that were unused to work, yet didn't feel sore. He sat down and began a routine to loosen his muscles.

Tyna returned and looked at him in dismay. *That furrow was going to become permanent*, he mused.

"I told you to rest. You could have a serious brain injury, or worse."

"What could be worse, death?" He chuckled.

She knelt down next to him as he sat there with his head over his right knee, relaxing his back. He gazed at her in silence for a moment, digesting a stream of memories that came at him only by concentrating.

It was all familiar in an abstract way. Tyna, this light hill nestled amongst a sea of other mild hills, why he was out here—to round up horses—yet it seemed strange. Not peculiar in that it was out of place, but as if he were reading about it in a book. Distant. He had to think, to look it up as if in a dusty tome, to remember his own name, even after hearing it. Lerence.

Concussion. Despite feeling fine, it must be that.

He was Tyna's older brother. Brother, not husband. Step-brother. Not lover; a sense of sadness at that, as if he'd just discovered that she wasn't available. Why did he have to think so hard to remember? He rubbed his head again and licked his lips. Some Hrýll brandy would help.

Staying seated he stopped stretching and looked around a second time. If he drank in the surroundings often enough, maybe it would begin to feel right.

Rolling hills dotted with huge oaks spreading their umbrellas of branches and new leaves. A light breeze rippled the sea of grass, still green from spring rains. The wind shifted and cool current from the mountains washed over them. Lerence shivered, but did not feel cold.

She wiped the back of his head with a corner of her shirt dipped in water from the canteen filled from the nearby stream, her firm stomach visible as she pulled up the corner to reach his head.

"Don't move." She parted his hair and examined his scalp.

"How?" She gradually pressed harder on his scalp, searching almost franticly for something.

"What?" he asked.

"I can't find the wound. Your hair is soaked in blood, most of it dry now, but I can't find the cut. No swelling either."

"It must have been less serious than it seemed. Sometimes minor scalp wounds bleed a lot. There are all those surface blood vessels."

"No, I was scared. By the Sea, Ler, I felt broken bones, I swear it. You were out for over an hour. I even thought you'd stopped breathing at one point. I tried pumping your chest and breathing into your mouth, as the healers from town taught us." She paused, embarrassed at the way she was rambling. "I even prayed to Pé that your soul would be allowed into the Sea of Souls," she murmured as she probed once more.

Lerence was silent. The latter reference caused strange images to cross his mind. A battle? No. Not just one battle. The name Pé evoked memories, but no face. Battles, he remembered, many battles. Pé, she'd said. The Soul God?

Prayer? No, she should not be praying. Dangerous. Why? He couldn't remember, but prayer to the gods was dangerous. He shook his head to clear it, then rubbed it. Tyna must have panicked. She didn't look like the panicky type, but the sight of blood can sometimes distract even the best.

"Let's get back to the house. Mom must be worried about what's taking so long," he said, rubbing his head.

Worry about Pé and gods later.

Tyna nodded and helped him to his feet. He smelled the perspiration on her mixed with light spice. *If she wasn't my sister....* He smiled at the inappropriate thought. She would laugh, probably hitting him for even thinking it. He couldn't remember ever having such feelings before, but he was having trouble remembering anything.

The horse, who had caused all this, placidly chewed on grass nearby. During the hour he had decided that there was no real danger from these two. The five mares were nowhere to be seen. It was as if the bay were saying, "We have unfinished business, you and I."

"He's just a young stallion, full of ego and fight. Just needs to be talked to, learn a few manners. Learn I'm not trying to hurt him," Lerence said.

Tyna's eyes widened.

"He tried to kill you, Ler. It's a wild animal. We are in over our heads with a huge horse like that. I should have seen it before."

"He reminds me of Maurgen," Lerence said.

Tyna tilted her head. He could see she was reassessing the whole concussion. She was worried he was losing it. He rubbed his head. Was he?

He looked again at the rolling hills of the family ranch that stretched for marks in all directions. The occasional tree and line of bushes marked the year round creek that flowed through their land. It felt like a dream. Maybe a drink would clear his head. Something with its own kick, he smiled to himself. He closed his eyes and swallowed, almost tasting the smoky bite of that Hrýll brandy.

He opened his eyes and refocused on the horse. They needed horses. They needed this one. If the horse bolted now, there was no stopping it. It might go for marks without stopping.

"I'll get him."

"No, you're nuts. You were never good with horses Ler, I should have never let you try the first time. I still can't believe you are alive, let alone fit. You aren't. You're in shock or something. No, let's get home and wait for some of the hands to get back. We'll try again then."

Never good with horses? That felt wrong. Very wrong. No specific memories, but he felt that he had a special connection to horses. Yet, Tyna was telling him he was never good around them. When he thought carefully about it, he could not disagree. Lerence was lousy when it came to horses. He was thinking of himself in the third person. Closer to the surface was a memory of a herd so large it turned the plains into a dark roiling mass, with him riding a black stallion in the lead. That felt right, but it was no memory of his. Of Lerence's? No. A story perhaps.

"No. I need to."

Something in the tone of his voice convinced her to cease protesting. The furrow in her brow was now broken by a raised eyebrow and a look of fear. She watched him, head cocked, her own rope ready, as he approached the horse.

Lerence started talking to the horse in a low voice and approached it from an angle. He kept his head low, without meeting its gaze, and kept talking. Soon he was next to the horse and rubbing its chin. Lerence slipped the rope over the stallion's neck and it raised its head in protest, but a few more words and it lowered its head and allowed Lerence to tie a second loop around its nose, forming a field halter. With his left hand he grabbed a handful of mane, his right rested on its back. In one fluid motion he was on top of the horse. It jumped slightly in surprise, but quieted down soon as he spoke to it some more. He rode back to Tyna.

She was looking at him with mouth agape. Her furrow was completely gone. She really was beautiful.

"What?" he asked.

"What language were you using to talk to the horse?"

"What do you mean?"

"I heard some of what you were saying and it was not common tongue, nor Zethician. What was it?"

"The wind must have garbled it."

"Well, then explain how you got on the horse."

"You saw me. I mounted by the mane and a small leap."

"That horse has never been ridden and not long ago cracked your head. Now you are riding it like a tame draft horse."

Lerence grinned. "I guess the kick calmed him down. Want a ride?" He held out his arm for her.

She shook her head. Narrowed eyes looked at both him and the horse.

"Not a chance. I'll walk along beside you until we get to the wagon."

The spring grass had the smell of freshness. New. Reborn from the roots of the old grass. Rich earthy scents mixed with the smell of life. No other farms or ranches within sight. *That's because the nearest one is many marks away. Why didn't I remember? I had to think about it.* He stroked the bay and thought of horses. Horses were hard to raise on Nakana. Legend had it that horses came from one of the other planes, but which one no one knew. Not that it mattered, no one knew how to travel from one plane to another, except maybe the gods. Lerence felt a wave of … anger? Why did he feel anger toward the gods? The stallion hesitated, sensing Lerence's mood. He patted it on the neck and muttered something without thinking. Tyna looked up at him, the furrow was back.

The knowledge of horses flowed more easily than his other memories. He rubbed his face. Horses were more like the other races, such as the old ones. Low fertility, but long lived. As they walked and rode, Tyna kept looking at Lerence as if he were mad. Finally, growing tired of her stare he turned to her.

"I am going to ride up ahead and scout around."

"Scout around? For what? There are no dui mar here."

Dui mar, the death cats. No, they would not bother him.

"Oh, just in case," he smiled at her, hoping to remove that frown.

He nudged the horse with his knees, not bothering to touch the rope reins of the field halter-bridle combination. The horse responded as if reading his mind with a smooth canter.

Tyna stopped and watched as her brother floated, one with the horse, over the hill. Fists resting on hips, she gazed until he was out of sight.

Chapter 2

"I'm telling you, Mother, he rode the horse as if he were one of the Tarin show cavalry," Tyna said.

"Nonsense, your brother is a terrible horseman. I don't know why you let him ride at all. You must've been too worried about his head and then too relieved that he was alright. You need to protect your brother, he is not as skilled as you are … in many things. Finish up in the quarters and come in and help with dinner."

Despite being six inches shorter than Tyna, Sera Valence pushed her daughter out the door as if she were a small child. Sera didn't have the fiery red hair of her daughter, but she had some of the same strength of will.

Tyna stomped out of the main house. Dinner would be a large affair today as the hands came in from the work in the distant fields. She would have to deal with twenty hungry men and women who had been working hard and sleeping in tents for ten days. She went to the worker's building and made sure that the beds were made and that the linens were stacked. There were two houses for the workers, but since the Tarth War one of them stood empty. Each was almost as large as the main house and housed twenty. The broad porch overhand extended on all sides, providing shelter from the rains and the sun. The ranch was isolated, so each of the two bunk houses was quite self-sufficient, with ten bedrooms, a sitting room, and two showers and two toilets. There was even a small kitchen in each, but generally everyone ate at the main house. Tyna frowned at the unused building. The shortage of hands was putting a strain on everyone. She hoped they would be able to hire more, soon. It would be nice to open up the second house, which was beginning to have that abandoned look. The benign neglect of the unused.

She checked the water flow in the sinks and the toilets. After ten days they sometimes clogged with debris from the stream diversion that was the source of water. The old pipes and fixtures were her grandfather's design, and, while ingenious, they were suffering from age.

Since dad had died they were hard to manage. Father had managed with a strong, but fair, hand; which the workers had learned to respect. Lerence hadn't filled Father's shoes well. He had always been quiet and introverted. A bit of a bumbler. The pressures of trying to take over for Father this year had been a strain on them all.

Trying to capture and break that horse was something dad would have done. Lerence had been trying to prove he could step into his father's shoes. Tyna was sure he could never do that, but he tried. She'd been tempted to step in and take over more of the duties of running the farm, but couldn't bear to crush her brother's attempts. He was the eldest. Mother wanted him to succeed so desperately. Mom was sure that Tyna would get married and move away soon, so she pushed Lerence. Tyna was in no rush for marriage but didn't argue the point. The first priority right now was the ranch.

The rumbling of wagons, the whinny of horses, and the boisterous sound of voices approached. Stepping outside into the evening sun she squinted at the small caravan of workers approaching. There was one large wagon, with three passengers, another smaller wagon with one passenger and equipment and sixteen men on horseback. She waved at them. Before turning to go back to the main house, she called out, "Dinner in half an hour." They waved back and the chorus of enthusiastic voices told her that mom had better have plenty of food on hand. Saan, the de facto leader of the hands and self-appointed suitor broke out from the group and rode up.

"I'm glad to see you, Tyna. I was worried you might be in town," Saan said, his eyes running over her from top to bottom and then back again. She did her best to smile. He was a good hand, but that was about all he was good at.

Tyna served wine with the meal. It was a reward for the group's hard work. Since the war, wine was scarce. She was about to walk on past Lerence when he stopped her.

"Pour me a glass too, Tyna."

She looked at him in astonishment. He didn't drink. Never had. Their mom looked up from the other end of the table where she was serving corn and bread. She locked eyes momentarily with Tyna and then shrugged and nodded.

Tyna poured Ler a full glass, just as she had everyone else. Only as she was leaning over him to pour did she realize that he had called her Tyna. He always called her 'Sis.' With a start she realized she had stayed near him after pouring, staring at him and smiling. She hurried on to the next in line.

Saan, sitting next to Lerence, jabbed an elbow into his ribs. "Finally trying to be a man, eh Ler? It'll take more than a glass of wine to do that." He laughed a little too loudly, along with a few of the others. A few looked a bit uncomfortable, while the rest did their best to simply ignore the jibe, pointedly eating their food.

Tyna was about to jump to her brother's defense, when Lerence replied in laugh that held no mirth and to her ears sounded dangerous. But, Ler was never dangerous.

"Oh that wasn't my goal. My goal was to kill the stench of you sitting next to me."

He then tilted his head back and drained the glass and held it up for Tyna to fill again. He never took his eyes off of Saan. Saan was taken aback. Tyna stayed where she was, watching them both. What had come over Lerence? Saan was the meanest of the group. Dad had almost fired him twice for starting fights and injuring several of the workers.

"Leave him be Saan." Her mother shook a spoon at him from the other end of the table.

Saan couldn't let it be. He could never let anything be. He had to be the toughest of the group. He wanted to take over for dad and resented Lerence. This was the excuse he had been waiting for. He pushed back from the table, stood up, and lifted his arm.

"I think you just haven't had a good enough sniff, Ler. Let me help you."

He reached to grab Lerence's head.

No one at the table was quite sure what happened next. Tyna thought she saw her brother grab Saan's hand, twist it behind his back, force him to the ground and kick the bent arm sharply. She thought that's what happened. All she was sure of was that Saan was on the ground crying in pain with a broken arm and Ler was holding out his wine glass.

"Mind refilling this, Tyna?"

The silence of the group was loud. Tyna's hand trembled as she filled Lerence's glass. She stared deeply into his eyes and saw fear there. Not fear of Saan, but fear over what he had done. Where had he learned that? Father had been tough and large. It was where she got her size from. But, Dad had been a purely physical force. The men had respected him as they respected a tornado. There was no respect in their eyes now, but fear and confusion. Things were out of their natural order. Mom broke the silence.

"Noran, you know the most about medicine. Set his arm and take him to the bunkhouse. When he is able, we'll send him on his way."

"No. He can stay. He was just unwinding after a hard week. I overreacted." Lerence finished off his second glass of wine quickly and then turned and bent over Saan. Quickly, before Saan could protest, he set the arm; the crack made Tyna wince in sympathy. To Saan's credit, he did not pass out.

"Tie it lightly to a board. Don't cut off the blood supply, but keep it immobile."

With that, he strode out of the dining room and upstairs to his own room.

* * *

Tyna and her mother, Sera, sat in the living room by the small spring fire in the fireplace. Not that it was cold enough to need it, but with the windows were open and the light breeze it was cool enough to fight off the heat of the fire that they both enjoyed. Tyna spoke first.

"Something happened after the horse kicked him."

"It makes no sense. A blow like that should have made him weak and confused. He was more in control than I've ever seen him. Not even Cam could move that fast," Sera said.

Tyna thought she heard a note of pride in her mother's voice, but, looking quickly at her, she didn't see any expression on her mom's face.

"We can't afford to lose Saan right now," Tyna said. "Not with so many lost against the Tarth war and now the raids from the remaining band are causing many to go to Zethicia and join the army to help," Tyna said. Men joining a standing army, Zethicia's first. It was getting harder and harder to find help.

Her mother's face twisted in rage as she spit.

"We need to wipe the Tarth off the face of Nakana. They are daemons who deserve true death."

Tyna understood her mother's anger. Hatred. It coursed through her again at the reminder of how he'd died. Thousands died in Zethicia's Folly. Even hundreds of Katar from The Cities had died. It was hard to fathom hundreds of Katar in one place and even harder to imagine a force strong enough to kill them. How could the general have sent them against such daemons? She blamed that general, Barnus Dartia, as much as the Tarth. It was he who had ordered the attack. A test of the Tarth strength. Suicide.

No remains had been returned to the family. They later learned that the remains were too gruesome to return to most families. Thank the gods that the main Tarth force had once again been banished to some distant and hopefully destructive plane. The Katar claimed that they had been banished even further than 'Hell.' Yet, rumors were that the rebels and a young thief had been instrumental in the banishment. Some said the Katar had nothing to do with it. If so, Tyna thanked that thief, as she had a hundred times over the past year. As many in Tarin did, preferring to think a thief had saved them rather than the Katar.

A thief born on the eclipse of the five moons. Even in Tarin the priesthoods had been buzzing with it. The eclipse occurred only once in ten thousand years. Still other than the rarity, no one thought much of a child born on that day. But afterwards, over the years, all the children born that year had mysteriously died, many of them violently. Almost all of them. This made the thief's birth date part of the legend. Tyna wasn't sure if she believed it, but she liked it.

The Katar had immediately abandoned Zethicia to return to The Cities to put down a rebellion that had flowered during the war. Thus, Zethicia maintained a standing army for the first time in millennia. Mother forbade Lerence from joining up, not that he was so inclined.

Tyna shook herself out of her reverie faster than her mother.

"I should go and talk to him. Something is wrong and maybe he'll talk to me."

Her mother agreed.

"Bring some wine with you. It would seem he has acquired a taste for it." She smiled a tight smile.

Tyna brought a bottle and two glasses with her. She hesitated in front of Lerence's door, gave it a short knock and entered. Lerence had never minded her barging in, but today a knock seemed prudent.

Lerence paused from his pacing and his face lit up on seeing Tyna. Or, was it the wine? Tyna smiled and sat on the side of the bed.

"How are you feeling?"

"Better, now that you're here."

"Where did you learn how to do that to Saan?"

"By Nu Arr's damned luck, I have no idea."

She winced at the slur. The God of Luck wasn't one to be trifled with. A curse by him, or his priesthood was often considered worse than death. Lerence wasn't given to cursing.

Lerence laughed. "Don't worry Teen, they really can't hear everything you say."

"That is not what you would have thought yesterday."

"Really? Yet, I know it to be true. I am not sure why, but I know it."

He sat down next to her on the bed. If it had not been Lerence, she would have sworn he was looking at her breasts and her legs. She poured wine into both glasses, handing one to him.

"Don't drink it too quickly; I only brought the one bottle."

Lerence smiled and sipped the wine. "Not bad. We should smoke some Hrýll nart weed in the barrels. It gives it a better flavor over time."

How would he know that? He knew nothing about wine making. Much as she loved her brother, she knew he was generally useless around the ranch.

"Lerence, something happened when you were kicked by the horse."

Lerence nodded.

"I know. I have these strange feelings; almost memories." He laughed. "I thought a blow to the head was supposed to cause amnesia, not cause *extra* memories."

"What memories? Wine making? What else?"

"Almost muscle memories. Instinctive stuff. The horseback riding. The fighting with Saan. My hand has been twitching all evening. I would swear I'm used to having a weapon nearby, ready to grasp."

"Anything else?"

"No."

He looked away. She thought there was the slightest flush in his face. Not sure why, she felt embarrassed herself. They both sipped their wine in silence. Tyna got up to leave, leaving the wine bottle behind. At the door she turned back to her brother.

"I'm not sure I like this sudden change, Lerence, nor I suspect do the workers. Yet, I'm not sure I dislike it either."

She closed the door behind her, but stood in the hallway for a moment. She considered returning and trying to talk to Ler some more, but felt that flush of embarrassment again. Soon, the sound of pacing could be heard from her brother's room and she left, pushing a loose strand of hair out of her eyes.

* * *

It was traditional for the head of the house to go into town for trading. After Lerence sold the last batch of livestock for less than half their worth four months back, Tyna began accompanying him. This time there were five horses they were selling, a year's wages for all of the workers if they got a good price. With the winter wheat harvest from the northern fields the ranch would have a profit for the first time since Father died. Tyna and Lerence rode in the lead wagon, with the best wheat and the five horses, while ten other wagons followed with the rest of the wheat. Saan, due to his broken arm, had stayed at the ranch. It had been three days since the dinner incident.

One incident since then stood out in her mind. She had been leaning over an almost empty feed barrel, filling a bucket for the chickens. Standing back up she saw Lerence across the yard staring at her, with bulge in his pants. She turned away blushing and when she glanced back he was walking briskly in the opposite direction.

She was not stupid or foolishly modest. She knew that despite her height she was a striking woman. Dark skinned as most northerners were, she had a red hair that many found enticing because it was so rare in the warm north. Her breasts were large, but not extremely so. She was lean and strong from ranch work. Her green almond-shaped eyes received many compliments. She'd had several offers of marriage, but none of the men lived up to her standards that included intelligence, strength and she reluctantly admitted a version of her father. Sex, on the other hand, was something she indulged in occasionally, sometimes with those same men who offered marriage. Her mother, not naive, had shown Tyna how to control her body to prevent pregnancy since she was twelve. Some women worried this needlessly drained *ka*, but most felt it was such a small amount that it was worth it. Still, even casual encounters were hard to come by out here. The visits to town, or the gathering of several ranchers for a party were too infrequent.

All this came to mind as she watched Lerence walk away. Would he satisfy his urges with Broanna, the young field hand who was the only woman working for them to ever turn back Saan's advances? She felt a strange stab of jealously, which disturbed her as much as the thought of Broanna and Lerence together.

Before they left Lerence had searched for their father's sword. It had been returned after his death to the family. No body, just the sword. Even that had been a huge sign of respect for the family, as steel was quite rare and expensive. Tyna was puzzled by Lerence's sudden need to wear the sword. He had never been very good at fighting unarmed, let alone with weapons; the breaking of Saan's arm none withstanding.

The trip to Tarin was uneventful, despite everyone staying on edge since the aftermath of the Tarth war. The few Tarth that had escaped the banishment were terrorizing smaller cities, towns, and isolated ranches. Some thought thieves were using this as an excuse to cover their tracks, others said the old ones, the non-human races were all rising up against man. Regardless, things were more dangerous the past year and riding with goods meant riding as a group.

The weather held and they made good time.

Tarin was somewhere between a town and a city. The last town before the big outer ranches, it was a key trading nexus. From Tarin goods moved to and from Zethicia, the biggest city on the Muglanth plains. Unlike Zethicia it had always had a standing military, albeit small, the legendary Tarin riders. Horses were so expensive that a standing cavalry for a military was unheard of anywhere else. The proximity to the big ranches gave Tarin access to more horses than the rest of Nakana and the trade provided the sintar to pay for a standing military. It also meant that trading horses was something everyone was moderately good at.

Tyna prepared to do the bargaining with the horse trader they dealt with on a regular basis. Siltan was a widower. She brushed her hair and made sure some of her bosom showed. She was not afraid of using her looks to confuse the man. It had worked in the past.

Lerence would not hear of it.

"It's time I carried my weight. You shouldn't have to sell your body to get a fair price."

"First, I don't sell my body, like a whore, I simply distract him. He's a lonely widower and a nice enough man," she said. She held up her hand as he opened his mouth. "Second, do you remember the last time you bargained with livestock?"

"I don't like it," he said and looked her over in a way that sent a strange tingle down her spine.

Without further word he strode over to the horse trader. Tyna was not sure which emotion was the strongest, anger that he just took charge, amusement that he was protective of her, the strange feeling after his look, the fact he implied she was a prostitute, or worry that he would screw up the barter.

Lerence spoke softly and heatedly with Siltan. Tyna could not hear what he was saying. The trader looked over the horses and pointed to the legs on one. This started another round of heated discussion. Then to Tyna's astonishment Lerence walked over to the stock that the trader had in a coral. Pointing to one of the horses, obviously lame, he spoke briefly. The trader's mouth smiled slightly and he nodded.

Lerence returned with a wad of sintar and the lame horse. Tyna could not restrain herself anymore.

"You traded for *that*?"

Lerence looked at her and smiled. There was something in his smile that made her momentarily forget he was her brother. It caused her to smile and lean closer. He nodded and held up his hand to stop her from speaking more.

"Yes, but before you get too upset, I did get six thousand sintar for the horses."

"Six?"

"Yes. Admit it; you would have been happy with five."

She nodded. The horses were good, but wild and untrained. Five thousand would have been fair. But, what use was a lame horse?

"It's a tendon strain. I'll be riding him in a month."

"How can you tell, you didn't even feel his leg? You know as much about horses as I do an Arbeneth brothel." She stopped and flushed at the look on his face. "Don't even think of saying anything to that," she snapped.

They traded the rest of the goods at a nice price and headed for the inn they stayed at for these trips. The Ne Mar was owned by Gar, an old friend of their father's. The worse-for-wear pelt of the giant black wolf that the inn was named after hung above the large fireplace. The fireplace was more for show than anything else. The northern Muglanth plains were warm year round and the town of Tarin was not so close to the mountains as to truly get cold, although the view from the window showed that even in the north at higher elevations snow was visible. Gar greeted Lerence and Tyna warmly.

"My young Valence family, it is good to see you. You have been trading? Good, good. Tarin needs the goods. Indeed. Indeed. Since the war and the continued threat of the remaining Tarth, we get heartened with another season of trade." He saw the sword strapped on Lerence's back and frowned. "Where did you learn to wear a sword like that Lerence?"

Lerence looked startled. He thought for a moment and then shrugged.

"It seemed a natural way to wear a sword. It gets in the way less. Why?"

"It is the way of the Katar. Most do not wish to imitate the Katar even here … nor do many Katar take kindly to the imitation."

Lerence looked angry. Not at Gar, but at the thought of imitating the Katar. Then he shrugged again. "I'll warrant they did not invent it. I will stay with it for now."

Gar shook his head and went off to fetch some dinner. He called out to his wife Jeene to ready two rooms for 'family'. She came running out and hugged them both. After hugging Lerence she stepped back.

"You've changed Ler." She eyed the sword and looked to Tyna who raised one eyebrow. Jeene stared into Lerence's eyes and suddenly stepped back. She shivered. "I must be coming down with a cold. It is good to see both of you."

Three more customers entered and she bustled off to tend to them, her large matronly breasts bouncing out of sync: first one rising then the other would rise as the first fell. Tyna grabbed Lerence's arm and guided them to a table.

22

Dinner was good, simple fare: sticky stew, with as much meat as potatoes and vegetables; beer, which Lerence drank large quantities of; sweet cheese for desert.

The crowd grew as dinner wore on. More and more were there for beer, wine, or stronger alcohol. Soon, men were hitting on Tyna. She fended off the first five without incident. Lerence was scowling more with each occurrence.

"You would think that they see someone is with you." He muttered.

"Maybe they can tell you are my brother."

"I doubt they can even tell I am here."

Tyna laughed.

"It is sometimes nice to be desired."

"By these?"

He swept his arm expansively.

She laughed again.

"We are part of *these*. What has come over you Lerence, you never worried about my honor before."

"Perhaps I did, but simply did not voice it. As you grow more attractive, your honor needs more defending."

Tyna flushed slightly at the compliment. From her brother, she reminded herself.

Two young men at the table behind Tyna were talking just loudly enough to be heard. She didn't normally eavesdrop, but she was trying to get her mind off her brother and how much he had changed.. She stared at his face as she listened to the conversation.

"What's the point? I was born poor. I'll die poor. Why not end it and hope that next incarnation I am born rich and powerful?"

"Yeah, but what are the odds that you end up rich and powerful the second time around?"

"Then try again."

Tyna looked at Lerence, who was obviously catching the conversation. He was scowling and shaking his head.

"You don't approve of their line of thinking?" She asked.

"They're idiots."

"Why?"

"They sound like followers of Pé, the so called Soul God."

"So called?"

She didn't know how much she believed in the power of gods, but the gods were real. How could one deny it? There was too many who had seen them, or their interventions.

"There is too much unknown in a life. Why waste it on the hope of reincarnation. Hope, not certainty. There is no guarantee. That and one loses what is the essence of one's self. The memories, the experiences, the way of thinking. It is death, if not true death. Death is not something one embraces willingly, as if it were no worse than life. Incarnation could take generations, with your essence stuck in a sea of nothingness."

"Ler, I have never heard you so philosophic."

He laughed, rather darkly.

"Death is the end, whether you eventually get reincarnated, or not. More often than many realize, it is true death. The gods and the Katar see to that."

Tyna looked around nervously. No one appeared to have heard him. What was getting into Ler? She'd never thought about the gods, or reincarnation, much. She felt her father's *ka* would come back. She had to believe that. They were ranchers, away from any temple, and her father had never been one to waste money on donations or time and *ka* on prayer. Still, everyone believed in reincarnation.

She looked into his eyes and his brown irises flashed gold momentarily. For an instant he looked older. Paler skinned and … not sad so much as weary. During that moment, he was not the carefree, inept, brother she knew.

Perhaps a good night's sleep was what they both needed.

* * *

That night Tyna's dreams were troubled. She saw her brother lying on the ground, his head bleeding from the horse kick. She could feel the ruined skull beneath her fingers. Then he opened his eyes and stared at her. His eyes were golden. Gold on gold, the iris almost invisible against a yellow sclera that should have been white. He pulled her closer. She resisted. Closer. She struggled, then stopped. She was kissing her brother. Kissing him with unsisterly passion. She could feel his dark energy, his strength that flowed from beyond his natural *ka*. She closed her eyes and was consumed by it. Drained. Weakened and needing to consume him in return. Merge.

She awoke with a start, dripping with sweat.

The sharp intake of breath she heard, as she sat up, was not her own.

Chapter 3

"She is very beautiful. Her movements are fluid, like a fast and well trained dancer," said Oonie, the old Hrýll, who sat next to Tsom. His thin fur glistened with the sunlight; an oiled amber tan which blurred his human-like features.

Tsom nodded. He'd been thinking along the same lines. From the distance of their seats, a hundred feet off to the side of the newly cleared circle within the trees, Larrina, her raven hair tightly bound, was a young dancer. Her wooden training sword was simply one of the props of the ballet. Her body bent and glided away from her opponent's sword, then she pivoted around her own sword which held off a second attacker. Then, as if brushing a dance partner with a tender hand, her own sword left a trail of red across her opponent's chest and then a gentle red dot on his forehead as punctuation. From a distance the slow drying red paint looked remarkably like blood.

"You are fortunate that she has taken you as a lover."

Tsom didn't know he was still capable of blushing. He was twenty, even if his body looked like a man in his late fifties. The blush gave away his half Kinel blood, emphasizing the skin color difference on his two toned face, the darker skin of his neck and chin vanishing to a peak between his eyes. He replied with forced casualness, as if this were the topic of everyday conversation, hoping that the old Hrýll did not know much about human embarrassment.

"I suppose it's because Lanos and Alanar are both dead and she needed me as much as I needed her."

He leaned back on the grassy rise that made a natural amphitheater of the clearing, resting his weight on his two artificial hands. The complex wooden fingers were covered with thin leather gloves, making them look almost real.

"No, my friend. It is because she cares for you and knows you need healing. You are fortunate not just in the opportunity to make love to her; it is the healing I was referring to. Larrina's talent is healing in the old Kinel way." Oonie paused and smiled. "Although, she is beautiful for a human, or Kinel."

Heal the internal scars? Tsom didn't think that sort of healing existed. Shara, his first love, was gone. Gone and nothing he could have done to save her. Could anyone heal that? Heal the pain of loss and the pain of having let her die?

Tsom bowed his head briefly, so that Oonie couldn't look into his eyes. He had shown too much emotion already.

The pain of Shara's loss was still there, but Larrina had eased it. She had come to him one night and simply crawled into bed with him. She had held him and let him cry on her breast. That night he had simply curled in her arms and slept. The next night she had guided him into her and he had not objected. She was old enough to be many times his great grandmother, but she looked younger than he did—now. Kinel agelessness. With Oonie's words he realized it was true; each night they made love he awoke slightly more whole. He had not looked in a mirror in some time, but he felt better than he had in months.

"I've often wondered if that is Larrina's true Kinel power, healing. She has always been good with teas and herbs and I admit that the pain has been less. I even seem to have lost the phantom pain of my lost hands," Tsom waved his right arm in the air.

"More so than you guess. She heals souls—restores *ka*. I know of no other who can do so. There were such, before mankind, but she may be the last. You and she are the last of the Kinel and the Hryll are dying. Perhaps you two will breed?"

Tsom blushed again. Oonie did not mince words, perhaps it was the Hryll way; he was not too familiar with the old races. Maybe it was just the language difference.

"If she has that power, why doesn't she heal others? She could be rich with that power. Or, she could save the Hryll and Sryll who are dying from their over use of *ka*. The Katar have killed you with their demands, maybe she could help."

Oonie shook his head sadly.

"I wish it were true, my friend, but I understand her power. She heals only men. Only those she loves. I think this is why Alanar had begun to change. She loved him for a very long time. He was not human, nor Kinel, so it is hard to say if her power extended to him. Still, the last time we met I sensed a difference. 'Tis a pity that he did not survive long enough for us to see if he had truly changed."

Was Oonie blaming him for Alanar's death? Did he know the truth? He had told no one. What would Larrina do if she knew? Oonie spoke again, resting a hand on Tsom's wooden hand.

"Many would say Alanar deserved to die many times over, for his past sins," said Oonie.

"I wouldn't know about past sins, but he played a dangerous game negotiating with the Tarth," said Tsom, closing his eyes.

"Especially with his history. I only regret the lost opportunity to defeat the Katar. His power and leadership are needed now. You did what you could to save him. I know he was your friend," Oonie said. Tsom opened his eyes and looked for traces of irony on Oonie's face. Would they look the same as a human's?

"Let us watch our dancer dance the dance of combat. There is irony and sadness that one so gifted in healing is teaching others how to kill," Oonie continued.

All smiles were gone as Tsom and Oonie watched Larrina. She was fast, but more than that she was skilled. As a thief, he had been very quick,. He also had natural skill in combat, born of thievery and survival. Her skill was different. He had relied on reflexes and instinct. This was skill and natural talent honed by practice. Practice that spanned may of his lifetimes. Yet, watching her grace, he felt as if he were the old one, clumsy and stiff.

The clack and crash of the wooden swords sounded like a percussion tune. There was a rhythm to the practice that was unpredictable, but nonetheless tangible. In the few short weeks that they had been camped here the practice ground was already well packed, with the grass losing its last battle against the relentless feet.

Tsom had once asked why she used wooden swords and not real swords. Unlike some of the martial arts instructors in camp, Larrina refused to risk major injury for most training. 'What is the use of a well-trained soldier that is crippled?' She had said. He flexed his mechanical hands, using his arm muscles to move the ingenious mechanism; he squeezed, but felt nothing. Did she see him as crippled? He rubbed his right wooden hand on his left one. Wood on wood. *Maybe I can start a fire if I rub hard enough*, he thought bitterly.

Oonie tapped his hand and gestured toward Larrina and her pupils.

Next was a lesson in many against one tactics.

Ten women surrounded Larrina. She waited, making random small movements to force the group to stay slightly unorganized. Once they were close enough to get in each other's way she charged the knot. The three women there got entangled trying to get Larrina. She knocked their swords into each other, but didn't go for a killing blow. That would have slowed her down. She suddenly fell backwards in what was really a controlled roll. Her sword close to her body she still managed to roll gracefully and knock down one of the two women coming in from behind. The other hacked badly with her own wooden sword. Larrina holding her sword raised, but tip downward, deflected the clumsy chops without expending any energy. Leaping to her feet she slashed at the fallen woman and charged the group again, only now she was on the outside of the group.

The trick was to stay on the fringes, attack, retreat, and circle. It took energy, but used the milling of the group against itself. She was injuring them, not going for the kill. Keep on the move. The referee on the side called to the injured if they violated movement of their injury.

Soon the group was down to three. They tried to corner her, but she didn't let them circle her. Despite the past ten minutes of intense fighting, Larrina was breathing no harder than the three.

Suri, one of the women left standing was calling orders to the other two. With only three of them, they could act in a coordinated fashion.

"Wear her out. She cannot cull us off like a wolf does." Suri grinned at Larrina.

Larrina grinned back. Tsom winced for Suri. That was no healer's smile.

Larrina's wooden sword hit Suri in the chest hard enough to knock her down. The paint left a red mark over her heart. She had thrown it. One of the other two attacked Larrina. Larrina grabbed her hand and danced to the side. She yanked her opponent's hand down then twisted. To keep her wrist from breaking the woman fell. Larrina plucked the sword out of the fallen's hand and slashed down before her opponent had an opportunity to rise. The red paint appeared across her legs and then her back.

Her last opponent, instead of charging while Larrina was engaged, was holding her sword blade in one hand and tugging at the hilt with the other. Tsom didn't recognize her, which was not surprising given the number of new recruits—refugees—from Argn that came in weekly. Suddenly, the wooden sword was black, reflecting the sunlight that struck it. The strange woman tossed the false wooden covering aside and attacked.

Tsom leapt to his feet, manifesting his mind hands. Oonie grunted in surprise, feeling the *ka* and seeing the black sword simultaneously.

"Larrina!" Tsom yelled, needlessly. Larrina had already seen.

"Ptroni," hissed Oonie.

He grabbed Tsom's arm, which was raised pointing at the stranger.

Tsom ignored him. Larrina was the best fighter he knew, but she was tired after hours of training. This woman had waited until now, knowing she was vulnerable and thinking no one could stop her in time. Well, his mind-hands could. He could squeeze her heart faster than she could attempt her attack.

Tsom reached. A year ago this would have drained him and he would have been slow. Now, it took an instant. He reached her back and went in for the kill.

The pain was sudden and intense, as if he had dipped his hand into boiling water. He pulled back, falling over.

"Ptroni. It will affect your hands. Don't let the sword touch your mind-hands." Oonie was pulling him to his feet.

"Forget about me, save Larrina."

"Others are already trying…and failing."

Tsom watched in horror. He manifested his hands again. The left one caused so much pain he dropped it, but maintained the right one.

Suri and the others had quickly seen what was happening and rushed the strange woman. They had forgotten the lesson they were supposed to be learning. The black blade was fast and a single touch seemed to kill. Suri's face was already black and distorted as she fell to her knees. Five of her companions were already down. Larrina was yelling at the remaining group to back off.

"Is it poisoned?" Tsom asked as Oonie rested a warning hand on his wooden one.

"Not poison, worse. It destroys *ka*. Annihilates it. Your hands are vulnerable."

"But, I did not go for her sword, I went for her heart."

"Look at her carefully; she is wearing armor under her shirt. At first I assumed it was padding for training. It's a millennia's worth of Ptroni. "

Her head was not covered, neither were her legs. He could still do something.

Oonie pulled on his arm again.

"Careful, if she slashes at your arm while you try something, it could kill you. Even rolling around while you attempt to hold her could hurt your mind-hands, could even kill you."

Tsom hesitated for the barest moment. Then, it was too late, Larrina was between him and the woman. He had passed through objects before with his hands, but Larrina was sensitive to them. The merest distraction might make the difference and kill her.

Larrina and the woman were dancing, but this was no training exercise, it was a dance of death. The woman did not charge Larrina and Larrina neither ran away, nor attacked. She held on to her wooden sword and kept moving. The sweat that moments before Tsom had found stimulating was worrying him. How tired was she? Her opponent would strike soon, for the others were running for help and help would include bows.

The strange woman shifted her sword to her right hand and shoved her left into a pocket.

Movement slowed. Or rather everyone but the woman and Larrina slowed. Tsom felt his head ache and his stomach cramp. He knew this feeling.

Katar. By the Sea, the woman was wearing a ring of the Katar. Draining *ka* from all those around her and speeding up her movements. Tsom violated his old promise to Larrina and countered the influence of the ring. He spread his manifested hands wide and pulled the *ka* he felt toward him. He was hurting everyone around him, but it did not matter. He had to help Larrina.

He reached out and touched her just as the stranger closed in. He channeled the *ka* into her. Larrina's face betrayed a look that combined anger, anguish, and thanks all at once, but her eyes never left her opponent. Her Kinel coloring was flaring, making it look as if she were wearing a mask. The darker colored skin was red brown, while the white skin around her eyes grew whiter.

Larrina swatted the black sword aside with her wooden sword, not trying to block, but to deflect. She then stepped in close, dropping the wooden sword to free her hands for close combat.

It almost worked.

Chapter 4

Tyna managed not to scream. Someone was in the room with her. She didn't want to give away that she was awake. She tried to see, but the room was on the south side of the inn. No moonlight. It was the quiet side room that Gar reserved for friends. A board creaked. Was it near, or on the far side of the room? She was only wearing her under garments. Stupid to be thinking about what this intruder might see. He, or she, was not interested in her body—she hoped. The money? But Lerence had the money. She considered bolting for the door.

The hand wrapped around her mouth with force. The smell of a sweaty animal, like a horse hit her. She struggled silently, kicking and lashing out with her legs. At least once she connected, but her assailant made no noise and kept its hands over her mouth and was now pinching her nose. She reached, trying for the eyes. Her arms were long, longer than her assailant's. There, an eye. No mercy. She dug. The creature let go.

She drew in a huge gasping lungful of air and forced a scream out as she rolled off the bed, staying on the ground ready to kick upward. Shouts quickly echoed in the hallway. She kept quiet, not giving her position away. The south facing window exploded outward and a faint outline of a form, jumping through was visible. Moments later her door crashed inward. Lerence stood in the doorway in a fighter's stance. A stance that a few weeks ago would have looked incongruous now seemed natural for him. The light of the hallway glow globes framed him in a strange aura; it was almost as if his eyes were burning.

He ran to the window and looked out.

"Gone," he said as he came back.

Gar and others were just entering the room. Some had clubs, some knives, Gar had an old sword that looked like it had not been used in his lifetime. Lerence gestured to him to get some light in the room. Gar lit the lamp near the door and then went for a glow globe while Lerence examined Tyna as best he could. His gaze and touch were clinical, caring, and competent. Her brother was one surprise after another.

"He left this." Tyna dropped an eye into Lerence's hand. He did not flinch, or jump. He really was rising to the occasion; so unlike Lerence.

He looked at it closely. Then sniffed the air. Then he sniffed her face. She could smell whiskey on his breath. Lerence was drinking hard alcohol now? His mouth was near hers and she resisted the illicit feelings. He sniffed again and spoke.

"Kami."

She looked into his eyes for a moment. They flashed gold briefly. Fast. The after image of a blink. Those eyes were magnetic. She leaned back, away from him. These thoughts she was having were positively incestuous.

"How do you know? You've never smelled a Kami. We have only heard of them from the traders and the soldiers returned from Zethicia."

"That must be where I know it from. They said the smell of them was strong, like a horse sweating, yet not quite the same."

He got up and went back to the window, staring out as if it would give up its secrets under his scrutiny.

"Why you? Why would a Kami be sent for you?"

"I don't know, because I'm special?" She grinned from her perch on the bed.

He turned and grinned back. "You are indeed." She felt a strange thrill. Was he taller? In the poor light of the room she might not have even recognized her brother.

The others milled about until Gar returned with the glow globe and herded them out. Then he turned to Tyna.

"My poor girl, you must take my room tonight and we will sleep in one of the guest rooms." Tyna protested, but even Lerence seemed to think it was a good idea. As the adrenaline wore off Tyna found herself yawning and her protests faded.

"Yes, yes, I'll go. I appreciate it, old friend." She patted Gar on the shoulder and shivered.

She then realized that she had been sitting there in her undergarments the whole time; she blushed and grabbed her robe. She turned in the doorway and glanced back. Lerence stared out of the broken window. He was tapping the point of his sword absently into the floor. Her eyesight was good and she thought she saw a pattern to the damage on the floor, where the sword point had hit a number of times. A crescent moon shape. The tip of the sword fell seemingly without thought, but she saw that it never strayed. Suddenly, the tip snapped. *Father will be outraged*, she thought, then remembered.

Lerence lifted the sword and looked at the tip in surprise.

"Oh, it's steel," he murmured.

Of course it's steel, she thought, what else would it be?

Gar called from the stairway. She left.

* * *

Synr ran into the night, silently despite the pain from his eye socket. It wasn't bleeding much, but there was intense agony combined with a terrible itch. He knew better than to scratch the damaged crater in his face. He held his hand over the wound. What little blood came between his fingers darkly matted his light fur. Even at night no one would mistake him for human. He had a fast, simian, rolling gait, rounded shoulders and fur thicker than a Hrýll's. Breathing hard, he ran his tongue over his sharp pointed teeth and lips.

He stumbled. His depth perception was off or the pain where his eye once resided was distracting him. He relied on muscle memory to keep him going without a fall. The town full of lax humans never noticed him.

Once he was into the forest of the rolling hills he slowed down. His breathing was slightly labored, but not too loud. He cut a piece of leather off of his tunic and fashioned a crude patch for his eye. A woman. A human woman had done this to him. It was an embarrassment and hard to comprehend. Bal'alam would not be pleased that he had failed to bring her to him and the nar Tarth. He shuddered at the thought of a nar Tarth. The Tarth masters were strong, but the females were fearsome and unpredictable. The Kami were not used to females wielding so much power. He could smell his own scent, one of fear. Rubbing his eye patch he decided that the Tarth and humans were more alike than he had first supposed. Their women were strong, stronger than female Kami.

Later. With reinforcements. He would find this tall woman again and fulfill his mission. Any human who would interrupt them then would die. He cupped his hands to his mouth and made a yowling call. It was the sound of a cat in heat, or an animal dying, but not one the Kami was used to making.

There was no noise, but the Kami's nose was good. He spun around and looked the giant cat in the eye. Not as powerful as the death cats from Hell, the dui mar of this world were still fearsome. In this world, with some help from the 'goddess,' they were also tame around the Kami and the Tarth. Grinning, showing his canines, Synr leapt onto the giant cat's back. The cat growled, but waited. He leaned over and whispered his command into the cat's ear. Only a leaf stirred on the ground where they had been.

* * *

Bal'alam was frustrated. These Yanín made no sense. They had no honor. These negotiations were going nowhere. He pounded his fist on the table, there was a cracking noise, but the wood held. It was crudely built, from fresh oak. The Tarth were not craftsmen and the Kami were not much better. His face was flushed, making his normally pale pink almost as red as the normal Tarth pigment. Bal'alam stood his full six feet, extremely short for a Tarth, and stared the Yanín, Kulakoonstru, in the eyes. Red eyes, within the chitinous mask of a face, the double layer on its skull looking like a white cap.

"Why do you serve these inferior humans? The filthy Katar? They are sheelem leeches. I am willing to ally the Tarth and the Kami with the Yanín. Together we can destroy them," Bal'alam growled.

Bal'alam leaned forward at the end, staring into the Yanín's unflinching gaze. Damn. No human would stand there fearless. He wanted the Yanín on his side. Of all the races, they were worthy as allies.

"You offer no pay," Kulakoonstru said impassively.

The same thing over and over. Pay. This was the future of the world. The Yanín were dying off too. All the old races died in the wake of the fast breeding humans. He momentarily wished that the traitor Be Na Tarth was here. He was clever at these things. He could persuade others with means other than force. The stupid traitor had fallen for Alanar's trickery and was now either dead or banished again. But, the Tarth survived—because of Bal'alam. *He* had led the small band to freedom. *He* was more patient than Be Na Tarth had given him credit for. *He* was gathering allies. When the time was right … then mankind and the Katar would pay. Allies. He needed the Yanín. What could he offer them? They were not normal. Not sane. But, they could fight.

"The Yanín do not need money, not really. You do not need qenar, or talismans. What do you really need? What do you want? Kula, what is it that you crave, above all other things?"

Kulakoonstru stood impassively. His legs bent backwards at an impossible angle. *How could that be comfortable?* Bal'alam thought. Those double joints were disconcerting. Watching them walk was almost painful.

"The Hrýll." The Yanín finally spoke.

"What of them?"

"We destroy them. All."

Bal'alam sat down. The Hrýll were the talisman makers. Why would the Yanín want them destroyed? Even the Tarth had planned on sparing the Hrýll. They were no danger to anyone if left alone, it was only Alanar who had persuaded them to join the rebels. Once mankind fell, the Hrýll were useful. Only they knew how to bind *ka* to objects so that quenar could be used. Talismans were key to civilization.

Bal'alam stared at the Yanín. He wore only weapons. No comforts. Their only real luxury was a foul whiskey that only they would drink. The Yanín were warriors. Hand to hand. They were the best, well maybe second best, warriors on Nakana. Bal'alam nodded to himself. No talismans and the battle was pure. The Yanín felt it was cheating to use talismans or *ka*. They had a strange sense of honor. They hated the extinct Kinel as much as the Katar. It was offensive to them for a race to use *ka* directly. That was worse than the Hrýll or their cousins the Srýll. Rumor had it that the Srýll were done for already, over used by the Katar: no one young enough to breed. Of the races that manipulated ka, that left only the Hrýll. Was it worth it?

The survival of the Tarth was worth anything.

Bal'alam nodded in acquiescence.

"Agreed. We destroy the Hrýll along with the Katar and the humans."

Bal'alam wasn't sure, but he suspected that he'd just seen a Yanín smile.

Chapter 5

Larrina realized her instinctive mistake almost as soon as she closed in. This woman—Näsal she had called herself during introductions at the beginning of training—was not fighting to live. She was fighting to kill. She never expected to make it out of the rebel encampment alive. All this woman had to do was strike her with the blade. Her opponent would take insane risks and as a Katar she was extremely well trained, and had the damned ring that all Katar wore. Now, Larrina was well within striking distance of the black Ptroni blade. One mistake and she was lost.

The back of her mind could feel Tsom's hand hovering, it radiated *ka*. Why hadn't he simply crushed her heart? Or brain? He must know something she didn't. Yet, he was there. He had broken the Katar ring's drain on her and had funneled enough *ka* for her to move as quickly as Näsal. That meant he was draining *ka* from those nearby. She had to end this one way or the other quickly. Tsom was hurting too many people trying to save her.

She went for an amateur's move; she grabbed the woman's sword arm with both of her hands. Surprised, Näsal was expecting something more sophisticated and didn't immediately react, giving Larrina the extra moment she needed. She stepped in, lifting with both her hands to the left she twisted her head, and bit Nasal.

On the neck.

On the carotid artery.

Näsal clubbed her with her left hand, but Larrina held on to her throat with her teeth and the sword arm with both hands. She was ready for the knees and ignored the pain, but was unable to prevent Näsal from throwing them both to the ground. She felt Tsom's touch leave them as they rolled. The damned Katar must be wearing Ptroni armor. That was the only explanation as to why Tsom had not killed her already and why he refused to maintain contact. She hoped he was not too badly injured from the discovery. That much Ptroni would cost a fortune. They must really want her dead. The ring tried to heal its owner. Larrina could feel the blood thickening and the artery in her teeth try and close. She shook her head the way a wolf shakes its prey.

To the end, Näsal fought to get her blade to cut into Larrina. Larrina kept her teeth clamped for a good thirty seconds after all movement stopped. The damned ring was keeping everyone at bay and Näsal alive. She then let go and rolled quickly backwards, letting go of the Ptroni blade arm at the last moment. Näsal didn't move.

As the effect of the Katar ring wore off, the onlookers moved forward. Oonie stooped and picked up the wooden sheath, made to look like a sword. A small piece of wood was torn out at the base.

"Probably what saved Larrina's life," Oonie said. "The false cover was jammed on, Näsal was having problems removing it."

Tsom met Larrina's eyes. She gave him a weak smile, waved him to join Oonie, who was examining Näsal's body..

"That is more Ptroni than I have seen in many lifetimes," Oonie muttered.

Larrina was already by the bodies of her fallen students. Tsom let her be. She had a grim look. Her face coloring was still flaring, creating a mask of anger.

"Our respite from conflict is over," she said through clenched teeth.

Oonie looked at her with sadness. Tsom could almost hear him say something about how a healer should not be fighting.

Tsom sensed the scout almost at the same time as she entered the clearing. He could sense changes in ka, at close proximity, when his mind hands were manifested. She was agitated and interrupted their mourning, not really seeing the devastation.

Tsom didn't recognize the scout. She was gasping for breath.

"Tarth…to…the…north." She had her hands on her knees. As she sucked in more air she noticed that the women whom she thought were training were actually dead, one with her throat ripped out. Her eyes widened when she saw the blood dripping from Larrina's mouth.

Larrina wiped her mouth on her left arm. She grabbed the scout by the shoulders and nodded briskly, acknowledging what the scout saw and simultaneously forcing her to pay attention.

"You're sure that it was Tarth you saw?" asked Larrina.

"Yes, ma'am."

"How large a party?"

"Not large, ma'am. They were attacking a caravan between Zethicia and one of the outlying towns, Tarin. I came as fast as I could, given the instructions that any sign of Tarth should be reported immediately."

"You did well Lyn. I did not think that the remaining splinter band of Tarth would be content to hide in the mountains for long, but one hoped. What stood out as strange with these Tarth, if anything?"

Lyn looked puzzled. Tsom understood her confusion; wasn't the mere existence of a Tarth strange enough? Daemons from legend come back to trouble them. Daemons who wanted to destroy all of mankind, claiming that the Tarth were the first race on Nakana and all the other races invaders?

"The Tarth raiding party I saw had dui mar, death cats, with them."

Larrina's smile, at knowing there had been more, held no real satisfaction.

"Hallam's influence. The goddess of nature is allied with the Tarth. The other gods cannot be happy about that."

Tsom suppressed a shiver. He still had a tendency to think of the gods as … well … gods. Larrina and the late Alanar had not. Maybe it was because she was pure Kinel. Only the Kinel were able to manipulate *ka* directly, like a god, but it was only their own ka, not another person's. Legend had it that the Kinel had battled the gods and the Katar millennia ago. Their power had been great, but the Kinel were now gone, exterminated by the Katar. Tsom felt his old anger rise. The Katar had murdered his parents and now they were trying to assassinate Larrina.

Only Larrina and he remained; and he was only half Kinel. He could manipulate *ka* directly, without the aid of a talisman. At a price. Tsom looked at his dried and aged skin on his arms, where they connected to the mechanical hands. The price of learning had been steep.

He slowly pushed his way toward Larrina, the small crowd giving way when they saw who it was. He reached her as she finished sending the scout off. Despite the pain he manifested both hands again and pulled her to him, burying his face in her hair. She was stiff and trembling, but slowly softened in his embrace.

"I'm sorry I didn't do more," he whispered.

She shook her head against him and slowly pushed back. Her lips were still pink from the blood of the assassin, but he kissed her lips lightly and she smiled. She reached and touched his injured, manifested hand.

"You did enough," she said.

Tarth. This would complicate things. Larrina would get distracted from the main goal of destroying the Katar. This was a small band, even if they were fearsome they should be ignored. Destroy the Katar, then worry about the remnants of the daemon race.

He glanced down at the creak of wood. He had unconsciously clenched both mechanical hands until they groaned with protest. Was Barin, the maker of these hands, still alive, or had the Katar killed him too?

Chapter 6

That evening, under the three moons of spring, almost early summer, Larrina called forth a council. Tsom had been part of the rebel council ever since the confrontation with the Tarth in Zethicia almost a year ago. He was respected and his apparent age was an advantage in this instance. Many thought he had been with the revolution for decades. Those who knew the truth respected his sacrifice. They looked to Larrina for true leadership but listened when he spoke. He wondered if his two-toned skin, visible to those who knew he was Kinel or were not affected by the chameleon effect that protected Kinel, had anything to do with the respect and touch of fear.

The meeting was held outdoors as none of the rough buildings was large enough. The breeze in the trees was cool. The massive trunks had never been harvested and stood powerful. Older than the gods, if Larrina was correct. Their canopy of needles kept the heat of the sun out during the day so that the wood never absorbed the energy. So unlike his city days growing up.

The mountains, the Web of the Gods as the Hrýll called them, were near, their influence was evident in the afternoon winds. Oonie looked over at Tsom, as if sensing the direction his mind was taking. The representative of the Hrýll was not a leader in the way humans defined it, but when Oonie suggested that the Hrýll do something, they did. They were so human like physically, yet impossible to fully understand. If they shaved their fur, would Tsom be able to read Oonie's expression? Tsom thought even then he would not be able to read Oonie.

Oonie smiled and nodded at Tsom. His wife, Tiar, wasn't present. Recently, she was often missing. Tsom wondered what she was so important that she would miss a meeting of the full council. Perhaps something happening at the Hrýll homeland required her attention.

He shivered. Was it really cold, or just part of his old body losing its ability to heat itself? Or fear at the next steps they would be taking. He had always groaned how the elderly were wearing sweaters all the time. Now, suddenly, he was one of them.

Tsom eased himself to a sitting position. His joints ached. He thought about using his mind hands to ease himself gently onto the ground, but caught Larrina looking at him and decided against it. She could sense *ka* activity too. It seemed to be something in their shared Kinel blood. The manifestation took very little now, but Larrina disapproved of even that waste of *ka*.

"This assassination attempt shows that the Katar are feeling desperate," Larrina started out. Several of the council grunted in agreement.

"We need to cement our relationship with Zethicia, at the very least ensure that they do not move against us. If Zethicia recognizes us as the legitimate government of Argn, we have a chance. The Katar know this and they know I am the one to negotiate with Zethicia."

The council shifted uneasily.

"Now raids by the remaining Tarth have been reported in the northern Muglanth Plains. If I can provide intelligence on the Tarth to Zethicia and commit some of our force in return for Zethicia's alliance, then the Katar will be … amenable to a negotiated settlement on Argn." Larrina paused for a deep breath and to see how her words were effecting the council.

Tsom, normally reticent to speak, stood and, at Larrina's nod, spoke.

"This plan sounds close to what Alanar proposed a year ago and look at that disaster. The Tarth loose will keep Zethicia busy and they will request Katar aid again. Let's use that to focus on Argn while the Katar are still weak."

Larrina frowned at Tsom as she leaned forward, her right hand gesturing to the group. "Alanar did not betray us, no matter what some may think."

Tsom fought nausea and anger. She did not know the full story and he wasn't going to tell her. He avoided Larrina's eyes as she continued.

"He was willing to negotiate with ancient enemies for the sake of defeating the Katar. We need to keep that potential open. I can both assess the Tarth threat and negotiate with them, or Zethicia, or both. We need allies."

"With the Tarth?" yelled one of the council.

"They're alien. Not human," shouted another.

"Neither am I," said Oonie, standing. The council fell silent. Some looked down in guilt. Oonie and the Hrýll had been key to the success the rebellion had so far. The flow of talismans was crucial and they all knew the cost to the Hrýll.

Larrina's journey would take weeks, maybe months, and she would have to stay off the roads. They were too heavily guarded and full of caravans, now that the gateway between Zethicia and The Cities was destroyed. Tsom's stomach churned once again, thinking of Shara. Larrina was adamant that she could blend in with her Kinel chameleon effect. She knew more of the rebel network than anyone else and could use her connections in Zethicia. Many of the Council worried that Larrina could be betrayed in Zethicia. The possibility of her capture or torture was very real, even more so after the assassination attempt. Larrina pressed on.

"Only a small group can move unnoticed and with any speed. We may be able to forge an alliance with Zethicia to protect them against the Tarth so that they are not forced to ask for the Katar again. They already owe too much to the Katar, they would like to keep what independence they have. Over time, we may be able to persuade them to completely break free. I will take Tsom. He knows Barnus, the general of the Zethician forces."

The council argued some more, but Oonie's siding with Larrina cemented it. Most knew that she had already made up her mind. They finally managed to persuade her to take five of the best fighters with her. All were trained women from Argn who had a special allegiance to Larrina from the early moments of the revolution.

Larrina accepted the compromise and discussed actions the council might have to take while she was gone. Administrative details weren't of interest to Tsom. He grew tired and trusting that Larrina would tell him what he needed to know, he excused himself and stumbled off to their semi-permanent shelter. The damp smell of the forest was intense as he made his way by the light of two of the evening moons, the third evening moon having set already.

* * *

Larrina crawled into bed with Tsom, her unbathed, salty smell mixing with her spice perfume. She favored the perfume fashion of Argn, where she had lived so long. She lay next to him and rubbed his back gently. Gradually her hands strayed and rubbed other parts of his body both gently and demandingly.

Tsom stared into Larrina's eyes as they made love. She had been surprised the first time at his skill at love making, knowing how young he was chronologically, despite his aged body. He'd told her of the years he'd been raised by the women of the brothel and that they had shared some of their secrets. She'd mildly scolded him the first time he had used his manifested hands to touch her where no normal man could while in that position.

They were moving slowly. She pulled him in deeper and breathed in his breath as he exhaled and then he took in her breath. He could sense a small amount of their *ka* mixing. He'd never told anyone of his ability to sense emotions within the *ka*. With Larrina there was the twinge of guilt, but he was afraid it would change the way she was around him. Part of him suspected she knew.

He could feel the healing love in the way she enveloped not only his body but his *ka*. It was as if she pulled some other part of him into her warmth where he healed. Now that Oonie had explained it to him, he could actually understand it.

As she slowly climaxed Larrina suddenly stiffened. Not the contraction of muscles that was part of her orgasm. Her eyes were wide with, fear? No. Surprise and disbelief. Slowly she pushed Tsom off of her. Tears streamed down her face, dripping onto her breasts. There was a look of terror, sadness, and longing in her eyes. She saw the unspoken in his face.

"I momentarily sensed …" she hesitated and then looked ashamed for hesitating "…I felt as if I was with Alanar. No, no Tsom, it is not that I was wishing it was him. I momentarily was in a time shift. Literally as if I was with him. As if it was long … very long … ago." Her face was trance-like and she was gazing unfocused past him. He glanced backward at the dimly lit wall and back to Larrina.

Despite Oonie's speculation on Alanar and Larrina, Tsom had not seen them as lovers, merely close friends. At the time, she had shown every indication of being drawn toward Lanos. Once again Tsom was jealous; jealous of a man he'd helped kill. If she knew, she would never forgive him. The knowledge that she still thought of Alanar froze his speech. He had nothing to say.

Larrina slowly focused back Tsom.

"Oh, Tsom. I don't know what came over me. You know that Alanar and I were friends for an incredibly long time. It must be the stress of the day and the assassin with the Ptroni blade. It is very similar to the one Alanar gave me."

He nodded and touched her with his mind hands, to feel her face and emotions. She smiled and didn't scold him for the minute waste of *ka*.

"Let's go to sleep," he suggested.

Despite his craving her more than ever, they didn't make love again that night. He couldn't stay mad at her for long as she wrapped her arms around him and brought his face against her chest. Soon he was drifting asleep in a deep unconsciousness that was only possible when he was beside her. He didn't feel the wetness of her tears as he drifted off.

* * *

Larrina's hands trembled as she packed. The strange vision last night worried her. The last vision she had had was centuries ago, when her mother was still alive. She shuddered at the memory. Tsom entered the tent, but she kept packing. He watched for a moment then spoke.

"Just the two of us?"

"Yes, we'll be faster and harder to notice. I haven't told the council. Our bodyguards are expecting that we leave tomorrow. Are you up for it?"

"Of course. I feel better than I have in … months."

Tsom walked up to her and rested his forearms on her shoulders. She knew he hated to touch her with his mechanical hands. She was grateful he had learned to control some of his power. She had seen too many Kinel burn out while young, especially without training. Who would train Tsom's children, if he had any, she wondered. Once again she mourned the extinction of her race.

Tsom wrapped his arms around her and squeezed.

"Is there something wrong?" he asked.

"Nothing. Why do you ask?" She knew he could sense her feelings through the aura of her *ka* using his hands, if he tried, but he didn't.

"I thought I saw you tremble. I don't think I have ever seen you tremble."

"You must have been mistaken." She held out her hand in front of him. It was steady.

Tsom manifested his hands and held hers between his two incorporeal ones. He ignored her scowl at the minute waste of *ka*.

"Incredibly steady. Hard. Rock hard."

He placed his right mind-hand on her cheek. She knew it still pained him to use his right hand, after brushing against the ptroni. Her eyes darted to her short sword, lying on the bed next to the saddle pack. The jeweled handle contrasted with the dark black scabbard. Her own wealth and storage of death. Her face softened.

"Tsom, I'm just wound up. I'm worried about the encampment when we are gone. Worried that you are stretched thin. That's all."

"Of course." Tsom wiped a tear she was sure was not there off of her cheek. "I had best finish packing too."

As he left, she noticed that he kept his hands manifested and pushed aside the tent door long before he reached the exit.

* * *

The Web of the Gods always made her hair stand on end. There was a power in these mountains that was older than time. Only Alanar had been comfortable hiking them. The heavy forest of the foothills thinned to scattered mountain trees. Here they were spaced further apart, forced to find nourishment in thin soil and rocks. Larrina and Tsom followed a river to a narrow pass, Varnin's Trap, through the major arm of mountains that stretched to the southeast. Using the pass would cut three weeks off of their trip, but Larrina wasn't thrilled at the prospect. She knew the meaning of the pass's name better than most. Still, it was off the roads and less likely to have Katar, Tarth, or thieves.

She glanced at Tsom. He'd been a thief once, but not like these. Until Tsom had joined the revolution he'd never killed anyone.

Strange creatures roamed the mountains. Alanar once told her that the Web was a weakness between the planes. Occasionally, creatures would stray between the planes. He'd hinted that this was where mankind had come from. A migration from some other world. Even the Kinel, he had said, probably had drifted accidentally to Nakana.

'What about the Hrýll, or the Tarth?' she had asked, resting her head against his chest, slowly tracing one of his scars with her finger.

'They are the old ones. They have been here for longer than anyone can remember.' His hand drifted down to her bare ass, stroking from one cheek to the other. Then he slid his hand up to her breasts. She rolled more on her back to give him better access to the rest of her body.

'What about you, Alani? Where did you come from?'
'I wish I knew, Lar. I wish I knew, but I'm here now.'
Yes, he was.

Larrina noticed with a start that Tsom was looking at her intensely. She centered her mind quickly, calming her heartbeat and going almost into a trance. This avoided an embarrassing blush at her recollection of a day so long ago. Using a leg command, she sent her horse forward at a trot. She knew her horse's trot was smoother than Tsom's. Hopefully, he'd focus more on riding than her. She wiped the dampness off of her neck and surreptitiously smoothed her nipples down from their erect position. Given time she could control her body, the motion simply sped the process up.

The sure-footed horses avoided several potential disasters as the ground gave way on a narrow path. Larrina had learned from Alanar how to pick horses. She'd once thought that horsemanship was only a natural talent, but he'd laughed and said the only thing natural about riding horses was falling off. Some learn faster, but everyone needs to learn. Use the grace and balance she had from being a dancer to ride, Alanar had told her. She'd learned then and had never stopped learning.

Each step of the horse was reminding her of Alanar. She couldn't get him out of her head. As a Kinel, she was used to outliving everyone. Of friends dying. But Alanar had been different. He was older than her. Even when he'd been failing, letting his body get old and sick, she had never thought of him dying. When he'd disappeared with the Tarth she'd accepted his death because it had been war. Now, he was in her head—and she was comparing Tsom to him.

Tsom was not bad for someone who had only ridden for a year or two. He had an incredible balance, was light, and, despite his appearance, was lithe and strong. His muscles tired more easily than they had two years ago, before he had been drawn into events, or caused them—depending on if you believed the stories. Born on the eclipse of the five moons he was considered a catalyst by the priesthoods. To the rebels, he was simply an enemy to the Katar.

The path widened and they entered a small valley. She tightened her legs and her horse broke into a relaxed trot, leaving Tsom momentarily behind.

Larrina glanced back and watched Tsom impatiently force his horse into a short canter then a trot. He was so young. His emotional pain and injuries were so deep. He'd lost so much *ka* and her herbs and teas could only heal so much of his physical damage. Only taking him as a lover could she heal the *ka*. She knew how her power worked, though not why. As far as she knew, she was the only one who had ever restored someone's *ka*. Was it time to let Tsom go? Let him be a young man?

Part of her affection for Tsom was loneliness, he was half-Kinel. It's hard being alone in a crowd, the last of your kind. Maybe that was what had drawn her to Alanar also, all those years ago. He was the only one of his kind, as far as anyone knew.

"You're marks away," Tsom said, as his horse pulled alongside.

She smiled and nodded.

"I'm feeling my age, Tsom. Too many memories. Too much loss."

Tsom was silent in reply.

Only Alanar had been immune to her healing. Humans healed more quickly. Kinel, and Tsom, much more slowly. She had not had a Kinel lover in over a hundred years. She glanced at Tsom. He looked ten years younger than he had last year.

She pulled firmly, but not unkindly, on the reins as Lani tried to graze and walk at the same time. He was spirited. A stallion, not a gelding. She was the only one in the camp who could ride him. The other women made jokes about her and a stallion, which she laughed at with a small amount of pride.

The view was spectacular as they rose above the valley floor. Larrina's apprehension faded as she gazed across the valley and then down the valley. The wild cry of an eagle overhead, circling for an opportunity. The smell of no campfires, no city, and no people. The sun was heating up, now that they were out of the heavy forest and she could feel sweat on her back and trickling down her chest.

Lani snorted and his ears rotated forward, then rolled back pinned flat against his head. His muscles tightened under her.

Her sword was in her hand. The polished black blade reflected the sunlight. Her nose dilated. Her eyes went side to side, then up and down. She didn't make the mistake of looking only at eye level for danger.

Dui mar. A death cat. At least nine hundred pounds. She'd heard that the record size was over twelve hundred pounds. Motionless under a the large tree ahead, it's gaze fixed on them. Its tawny, lightly speckled, hide meshed with the dry grasses. She fought Lani, preventing him from spinning around and bolting. Even on flat land a horse couldn't outrun a dui mar.

Tsom had a harder time with his mare. He sawed on the bit with his mechanical hands and then she felt the *ka* as his hands manifested.

Don't squeeze its heart. There is something more than meets the eye here, she thought. He seemed to sense her intent and did nothing. She forced her mount closer. It was rumored that dui mar were intelligent enough to understand you. She spoke.

"Leave us and we won't harm you."

She tapped her sword tip to her bow to emphasize the point. Of course, the bow was not strung.

To her shock—and she didn't shock easily—the cat spoke. "So the catalyst still lives." Its voice was scratchy, with the sounds requiring lips not coming out well, but it was intelligible. It seemed in pain as it spoke.

It shifted position to get a better look at Tsom.

Both horses stopped panicking, almost as if they'd been drugged. Tsom moved his mare next to Larrina. He looked a question at her. She shrugged.

"You know us?" Larrina asked.

"The band of Tarth survived, as you know. They wish to destroy all of mankind. While I am not opposed to this, I see that the goal is perhaps too ambitious. I'm willing to compromise."

The big cat paused, to let its throat recover.

"You're Hallam, the goddess of nature," Larrina noted.

"Your inflection on goddess is insolent. But, you Kinel were always insolent. Yes, I am using one of my creatures as an avatar. You need not try and kill me; all you would do is destroy this helpless cat."

The cat did not look too worried. Helpless was not the word that sprang to mind when looking at a cat that weighed close to a thousand pounds.

"What are you proposing?" asked Larrina. Hallam had something in mind or she would not be troubling to find them and talk to them.

"For a long lived race, you're rather impatient. My goal is the destruction of the Katar and the gods of mankind. Mankind itself need not perish. Ally your rebel forces with us and I will persuade the Tarth to spare mankind."

"That is basically the deal Alanar offered the Tarth and he was betrayed and destroyed."

"*I* was not part of that deal. I want the gods destroyed, not just the Katar. There are fewer Tarth now and I can be very persuasive. They will not betray me."

"What chance do we have against gods?"

The cat laughed. At least that is what Larrina assumed it was. Of course it could be the hunting cough of the dui mar. Then it continued.

"Larrina, yes I know who you are." The cat coughed again and Larrina almost felt sorry for the strain its vocal system must be under.

The cat continued.

"You know better. The other gods are weak. Stop the prayer. Stop the worshipping and the gods will be further weakened. Your race's war ten thousand years ago was at the height of the gods' power, now they will be no stronger than the Katar and fewer in number. This time, I will be helping.

"Alanar had the right idea, but I agree, he was betrayed. Lanos should never have brought the Sphere of Banishment into the encampment. If he had simply destroyed the sphere--neutralizing the Katar's only weapon against the Tarth-- the Tarth and Alanar may have succeeded."

Tsom knew the full story was slightly different. The sphere, an ancient Hrýll artifact transported those within its radius to another plane of existence. Even Oonie didn't seem to understand how it worked. But, it had been Tsom who'd activated it, not Lanos.

"The Tarth can't be trusted." Tsom watched Larrina as he spoke. "The attack in the north a year ago verified that. You were there, part of it. We all saw the birds and the other animals involved. Why should we trust you? It was you who convinced that faction of Tarth to betray the rest." The last sounded more pleading than convincing.

"No one can be trusted," a small cough, "but if our goals overlap enough then we should still be able to cooperate. You should know that the Tarth now have the Yanín as allies."

Larrina and Tsom looked at each other simultaneously. One Yanín was like five well trained soldiers. This made up for the loss of the Tarth's main forces. Another war was coming, and, once again, the rebellion would have to choose sides.

"I know you still have the sphere. Destroy it!" The last a loud yowl from the death cat as its throat gave out momentarily.

"We would be foolish to do so," replied Larrina. No need for the bitch goddess to know that the sphere was already destroyed.

"It's a dangerous tool," the big cat resumed. "It should never have been created. All the artifacts from those times are dangerous. It could backfire, drawing others from the planes. It is an ancient artifact that no one fully understands. Nonetheless, our tactics will take it into account. Even you," the cat looked at Tsom, "with your wondrous hands will not be a match for a three pronged attack. Your power was a surprise. You would have to sacrifice too many of your own to banish us. We will fight a guerilla war of hit and run. We will find and destroy the sphere—or destroy all of you rebels—unless you ally with me. I know where your main camp is and where your small groups are. After all, I can see with my animals, great and small. Cooperate or suffer."

The last ultimatum had lost some of its threat by sounding thin and whispery. Larrina doubted the cat's throat could take much more. The goddess pushed the cat into further speech.

"All weapons are double edged. If the Tarth obtain the sphere then they might use it against you, or use it to find the main group of Tarth and try and bring them back. That would make it hard to bargain for mankind's continued existence. It must be destroyed. Show me the remnants of the sphere and ally with us."

Larrina thought often of the sphere and how thousands of Tarth and Alanar had simply faded into a different plane. If the sphere had survived, she would have destroyed it for this very reason. It was a moot point. Something about its last usage had damaged it. The Hrýll had no idea as to how to even begin repairing it. But Hallam didn't know that. Instinct told Larrina not to let Hallam know. The gods were no better than the Katar;. Except for this bitch, their power was fading.

Hallam continued.

"The smaller band of Tarth are a better ally than the entire race was. They have almost no women with them. They will die off eventually. Ally with them and save mankind. Let them destroy the Katar and their gods."

The cat pawed its face in frustration and pain.

"We'll consider your offer. It strikes me as strange that you care. You, of all the gods, don't need mankind."

It looked like the cat shrugged.

"The world would be lonely without beings such as humans. Humans are physically so similar to gods that I admit we must be related. The Hrýll are too strange. The Kinel are gone—except for you and the thief, and I think you are too old to reproduce." Larrina kept the pain off her face at the latter comment. "The Yanín are both strange and too aggressive. The other races are dying. Mankind could worship me, and, unlike the other gods, they would not pay for their worship through shortened life span. My power flows from the animals. I would be a benevolent god.

"Consider carefully and quickly. Now that I have found you on your journey, you won't be able to hide. I may change my mind about enjoying mankind's company."

The large cat leapt away from the tree and bounded up the hillside into the forest.

"You were considering allying with the Tarth, or Zethicia," Tsom said. "Does this change your opinion which to approach?"

Larrina stared upward, silent. An eagle screamed overhead, circling. Watching.

Larrina no longer found the bird beautiful.

Chapter 7

Tyna stayed on edge the next day as they prepared to return home. They had wagons to load and secure, but she kept stopping. Her eyes kept darting from side to side and her heart beat irregularly with every small surprise. She cursed herself for being weak. No Kami was going to come into town in broad daylight. Still, Kami meant the Tarth and the Tarth had killed her father.

Tarin was small by Zethician standards, but still well over ten thousand people. The town, Tyna thought of it as a town even at its size, known for its elite cavalry had many who were both hopeful members and past members. It would be suicide for any being allied with the hated Tarth to be seen here.

She watched Lerence, as she secured several barrels with a large mesh net. She'd never thought that she would be looking to him for protection, but he'd changed so quickly. That kick by the horse had morphed him into something more. He was hard to recognize—physically or by his manners—as her brother. She felt safe near him. He seemed taller than before—no he *was* taller. She was sure of it. Leaner too. He'd never been fat, but she noticed the muscles rippling on his arms and back as he loaded the supplies. She was sure she would have noticed those muscles before. One didn't get muscles like that in a few days, normally. He also now worked with father's old sword strapped to his back. It seemed natural there. Out of the way, yet very close. All his movements seemed graceful. Smooth. Unwasted. She realized that she wished this man was someone other than her step-brother. Wished it and sensed it to be true, somehow. It felt guilty, sinful. But she didn't deny the feeling.

Lerence caught her watching him and smiled and winked.

"Supervising?" he asked.

She jumped to help load one of the other wagons. Glancing back at him, she shook her head ever so slightly. After a few minutes, she stopped her loading.

"Ler, I need to run an errand. I won't be more than an hour. Are you ok on your own?"

He nodded with a questioning look. She pretended not to notice and, using her long legs, was quickly away from him.

It took her a few enquires to locate the temple of Pé, the Soul God, she'd never visited any of the temples in Tarin.

She was surprised at how small and rather plain the temple was. It wasn't tall, the entrance a simple double doorway. There no statues, or any artwork adorning the exterior. There was a small Y symbol above the doors and it took her a moment to recall that indicated the Rivers of Life and Death flowing into the Sea of Souls.

Since the Tarth War, when the gods had failed to help mankind against the native daemons of Nakana, the temples had all seen a decline, but this temple looked as if it had been neglected for far longer. Rumor had it that in The Cities the Katar and the gods had allied, using forced sacrifice of *ka* in lieu of worship, to crush the rebellion. She hoped that nothing like that would spread to Tarin. She, like many who lived outside of The Cities, had no love for the Katar. There had been enough killing in the past year. What mattered now was the ranch. That and to figure out what was happening to her brother. Step-brother, she reminded herself. Not really of my blood. It shouldn't be important. It hadn't been before, but now it was. Her feelings were less … wrong, knowing that Ler was not really of her blood.

The ante-chamber of the temple of Pé was empty of people.

Within the chamber were two doors. Above one was a stylized bent figure of a man wading into a river. Above the other was a baby crawling out of a river.

Life and death. She wracked her memory for a clue as to whether it was important to go through one door versus the other. Shit, she just wanted to talk to a priest. All her life she had ignored the gods, following her father's lead. Sure, everyone believed in the Sea of Souls and maybe the rivers of life and death, to some extent.

She strode through the door of death, as she expected she was supposed to. Then exiting she would be 'reborn.'

Inside the symbolism continued. The room sloped downward, almost as if it were an empty pond. The chamber seemed larger than the building would have allowed for; no doubt an optical illusion. In the center was a small pool of water and ladles set to the side.

She looked around for a priest. Did she have to drink and then be reborn to meet someone? Or was this all self-service?

Tyna fished a coin out of her pocket she tossed it in the misshapen bowl next to the ladles. There were a few sintar in it but not enough to tempt any but the pettiest thief. She drank deeply of the water.

It was good. Cool, crisp, with a tingle to it. She did feel better. Alcohol? No, not alcohol. She took another drink but felt no effect the second time.

"You are not a believer."

Tyna turned quickly. A handsome man of indeterminate years stepped out of the shadows. Like many men, he was just under Tyna's height.

"Are you a priest?" she asked, setting down the ladle.

"That title works." He smiled at her. She smiled back.

"I have a question about reincarnation."

He bent and took one of the ladles and helped himself, then nodded and indicated she should continue.

"Is it possible to be reincarnated into a fully grown body?"

The handsome man frowned.

"The souls returning from the Sea of Souls return only after they have recovered from the hardships of life and are ready to be born anew. It has no memory and is 'born' during conception."

"Conception? So if a man died and then came back to life, it is always his own soul that returns?"

"Ah, such as drowning and then after mouth-to-mouth the victim breathes again?"

"Yeah, something like that."

The priest looked thoughtful as he returned the ladle and walked toward the door of life. He beckoned her to follow. As she stepped out into the light she was momentarily blinded.

"The soul takes time to make it to the River of Death, a man who has drowned has his own soul returned. The longer he is dead the more likely that the trauma of the soul being pulled back will damage it. Those who were 'dead' too long are sometimes broken, never the same. If the soul enters the River of Death, it cannot return without spending time in the Sea of Souls."

"The wrong soul cannot be pulled back?"

"No. No, there are strands of *ka* that connect the soul to the body until entering the River of Death."

"So it is impossible for another soul to take its place," she pushed back.

The priest looked less than sure.

"I have never heard of such a thing. Impossible? Who knows what is impossible."

His gaze upon her was wandering past her face. Was he paying attention to her questions?

"So if someone starts having memories and acting differently, that is just the memories of a past life?"

Now the priest was standing a bit too close and Tyna took a step back. He took the hint and did not pursue, but she was sure he was interested in more than her spiritual wellbeing.

"It is possible, but only the Hrýll have consistently recalled their past lives. Mankind almost never remembers a past life. The soul returns to its own race, which may explain the Hrýll."

"What about half breeds? I thought the Kinel and men could inter-marry and bear children."

"Yes. We have all heard the stories of the first Tarth wars and the Kinel. Of course the Kinel are all dead. But, yes, it is true. I do not claim to understand all of the workings of Pé. However, it does explain why man and the other races cannot interbreed. Kinel and man did interbreed, so their souls must have been related. Perhaps the Kinel and man had common ancestors. Over time new souls are also created in the Sea. I have often wondered if that is why mankind does not remember past lives. We may be the new souls. Or we multiply so fast that more of our souls are new than not."

"If we are reincarnated do we resemble our past selves physically?"

"The Hrýll say that they can recognize each other from past lives. So, at least for the Hrýll, this seems to be true. I have heard lovers say they feel that they were lovers in a past life, but it is hard to separate romantic dreams from reality."

They spoke some more, but the priest seemed weary of her questions once it was clear that she wasn't going to respond to his overtures. She thanked him and made her way back to Lerence and the wagons. It was a long ride home and she had wasted over an hour without a real answer and left with more questions than she had started with.

After the first night on the road, Tyna's nerves settled. The next day she moved deeper into the wagon seat and a little closer to Lerence, who was driving. The horses were responding to him incredibly well and they were making better time than usual, probably four marks an hour. She gazed over the rolling hills and scattered trees. The road was already thinning to almost a trail. There were three or four huge ranches between their place and town. The traffic off of those ranches was enough to keep a trail in good condition, but not enough to justify maintaining a road. Some of the ranchers were rich enough to afford floaters for frequent use, making the need for a road even lower. She wondered how much longer the floaters would last; given the Hrýll alliance with the rebels. Their own ranch didn't depend on many talismans, but they weren't rich.

The wind stirred the marks and marks of grass, making waves that Tyna imagined must be similar to the ocean. She had read of the ocean and The Cities. She dreamed of what they must be like. Millions of people in one small area. It seemed incredible. Even the artifacts and talismans needed to support such a huge populace were hard to conceive. She wanted to see how it all worked. That and all the races that she had heard and read about. The Hrýll and the Yanín. She tilted her head back letting the long midday sun warm her face. She closed her eyes and daydreamed. The rhythmic sound of horse's hooves and the creaking of the wagon wheels were soothing. *Like the ocean waves lapping shore.* She smiled to herself and began to doze.

Thump.

Lerence's arm knocked her backwards; she went flailing into the back of the wagon.

Thump. Thump-thump-thump.

What was that noise? She tried to get up but fell backwards.

The horses were galloping. She saw Lerence standing with his sword in his left hand. *Since when did he use his left hand?* She struggled to get up in the bouncing wagon. There was a black blur. Both horses were knocked off their feet. The wagon rocked, slid sideways, and began to roll. She struggled to jump free as bags and boxes fell on her and about her and the wagon continued its roll, moving past the horses, yanking them viciously as they struggled to regain their feet.

Lerence landed on his feet as a giant cat turned on him. Blood dripped from its mouth. Its golden eyes glowed with intelligence. It didn't leap for Lerence. It bared its teeth and yowled.

Thwick.

An arrow went halfway through Lerence's right thigh. She screamed as she broke free of the wagon debris.

Lerence's right hand shot down and snapped the arrow off. He charged the cat.

Tyna couldn't move her arms. She turned her head to see three Kami. One wore an eye patch. She kicked out at him. Her actions were wild and uncontrolled, but it managed to connect. The Kami groaned but lashed out with his simian hands. He struck her twice, the second blow snapping her head back and pain shot up from her spine.

Thwick. Thwick. Thwick.

She now knew that sound meant arrows hitting flesh.

She rolled her head. Lerence. Oh, Lerence. Three more arrows found him, but he was still standing. She whispered his name as she passed out.

Chapter 8

Larrina screamed. Tsom bolted up, his hands manifested instantly. It was dark, but the light of two moons gently bathed the camp in cool white glow. Everything was black and white.

Larrina sat with her eyes open but unseeing. She screamed again less loudly. She held her thigh as if it were hurt, then she grabbed her shoulder. Then her side, near her belly button. Then her chest above her heart. She shuddered and slumped forward.

Tsom was stunned. He reached out with his left hand, the stronger of the two. He stretched for a long distance, stretching, sensing. A few animals. No strong *ka*. No sentient beings.

He *touched* Larrina. She felt injured at first, but as he desperately began to try and heal her by channeling his own *ka* to her, something he was not very good at, the sense of injuries was gone. A dream? Was her dream so strong that she had manifested something with her ka? She was breathing deeply. Either asleep, or unconscious. He pulled her close and wrapped a light blanket around her, encircled her in his arms. He kept his left hand manifested, just in case. No sentient being would be able to approach without him knowing. It was going to be a long night.

* * *

"Time to get up, sleepy."

Tsom woke with a start. Larrina was already saddling the horses. A pot of tea was steaming over a very small fire. Travel tea, she called it. It gave energy and woke him up. She had a tea for every situation.

"What happened last night?" he asked.

Puzzled, she looked at him.

"Your nightmare, what was it all about?"

"Nightmare?"

He told her what happened while sipping his tea. He needed it. He was exhausted. He fended off her scolding, for using his ka, with a wave of his mechanical hand. Her cheerful morning mood now faded, she listened silently, drinking her own cup of tea. Tsom couldn't remember a time when Larrina didn't have one of her teas close at hand. She had a mix for almost anything, but right now she seemed to take no comfort from her brew.

"Nothing like that has ever happened to me before," she said.

"Maybe it was just a nightmare."

"Maybe." She stared off across the valley, her eyes narrowed. Momentarily some of her age showed around her eyes and the corners of her mouth. Tsom felt a knot in his stomach, remembering that the Kinel looked young until their last years.

"Maybe it was Hallam, our friendly goddess?" he muttered.

"No. She only has power over animals and plants, not people. Our *ka* is subtly different."

"Another god or goddess?" he ventured.

"I've never heard of such a power among the gods. They can only affect mankind. They might be able to touch you, but they shouldn't be able to affect me. One of many reasons even the gods hated us."

Tsom remained troubled as they rode. First the visit from Hallam's minion, then the nightmare. He wished they were near the end of their journey. They were still four weeks out from the Muglanth plains. A lot could go wrong in four weeks. The first major town they would hit would be Tarin. The riders of Tarin were known even in The Cities. In Tarin they should have some protection from prying animal eyes and perhaps whatever troubled Larrina's dreams. The next week passed without incident. Animals watched them silently from the side of the road. First it was simply squirrels and rabbits; occasionally, an eagle that would circle overhead for hours.

Tsom manifested his hand to crush one of the squirrels. Larrina felt the *ka* and put her hand on his arm.

"Don't bother. No need to kill an innocent creature when she can simply jump her concentration to another near one. Why anger her? For the moment, she isn't trying to hurt us."

"For the moment." He grumbled as he dropped his hand.

In the evenings, animals would come up to their camp and lay themselves down next to the pot to be killed. Larrina would have none of it. Instead she would quietly tell Hallam to perform obscene acts on herself and make do with whatever they already had in their stores. After a few days the animals would simply watch, but not lay down next to the pot waiting to be killed.

After their dinner tea they usually slept well, but not in a stupor that would prevent fast awakening. One night Tsom craved Larrina enough to overcome his fatigue. He leaned over her, brushing hair from her eyes, kissing her eyelids gently. She smiled with her eyes closed, one hand under his shirt rubbing his chest. He unbuttoned her blouse and spent considerable time kissing and mouthing her smallish breasts. They were slightly salty from the day's ride. Yesterday they had spent time bathing in a small stream and she still smelled of the pine soap that Larrina had made.

Perhaps it was due to his lack of physical hands, but Tsom enjoyed using his tongue and lips to explore her. He knew every inch of her, but there was still the thrill of exploration as he loosened her pants. Larrina didn't help him, knowing he preferred to undress her himself. She kept her eyes closed with her hands exploring him, loosening his clothes, but not actually taking them off. She pulled the blanket over them to make a loose tent and keep the cool air off. He buried his face into her bare, hairless, crotch.

Tsom had been astonished the first time they made love that Larrina had no pubic hair. She had laughed lightly. "Kinel women have no pubic hair, nor hair under their arms, or even on their legs or arms. Kinel men have no chest hair or beard. Haven't you wondered why you don't need to shave?"

"I thought it was a side effect of my rapid aging," he said, thinking of the past year and his over use of *ka.*"

She laughed again and they soon had no time for more words.

Tonight she pulled his face up and kissed him. Suddenly she needed him inside of her and made it clear. He was happy to oblige. He became caught up in the moment and did not manifest his hands to stimulate her even more, tempting though it was. When they were both exhausted she wouldn't let him leave her. She pulled him deeper inside and whispered, "Stay." Time seemed to change flow and he didn't know how long they stayed joined, but as he rolled to the side, keeping her close, he kissed her eyes and cheeks. She was asleep, breathing deeply. Her face was covered in dried tears.

He lay there staring at her face, her chameleon effect down out here in the wilderness. The curved upside down "V" coloring on her face visible in the cool moonlight. The darker skin vanished to a point on her forehead, her high cheeks pale white, her chin and neck a dark chocolate. He knew that he had the same coloring too, when he did not use his own chameleon effect. His chameleon effect was stronger than Larrina's, honed unconsciously by his years as a thief.

"I wish I could heal you, as you have healed me," he whispered. He lay down next to her, his hand on her breast.

The owl, sitting on the branch of a nearby tree, lifted off silently.

Chapter 9

Tyna woke with her head bouncing off something soft, a warm pillow; a warm *furry* pillow. She opened her eyes quickly and tried to get focused. Black legs and a long tail. Bounce. Behind that a large death cat with a Kami riding it. She was *on* a dui mar. *Keep calm,* she told herself as the mere concept made her stomach turn. She tested her arms and legs. Yes, they were bound, but not cruelly. The blood flowed to her hands and feet.

Then it hit her. Lerence! She remembered the arrows. He was dead. Shot protecting her. She remembered the arrow buried in his stomach. First her father, now Lerence. The damned Tarth and their minions. If she could, she would kill them all right now. She turned her head and looked around more. No point in feigning unconsciousness when she was bound. She was the only human visible. All the other hands must have been killed too. Why was she alive? She shuddered. She had been the only woman in the group.

"Let me up, I'm going to throw up if you leave me like this much longer."

The cat slowed. The ride was quite different than a horse. The ropes binding her arms to her legs across the cat's chest were untied and she was allowed to stand. She threw up. The thoughts of Lerence combined with the aches in her neck and head were too much. The dui mar's nose twitched and it moved away a bit, a low growl rumbling from its chest and belly. Not a purr.

The Kami with the missing eye came up, keeping a careful distance. It bared its canine teeth, longer than the rest. She decided it was smiling. It spoke in common tongue.

"You're awake. Good. The cat wasn't happy with the way we strapped you to its back." He patted the death cat.

"Why am I alive?"

"The nar Tarth said you were needed." His grin vanished.

"Nar Tarth?"

The Kami seemed to grimace. His one eye darted to the other Kami, they all looked unhappy.

"The female Tarth. The companion to Bal'alam." The other Kami seemed to perk up at his name.

Tyna rubbed her neck. So she was not to be raped repeatedly as she had feared. Still, it didn't look like pleasantries would ensue once she arrived to wherever they were headed. She eyed the forest, the three Kami, and the four death cats. Four, she had never heard of more than two and cubs being seen together. The rumors of Hallam allying herself with the Tarth must be true. Gods fighting amongst themselves. This did not bode well for mankind.

She was concerned for one member of mankind in particular. Tears for Lerence would have to wait.

They let her drink water and eat a little bread, which was remarkably tasty. Then they put her on one of the dui mar. The one-eyed Kami, who called himself Synr, told her to wrap her arms around the cat's neck and hold on tight.

"The cats bound in long leaps. Nothing like a horse. Stay on, or we'll tie you on again."

The cats went in spurts. They were sometimes faster than horses, but needed longer resting periods in between. Occasionally, they would stop and let the dui mar hunt, which took very little time. The Kami would share in the meals; after her initial revulsion she ate some of the badly roasted meat. The smell of the burnt outside roiled her still sensitive stomach, but she knew she needed the energy.

They stayed to the forests, working their way east. They were on the edge of the Muglanth plains, moving closer to Zethicia, but staying north, in the forest that ringed the plains. It struck Tyna that the area was a perfect raiding location; hit the towns near the edge of the plains and then fade back into the dense forest.

After five days of travel, they arrived just before dusk. No clearing, just a thinning of the trees, but suddenly they were among Kami and Tarth. The smell of the Kami was borderline overwhelming and Tyna fought back nausea. There were dozens of small tents. A man watched them as they arrived. His head rotated a full 180 degrees and both of his arms bent the wrong way so that they appeared to reverse themselves to fit the direction of the head. He also bore a strange white cap. A Yanín. She'd heard of them, but never seen one. As she stared at it, it returned her gaze without blinking. She remembered that all Yanín in public were male. He walked toward her, what would have been backwards a few moments ago, but now seemed forwards. The three Kami guiding her tensed. Synr's grip on her arm would leave a bruise.

The Yanín stopped a few feet away. It stretched out a leathery hand and touched her belly. She tried to step back, but the Kami held her in place.

Suddenly, a short Tarth grabbed the Yanín's wrist. It was short by Tarth standards, but still over six feet tall, taller than she was by a hair. He was a lighter red, almost pink. But very muscular. The Yanín's eyes narrowed and its arm/hand spun in place, now palm up and it grabbed the Tarth's wrist. They stood this way for several moments. She could see the muscles on the Tarth bulging. He spoke through partially clenched teeth.

"Kulakoonstru, she is for the Tarth."

"Yes. I understand. You may release my arm, Bal'alam. Now." The Yanín was lisping lightly, due to its lips being hard chitin and its tongue that was shorter than a human's. It chose its words carefully and spoke slowly.

The Tarth relaxed his grip and the Yanín pulled back its arm slowly. Tyna had heard that a Tarth could shatter wood by squeezing, yet the Yanín had shown no emotion, no pain. It reversed its head, knees, and arms again and walked away.

The Tarth called Bal'alam looked at her while rubbing his wrist.

"So you are the one we try this time, eh? Bigger than the others. Stronger. Not bad looking. It would not be bad if it worked this time."

She felt cold. She thought about spitting in his face, but it would only accomplish a short spurt of satisfaction followed by a lot of pain. She decided on silence.

Bal'alam waited a moment for her to respond. Then he nodded. In a language that she could almost understand, he commanded the Kami and gestured toward one of the tents. Synr tensed again, causing her arm pain. Not good at all.

Synr pushed her into the tent. Glow globes lit it brightly. So, the Tarth didn't mind using talismans, despite the rumors to the contrary. The female Tarth … what was it the Kami had called the females, nar Tarth … the nar Tarth was beautiful. She was taller than Tyna, maybe six feet four. Lithe very feminine, she was a darker red than Bal'alam. The dark red seemed more the norm for the Tarth. Almost a brown red. Very high cheekbones gave her face a heart shape. Her smile held no warmth, but was not cruel. She gestured to the Kami, who gratefully backed out of the tent.

The nar Tarth came up to Tyna and sniffed.

"You are in your fertile period."

Tyna blushed. Could she really tell that by sniffing? She stayed silent. There was still no benefit to talking.

"Not stupid. I see it you your eyes. What's the point in talking, right? I'll be blunt, human, you will either live or die soon. I hold you no personal grudge. If you wish to speak to me, you may address me as one woman to another. As See'arr."

"OK, See'ar. How do I live?"

See'arr laughed. No mirth.

"Good. You are direct too. Strong. Tall." This seemed to be a thing with the Tarth. "You might be the one."

See'arr turned and walked to a cabinet. With her back toward Tyna, she spoke.

"Kami and Tarth guards completely surround this tent."

She returned with a cup. It was full with a liquid.

"Drink this. Don't refuse, forcing it down your throat would not be pleasant."

Tyna took the cup. Visions of throwing it in See'ar's face occurred to her. She tried to resist sniffing it, but couldn't. It smelled familiar. Poison? She took a deep breath and swallowed it all. Then she asked what she was afraid to ask before.

"What is it?"

"Its main ingredient is my blood." She waited, poised to prevent Tyna from throwing up. Tyna gagged a bit, coughed once, but held it in. Best to not have to drink another one.

"What else was in it?"

"That would be hard to define. Shall we say that I shaped it with my own *ka*. The *ka* of the Tarth is very strong. We cannot shape talismans as the Hrýll do, nor can we use *ka* as the Kinel do, or did—where one ability predominates and becomes easier and easier to use. Yet, sometimes, we can attempt one shot creations with our own *ka*. Very rarely they work. It is good that you did not try and throw up—I had no replacement."

Tyna tried sticking her finger in her mouth, but See'arr caught her hands.

"It's too late. It only takes a few minutes. It is coursing through your system now."

"What have you done to me?" Panic overcame her control for the first time. She'd held herself together so well. She'd prepared herself for the worst on the ride here. She'd rehearsed her emotions. But this was sounding worse than death. Death could be clean. One went to the Sea of Souls and would be reborn, if the priests did not lie. What experiment was this?

The pain was sudden and extreme. It felt as though someone had knifed her in the groin and then reached in and clenched. Like any woman, she'd been taught control over her reproductive functions at an early age. She fought for control. It felt like her uterus was being ripped out. She dropped to the floor. See'arr was looking down with a clinical eye.

Something was grabbing her stomach and crumpling it like a paper, then chewing on the crumpled paper. She grabbed See'ar's leg and pulled herself up. Standing, swaying with pain and nausea, she grabbed See'arr by the neck with both hands and squeezed.

"What did you doooo?"

Ignoring Tyna's stranglehold, See'arr looked at her with a small smile. "You're strong. Very good."

She felt a warmth spill over her legs. Damn, had she peed on herself? She looked down, holding herself up by the grip on See'ar's throat. Blood. She was bleeding. What in Pe's rivers was going on?

The next cramp was too much. More blood. She felt her grip loosen.

Lerence, I may see you sooner than I thought.

Chapter 10

Five moons. Swirling. Five moons? That was strange. Rare. All five of Na-kana's moons shouldn't be visible simultaneously. Not here. He blinked and the five moons resolved into three.

Lerence sat up. He felt good. Coiled energy. Refreshed. Renewed. Why was that strange? He looked around. Nearby was an overturned wagon with two dead horses. Further away two other wagons, beyond that seven more. Ten wagons. He rubbed his head. Ten wagons. That number sounded familiar. Wagons. Trading. Town. Tyna! He ran to where he'd last seen her. Nothing.

Something else was wrong. The grass, it was all black and dead. And, he was running. He felt where he had snapped off the arrow in his leg. There was a hole in his pants, but no wound. Shoulder. Stomach. Chest. All the same. Holes in the cloth, well healed scar tissue. He went back to where he'd first awakened. There was a withered corpse of a death cat, its fur gray. Further away was another. He walked in ever widening circles. Some bodies were withered and aged, some were simply dead.

Underneath one of the wagons, crouched in a fetal position was a withered body. Saan, by his clothes, but he would have never recognized him otherwise. He was mummified, almost a skeleton.

There were five Kami bodies also. All withered and aged.

Lerence rifled all the bodies. A good longbow and some arrows. The swords were not bad, but his father's old sword still felt best. He found the money from their trading. The attackers hadn't been after the money. No body of his sister. Of them all, they had only taken her. If they took her, she might be alive. His racing heart slowed.

The circle of dead grass, dead trees, dead Kami, and dead dui mar, extended for over a hundred feet. Even the insects were dead.

Lerence rubbed his head, failing to find the small bump where the horse, not so long ago, connected. This was feeling very familiar and it wasn't good. He felt cold. Guilty. He shook his head. No time to search fading memories. All he could think of was Tyna. He had to find her.

He found the tracks of four dui mar. One set of tracks the lopes were short and deep. It had been carrying something. He followed the trail easily, at a trot, in the light of the three moons. Physically, he felt great. Energized. As if he could run for days.

At sunrise he didn't slow except for a drink of water. It didn't occur to him that he'd been jogging for over ten hours and wasn't tired. He kept moving. The terrain changed from scattered trees to a full forest. The fir and pine were spaced widely as the trees were ancient and the underbrush received little light. A shadow of a memory flashed before his eyes of a similar forest, recently devastated from war and fire. He blinked and it was gone. The trail was still easy to read. He breathed easily in the cooler air under the canopy of trees and maintained a fast pace. Night tracking would be harder here, best to keep up speed.

Nightfall.

The partial light of two moons filtered weakly through the branches and he slowed to a fast walk. He wasn't really tracking anymore. The path the big cats were taking was straight and he risked staying in one direction and looking for the occasional sign. He was gaining on the dui mar. They rested more than he did. Except for water he felt no need to eat.

Finally, he lost the trail. Given the light, he would have to wait until sunrise to find it again. Lerence sank next to a large fir tree. He braced his back against it. He slid his sword out of its scabbard and onto his lap. He didn't feel tired, but fell asleep instantly.

'What's your name?' the beautiful woman asked.

'Death'

'Where did you come from?'

'The fields of the dead. They're all dead now. The Kinel, the Tarth, the Ricone, the Hrýll.'

'Not all. The battle you speak of was months ago. You're a survivor of that battle.'

'No, I didn't survive.'

She took him into her arms and led him away. After a time—the next day, or perhaps the next month, or year, or many years—she spoke again.

'I'll heal you.'

'Why? I'm not wounded'

'Not physically.'

'Why?'

'Because I love you. Because I can.'

Lerence woke as the sun crested the horizon. Strange dreams. He felt he should remember this dream, it was important, but he soon forgot as he ran along the trail of the dui mar. The death cats. Death cats carrying Tyna. A corner of his mind, the part where his memories as Lerence lived, screamed at the insanity of it. Suicide. A larger part of him welcomed the battle. Someone must pay for hurting her. He would enjoy making them pay. A fury was building within.

Two days later he slowed sniffing the air. Fires. Meat cooking. His stomach growled loudly. He was finally hungry, but he still felt strong. Time for that later. The breeze was from the east. He circled to the north where the trees were thicker. He walked silently, not wondering at the skill he was demonstrating.

Slowly he made his way to the fires. Tarth. A lot of Tarth. It must be the band that had escaped the Zethician War. Daemons and their furry servants. The smell of the Kami was overwhelming. He didn't see Tyna. Maybe she was deeper in?

No matter how he racked his brains he didn't know how he could get any closer. Both the Tarth and Kami had a keen sense of smell and neither covered enough of their bodies to offer a route for disguise. No time for careful plans. An inner voice said, the Tarth do not torture. He did not believe the inner voice.

When in doubt, go for the bold approach. He sheathed his sword. He found an old bag at one of the empty tents on the edge. He stuffed it with leaves. Carrying it as if it were an important package, he strolled into the heart of the Tarth encampment.

Things went well. A few Kami looked at him with suspicion, but he walked as if he owned the place. As if he was here to see the leader of the camp.

There were more Tarth as he neared the center of camp. Several started to approach him, but he looked past them as if he had his destination in mind and they were slowing him down. It worked. He began to relax a bit as luck stayed with him. That was his mistake. He bumped into a Tarth without seeing him.

"Filthy human, watch where you are going. What business do you have in this part of camp?"

The Tarth was huge. Dark red with muscles on top of muscles. His breath stank of something that smelled three weeks dead.

"I'm here with something for the woman." He held up the bag.

The Tarth reached for it, but Lerence pulled it back.

"I was told to only bring it to her tent."

The Tarth bared his teeth.

"Damn See'arr and her foolish dreams," he growled. His head jerked in the direction of one tent set slightly off from the others. Four Kami and one Tarth stood guard outside the tent. As he started walking to the tent, the flap opened and a tall female Tarth stepped out carrying a limp form. Tyna. Dripping blood.

Lerence let out a yell. A battle cry. A cry in a language that Lerence didn't understand. He was by Tyna and the nar Tarth in a blink. The nar Tarth dropped Tyna like a sack of grain and was pulling the sword out of the nearest Kami's scabbard when Lerence struck. He kicked the nar Tarth in the throat and slashed at the male Tarth. Lerence landed on the ground next to Tyna. His peripheral vision sent him a signal that she breathed.

The four Kami were now moving, but one was left handed and the other right. As those two disentangled Lerence lanced the third in the eye, twisting the blade quickly. The forth tried to simply slam its fist into Lerence, which he dodged by dropping to the ground and hacking at Lefty's Achilles. The blade cut only a fraction of an inch, but it was enough to partially cripple Lefty. The slash to the male Tarth had almost no effect.

Damn Tarth skin, he thought. It was worse than boiled leather.

Lefty's companion pushed Lefty aside and tried to stomp on Lerence, as if he were some small animal. Lerence shifted and jabbed with all his strength upward into the Tarth's groin. Slicing might not work, but a small point still penetrated enough. The Tarth was down. He rolled and leapt to his feet, charging the nar Tarth again.

A human would have been dead from a kick to the throat but the nar Tarth was simply angry. She yelled, her voice at least sounding hoarse, orders to the other Tarth running toward her tent.

"Watch out, he is Katar, or something like Katar. His speed and strength are not human. Shoot him. Shoot him. But don't injure the woman." She was yelling in Tarth, not common tongue, and Lerence understood her.

Tyna was important to them. It was a risk, but he saw no other alternative. He yanked Tyna over his shoulder and ran toward the last group of horses he'd seen. Thankfully, not all the Kami rode big cats.

"Don't shoot. You'll hit the woman. Catch them! Surly someone here can out run a human!" The big female Tarth coughed and wheezed. The throat kick must have done more damage than he'd initially thought.

He dug deep within himself for energy. He had to have more speed. Power flooded into him with a whiskey burn, making his muscles alive with fire. Behind him several Tarth stumbled and collapsed, groaning in pain as if something had suddenly injured them.

The horses were unguarded. The thought of guarding horses inside the camp must have never occurred to them. Anyone this deep into the stronghold was an ally, a prisoner, or dead. He threw Tyna over the back of a medium sized gelding and pulled himself up by the mane. Slashing at the ropes he screamed something in a language that he didn't understand. The horses all bolted, knocking down a few Kami rushing in. Behind him was a wall of Tarth. A carpet of angry red. On all other sides the sounds of more closing in.

Lerence held onto the horse's mane with one hand and, after he sheathed his sword on his back, he held Tyna with the other. Voices screamed. It took him a moment to realize that some of them were in his own head. He was repeating the words in his head without understanding them, but the horse moved faster.

Two of the dui mar caught up to him. The screaming in his head increased. He could understand it now. *Don't let yourself get wounded badly or they all die, even Tyna. You don't know how to control yourself. You. I. We. Just a little further. A little further. I sense the weakness up ahead. If we make it there, we can shift.*

Lerence leaned forward and begged the horse for more. His head ached. The landscape blurred from the speed, blurred from his fatigue, he blinked several times to get the wind tears out of his eyes. It really was blurred. He couldn't focus. The world was stretching: a painting on top of a painting. The horse stumbled and the blurring stopped. Just as suddenly, his head stopped aching. It was dark with a single moon overhead.

A single moon was rare, usually the moons rose two or three at a time. It had been two moons all this week. The landscape was rocky, lifeless, cold in all senses of the word. It was as if he were suddenly in the southern hemisphere, where--from the stories his father had told--it never got warm.

His horse stood shaking with fatigue and dripping sweat. Lerence dropped off the horse and lifted Tyna down. The horse just stood there swaying. He petted it, wishing there was something he could do. It had saved their lives. He stood there petting the horse and staring at the landscape. They were not near the Muglanth plains, he was sure of that. He had been born and raised there and this was nothing like it.

He was feeling weak himself now. The more he petted the horse the weaker he felt. Shock setting in. The horse looked better. It turned its head and nuzzled him. It was no longer shaking and its eyes were bright and alert.

Lerence felt tired. So very tired. He sank down next to Tyna and made sure she was breathing. He noticed the blood was all around her groin area. He should check for wounds. He really should. Tired. Need just a moment's rest. Then check for wounds. One moment …

Chapter 11

Arlec chafed at the delays. He was head of the Karn family, by the Sea, he shouldn't have to waste time with meetings. The other families should follow his lead. Had he not led them to victory against the Tarth? It had been his artifact that had saved the day. When the other Katar families had hesitated, he had ordered the burning of Argn to break the siege. Was there any doubt that he was the worthiest amongst equals? Was there any doubt that he was the natural leader of the Katar against their enemies? Their enemies: the filthy rebels, the rumored half-breed Kinel, the Tarth? He thought not. His sisters, those left alive, and the other Katar would acknowledge his leadership and power. Soon. Very soon.

The latest delay had something to do with the deployment of Katar guardsmen in Argn. The area in question was dominated by the religious and musical sect of women known as the Triansriat; strange fanatics that blamed men for all the world's woes. It was bad enough that the Katar of Argn granted women leadership roles, but hesitating over some minor sect with no god to back them up? He didn't give a whore's scream about the Triansriat, Argn had to brought back under Katar control.

He stabbed his pen at the map on his desk several times, punching small holes in the paper and smearing ink over Argn as the tip broke.

Why did this need council approval? So a few women died. Or a few women priests with no god to avenge them. What possible harm could come of simply knocking them out of the way?

Delays. He stood quickly, knocking his chair over. His father had always delayed him. He strode to the fireplace that burned with a preternatural flame. He threw the pen in and watched it burn almost instantly.

He, the Katar, needed absolute control of Argn. It was crucial. The rebels to the north of Argn were rumored to include the thief Tsom. The sooner Argn was under complete control the sooner they could concentrate on wiping out the rebels.

They must be destroyed at all costs.

That damned thief was the cause of his sister's death.

All costs.

Arlec returned to his desk in frustration. The glow globe cast its artificial light over his room and his desk, mocking the inability of the Katar to control the manufacture of talismans. The Hrýll had been punished for allying with the rebels, but not too severely. The need for new talismans was too great. Damn the monopoly the Hrýll had over the talismans. At least The Cities, and by association the Katar, controlled the source of fuel. The quenar. No talismans, no quenar. The Hrýll soon saw reason, but the quantity and quality of talismans were both down. Arlec was sure that would change once the rebellion was crushed. He knew they were syphoning off some talismans. It all came back to the rebels and Argn.

He rubbed his left hand's ring finger. Spinning the ring of the Katar around his finger. So powerful, he mused, yet that damn thief had stolen his ring effortlessly. As if Arlec was not Katar. Someday, that damned little thief would pay. Pay more than the loss of his hands. Someday he would die the true death.

His anger triggered the ring, very subtly. The soft glow should have given him pause, but he continued to brood; not knowing, or caring, the effect his ring was having. The servants within the building began feeling ill. Slightly off. The elderly excused themselves for the day. Nothing unusual at a Katar household; the risk for working for the Katar included early death and constant fatigue. The benefits of working for the Katar were the shadow of power and the high pay.

Arlec continued to toy with the ring. The black center diamond glowed in response. A knock on the door interrupted his brooding. His sisters, always a pair, entered. Larra and Piea lately caused him to wince. He knew it was due to guilty feelings concerning Shara, their dead sister. He had had no choice, but could never explain it to them. Their judgmental stares burned with a branding intensity. Something else he would eventually have to attend to. So be it. A leader often had to sacrifice personal relationships for the good of the group.

Larra spoke first. She was the eldest and still viewed him as the baby brother. She had stupid notions of female equality from her time in Argn and resented his ascension to power now that his father was dead. Arlec wondered if she suspected him. She was no fool, woman or not.

"Arlec, stop messing with your ring."

She held up her hand where her ring glowed in response to his. It was protecting her from the draining power of his ring, just as all Katar rings did. He jerked his hand up and now sensed that he had been so stressed that he had been inadvertently using his ring. Well, what of it? So a few servants died a day or two earlier than normal. Still, he knew it was frowned upon by the families and he relaxed his mental hold on the ring and the glowing stopped.

"Is that all you came here for?" he asked.

"It would have been enough." Piea replied, looking angry. "Father would have disciplined you for such meaningless use of the ring."

"Father is no more. I am the leader of the Karn clan now."

"You are the head of a clan." Larra responded. Her changing of his words was not lost on Arlec. He bit back an angry retort and waited.

"You must relax martial law on Argn and let Jern resume his rightful role in running the city."

Larra said this as she strode up to his desk and sat down across from him without invitation. She was quite attractive, but his sister and her feminine attributes would not distract him as they did so many other Katar.

"Jern and his two daughters let Argn go up in chaos. He can't be trusted. In these dangerous times we must rule with a strong fist, the control of the Katar, and Jern is too weak. Too maidenly."

He stopped, realizing his faux pas. Well, time his sisters started acting the way women should. He folded his arms across his chest and stared at both of them.

Piea, losing her normal self-control, spoke; her contempt audible.

"Arlec, you're being an ass. You know either of us could best you in battle and women have ruled Argn for centuries. Argn is enlightened enough to let both women and men rule and Jern knows that his daughters are as capable as any son of any of the families." She looked pointedly at Arlec, who felt a flush rising and was forced to control tapping his ring once again. She continued, "Argn fell because it was closest to the Hrýll and the rebel network was strongest both in Argn and here in Arbeneth…" she paused to emphasize the latter point, "… where this Alanar had a huge mansion right under our noses and where the thief Tsom, that you let slip free, came from. The thief that was able to steal your ring. Steal it and use it. Did you forget how the priesthoods were running scared? Don't go blaming Jern or the city of Argn for the rebellion. Blame the legacy of the Katar and our own stupidity."

Arlec trembled with rage. How dare she bring up his loss of a ring? He gripped the desk edge. Larra took over.

"Look, Arlec, you need to soften your stance on Argn. Now. The other families are ready to turn against you. The Sphere of Banishment is no longer under your control. While you were clever in ensuring that most of the other families lost more troops than ours, we are hardly strong enough to face all four. Argn is in ruins, let Jern focus on that instead of on you. He and his daughters are not to be trifled with. Don't forget that Argn trains all female Katar in fighting. Jern has allies in all the families." She paused and stared straight at him. She rose halfway out of her chair and leaned toward him. "You are my brother, but I am my own mistress. Do not push me Arlec." She leaned back and waited.

He hated when his sisters were right.

Only his control of the port that all the cities used, combined with his family now having both the largest force and the biggest financial reserve, kept them respectful. That and his alliance with the priesthoods. The zealots were still worried about Tsom, because of some prophesy that only the gods knew about. Still, the religious hunt for Tsom and his own were the same. He craved vengeance against the man who had stolen from him, helped the rebels, and forced him to act against his younger sister Shara. She had claimed to have fallen in love with him. A commoner. A Kinel half breed. Even if the old texts were true and traces of Kinel blood flowed through the veins of all Katar, he could not accept the Kinel as equals. In some ways the truth of the traces of Kinel blood in Katar made him hate Tsom more.

He nodded to Larra and forced a smile.

"Of course Larra, I concur with your analysis. Argn is cleansed of rebels, it does no harm for Jern and his clan to take over the day to day administration of Argn. We still need to rid the other cities of the rebel vermin. Please convey my wishes in this regard to Jern."

Larra and Piea looked at each other, not quite trusting what they were hearing. Larra got up and as one they left the room.

Arlec waited until they closed the door and then strode over to one of the many bookshelves in his father's ... no his ... study. He pulled down the book he had discovered last night. It was an old handwritten manuscript by one of his ancestors. It was on the Kinel race and the Katar. Shocking and yet potentially useful. If this Tsom was indeed Kinel it explained much.

Returning to his desk with the book he gazed at the fire that needed no tending and saw his father's image in the flames. The long knife that he had stuck in his father's eye was there. The accusing face flickered and disappeared. Arlec reached for his drink and reread about the destruction of the Kinel by the Katar.

Chapter 12

The weeks following their visit from Hallam were strained. Larrina's nightmares continued and she had a panic in her eyes each time they made love. "I'm afraid I'll have that feeling again, as if someone was in my head." He didn't need to ask who that someone was.

Soon, the feeling of wellbeing that always accompanied their love making was gone. Not the normal wellbeing of any lover, but Larrina's healing. One day she told Tsom, tearfully, to stop using his non-corporeal hands during love making.

What had he done? Why was she pushing him away? Was Alanar's ghost intruding? Tsom still missed Shara, but they had each other now. Larrina had helped him move on. Why was it that he wasn't good enough for her to do the same?

He knew in his heart it should be enough that he was better and that Larrina had shared herself with him, but it was not. He wanted her to be his. All of her.

One night, as they made love, Larrina bit her lower lip and turned away with tears running down her cheeks.

"Larrina, you're not even here. You're with a dead man."

She looked at him with sadness in her eyes. Then pulled away.

"You're right."

No, his mind yelled.

She hugged herself and laughed bitterly.

"I'm almost four hundred years old and I'm acting like ..."

She stopped.

"Kinel relationships were rarely for life, Tsom. We live too long."

"We've barely begun," he said, standing and buttoning his pants with his mind hands. "Yet, you cast me away as if we were human teenagers."

She bowed her head.

"He's alive, Tsom. Somewhere. He needs me."

"I need you," he growled.

"You want me. I've healed you enough. Your body will recover a bit more on its own now."

"That's not what I meant."

"Am I such a poor substitute for Alanar?" He took a step toward her, looked at her face and stopped.

She smiled at him as she dressed.

"Tsom, until you I had not been with a man for fifty years. You drew me out. Let that be enough."

Tsom thought of the change he'd seen Alanar go through in the months just before…before Tsom had banished him, or killed him. Oonie and Larrina had both been drawn to that changed Alanar.

"We were good together, but we can also be good as friends. You are still so young. I may have less than a hundred years left."

He kept at it for the rest of the night, but she refused to lose her temper and refused to relent. For the first time, in more months than he cared to think about, they slept apart.

Tsom's jealousy grew. He fantasized about how he would use his powers to destroy Alanar if he were still alive. Some nights he awoke to find hand imprints on nearby trees. The bark crushed into the wood. His dreams were manifesting themselves dangerously. Yet, he felt no weaker from the obvious use of *ka* in his sleep. Larrina appeared not to notice, but he suspected she did. She rarely missed anything when it came to *ka*.

The Muglanth plains were finally visible. Rolling hills of green for as far as the eye could see. The tall grasses rippling like waves, reminding Tsom of his youth and the docks of Arbeneth. Youth. In his head, he laughed. He was physically middle aged, but barely twenty. Youth was only a few years ago, before he had stolen the cursed ring that had changed his life.

As a child he had gazed out across the water many times dreaming of adventure across the seas. He'd never made it over the ocean, but in the past couple of years he had traveled further than he had ever imagined and seen more than most of the sailors who had enchanted him with their tales.

The air changed as they descended toward the plains. It was richer and moister. The smell of ripening grasses arrived with the occasional gust of hot air. The horses sped up, wanting to feast on the verdant vegetation of the lowlands, each stalk a meal compared to the slim pickings of the mountains.

The change let Tsom forget his anger and he gave his horse its head and let it trot down the mountain path. He ignored the cautionary calls from Larrina and suddenly the horse was galloping. Galloping downhill on a mountain path. Tsom knew this was not good. As he worked to control the horse the path gave way under its feet. Only two feet making contact, the horse had no way to maintain its balance. They fell.

Tsom was a thief. He was always fast on his feet and fast to react. He manifested his hands, lifting himself off the horse with one and grabbed onto a small tree rushing by with another. He was clear of the horse. He lowered himself down to the ground, momentarily proud of how well he had done that. His weight had not affected his ability to lift even when he had stretched his hands over twenty feet. His self-satisfaction was short lived.

Larrina was next to his horse, which was on the ground struggling. She rested her hands on its neck and spoke to it in a language Tsom did not understand. It calmed and turned its head toward her, its right eye focusing on her. It nuzzled her hand and waited. She pulled her knife out and slit its throat. Even from a distance he could see she was crying. She wiped the knife clean and sheathed it. Then she took the saddle bags and packs off, leaving the saddle on the horse. Standing, she walked past him without looking at him, her mouth an angry, thin line. She tied the bags on her horse and walking in front of the horse she started downhill.

Tsom took a step toward the horse's body. *We could have tried healing him,* he thought. *I would have been willing to use my ka.* But, he wasn't a healer and had never even tried on an animal.

With a bowed head Tsom followed.

Both noticed the birds circling over where the horse had gone down, but in silent agreement said nothing. The single eagle overhead also raised no comment.

They made their way toward Tarin. They needed another horse.

Three days out from Tarin they came to the edge of a blackened circle. All vegetation within the circle was dead. All small animals were withered and mummified. Larrina stood at the edge of the circle trembling. Her hand went over the edge and then returned to the green side. Tsom imitated her movement with his mind hand. He jumped back. No *ka.* None. A complete absence of it. He had never felt something like that before.

As he understood from conversations with Larrina, all life had *ka* of some sort. Human, or any of the races, had the strongest *ka.* Yet, even animals and plants had some minute *ka.* After their visit from Hallam; Larrina explained that of all the gods, Hallam could tap the *ka* of animals and perhaps plants. The other gods all depended on man. Not the other races, but man. Here, in this circle, was no ka, not even the background buzz that he always felt.

"What did this Larrina?" He was watching her as she slowly stepped into the blackened area and walked. He followed, fighting the unease that the lack of *ka* was causing. They topped a small rise and gazed at the wagons scattered before them. Dead mummified horses attached to the wagons. A few strangely not rotting corpses mixed in with mummified human corpses. Two dui mar mummies. The death cats looked strangely small.

Larrina kept walking until she was in the center of the blackened circle. Near the dui mar. She knelt and her hands touched the ground. Here the grass was green. A lush green. It was dense and thick. Larrina sat and pulled her legs so her chin rested on her knees. She was rocking back and forth a bit, shaking her head. Tsom waited, watching her. Finally, she spoke.

"He lives. Alanar lives. There is only one being in Nakana that can do this. He will have changed. If he had to resort to this, he will have changed. For better, or for worse; and by the Sea help us all if it is for worse."

* * *

Lerence opened his eyes to meet the gaze of two almond shaped emeralds framed by an explosion of red. He blinked.

"Lerence?"

Tyna. She must be ok. He blinked again and focused on her face. She was flushed. Her skin was a pale pink. Fever? He sat up, she had her arm under his head and neck and supported him. She smelled strange. Cinnamon and orange and musk. Like a mare in heat mixed with perfume. His head swam. Had he been kicked again? No, that was not right. He had been calming the horse.

"You aren't really Lerence, are you?"

He tried to focus on Tyna's face, but her smell kept intruding. His mouth was alternately dry and then he was salivating.

"What do you mean? Tyna, are you ill? You're feverish."

She pulled his head closer to hers. Her breath stank of musk. It was hot. Her lips were red, redder than normal. She was covered in sweat. He could feel his heart racing. His adrenalin increasing.

She smiled and with her lips inches from him replied.

"I can sense it. You are not really Ler. Even now you've changed. You're older, leaner, stronger. You survived the dui mar by the wagons. Your way with horses. Your sudden fighting ability. Who are you? You look vaguely like my brother, but less and less so with each passing day."

She tightened her grip on his head, her right hand twined in his hair. It was not threatening. Her neck muscles suddenly tensed. Lerence tried to protest her words, but some small part of his head nagged at him. The words he had been yelling out as they had fled. What had happened in the battle with the dui mar? He couldn't remember. He was having a hard time thinking with Tyna so close. She was burning up. He could feel the heat of her radiating in waves. Her smell was overpowering. He opened his mouth to protest. She pulled his mouth to hers and kissed him. Her tongue almost brutally inside his mouth. Her saliva tasted strange. It was very salty and sweet, yet burned like brandy. His vision blurred.

He began to pull away. This was his sister. Wasn't he Lerence? He felt his erection painfully pushing against his pants. She pulled back for a moment. There was confusion in her eyes. It was mixed with lust. She looked into his eyes.

"Your eyes. They are changing. Right now. They are gold on gold."

As she spoke she straddled him. His face flushed. He felt energy all around him with a concentration within Tyna. If he was not Lerence, was she still Tyna? She was a flame within flame. Her red hair surrounding her pink, almost red face. Heat radiated from her. His nostrils flared wide and his vision stayed blurry. She was unbuckling his pants while staying on top of him. He did not resist. Instead he pulled her closer and tasted her mouth again. So salty. So sweet. Where had he tasted that before? His head felt as if it would explode. A tiny voice said not to resist. Don't panic. Panic was bad.

He was inside of her without knowing quite how it had happened. His vision kept blurring. He saw Tyna's face then another woman's then another. Three women. All seemed familiar. As her sweat touched his skin he felt his heart race faster. She smelled stronger now. Her sweat reeked and it drove him mad. Blood. He tasted blood.

* * *

They lay exhausted and naked upon the spare ground. Their clothes lay ripped and scattered around them. They had made love continuously for four hours. They were in pain and Tyna was bleeding from between her legs. As they lay there, too tired to move, Lerence spoke.

"Tyna, they did something to you."

She tried to nod, but could not. With a sob, she croaked out a, "yes."

They were moving slowly toward each other. They both knew that it was to make love again. Love? No, sex. Not even at an animal level, this was self-destructive. She felt as if she would die of exhaustion, but she dragged herself toward him. He was doing better than she was. She had at first thought that she was trying to convince herself that Lerence was someone else. Gazing at this man, leaner than Lerence and with gold eyes, she knew it was true. Lerence had died when the horse had kicked him. This was someone else. Somehow. Then she stopped thinking. He was in her again and she felt a wave of new strength. She pulled him deeper, ignoring the pain and the groan that issued forth from one, or both of them.

* * *

"How long?" Lerence whispered.

"I think it has been over a day. The sun and the moons are not right here."

"When will it stop?" He asked as he gently pulled her head onto his chest. She could see he had an erection.

"I think I know what it takes. Ler, I need to call you something different, what should I call you?"

"Alan."

"Why Alan?"

"I don't know."

They were intertwined again. She was almost without sweat, having used it all up hours ago. Almost, but not quite. Alan, as she now would think of him, was looking bad. She knew that she was bleeding from her vagina, but it was a numb pain. While she would still crawl toward him as soon as physically able, she would roll on her back and let him do most of the work. They had tried alternating for the first few hours after the first session of pure madness and lust. It seemed an eternity ago. They had talked every few hours as they rested just enough to start again. They had joked about honeymoons and soreness. That first few hours of madness she knew that they both had not resisted. Even without the madness there was an attraction. Now, it was killing them.

"Alan, I think we are going to kill each other if we continue much longer."

She said this without emotion. She worried that all that remained of her was this thing beyond lust, but even the worry was emotionless. Alan seemed to be fighting. His emotions were there, under the surface, but it was as if he were afraid to let them out to comingle with the driving need they both were responding to. She no longer really cared. She no longer felt pain. She no longer felt anything.

He was silent as they moved closer and then together. She stared into his strange golden eyes as they had sex. He sensed that she was fading. He felt a core of rage at his impotence in his ability to save her blossom. Suddenly his eyes flashed. They turned momentarily black—the iris black upon a black sclera—then back to gold iris on white sclera, he pulled her closer and was deeper inside of her. She felt a massive wave of *ka*. She knew what *ka* was. All women did, they could sense life better than men. Women knew life from its first stirring. Alan was enveloping her in ka, it was overwhelming. It was an explosion. She was strong. Stronger than she had ever felt. She could feel him inside of her, she was no longer numb. The explosion of *ka* was now inside of her. She pulled him deeper and her nails drew blood. Her scream was primal and echoed across the barren rocks. It intermingled with his groan that sounded painful and relieved.

It had stopped. The self-destructive mating urge subsided. She could feel the emotions that had been subsumed by the mating madness come flooding. Within that maelstrom she felt love for this man. She lay exhausted in Alan's arms and as she fell asleep she whispered.

"I'm pregnant."

Chapter 13

Flana stormed out of her father's office, her green leather boots making a muf-
fled thump with each step. The greedy old fool was urging her once again to
cement her relationship with Arlec, even after all that had happened in the past
year. Father had as much as told her to make love to Arlec and hook him that
way if necessary. She pushed past the servants and ignored the offers of tea or
a bath as they saw her mood. Making her way to the outside door she yelled at
poor gentle Ulna.

"Get my horse saddled immediately."

Ulna blinked at her voice, but nodded. Ulna's limp caused a twinge of guilt,
but Flana's rage washed over it quickly.

She didn't want to use the ostentatious floater. She wanted all symbols of
wealth and power—symbols cemented with her body, if her father had his
way—to disappear. She wouldn't stand out on horseback and right now she did
not want to be part of the Showa family.

She knew she was expected to increase the power of the family by marriage.
It was what the women in the family had done for centuries. It didn't mean she
had to like it. Damn her luck in being born in Arbeneth instead of Argn. There,
at least, the women and the men both married for advantage. There the women
were leaders also. Openly, not behind closed doors as it was here in Arbeneth.
She doubted that Arlec shared power even behind doors and shuddered at what
else might occur there.

She mounted the horse effortlessly, pushing herself over the saddle more
than pulling. The saddle didn't shift. She knew she should check the saddle
and bridle, but she trusted her servants. Digging her left foot back on the horse,
she cantered off the grounds and into the outskirts of the city. Very impolite,
but she didn't care. Not today.

The Showa compound was as large as any Katar estate. It included several
marks of riverfront, with private docks and several luxury yachts. The area of

the city she entered was rich merchant class and the Showa were the richest. She headed south toward the city's main commerce docks. She enjoyed it there where she could think in peace. No obsequies from her so-called peers. No need to always be the lady.

She slowed down to a trot; best not to injure some poor pedestrian. Riding soothed her and she didn't force the horse to keep going as it stopped to defecate. Almost immediately the street cleaner appeared with his large cargo floater and shoveled the manure into the back. He caught Flana gazing at him and nodded politely. She nodded back, which surprised him enough to smile.

Arlec was a good catch. She knew that. A Katar marrying a mere merchant, albeit powerful one, was rare. The Karn family were incredibly powerful and Arlec was now head of the clan, after his father's unfortunate murder. Arlec blamed that young thief that they had bumped into over a year ago during Festival. She remembered the young man's face after all this time. He had seemed drunk, but there had been a mischievous wink on his face after he had knocked her down. It seemed hard to believe that he was a danger to the Katar and the priesthoods. She suspected Arlec's father had met his end from other quarters. How had the thief avoided capture all this time? Perhaps the Tarth War had distracted the Katar too much. Rumor had it that many of their irreplaceable rings had been lost.

Flana fingered her small family talisman depicting Ague, the God of the Seas, Showa's patron god. Her family contributed large amounts to that priesthood. Very large. Large enough that any family foolish enough to send out competing ships soon found that the ships would be lost at sea, with survivors a rarity. Flana knew that the power of the priests was real, if not omnipotent. She enjoyed the thought of a young thief flouting that power.

Arriving at the warehouse district she stabled her horse with one of the family warehouses. She ignored the protests of the employees that she should not wander the docks alone. She was known by enough of the people here that she felt no real danger. It was daylight and the dangerous scoundrels of the night would be sleeping off their drugs and alcohol from the night before.

The smell of fish and spices were strong, but not overpowering. The docks and the streets were sprayed with pressurized sea water daily. The smell was not rotten, just strong. Merchants from throughout Arbeneth and from the rest of The Cities were busy buying, selling and arranging transport. Her obvious expensive clothes drew the occasional look, but there were enough tourists and merchant women that she did not stand out egregiously. Her ubiquitous green was muted today. Her riding dress was a dark green, almost black. Her blouse was a pale light green, but not too bright. Those who knew her spotted the colors immediately and nodded and smiled. All so polite and all due to her family's power. She wondered what they really thought. What if the rebellion spread, would she be safe then?

She sat at an outdoor tavern and ordered a wine and fried squid. She loved the crunchy chewy combination and didn't worry about how it would affect her figure. She knew her figure and metabolism were enviable.

Two women sat down next to her. One on each side. She was about to protest that she wanted to be alone when they each laid their left hand on each of her hands. The ring with the five white diamonds and the black one in the center was introduction enough. Katar. She looked at each of them in turn. They were familiar. Yes, Arlec's sisters. Piea and Larra. Both were beautiful while simultaneously appearing dangerous. She would not be intimidated.

"You're Arlec's sisters."

The older one nodded. It was hard to concentrate on both of them at once, so she focused on Larra. Larra, she was sure, was the older one.

"We want to speak with you about Arlec."

Not these two also. Did everyone want her to bed and marry him? She scowled at Larra and then turned and scowled at Piea for good measure.

"My father has just been pressuring me to move faster with your brother. I don't need your pressure too."

Larra's left eyebrow rose a bit. She smiled. Her almost perfect teeth were flawed by a chip in one of the incisors. Flana wondered how she had chipped that tooth.

"You mistake our intentions. We are here to warn you against Arlec."

Flana became angry. So she was not good enough for their brother? How dare they? She was from the most powerful family outside of the Katar clans. Dozens of men and their father's had vied for her hand. Piea interrupted her silent tirade.

"Larra, she still doesn't understand. She thinks we're protecting Arlec," Piea said, a twitch of her mouth showing amusement.

Larra cocked her head slightly and then laughed out loud.

"Flana, we're warning you that Arlec is dangerous. You should not marry him for your own safety. It is not that we don't think you are good enough for him. We think he is not good enough for you. We have reason to believe that he murdered our father. He craves power and does not respect women. We don't want to see you become his next victim. Or your father."

They let this sink in. The fried squid arrived and Larra signaled for wine for her and her sister. The waiter, seeing their rings, scurried off with a stiff smile frozen on his face.

Larra did most of the talking, but occasionally Piea would chime in. They'd been watching her for some time. Ever since Arlec had shown interest in her. She was not surprised. All the powerful families had spies who checked into these things. Yet, it bothered Flana to have it spelled out in the open. Was nothing in her life private? Initially, they were trying to protect their brother. However, the past year the evidence mounted that he had been the one to murder their father and was indirectly responsible for the death of their younger sister, Shara. Little clues, including their own interrogation of some of the household guards, began adding up to larger clues. Through their own network they found a young man who had been paid to be seen the night of the murder. Unfortunately, he had met with an accident not long after they talked with him.

The story of how Shara was locked up and drugged by her own brother sickened Flana. The hints that Larra and Piea gave as to the other indignities she had suffered added anger to that.

Larra snacked on the fried squid that Flana was now ignoring, then she sipped her wine and continued speaking.

"You're not naïve Flana, you must know that the Katar are no longer united. Arlec has turned Jern, of Argn, against the other four families. Jern feels that they improperly destroyed most of Argn to get at the rebels. He feels weakened and threatened. The other families know this and most are allied with Arlec now, out of necessity, or fear. Within the families, many of the Katar women are divided in their loyalties. Loyalty to their family and loyalty to their shared training and camaraderie from training in Argn. All female Katar share a fondness of that colorful city, where women are equals.

"With the loss of a quarter of the Katar forces in the Tarth war, we are weakened. We must prevent a civil war between the Katar, but many of us refuse to let Arlec lead us into destroying both one of the families and the city of Argn to do it. We are recruiting women of power to join us. To join us in Argn and make it an unattractive target for Arlec."

Flana listened and meshed what she was hearing with what she knew. They were right, she was not naïve. She also knew more of the economic empire that her father ruled over than he suspected. Many of his spy network were part of her own. She fingered her sea talisman and spoke.

"What of the gods? I've heard that within the pantheon of gods a similar break is occurring. Hallam is allied with the remaining Tarth and would destroy all the other gods, even mankind. Pé's priesthood had been preaching blasphemies concerning the other gods, encouraging people to stop worshipping with prayer. Telling all who would listen that prayer was draining their life essence, their ka, and giving it to the gods. His priests are also preaching that the Katar are worse than the gods. That your rings drain us all of our ka, whether we pray or not. Whom do I trust? The gods? Which god? The Katar? Which Katar clan? The rebels? They were rumored to have allied with the Tarth before the banishment of Zethica."

Larra and Piea twisted their rings nervously. Flana noticed that the Katar all had that nervous habit. Arlec was the same. He had even rubbed his ring finger that day that the thief had stolen his ring. It meant they were nervous, or guilty, or both. Larra caught her gaze and stopped twisting the ring. She leaned forward and impulsively grabbed Flana's hand into both of hers.

"Some of the Katar are willing to change. The priests of Pé are telling the truth. We do drain ka, often indiscriminately. Most of the Katar don't even know that is how the rings work, or they don't want to know. But, not all of us.

When we achieve a peaceful balance between the families and the rebels, we can work on changing. We are not evil, but we need the power of the Katar to keep the Tarth, the gods, and the rebels at bay."

"But your power is killing us. That is what Pé's priests are warning us of. It is what the rebels tell us too. How can I ally with any of you? I agree that I can't marry your brother." The latter was now a truth. She'd been wrestling with her situation with Arlec and now she knew what she felt. If nothing else, this conversation made up her mind on this piece of her life. Larra kept her hand between hers and would not give up.

"I cannot promise you too much Flana. We will not create a power vacuum by eliminating the source of power of the Katar. But, if Argn and the women Katar succeed, we will change. It may take generations, but we will change the use of the rings. We will also force the gods and their priests to change. Over time. We need smart women like you as part of the leadership in Argn. You would be respected both for your intelligence and because they know you. They know you will have given up power to join them and they know you are used to giving orders. Your training as the daughter of the most powerful merchant within The Cities is valuable to us."

"And if I refuse? With what I now know of your plans? Can you trust me when you have an implicit threat built in to your offer?"

Piea was rubbing her ring furiously. Letting go of Flana's hand, Larra lightly slapped Piea's hand. Piea blushed lightly. Then she spoke.

"We let you go. You won't go running to Arlec, that much is certain. I can see it in your face every time I mention his name. Everything else we've spoken of is not so secret that someone within the families doesn't know it. They don't fully comprehend how it all fits, but they have heard it. You are just a commoner to most Katar. Even if you married and gave birth, it would be your offspring that was Katar, never you. You don't pose a threat if we let you go. There is no implied threat here. You are either with us, or a minor issue. We," she gestured to her sister, "are different than most Katar. By not killing you if you refuse, we at least plant that seed of truth within the important families within The Cities."

"I'm with you." Her blood was pounding in her ears, making her own words hard to hear. It was right. She felt it. These were women she could trust, to a point.

"Good," said Larra, pulling out a folded paper from her blouse. "You leave immediately. Here are introduction papers to Crissa and Mia, Jern's two daughters and de facto rulers of Argn and the joint Katar and non-Katar league."

"We have to come up with a better name," piped in Piea.

Chapter 14

Alan and Tyna awoke parched and ravenously hungry. Alan, the name felt almost right, was the first to rise. Pregnant. That's what Tyna said as they both passed out. A small part of his brain screamed that this was shameful. It would be a disfigured idiot child, born of a brother and a sister. Then he remembered she was not really his sister, just step-sister and from there his brain accepted, once again, he really wasn't Lerence. Not anymore. He shivered and found their clothes scattered nearby. They were worse for wear, but still usable and it was decidedly chilly. He gently covered Tyna with her clothes and let her continue sleeping.

Water was no problem. He followed the slope until a small trickle of a stream formed. Drinking his fill he returned to find Tyna dressed and rubbing her arms to warm them. The blood on her pants, in the groin area, was dried and cracked. She was still too pink, as if her skin had permanently changed color. She smiled tentatively at him.

"Alan?"

"Yes?"

She appeared relieved that he responded to the name. He held out his hand and helped her to her feet. They stood next to each other, staring into each other's eyes. He noticed that he was looking slightly down into her eyes. Strange, she had always been as tall as him. He glanced down to his feet to see if he was on higher ground. No. She seemed to understand what he was thinking.

"I told you. You've changed. You're definitely not my brother." The last had a hint of question to it. Was she not sure? He looked at his arms. He was darker skinned than before. More muscular. He'd never had rippling arm muscles, but he did now.

Pregnant. It hit him again.

There was something shocking beyond the fact that Tyna was his step-sister. He should not be able to father a child. He was sure of it. Yet, he could not explain why he was sure. His memories were becoming more confused, instead of less, as time went on. He rubbed his temples, as if that would help.

"I have his memories, but I have other memories. I ..." he pulled her closer and sniffed. No, no musky smell. No air born drug. That was gone now. Yet, he felt the attraction. It was real and didn't feel evil. She was not his sister. "... am not your brother. But, I don't know who I am."

He took her to the small stream and she cleaned up and washed her clothes. As she bathed, openly and unabashedly in front of him, they spoke of what the Tarth had done to her. Alan listened and asked a few questions on details.

When she was finished bathing, rather than let her shiver naked, he gave her his own pants and tied her wet pants around his waist as a loincloth. They would switch when her clothes dried. She was a large woman, but slim and he knew her pants would not fit him. As they changed he mused out loud.

"You're their brood mare."

"What do you mean?"

"They intend for you to facilitate cross breeding between the Tarth and mankind. You were to give birth to other Tarth. Tarth half-breeds."

"Why? Why would they want half-breeds?"

"Survival. Half-breed is better than extinction. There are almost no female Tarth left. They breed slowly and with so few the species is doomed. They may be better fighters than man, but they can't beat the numbers. Sheer numbers will win. This is their way out."

"So once I became pregnant, the need to mate disappeared?"

"Yes, that must be it. The Tarth males might not normally be attracted to you. Or perhaps it was something in the mixing of human and Tarth that went awry. Perhaps the idea was that not just one Tarth would mate with you. A brood mare."

Tyna shuddered and Alan echoed the sentiment. That nar Tarth, See'ar, had said that there had been others. Had they all died by rape? She rubbed her arms more. It was very cold. Did she love Alan? Or was it the drug, or whatever one called that concoction that she had been forced to drink.

No, that had triggered the physical lust, but she had to admit that something had been there for several weeks. Ever since her brother died—as she now thought of the blow to his head—she had felt differently about him. Did he love her? Or was it just male lust triggered by her sweat.

She dared not abort the child. Normally, any well trained woman could will the abortion, but what then? Another day of destructive sex? Neither of them would survive. Also, she was forced to admit to herself, she wanted this child. She could feel its life force within her. It was Alan's and she loved him. Would their mother understand? Would she believe that Alan was not Lerence? She had to. It was true.

Again, Alan seemed to be thinking along the same lines as she.

"You must carry the child, at least for now. I don't think either of us would survive another mating lust."

The horse had wandered off, but not far. It found a small patch of grass and leafy bushes near where the small stream petered out onto a small flat area. Tyna found the landscape and weak sunlight very disturbing. The lack of multiple moons made it all worse. In her desperation to find something familiar, she focused on the mountain ridge in the distance.

"Alan, that ridge. If we were home that would be the Arm of Glannon. The range northwest of our ranch. Look at the three peaks on the left, each one slightly larger and taller than the previous. And the hills to the east, the Hand of Glannon. Except that there is no green here. They are snow covered. Barren. Cold."

He stepped behind her and wrapped both arms around her as she was speaking. It was warm and comforting; she paused momentarily to absorb the feeling. He followed her hand and she could tell he was getting excited as he recognized the features too. He turned and called out to the horse in a language she didn't recognize.

"What is that language Alan?"

"I don't know its name. I used it when we were fleeing, when you were unconscious on the horse. Since then, and since …" he looked cautiously at her, almost shyly. "…since the last time we made love and you conceived, I am remembering things. I think that the language is one I used to speak. To horses. A long time ago. A very long time ago."

She was silent. A long time ago? Yet, that confirmed her feeling, her knowledge that he was not her brother. A spirit that took over his body as he died from the blow to the head? A ghost that was not a ghost? He was alive. He was a man. As he spoke she felt very young and that he was very old.

The horse trotted up to Alan and let him groom him with his hands. Alan checked his feet. All were sound and no rocks. The Kami did not shod their horses, but the hooves were in good condition. He gestured for her to mount and she momentarily thought of arguing with him, but she felt how weak she was. He looked older, leaner, but no longer weak. As if he were using all fat up to gain energy. She touched his cheek and then mounted, with the help of a boost from behind. Alan pointed to the mountain ridge.

"The Web. It is part of the Web. We must go there to get back home."

"The Web?"

He shrugged. "The Web of the Gods. I don't remember all of it, but the mountain range that the Hrýll call the Web of the Gods is the key. Parts of the mountains lay on other planes simultaneous to their existence on Nakana. From Nakana one can go to them all, but from each plane there is often only one crossing. One to Nakana. If one takes the wrong crossing then you are on yet another plane and from there it may be more difficult to find the way back to Nakana."

She looked at him, slightly frightened. She had wanted proof that he was not her brother, but now he was changing by the moment. Strange languages and strange knowledge. He looked up at her and rubbed her leg.

"I don't really know what I know Tyna. It comes in pieces. I feel that we can cross over the same way that we came here, but at a different place. That is all. I'm not sure why I know this, or if it is dangerous, or even how it will be done, but I know it can be done."

She smiled reassuringly at him and touched his hand as it rubbed her leg.

"Then let's go. And let's look for some food along the way."

* * *

Tarin was not what Tsom expected. He thought it would be a small backwards town, full of uneducated and primitive people. After all, they were a thousand marks or more from The Cities and hundreds from Zethica. He expected poverty and lack of sophisticated talismans. Yes, compared to the many millions of The Cities, it was tiny, but not simple.

Everyone rode horses. He had never seen such a concentration of horses per capita. The town, while obviously not Zethica, was prosperous. The last trading city before the mountains it was the nexus of trade from a variety of large ranches. What surprised him was the glow globes on the street. He had expected torches, or lanterns, or something equally primitive. Yet here they were, just as in The Cities themselves. Glow globes lighting the street. They were a mixed lot of globes: different styles and varying quality. Some faded randomly in the light they gave out. A few gave off bizarre patterns, rather than a uniform glow.

What surprised him most was the races. He thought of The Cities as the center of everything, yet here was small city with such diversity. Yanín walked the streets, as did Hrýll. There was a tall pale man with strange tattoos covering his body. He was over seven feet tall and moved with a strange stumbling grace. If that was not strange enough, when he drew near the Yanín, the Yanín gave way. The Yanín gave way to no one. Tsom looked to Larrina for information.

She had relaxed a bit as they entered Tarin and he was glad that she was no longer making a point of his stupidity with the horse. She saw his questioning look.

"Riconé."

"Daemon controllers?"

She smiled and shook her head.

"Not the Tarth if that is what you're thinking of. The Riconé have power over the mountain daemons. The semi-intelligent giants of the mountains. Eight or nine feet tall they resemble a man, but are violent. Except around Riconé. Somehow they control them."

"Why do the Yanín give them wide berth?"

"The Yanín are superstitious. They are afraid that the Riconé can control them too. Legend has it that the mountain daemons were once an intelligent race of fierce warriors. They waged war against the Riconé and their punishment was stupidity and slavery."

"Why haven't I seen any Riconé in The Cities?"

"The Cities are too far from the mountains and too populated. The Riconé, as with all the races, are dwindling in the face of mankind's expansion. They stay in the mountains and trade with the smaller towns near the foothills."

Tsom considered that he was half human himself. At one time he had thought of himself as fully human. Yet, the more he knew of mankind, the more he thought of himself as Kinel.

They made their way to a tavern. It was nothing fancy, but seemed in good repair and well kept. It was called the Ne Mar and had a faded painting of the giant wolf on its sign. The owner, a man named Gar, looked strangely at Larrina and glanced from her sword on her back to her left hand. He seemed relieved after glancing at her hand and warmly sat them down at a table.

"Welcome strangers. What brings you to Tarin this good day? Beer? Wine?"

"Horses. Wine." Larrina replied. "Valence vintage if you have any."

"Indeed we do. You know your local wines. Indeed. Horses. I would recommend Torlan as the fairest of the traders. If you know your horses. He will test you, but when he sees you know your stock he will trade well."

"Thank you master Gar, we appreciate the tip." She smiled and even Tsom's heart skipped a beat. When Larrina turned on the charm it was hard to resist. Gar stuttered and flushed as he hurried off to the bar to fetch the wine.

"Valence vintage? You have been here before?"

"Many years ago. I was not certain it was still available. The family may have sold, or perished, or moved on. I am glad that it has not. The wine is excellent and not known outside of Tarin. It is made on a large ranch to the west of here. On the edge of the mountains."

Gar returned with the wine and was all smiles.

"Yes, an excellent wine. The family is good friends with me. The son and daughter were here recently to trade for the season and brought horses and wine. Indeed. Indeed." He looked at Larrina's sword, a slight frown. Then he continued.

"It must be becoming a fashion to wear swords like that. I thought only the Katar wore their swords in such a manner, but young Lerence, of the Valence family is also sporting his sword that way. Indeed. Indeed."

Larrina raised an eyebrow slightly and leaned toward Gar all smiles. Despite the long weeks on the trail she smelled of spices and femininity. Tsom felt a wave of lust and jealousy. They had not made love for over a week. He craved her. Larrina place her hand on Gar's and laughed.

"Really, I thought I was the only one. I know the Katar favor the style, but I simply find it more comfortable. I doubt the Katar invented it."

Gar looked mildly startled. "Indeed. That is what young Lerence said. He seemed offended that I even make the connection to Katar. I had never known Lerence to use a weapon, but when the incident with his sister occurred, he seemed quite in control. Quite. Indeed. He moved like a warrior. Quite surprising. Quite. And he guessed that it was a Kami. Ridiculous of course. No Kami would dare enter a town the size of Tarin. Indeed. Ridiculous. Still, he seemed certain. Quite changed. Lerence has grown to take his father's place, Pé take his soul to the Sea."

"Interesting. I would like to meet this young man someday. You say he is from the Valence family? My mother once visited them, years ago. Are they still the last ranch on the westward road?"

"Indeed. Indeed. You know your way around here madam …" He waited for a name. She did not hesitate.

"Senita, of the Alanar family."

"Indeed a pleasure madam Senita. Indeed." He scurried off to tend to other guests but remained attentive to their table.

Larrina leaned back and sipped her wine. She looked at Tsom.

"It would seem that your powers as a catalyst remain. We are here by no mere coincidence."

Tsom raised both eyebrows.

"I suspect that this young man Lerence is Alanar. While many do actually wear their swords as I do, few use that exact phrase concerning the Katar. After all, he was the one who taught them to wear swords like that."

* * *

Hallam paced her new compound like a caged cat. The animals nearby were nervous, picking up her mood. She had relocated her compound here, deep within the mountains, after making her move against the other gods and through them against mankind. They might try and retaliate. No need to make it easy.

The area did not have the centuries, which her previous compound had, to bend to her will. The plants were trying to change as she had willed them too. The local fauna was on guard against intrusion. She remained strong, not dependent on mankind as her fellow members of the pantheon were. Pé might be less dependent, but even he needed mankind. Soon, mankind would perish or cease to pay homage to the gods and that would leave only her. She purred lightly, a habit she'd picked up only in the past hundred years.

See'ra, the nar Tarth, had sent word that the latest attempt to change a woman may have been successful. The fool had let the woman escape, but the woman lived past the initial moments of taking the serum. The woman was stronger than the others. See'ra said that the Kami could smell her fertility. They had been drawn to her even though she was human. There were plenty of humans. Others would be found, if necessary.

Hallam smiled as she prepared another batch of the draught. She could bring any animal into heat, but not human. So, they had to make a woman slightly less human. The Tarth needed breeders, so the woman had to be compatible with Tarth. Hallam cut her wrist and poured the blood into the bottle which already contained the blood of See'ra. The proportions needed to be just right. She willed her *ka* that was more animal than human into the blood. She could feel it gain a life of its own. She willed it into a state of fertility. Of permanent heat. More *ka* flowed from her, to the bottle.

She stopped and wiped her wrist. The wound closed rapidly. The nearby deer staggered, then died, as its *ka* was drained for the task. Soon mankind would be no more. The Tarth thought they would gain dominance by multiplying with half breeds, but little did they know that unlike humans and unlike Tarth, these half breeds would answer to her. A source that could willingly funnel its energy to her as humans did to the other gods. They would have more life force than either animal or mankind and it would be hers.

She called the eagle down from the tree and tied the capped bottle to its leg. In her mind she pictured the Tarth encampment and its location from here. The eagle leapt upward and with several strong beats of its wide wings was on its way.

Chapter 15

Food was becoming a problem. Tyna was dying, starving. Her tall wiry frame needed food just to maintain her weight. The past few days had taken its toll. While the baby within her was only a day or two old, she worried that she was depriving it at a crucial time.

"Alan, I need to eat soon."

He nodded. He was too tired to speak. She regretted saying anything. She had asked him to find food several times already today. He was fading faster than she. He was walking while she rode. Finally, he halted the horse.

"Wait here. If I'm not successful, we eat the horse."

He helped her down and she didn't protest his plan. The horse had saved their life once before. It might be called upon to do so one last time. She patted the horse's neck and then sat braced against a large rock. That is all this place was, rock and some grass, and cold. She pulled up her knees and fell asleep.

'Eat. You are too skinny; no man wants a woman so skinny. Eat.'

'Yes mother.' The roast beef and lamb and potatoes and carrots were heaped on her plate. She knew that men already found her attractive, but the food smelled so good. No need to worry about gaining weight. More meat. More potatoes.

Wait. Her mother was burning the food. Throwing it away.

'No, don't throw it away. Stop. I'll eat it. Don't burn it.'

Tyna opened her eyes. Alan was standing over a small fire of grasses and small brush. The skinned rabbit was burning slightly on the outside. She began to drool. Spitting as she tried to speak, she called out.

"It looks done to me."

She moved over on her hands and knees and grabbed the stick from him. He grinned more as she yelped at the burn, but she tore into the flesh and swallowed the piece without chewing. Without thinking she greedily ate the entire rabbit. Realizing what she had done she started to cry and apologize to Alan.

He pulled five more smaller rabbits out from behind a rock and began to roast another. She laughed and wept at the same time and laid her head on his lap as he cooked.

They smoked the two remaining rabbits for travel. Then they slept. Tyna's dreams were troubled by visions of Tarth laying on top of her and raping her. She awoke desperately and pulled herself closer to Alan who always seemed to be awake. He stroked her hair and whispered in a language she could not quite understand, but it was soothing and soon she fell back asleep.

With the renewed strength they made better time and Alan was able to hunt with more energy. The strange light and cold no longer bothered her and after a week she felt as though she'd healed enough. They made cautious love that evening by the small fire. Cautious at first, but as she sweated with their love making he became more intense. Nothing like the days of wildness a week before, but she sensed that he was swept up by something in her scent. She did not care, much. Neither did he.

Over the next week she only had to think of sex and they were intertwined. They both knew that there was something affecting them, but neither minded. Each time they made love Tyna sensed the baby within her more strongly. It was as if Alan was pouring some of his life force into the baby, through their love making. Her skin stayed a pale pink and now that she had food she noticed that she was incredibly strong. Her muscles grew more defined. Her breasts grew firmer and slightly smaller.

"Alan, do you still find me attractive?" She stood bare chested, dressing after a bath in a stream.

He stopped from packing the horse; they now had a small pack made of animal skins. He gazed at her and his eyes flashed gold. He began to move toward her and she giggled and splashed water at him.

"That is not what I meant."

"No? How else can I prove to you that I find you attractive?" He had her in his arms and she pushed back while laughing. No matter how strong she felt, he always felt stronger. They sank to the bank of the stream.

"What have we here?"

The voice brought both Tyna and Alan up instantly. Alan felt for his sword, but he was completely naked. He looked around. There were ten men and two women. Four of the men had bows with arrows nocked and ready. Tyna reached for a rock and then thought the better of it.

"It looks like your sword is ready stranger. Don't attack or I will be forced to defend myself." This was from one of the men without a bow. He might be the leader, but the others did not seem to give him any special deference. A few of the others laughed at his joke.

Tyna was shaking, but it was not with fear. She would not let these men take her alive. One of the two women walked over and threw her clothes at her.

"Don't worry dear, they will not harm you. Not if you behave." The woman was not unattractive, about forty. She was worn looking. Her skin was pale, as was the color of the entire group. She dressed quickly and nodded toward Alan.

"What about him?"

The woman looked and shrugged.

"He is handsome enough, but we have enough men. Too many men."

That was all she needed to hear.

She leapt onto the nearest bowman. He tried to let loose his arrow, but her body was pressed against the bow and the arrow only nicked her skin as it and the bow went flying. She kneed him as hard as she could in the groin and pulled at his sword. Two bodies slammed into her as she began to pull the sword free.

Alan had taken out two with his hands and had a sword. He managed to knock down two arrows in mid-flight. The third hit him in the stomach.

The men were not fools and backed off rapidly, yelling to the bowmen to shoot again. Alan charged one and Tyna shook off the two men, seriously wounding one with the newly acquired sword in the process, and then charged another of the bowmen. One arrow missed and Alan amazingly knocked a third arrow down. Another found its way into his back. He stumbled and screamed in rage. Rage and fear.

She could see that he was afraid, but it was not for himself. It was for her. He yelled for her to run.

"Save yourself. Run. All will die. Run."

What did he mean? She killed the bowman and ran toward him, not away. Two more arrows hit him and now the cowards with the swords were closing in.

She felt the force slam into her. She was knocked down and felt weak. Looking up she saw the men moving in slow motion. There was agony in their eyes. And fear. Alan stood with a snarl on his face pulling the arrows from his body as if they were minor annoyances. The wounds sealed up and healed as she watched. His eyes gold on gold were flashing. She could feel the pull of her *ka*. Alan was the center of a vortex pulling all life toward him. Wrenching the *ka* out of the living. Killing with true death. Total destruction. No rebirth. No travel to the Sea of Souls. She could feel it and knew it, a primordial knowledge of destruction.

"Alan, stop. You are killing me."

He did not hear. He swirled his sword around his head and charged the men who were already falling. She felt her own *ka* slipping.

Then, she felt something within her pulling back. She struggled to her feet and staggered to Alan. The sparse grass was black. The men and women were feebly struggling, old and dying. She felt the baby within her feeding off the same energy and sustaining her at the same time.

"Stop Alan. Stop!" She put her arms around him and pulled him to the ground. His contorted face and gold eyes were unseeing. He swung his sword to strike. She caught his hand in her own. She felt more energy flowing to her from within her belly. Slowly she pushed his sword arm down. She kissed him. It was all she had left.

His arm slackened and the enormous tug of war between him and her belly subsided. He fell unconscious.

* * *

Alan awoke with his head on Tyna. She was asleep. As he moved she opened her eyes and sat up. They were surrounded by blackness. Dark grass and mummified bodies. It was like the wagons. But, Tyna was alive. How was she alive? Some part of his mind said that this was impossible.

"What happened?" he asked.

"You don't remember?"

He shook his head. Somehow, he was responsible for this. He felt it. This had happened before. Many times. Too many times. But, he felt that she shouldn't be alive. No one should be alive. No one ever was ever alive, even those he loved. Flashes of friends and lovers, all dead, passed through the shattered shards of memory.

"How?" he looked at her.

"The baby. Whatever it is that you did, the baby has the same power. It protected me. Oh, Alan it's a terrible power. I feel sick that I was a part of it. They are *true deathed*. All their *ka* is gone. I could feel it as you did it. As our baby fought back and did the same."

He looked around, the echo of Lerence was shocked. True death. The Katar used that as the ultimate punishment. Mothers told their children horror stories of *true death* to scare them. Everyone knew that when they died they went to the Sea of Souls to be reborn. The gods promised it. Even the other races believed. He shuddered. Tyna shuddered also.

He looked at her. She was different. The pink color was gone and her normal coloring had returned. Her large muscles had faded back to her wiry ones. He looked at her eyes. Still green, but he could detect flecks of gold. His eyes were drawn to her stomach and her eyes followed his. She was huge. She was less than two weeks pregnant but looked nine months. Tyna's eyes widened and she placed both hands on her stomach.

"Alan, what have we done?"

With that she went into labor.

* * *

"What do you mean, 'she's gone'?" Growled Arlec.

"I'm sorry sir, but that is what the household servants told me. The entire house is in an uproar. There is even a reward posted for finding her or information leading to her."

Arlec rubbed his clean shaven chin. It jutted out in strong lines, similar to his father's—as seen by the portrait of Devon behind him. He would love to take down that stupid portrait, but he had no excuse to do so. Flana missing? It seemed inconceivable that any violence had occurred to her. She was a noblewoman, rich and well known. He felt some worry for her, but primarily he was annoyed. She would turn up after slumming, as she was prone to do. He refused to get worried. If she wasn't so beautiful and rich, he would have moved on long ago. She was too independent. Too much like his sisters.

"Well, send our condolences and have a few of our people join in the hunt. Look for her at the docks, she has a bad habit of hanging out there. I'm sure she will turn up."

He had been looking forward to a distracting dinner with Flana tonight. He knew her father had been adding to his own pressures on her and tonight he was going to take the game to the next level. Women were an enjoyable game, if sometimes tiresome. With Flana he often had to take out his frustrations at the brothel. The discreet one, where they knew him well. Someday she would be his. Her father's ships and power would complement the Karn family's well.

Arlec returned to his research. Why had his father hidden so much from the rest of the Katar? He was a craftier old man than Arlec had given him credit for. There was a wealth of information here, if one dug deep enough. It was obvious why he had hidden the secret of Kinel blood in the Katar families. That would have made the genocide much harder. Too many of the Katar would have balked. The research that Devon had done on the Kinel powers; that was leading to some interesting ideas.

If the thief Tsom was a half breed Kinel as most of the evidence indicated, and he had these new and interesting powers such as manifesting invisible hands and arms, then why couldn't a Katar do something similar. The Kinel blood may be weaker within the Katar, but it was there. The Cities were full of stories of someone doing some fantastic thing without the use of a talisman. Surely, it must be the Kinel blood intermingled with human over generations. After all the Katar were known to occasionally have bastard children they never acknowledged. Most were brought into the Katar structure as minor guards, or low ranking officials, but some must be lost.

Devon's books warned that Kinel were prone to burning themselves out. Using too much of their own *ka* in the discovery of their own powers. Arlec rubbed his ring absently. All senior Katar knew that the rings drained the *ka* of those around them. The wearer of a ring would not have to worry about draining himself. A few commoners might suffer.

Unfortunately, the handwritten books didn't explain how the Kinel would discover their powers. Could they choose whatever power they wanted? What choices were available? It wasn't clear. Devon wrote that it had been very rare for a Kinel to have more than one significant power and that patterns emerged. Healers tended to have offspring that were healers.

If the Katar could use powers without the aid of Hrýll talismans, then the Hrýll would lose their last hold over mankind and the Katar. True, the talismans would be useful, but in a war, or in an emergency, the Katar could use their powers directly. A few citizens might perish, but the good of the whole would be served. If only some Katar knew how to use powers. Arlec rubbed his ring finger again. He would have to start experimenting.

The Katar families had ruled for thousands of years. The head of the clans had remained the same family throughout that time. It stood to reason that each of the five families had more Kinel blood in them than the minor families allied to each of the five. There must be some natural power in the Karn family that Arlec was missing. Some clue.

Karn was the ruling Katar family of Arbeneth. The sea port. Trading. Sailing. Commerce. Why the sea port? Why had the early Karn families chosen this city to rule?

Arlec strode to the library's main window and stared out over the city and to the sea. *What of the gods?* He thought. Are they Kinel also? The concept seemed very similar. Were the gods suppressing Katar powers somehow? Yet, the gods had no power over the Katar rings. Arlec worried his ring on his left hand. Why had the Karns come to Arbeneth?

He pulled volume after volume off the shelves. Lists of family members. Accounts of wars. All the Karn family heads seemed to have kept accounts of their lives. Most were utterly banal. The dust storm he was creating was making him sneeze and his throat dry. The waning daylight made him stop and activate the glow globes. He called for the butler.

"Some tea and a light snack. I will not be having dinner in the main dining area."

"Yes sir."

"Jem, your family has served ours for how long?"

"Twenty generations sir."

"Do you have any idea why the Karn family chose this city? This location?"

"None sir. Our family served yours since the Karns left the island."

"The island?" Arlec gave the butler his full attention.

"Old Arbeneth, sir. The island, as we all call it. The Karn family still owns land there, sir."

"Yes, yes. The ruins in the swamp. Thank you Jem."

"Yes sir." Jem gave Arlec a small nod and left. He did not remark on the scattered books lying strewn about, although his eyes betrayed his curiosity.

Arlec renewed his search, but focused on references to the island. He kept at it through his tea and light meal. He poured himself brandy and kept at it. It was nearly sunrise when he found something.

The common tongue was different than that of today, but he could still read it. He had almost thrown it into the growing pile of rejected books. He had been about to call it a night, or a day as it were, right after skimming this one last book. He had been so tired that he almost missed it.

We have ruined the lands around us forever. It will take centuries for the people and the land to recover, if ever. We have fended off the gods, but at what cost? Are we as evil as they are? Better we should ally with them and share dominion over mankind rather than destroy mankind. The Karn family will never again summon forth the undine. Ague of the seas has agreed that if we give up this power, he will guard our city and our ships. We will be the blessed of the sea. We will give up our historic site on the isle of Arbeneth. It will remain as a reminder of our abuse of power. The isle surrounded by water both salt and clean. Time will heal our misuse, our sins. May the other families make a similar peace with the gods.

Undine. So there was such a thing. The sailor's stories had roots in truth. Sprites. Elementals. Water beings. And the Karn family once controlled them. The destruction must have been either the use of too much ka, or a battle between the Katar and the gods. Interesting.

Arlec rubbed his ring and gazed at the eternal fire in the fireplace. Arlec was aware, as were all the families, of the internal strife amongst the gods. Pé babbling on about the gods drain on humanity and Hallam's attack on both the gods and humanity. Arlec could still show them that he was the one that would save them all—again. In return, he would rule them all. As soon as he relearned the powers of his family. No time for sleep. He must find out more. He ignored the images of his father and his sister Shara dancing in the flames of the fire. Their sacrifice had been necessary. For the good of the family. For the good of Katar. The Katar would no longer worship gods. They would be gods.

Chapter 16

"Hallam, is a bitch."

Thwick.

"A fool."

Thwick.

"A traitor."

Thwick.

Three darts were neatly arranged in and near the bull's eye. Nu Arr, the god of luck, smiled at Ague's toss.

"I think we all agree on that point, Ague." He strode over to the board and removed Ague's darts. He strode back and handed them to Ague. "I don't want to damage your darts."

Nu Arr closed his eyes. If they were open then there would be too much skill involved, for his power to work it had to be luck. He stood sideways and threw all three darts at the same time. All three hit the bull's eye. Ague cursed, but not too vehemently. They had no bet on the game, only a fool bet against Luck. He moved with fluid motion to the open bar and poured a large glass of Hrýll brandy.

Met, the weather god, lay on the couch off to the side. It was his grounds they were meeting on and of them all, he felt the most at ease. It had been his domain for centuries and the other gods knew he had the advantage here. Not that they were going to try anything, but one could never be too safe.

The temperature and humidity were perfect. The sun shone through the top of the room, there was no roof. It never rained on this spot. This open recreation room was less of a room and more of a walled off area. Met's entire domain was open to the elements. The recreation area had a swimming pool, gaming spots, and numerous female 'priestesses' whose sole function was pleasing Met. While he looked at ease, he was as worried as the other gods.

This was their first major conclave in millennia. After Hallam's trickery and her allying with the Tarth, the gods were finally convinced that Nu Arr's fears were a reality. It was a time of change. Major change. Mankind wasn't worshipping as much, which meant they were growing weaker. They were becoming mortal. Met shivered. All of them but Hallam were effected.

"Perhaps we should have helped more overtly against the Tarth," Ague said.

"Easy for you to say, you wouldn't be expected to help. No seas near the Muglanth plains. No, you still have your worshipers in Arbeneth. The sailors will always worship a sea god," Nu Arr muttered.

Met smiled wryly.

"Just as people will always wish for good luck. But, will they pray with our talismans in their hands? Will they channel their *ka* to us? We need to force the issue. You know we do," said Met.

There was no rushing a god. We have lived too long, he thought. We don't act quickly. They would debate this for weeks. He shrugged internally. They were weakened, but they were hardly on their death beds. If mankind stopped worshipping, how long would they live? Centuries at least.

"It does seem, somehow, unfair doesn't it?" laughed Inlas from the side of the pool. She was not actually in it, but looked as if she had recently emerged. Droplets of water were dripping from her almost nude frame, all an illusion. None of them could remember what she really looked like; her power of illusion was always on, always bending their thoughts, or desires. Met groaned inwardly, as his unrequited passion flowed through him. Even though he knew it was exactly what Inlas wanted, he could not control it.

They all knew what she meant. Here they were, immensely powerful, yet in fear of the very beings that gave them power. Man. Without man's *ka* they were more mortal than any human. All the gods knew that for them any death was true death. No rebirth. Not even Pé, who often sat by the rivers of Life and Death, could change that.

Pé was not among them now, although he had visited recently, for the first time in centuries. He would not be persuaded to leave his rivers for long. The self-important, pompous ass thought that he was the only god who served a valuable role. As if the rivers would stop flowing without him. When was it that he'd discovered them? No matter. The last time he had blessed them with his presence, a year ago, he was quite agitated. He'd been ranting about the destruction of Talanas.

"Talanas? He's been dead for a thousand years, or more," Met said at the time. "He has no source of ka, he never even tried to become a god. He must have aged and died."

"No," Inlas had warned them. "I've seen him, calling himself Alanar, allying with the Hrýll. He's changed, I almost didn't believe it was him. Somehow he has been reborn, many times." Even now, Met did not question why it had taken Inlas so long to inform them of this Alanar, who was perhaps Talanas.

No, the hope that one of the original party was still alive, was what they all focused on. If one could survive without stealing ka, then perhaps they could too. Perhaps the gods did go to the Sea of Souls. Inlas dashed those dreams.

"No, not from the Sea of Souls. The Hrýll were clear on that. No, he somehow was reborn in the same body. Oonie said it was his curse."

She had been pretending to be a Hrýll woman, of all things, and witnessed this while visiting her 'husband,' Oonie. Hard to believe. Talanas. Their old nemesis and savior.

Pe's news was perhaps all the more surprising, given Inlas' proclamation. Pé claimed that he'd destroyed Talanas, or Alanar as he called himself, on the River of Death only weeks ago.

"I thought none of us ever traveled the Rivers of Life and Death, after we die?" Met asked.

"We don't. I'm sure of it. But he wasn't really one of us, was he? He could travel between the planes, where even we can't. I think he had a plan, but he was weakened. Weaker than even the other souls in the River. A remnant of ka," Pé replied. He looked pensive as he said it. As if he regretted destroying the remnant of Talanas.

"You travel to the Rivers, isn't that same the same as his power?"

"No, you know it isn't. The Rivers call me, just as the weather, or the sky, calls to you, or healing to some humans. It's in our blood and we don't even know how it works."

"Nor do we care," Inlas purred in a sultry voice. "He's gone, finally. He scared me. The Hrýll seemed to think he'd changed, become less evil, but I am glad he's truly dead. I'm glad Pé made sure he couldn't enter the Sea. His soul doesn't deserve rebirth."

"As our souls are doomed to never do either," Pé reminded her. "Immortal only as long as we can syphon off their ka, we're the weak ones."

That had been a year ago. A year and they still hadn't formed a cohesive plan. At least they were all afraid now. All feeling the waning power.

Inlas stretched out on a soft outdoor couch, tempting as always, out of reach as always. She wiggled her toes and flexed her leg muscles. Met turned away, forcing down his growing lust.

"Did you know that the average lifespan of a man has gone down in the past one hundred years," said Luck, idly flipping a coin over and over to heads.

"That isn't us," protested Met.

Inlas laughed. It sounded bitter, which meant either she intended it to sound that way, or her illusion had faltered. Something was distracting Inlas, Met thought. She is acting almost as if she were in love, which for her was ridiculous.

"Of course it is. We let our priests syphon off some of the *ka* for their own power. We give the priesthoods autonomy. What do you expect? Between us and the Katar, it's a wonder it's only ten years," she laughed again. The bitterness in her tone was stronger.

"Mankind breeds quickly. Even with the drop in lifespan, they multiply," said Met, shrugging.

"True, but to maintain that population they destroy the old races, in particular the Hrýll. Without the Hrýll, no talismans. No talismans, no civilization. Not as we know it. Think about something as simple as glow globes. What would happen if everyone fled to their hovel at night? Unable to read, or walk the streets safely, or manufacture things after dark."

"More irony. I can call up a storm with lightning, yet I can't create a simple glow globe on my own," Met growled.

"Yet, we allow man to destroy the Hrýll slowly, the very makers of those glow globes," said Inlas.

"You've grown fond of your mortal lover," accused Met. He felt the flash of rage that a mortal was bedding her and she still refused him.

For a moment the omnipresent illusion surrounding Inlas wavered. The woman they saw was no less beautiful, but looked scared and vulnerable. It was just a flicker.

"Perhaps we need to destroy the Katar ourselves," Ague said. "Then mankind will be beholden to us and no longer feel the strain of their drain on *ka.*"

"Because we did it out of the goodness of our hearts," said Inlas. Her laugh was beginning to grate him.

"Are you forgetting, the Katar have those damned rings. They dared fight us once before," Nu Arr added.

"But, they have lost over half their number and their creator is now dead," Inlas emphasized her statement with a subtle increase of a feeling of confidence. Met glanced around to see if he was the only one sensing her manipulations. Did it matter? Perhaps they all agreed and only needed her prodding to act. He remained silent.

"Perhaps we should adopt Alanar's original plan," Inlas said. Met felt more of her manipulations, the scent in the air, the way she looked sincere and wise. "We let the Katar and the revolution and the remaining Tarth weaken each other, then step in and clean up. Either way, we can't let the Katar survive. They will destroy both mankind and the Hrýll, whom we all need, if they continue to rule."

The others nodded thoughtfully. With Talanas not part of the equation, then the opportunity of finally ridding themselves of the Katar and their damned rings seemed an opportunity too rich to pass up. Hallam could wait. She was only one goddess whose only real power was manipulating animals. They could deal with her at their leisure.

Inlas lay back on her couch and smiled. If it had been a little quieter the others might have heard the purring of a cat in the distance.

Chapter 17

Tyna screamed and gripped Alan's arm, pulling him down. He grimaced with pain, but held her and leaned closer. She felt as if this child was ripping its way out of her. *She was paying for the sin of loving her brother*, she briefly thought. Then she looked at Alan and dismissed the idea. Alan's eyes were constantly glowing and flashing gold. His features were sharp, with cords of muscle visible on his cheeks. There were only traces of Lerence left on his face.

The relief from the pain was almost orgasmic. She shuddered and her body relaxed. A feeling of wellbeing and warmth spread through her and she lay back with a smile.

"Well?" She asked, looking at Alan, down by her legs.

The bloody squirming being was both beautiful and scary. She was strong for a newborn. Tyna had helped with childbirth before. This small girl was strange. She was very pale skinned, white pink, almost albino. Yet, her eyes were like Alan's. Gold flecked. Both Tyna and Alan were dark skinned, although since the Tarth had forced her to drink that blood Tyna had taken on a red ting. The girl's eyes were more almond shaped than either of theirs. The girl grabbed a hold of Alan's finger and pulled. It was strong enough to move itself! She then began to cry and Alan wiped the last of the blood off it with his shirt, cut the umbilical, and handed her to Tyna. She looked at him questioningly. He caressed her breast and said with a grin. "I think she's hungry, let's hope those work on an accelerated time frame also."

* * *

They called her Rosea, after her grandmother. She was a sturdy baby who did not slow them down too much as they made their way to the mountain ridge that Alan continued to feel was their gateway back to Nakana. The land became more forested, but still felt different from where she felt they were, or should be – if they'd still been on Nakana. The mountain peaks looked right from a distance, but the flora and fauna were still off.

Without the horse their speed was slower than before, but not much. Horses tired more easily than a fit human and now that they had both been eating again they were both strong.

Since the first day Rosea did not cry. She was constantly hungry. Finally, Tyna rigged up a sling so that she could simply suckle on her breast constantly. Her body seemed to respond to the need and was producing more milk than she thought was normal. Alan hunted more to keep up with Tyna's own ravenous appetite.

Nights they slept the sleep of the exhausted. Yet, they both found energy for continued lovemaking, usually at dawn as they woke with new energy. At first Tyna was slightly embarrassed to have their baby watching while they made love, but soon she got over it. Rosea seemed disinterested after the first few times.

Neither of them spoke of the day that Alan had killed the party of kidnappers. She knew it had been self-defense, but the horror of *true death* still bothered her. Alan continued to change since the event. His body seemed to respond to the pressures of travel extraordinarily well. He grew a beard that came out pure white in color. Not gray. No streaks, but pure white. He kept it fairly well trimmed with his knife and despite the lack of color it did not make him look much older. She was not sure if she liked him clean shaven or this way. With the beard he was even less like the brother she still occasionally thought of.

They reached the ridge two weeks after Rosea was born.

Alan seemed to see a pattern in the rocks and chose their path as if he had been here before. Tyna was curious as to what he was feeling or remembering.

"Do you sense something, or simply remember it?"

"Both. I suddenly feel like I am within a slowly moving river. The current is taking us in one direction. As we walk, I occasionally feel as if a cross current intersects our path, but this is the strong current. This current feels like Nakana."

After one day of walking in this current Alan grabbed her.

"Hold on to me as we walk."

The terrain became blurry, as if smoke were in her eyes. They kept walking and she felt nauseous. She felt a current now. Something was pulling her in one direction, but Alan grabbed her and pulled her along another.

"Not that way. That is a side current. It will suck you in. Pull you toward Hell."

"Hell? I thought that was simply a myth to scare children."

"Hell is real. It is a plane that is easy to get to, but very hard to leave. It is where the Tarth were banished to."

"Alan, I feel these currents too. How can we be sure we are in the right one?"

She felt him shrug, but he did not say anything. He simply dragged her along. Suddenly her eyes came into focus. Heavy forest. The smell of fir trees and water. Warmth. It felt like home, it felt right.

"We're back." Alan announced.

Rosea began to cry.

Chapter 18

Damp decay surrounded Arlec. He was within the old family compound in Old Arbeneth. Alone. Since the war with the Tarth and his power play with the other families, he rarely went alone. Assassinations between the families were not unheard of, if fairly infrequent. Since he was searching for keys to the family power of the past he didn't want others to know, even guards.

The smell of fungus, rotted wood, and stagnant water was everywhere. No wonder they had abandoned this compound. It was a worthless swamp. The entire island of the old city felt like it was sinking into the river. Maybe a thousand years ago it had been better.

He picked his way past the mounds of moss that at one time must have been outbuildings. Unconsciously he had his hand on his sword. The huge trees obscured the sun and kept the moisture in the air. A large snake dropped off of a branch in front of him and he half pulled his sword out of its scabbard, the wood lining the metal scabbard already swelling with moisture. With a soft laugh he kept moving toward the stone ruins of the old main house.

His continued search within his father's library turned up very little additional information on the Undine. The old families had more backbone than the current ones, he thought as he pushed past the heavy vines at the threshold of the collapsed manor. One had to protect ones power, at all costs.

Arlec hadn't known what he was looking for before coming here, but the large well on the interior of the fallen structure immediately beckoned him. It was covered in lichen and moss, but as he approached it became clear that it was made of jade. Solid jade. The mineral was what qenar was bound too. This much jade indicated a potential talisman. The entire well might be a talisman. Qenar simply needed *ka* as a catalyst to be used as a source of power. Arlec stroked his ring and smiled. If there was not enough *ka* in his ring, then he would bring a servant here. One without any close family.

Arlec placed his hands on the rim of the well wall and looked over the edge, not really expecting to see anything. He was surprised to see water close to the surface. Then he noticed that his ring was glowing. Danger? Or was it interacting with the well?

He sniffed the air above the water. It smelled pure, cleaner than the rest of the air of this putrid bog. Without thinking he dipped his hand into the well and cupping it he took a drink.

The effect was immediate.

Cold fire moved through his belly to his limbs. His vision blurred. Not the blur of drunkenness, or eye irritation, but something else. He was seeing double. The moss, the trees, were all there in double image, overlapping imperfectly. The ruins were not there, but the well was clearly visible as two wells. He blinked to focus and instead of making things better, it made them worse. The images that were not-of-here became stronger. He glanced at his ring, as all Katar were wont to do. It was glowing brightly.

It was the voice that allowed him to focus on the being, otherwise he might have never seen it.

"Karn. You have not called to us in a long time. What is it you have contacted us for?"

To the left, rising out of the ground was a short pillar of water. It was only visible within the echo of images. Without understanding why, he knew that this is where the voice came from.

"It is time for the Undine and the Karn to ally once again." He hoped that he struck the right convincing tone that he knew what was going on.

"Ally? A strange word for masters to use with their slaves. We await your commands."

* * *

Larrina and Tsom returned to the blackened grass near Tarin and walked amongst the wagons and withered corpses. Their new horses had refused to enter the area and were staked nearby. The corpses were just beginning to rot. Tsom was surprised to hear Larrina speculate that this must have occurred weeks ago.

"Surely the corpses would have been more decomposed?" he commented.

"No, this is the effect of Talanas … Alanar. Everything was killed, even the worms and the small things that eat away flesh. It takes some time for the wind to carry enough new life to complete the cycle of death. It is indeed Alanar, still alive. I know of no other who could do such a thing. Almost no other."

Tsom flushed at the latter. He had once created a very similar sort of destruction, almost killing Larrina. It was similar, in many ways, to the power of the Katar rings. He would never do such a thing again. It was evil. It destroyed indiscriminately. It was why the Katar assassin's ring had been destroyed. So Alanar was alive? By the Sea, it never occurred to Tsom that he could have survived the Tarth.

The feeling of relief over not having caused his death, battled with feelings of jealousy and worry. If Alanar lived, what of the Tarth who had been banished with him? Yet, from what he could piece together, it seemed that Alanar was also the son of some local ranching family. How could that be? Even Larrina had been puzzled at this last bit. She simply shrugged it off for the moment.

"When we find him, we can ask him."

Ever the pragmatic. Tsom sometimes wished that Larrina was more like other women. Women that were talkative and romantic and not so practical. Even at the brothel, where he was raised, women were different from Larrina. Maybe it was her great age. She was so much older than him that perhaps she had lost some of the normal qualities of human women. Well, she wasn't human, so that also explained it.

Larrina scoured the perimeter of the circle of death. The edges had grass slowly growing back into the circle. Tsom saw no signs of anything, but believed Larrina when she said that there had been Kami and death cats in the area. She was set on going after the trail, but he balked.

"Didn't we come here to negotiate with Zethicia? We have a lot of people depending on us."

"It can wait."

"Larrina, you're acting foolishly. When has any single individual mattered more than the group, the cause? We have a mission to complete. Wasn't that Alanar's mission, the rebellion?"

She paused as she prepared to mount her horse, then she nodded her head slowly. Lani, the big stallion, backed his hindquarters a step to lower the saddle for her. She mounted and stared off in the direction she'd indicated to Tsom as the direction both the death cats and the man on foot had gone. Her hand trembled slightly and Lani pranced in the direction she was gazing. She touched the reins lightly and he stopped, looking confused, but calm.

Tsom barely caught her quiet, "What do you remember, how much have you lost this time?" She then wheeled her horse toward Zethicia and Tsom scrambled to follow. He knew the tears in his eyes were for a different reason than hers.

* * *

Barnus gazed at the beautiful woman across the table from him. This was the woman that Lanos had told him about, before he died. One of the leaders of the revolution. Tsom he knew, from that fateful day. The 'boy' looked better than he had then. Slightly younger and less used up. Still, he was to the casual observer a middle aged man. The young man had given up much, although Barnus's sons had given more.

"Why do you approach me and not the governor? I'm simply the commander of the forces, the governor makes the final decision on how the military is used."

Larrina laughed, a musical sound, which held no mirth. Her breath smelled lightly of undefined spices. She was mature, but definitely desirable. He'd been happily married for thirty years, was she using some sort of drug in her perfume to confuse him?

"Please, Barnus. We both know that governor Courie is cowed by the Katar. She is just happy that they are out of your hair for now. But, they are demanding payment for their 'protection' with the Tarth and you know that once the gateway is reopened that they will try for complete control of Zethicia."

Barnus agreed with her, but what could he do? Zethicia was not run by the military. It was a civilian government. Elected. The military was already rapidly shrinking as the raids by the small Tarth band, or bands, were more annoyances than real war. The drafted soldiers had to be allowed back to their fields and trades. Zethicia was not like The Cities. It did not have the wealth to keep a real standing army. It was large enough, but agriculture was its main trade.

"Look, Barnus, I know what you're thinking. I am not asking for a formal alliance. I am asking for your alliance and those loyal to you. When the time is right."

"What use is that? I can't speak for anyone other than myself."

"Nonsense. Your reputation is well known. There is a significant portion of the military that would follow you, certainly the core standing army. They would trust you. I just need to know if you're with us. If not, we have to assume you are against us and for the Katar."

The last stung. For the Katar? He feared the Katar and was for peace. Peace was welcome after the short, but bloody and destructive Tarth war. Entire towns burned to the ground. Sons lost. His nose twitched at the memory. This woman wanted more war. More fighting.

Barnus recalled the war meetings with the Katar, only a year or so ago. He remembered the new head of the Karn family, Arlec. That one craved power. He would be back. Once the revolution was crushed, they would return. This Arlec would not be content with The Cities.

"When the time comes I will ally myself and those I can persuade. We stay within the borders of Zethicia. No invasions of the The Cities, for either side."

"I would not ask for more." She stood up as if to go.

"You're leaving? You're of course welcome to stay as my guests. I had quarters prepared." Barnus looked to Tsom to see what his reaction was. Tsom was watching Larrina intently.

"I am afraid I have urgent business elsewhere."

Tsom frowned, his chin dipping down to his chest. Barnus would have said that he was angry, or jealous. It was no business of his.

Chapter 19

"You dared to tamper with my potion?" Hallam screamed at See'arr.

The Tarth calmly looked at her, almost down her nose.

"Your previous attempts were killing off the frail humans. I felt the blood of a Tarth would strengthen her and make her more attractive to Tarth."

The implied insult was more than Hallam could stand. She was not used to any mortal standing up to her. Without thinking she back hand slapped See'arr. The blow would have shattered the jaw and snapped the neck of a human. The Tarth rocked back with the blow and faster than Hallam thought possible she struck back. Unfortunately, the instinct of a Tarth is not for simple blow for blow exchange.

Both Hallam's and See'arr's eyes went wide. See'aar's open hand was buried to the wrist just below Hallam's sternum. A death blow aimed at hitting the heart. See'arr pulled her hand back, her mouth a small 'o' and her eyebrows rose. Hallam staggered back and tapped her vast reservoir of *ka*. She visualized her body mending, the flesh and skin melding back. The horses tied up outside felt the draw upon their *ka* and neighed in terror as their life force fled. Several squirrels fell from the trees, dead. Hallam pulled on the *ka* of the animals in an ever widening circle. Using her own inner *ka* was dangerous. It would weaken her. Age her, if only minutely. Now that she had bought a little time in stopping the internal bleeding, she could use external sources for her healing.

It was over in a few moments, but Hallam felt more tired than she had in decades. Damn these Tarth, they were strong and had no respect for gods. Still, she needed them in her move against the other gods. She forced a smile on her lips as she pulled part of the torn blouse off her now healed wound, to demonstrate that she was unharmed.

"I am only upset because from what you describe it will be hard to reproduce the exact formula used on the woman. If she lived, as you say, then it will benefit the Tarth if you find her. Alive. She could be the crossover breeding stock between human and Tarth. Her children could be fertile to both races. Her blood might even be used for another attempt with another woman."

See'arr smiled back, but Hallam saw no warmth there. Speculation. Cunning. Perhaps an acknowledgement that Hallam was right. No, there was less respect in her eyes than there had been before; she had seen the momentary fear in Hallam's eyes. I will need to watch my back around this one now. She sees me as vulnerable, Hallam thought.

They strode out of the tent continuing their discussion. The presence of a god within the Tarth encampment did not have much of an effect. The Kami watched her intently, but with no fear. She had briefly tried touching the Kami to see if she could tap their *ka* as she could some animals that were intelligent, such as the dui mar. No, the Kami must be too much like other humanoid species. She could not tap them. Her nose involuntarily twitched at their smell. The sweaty horse smell mixed with some other animal that she could not identify.

The most of the Tarth glared at her. To them, goddess or not, she looked human. Yet, they kept their distance and nodded respectfully to See'arr. It was her they respected, not Hallam. Well, if this experiment with the woman proved successful, then she would not have to worry about the Tarth, in the future. After the other gods were defeated, then she would focus on the Tarth and the seed she'd planted. She doubted that the tainting of the formula by See'arr would affect that. Her own blood was in there. Her smile broadened to a genuine one, causing See'arr to look at her slightly askance. Yes, she could tolerate the Tarth arrogance and lack of fear for now. A few decades from now would be different situation. What were a few decades to her? Several of the male Tarth looked at her as they heard an audible purr emanate from her chest.

* * *

Tyna slumped against Alan, holding the crying Rosea close to her chest. Rosea's hands and mouth groped for her breasts, but she was too tired to help her. Alan guided Tyna to a fallen tree to sit down.

"Walking the web takes energy, *ka*. You will be tired for several days."

"Are you remembering more of your past Alan? Who you really are?"

Alan rubbed his face. His brows were furrowed and his eyes were squinting as in pain. He looked at Tyna and touched her face with the tips of his hand, brushing a strand of her red hair away.

"No, not really. I have feelings. I seem to 'know' things when they directly apply to the situation, but I do not really recall. I even have a hard time recalling what I have told you concerning some things I thought I was remembering. Especially since the time we fought the bandits and my strange dark power manifested itself."

Both Tyna and Alan shuddered slightly. Rosea stopped crying as she found her breast and warm milk. Tyna rubbed her fuzzy head and marveled at her

106

movement and ability to hold her head up on her own. The pinkness in Rosea's skin had not faded; she was strange pale baby, not the dark brown of both her and Alan. She recalled the liquid that the Tarth woman had forced her drink. She had another question for Alan, but the warm feeling of contentment as Rosea suckled put her to sleep before she could ask it.

Alan looked down at her leaning against him, starting to slump forward on the fallen tree. He lowered her gently to the ground, careful not to disturb Rosea, bracing Tyna against a large low branch still intact on the tree. Rosea's eyes followed his every move. Alan tousled her hair and stood, the frown returning to his face and his brows furrowed. Standing he began to circle the area.

To the west he could feel the flow of the invisible stream they had just left. This felt right. To the north he felt as if a damn had broken within these strange streams he could sense. Something was not right up there. He stared off to the north, knowing that seeing something was unlikely. The rush disappeared as suddenly as it had appeared upon his senses. He felt a chill and unconsciously rubbed the ring finger on his left hand.

* * *

Tsom was tired. He ached for his lost youth of just a couple of years ago; the ache was mental and physical. Growing up on the docks he was not an experienced horseman. He rubbed his butt and knees as they rode. Despite the past year of running with Larrina and the revolution, he still preferred a carriage or his own two feet.

They were riding cross-country over the vast rolling hills surrounding Zethicia. The beauty of the Muglanth Plains, its sea of grass dotted with massive oak trees was lost on him. The earlier trip across the mountains was still fresh in his mind and he knew that weeks of uncomfortable sleep were ahead. Sleep alone. He clenched his jaw. His horse responded to his tenseness by breaking into a trot, causing his sore body to protest and he concentrated on relaxing.

Larrina stayed in the lead. Her tight riding tunic showed off her slim back and narrow waist, accentuated with the sword strapped there. As he watched she let her reins carefully fall and reached behind her saddle. A small but very heavy bow was there. Larrina had asked Barnus for it as they left. He remembered being surprised as he had never seen Larrina use a bow. Of course when he had first met her he did not know she owned a sword. She was a healer, and herbalist, and still strange to him despite being half Kinel himself. His simmering mood had prevented him from asking her what it was for.

She now fitted an arrow against the string and in one fluid motion stood in a half crouch in the stirrups, aimed in the air, and let the arrow loose.

Tsom looked up and saw the silhouette of a raptor, possibly an eagle. The arrow, astonishingly, found its mark and the eagle fell fluttering to the ground. Without bothering to inspect her kill, Larrina changed direction of her horse and broke into a canter. Tsom struggled to keep up.

Larrina regretted having to kill the eagle, but she didn't want Hallam spying on their every move. Not anymore. This would buy them some time. It would take Hallam days to find them. Larrina knew that Hallam needed to devote some concentration on each animal. The animals were not sentient enough to take an order and act on it on their own. Humans thought of Hallam as a goddess who controlled all animals and even some plants, but Larrina knew that wasn't true. The battle in Zethicia had shown something of her limits. Thousands of birds and hundreds of large animals yes, but only in gross group movements. No individual control. No subtlety. Unless she already had full control of another animal other than the eagle, than they were safe from her prying eyes for a while.

She maintained a canter for at least fifteen minutes and then alternated between trot and canter. Tsom struggled to stay with. She knew that he must be in pain, inexperienced as he was riding, but it couldn't be helped. When she finally allowed the horses to walk, Tsom pulled alongside of her.

"So we are in search of this Lerence, who you think is Alanar?" Stating what he already knew.

"Yes. If he is truly in the body of someone else, then he will need help. His memories will be worse than before. He will be vulnerable to his own powers."

"You are looking for him only out of concern for his own wellbeing then?"

"His wellbeing and the wellbeing of Nakana. Alanar can be a dangerous man to many … if he cannot control himself."

"Then why do you love him?"

Larrina looked sharply at Tsom.

"Who said I love him? He is an old friend, in need."

"He's dangerous to us all. He was better off dead. If he lives the main body of Tarth may live. Mankind is in enough danger with only the small band of Tarth that survived the banishment. Let's hope that you're wrong. How could he have survived? I thought that where they were sent to was sure death?"

"I don't know. It was a plane further removed than Hell, which all assume is worse than Hell. Yet, few know much of the planes beyond Nakana."

Tsom's horse stumbled and he was silent for a moment.

"Larrina, Oonie called you a healer and said it wasn't right that you were now a warrior. I know you hate the Katar and all they have done to destroy our race, but is hate really a way to live?"

Larrina looked at him and smiled.

"Tsom, you have grown and healed yourself. A year ago you would have destroyed everything in your path for revenge. Now you try and talk me out of continuing with the revolution?"

"I just don't want to lose you. I have lost enough."

You have, she thought. *I too am afraid of losing again. This time I fight to hold on.*

Chapter 20

Arlec liked the sound of the word, 'master.' So the Karn family ruled over the Undine? How could his father have hidden this from him? Such power. With this sort of power why wasn't the Karn family in charge of all the Katar? Did the other families have some similar hidden power? He didn't think so, but if this could have been hidden from him than perhaps other secrets were there to be discovered. It was a shame his father had to die before revealing these and other secrets. Did his sisters know of this—no, and he would have to insure they remained ignorant.

The Undine pulsated in front of him. The pillar formed itself into a roughly human shape. Without moving its 'legs,' the being flowed closer to him and spoke.

"You have the look about you of one from long ago. What is your name Karn?"

"Arlec."

"Ah. Strange. It is said that humans, or perhaps all mortals, are sometimes born again. You had an ancestor of the same name. He too called upon the Undine."

Arlec tried to remember an ancestor that he might have been named after. The name was not so uncommon, yet he couldn't recall hearing any story of an Arlec in the family.

"While that's interesting, Undine, it doesn't seem pertinent. Tell me, how many Undine are there? Are they all under my command?

The shape of the Undine oscillated in size several times. Arlec realized it was laughing, or imitating laughter. He held his tongue. Shortly the Undine replied.

"Ah, you do not really know, do you mortal." It paused and the ground around Arlec erupted in a shower of water and dirt. The water surrounded him and rose quickly. He fought panic. The water rose to his waist and he attempted to move, but the water seemed to press upon him. He was trapped. He was a good swimmer, but swimming was not an option.

"Stop. Stop in the name of Karn. Stop, I command it. I order it."

The Undine chuckled, a watery, gurgling sound. Yet, the water did subside and he felt he could move again. It did have to obey him.

"Yes, I, we, do have to obey. But, be forewarned mortal. We obey the letter, not the spirit. Your ancestors knew this. So will you. As to your questions ... who knows. The Undine are immortal, but we do occasionally die from external causes. Your god of the sea killed many of us, as you should know. Perhaps there are more of us created somewhere else, perhaps not. There are perhaps a thousand of us left. Maybe more. Maybe less. Sooner or later we will all hear your orders. And obey. Do you have orders?"

Arlec thought furiously. It would seem that the Undine did not obey quickly, nor with great willingness. He should plan. Yet, he should see what these water spirits were capable of.

"Gather the Undine here. First I want you to rebuild this manor to its former glory. Then I want at least five hundred of the Undine here within a month and I will have orders for you all. Do it. I command it. Do it well and no tricks."

With more confidence than he felt he spun on his heal and strode from the swamp. The sound of underwater laughter was not comforting.

* * *

The council chamber was unnaturally cold. Arlec pulled his sweater tighter and signaled for his aid, Garron. Garron was of the Trias clan, one of the minor clans affiliated with the Karn clan. Arlec knew Garron had ambitions and planned to use that to his advantage. He was huge, almost seven feet tall, with a sloping forehead, bushy eyebrows, and a full beard. His appearance was frightening to many, but deceiving. To assume Garron was unintelligent was a mistake. A mistake that many made.

"Garron, see what is keeping Jern," Arlec said as he slipped a small note into Garron's hand.

The Katar hold on The Cities was being slowly restored. Jern, head of the Tanec family had suffered the most. The city state of Argn had fallen to the rebels and many sympathizers still remained. That was what came with having women control so much of the city, he thought. Even Katar women there were too lenient. Argn was too wild and loose. Soon, if all went well, the Tanec would no longer be in control of that city. Arlec would have a loyal ally in place.

Assassinating a Katar was not easy, but not impossible. Even the healing powers of the rings were incapable of fixing a well-placed arrow, or brain damage, or similar mortal injuries. Even the Katar suffered 'accidents.' His father had suffered such an accident.

Arlec's reverie was broken as Jern came in with his two daughters, Mia and

Crissa. Their looks made him feel guilty, as if they knew something. Their bright colors out of place with the rest of the council. He thought of his remaining two sisters, in Argn helping with the quashing of the rebellion. He might have to deal with them soon. They still blamed him for Shara's death. Despite her association with that damn thief, Tsom, his sisters blamed him. That thorn had to be removed some day. The year had only lightly dulled his hatred of the thief. Yet, now the priesthoods seemed unconcerned with Tsom. Internal strife seemed to have taken over the gods and their priests. Fine, Strife fit Arlec's plans.

"Arlec, I still don't know why you insist that I be at these meetings personally. Either of my daughters is capable of dealing with the council on most matters," said Jern.

Jern looked tired. Crissa rubbed his shoulders and glared at Arlec.

Arlec forced a smile at Crissa, causing her look a bit confused.

"Of course they could. I have no doubt of your daughters' competence." More confused looks on both daughters' faces. "However, I wanted to follow the old traditions. As head of the Karn clan I ask you, as head of the Tanec clan for your daughter's hand in marriage to Garron, head of Trias family, which is part of the Karn clan. This marriage would do much to solidify relations between our two families."

Crissa's eyes went wide and her jaw momentarily dropped a fraction. She recovered quickly, although Jern jumped from pain as her hand dug into his shoulder.

"That is ludicrous," replied Jern. "My daughter and Garron have only the briefest of acquaintances. You know they have no interest in each other."

Garron entered the chamber at that moment. His bulk barely fitting through the door. His strong tenor voice sounding too mild for his size.

"The Trias family requests this under Katar law. The Tanec family is responsible for the assassination of my brother, trying to weaken the Karn clan. We demand recompense through marriage, or a duel to the death."

The ensuing uproar took minutes before enough order was restored for Garron to continue.

"I offer as proof the mind scanner Silan. He has scanned the mind of Jern's assassin and will testify that Jern hired the assassin." The silence was both for the strength of the evidence and the shock of a mind scan being done. A rape of the mind. Completely illegal, but if this were true than forgivable.

"Unfortunately, the assassin's mind was not up to the scan. He died. Silan has offered to allow a fellow scanner to read his own mind as to the truth of what we say."

All present knew that 'offer' was probably not the right word. Even a mind scanner was not immune to the effects of a mind scan. The talismans that allowed such an intrusion to occur were old. The Hrýll refused to make any more now. They were not intended for use by humans and tended to be damaging to the subject. Arlec smiled grimly, remembering that his own father had forced a mind scan upon him. Everyone in the chamber knew of that and would never dare to ask that he be subjected to that again.

After an hour of arguing and protesting the council recessed. Jern's face was twisted in rage and Arlec saw fear in Crissa's face. Mia's face was completely stone.

"You will have your answer in the morning Arlec," Jern said so softly that Arlec had to fill in a few of the words.

* * *

"Father, you cannot fight Garron. He is a brute. He will crush you," Crissa pleaded with her father, as they gathered in their guest quarters. The council met in Qenaril, as had been customary for centuries. The power of Qenaril lay with its control of the qenar mines. Given that the Telem clan was the only family to control two cities and was the wealthiest, it fell to them to host the council. Despite their financial power, Jern feared the Karn clan more than the Telem clan. The Karn had always been the most militaristic of the already militaristic Katar. Arlec was without morals, but Telem would ensure nothing occurred under his roof.

"I'm more experienced than he is. Arlec expects us to give in. You can't marry Garron. It is part of some scheme of Arlec's. He has all the cunning of his father and none of the honor, nor restraint. We must take a stand now." Jern all but pounded his fist on the table in their room.

"We should have him assassinated, at least then the charge would be real," Mia spoke for the first time.

"No, unfortunately, now the blame would instantly fall upon us. We cannot overtly move against Arlec," Crissa said, looking with some surprise at the sound of death in her sister's voice.

"What of his two daughters? We could threaten to have them killed?" Mia said, not letting it drop.

"No, Arlec would let them die. He feels threatened by them as it is," Jern said.

"I will marry the oaf. I'll ensure that whatever foul plan they have, that it backfires."

Silence. Jern considered. He could fight Garron, but he knew that despite Garron's huge size and stupid looks that he was an excellent fighter and shrewd. He had probably studied Jern's strengths and weaknesses already and Jern would not have time to do the same. If he fought and lost, then his daughters would be in the same situation in a matter of months. Now that Arlec had come out in the open in making a power play, perhaps he could counter future attempts. Arlec's weakness was that he underestimated women. Jern knew that his two daughters were better than most men in both fighting and intrigue. Crissa might actually be able to do more damage to the Karn clan married to Garron.

Jern sank into the chair. The Tanec chambers in the council building were simple and sparse. Easier to search for talismans that might be used to spy on them. He felt tired to his core. First the Tarth invasion of over a year ago, then the rebellion which was destroying his beloved Argn, and now this. Was this the change that the priesthoods had warned against with that thief? If so, he regretted that they had not been able to kill the young man right away.

"Very well Crissa, marry Garron. But, if he harms you in any way I will bring down the Karn family even if it means the destruction of all of the Katar. Do not underestimate Garron. He is smarter than he looks and while he is no doubt a tool of Arlec, he has a mind of his own."

* * *

Arlec was only mildly surprised that Jern allowed his daughter to marry Garron. The old man wasn't a fool, he probably guessed at some of what was going on. He had thought that Crissa would protest and force Jern's hand, but evidently the old man had more control over his daughters than Arlec believed.

The wedding was a simple affair. Rushed. The Lord Priest of Ague, God of the Seas, presided over the ceremony. Arlec had insisted that the ceremony take place on the island of old Arbeneth, on the grounds of the ancient Karn compound. Those attending were astonished at the newly erected manor and the grounds surrounding it.

Multiple fountains adorned what only recently had been swampland. The old stones of the ancient manor were scrubbed clean. A stream flowed from a natural spring on the eastern side of the new building.

Marsan, Lord Priest of Ague, stood upon the dais erected for the event. He kept staring at the two fountains flanking him. His brow was covered in sweat and he rubbed his staff of office which was clenched tightly in one hand. Arlec watched the priest intently. *What was he sensing?* He wondered. Could he possibly know of the Undine? His god was of the sea, of water.

The small crowd finished assembling. Garron stood in front of the priest, a small smile playing across his lips. Jern stood next to him, his face chiseled in stone. Occasionally his Katar ring glowed for less than a second, with the other Katar's rings flashing in response, protecting their wearers. Arlec tried hard not to laugh out loud. He clenched his jaws in the effort, but a smile still played on his face.

Crissa walked down the path to her husband-to-be. She wore a festive dress, with reds, orange, green, brown in stripes radiating down from her waist, while from the waist up the dress was an aqua blue. Her step was firm and her chin high. Jern looked at his daughter and smiled, but Garron frowned. Arlec saw the frown and tried to remember his lessons on Argn and their tying meanings to every color. Garron saw something there that he did not. Well, no matter, she was marrying Garron and that was what was necessary.

The Lord Priest evidently saw the same thing as he raised an eyebrow when he saw Crissa. When she stepped next to Garron the priest hastily began the ceremony, as if in a hurry.

"Family and witnesses we are here to wed Garron and Crissa in the ancient ritual of marriage and bonding of the Katar. I call upon the Gods of the Katar and the powers of the Katar to seal this marriage and bind these two to each other." The orb at the top of his staff of office glowed as did all the Katar rings.

"You are now husband and wife," declared the priest, not bothering with any flowery additional phrases. Everyone knew that the marriage was forced. The priest stared at the two fountains once again and hurried off to his floater at the edge of the property. He kept glancing back as he walked briskly down the winding path which followed the stream. He did not notice as parts of the stream seemed to stop moving momentarily near his feet and water flowed out of the stream, almost touching him, but never quite reaching him. Arlec thought he could hear a gurgling laughter from the two fountains.

The priest hopped onto the floater and commanded his lower priest to leave immediately. The water flowed back into the stream and merged with the current.

Chapter 21

"Lord Ague, I swear I sensed something on the Karn estate. A presence that echoed of your own, but was distinctly different."

Marsan stood uncomfortably over the pool of water, his god's image gently rippling within the liquid. The orb atop his staff-of-office glowed. The glow was weaker than it should have been. Both the priest and his god knew that the number of worshippers actively paying homage to any of the gods had declined noticeably the past year. Both had their reasons for fearing the decline.

"I have felt the presence of the Undine. Arlec has used his family's ancient hold over the water daemons. It's the only explanation. Without explicit summoning they would be unable to cross from their plane to Nakana. The man is a fool. His father should have told him more about the Undine. Surely even a power hungry Katar would have had more sense, if he knew the consequences. Unfortunately, my priest, I am unable to do anything about this at the moment. Hallam continues to harass us with her animals and her plots. We are all focused on defeating her. Until then, the Undine will do what they always do. This will undoubtedly be Arlec's bidding for now, but soon it will be for their own purposes. All too soon."

Maran shivered, despite the warmth of the air. His god was not going to aid him, or his other worshippers. At least not now. His congregation, what remained, believed the lines he fed them concerning the difficulty understanding the ways of a god, but he understood. His god was afraid. Afraid of another god. Afraid of the Undine. More prayers would go unanswered and only his own ability to interfere, with the power of his staff, would provide any 'divine' intervention. The less people prayed, the less power the staff and Ague had. It was a vicious cycle and he didn't like the rapidity in which it was deteriorating.

He turned away from the pool which now only held his reflection. Rubbing his hands together in instinctive warmth generation, he tucked his staff of office into the crook of his left arm. He shivered again. He must not let the thought of the struggle between the gods disturb him so much. All high priests knew the limitations of their gods. At least he was not alone in his fear.

From the pool behind him slowly rose a pillar of water. Maran angrily shrugged off another shiver. He did not see the orb on his staff flare. The pillar grew two massive arms and reached out. There was no scream, as Maran's mouth was full of water. It was over in moments. The water within his body flowed out of him. Orifices ruptured. The pores on his skin turned to sieves with the force of the flow. The Undine, finished, pulled back into the pool.

The junior priest found the dried sack of skin and bones next to his master's broken staff of office. Gagging, he ran from the room. The icy feeling did not register on him until later, when he described the scene to the new Lord Priest, who hardly seemed pleased with his promotion.

* * *

The living water swelled with the *ka* of the priest. He was enjoying this return to Nakana. The Karn had changed. They were weak. Almost human in their weakness. Had the Katar changed so much? How long had it been? Time was nearly meaningless to an Undine, yet he knew that many of the mortal races changed over time. The Katar known as Arlec had some of the old power, but it was diluted. There was just enough power there to hesitate striking the hated Karn. He would probe first to see how much power and knowledge remained. When the time was right then the Undine would strike.

The river felt good. The water here was so full of life. So easy to tap the energy. One had to be careful not to overdo it. Too much at once could be too intoxicating. Overload his ability to absorb.

He traveled thousands of marks, no destination in mind. Nakana, the nexus of the planes and home to this foolish Katar who bid him to use whatever means necessary to accomplish the tasks he had set upon the Undine. He imitated the laugh of a human, sending small waves of force through the water.

He sensed the power of Ague as he flowed near a ship. The power was tenuous, but tangible. Jumping Water could sense the power in the waves, the imprint of Ague. His old foe had grown weak. Humans called Ague a god. Jumping Water did not. Power over the sea was simply power over water. The Undine had power over any body of water. Ague only over salt water. True, Ague had reserves of *ka* that the Undine could not hold within themselves, but Ague was not truly of the water as they were. To the Undine, Ague was simply a strangely powerful human. An interloper.

He recalled the time Nakana had been without mankind. When only the Tarth and the Old Ones roamed the planet. The seas and the waters were left to the Undine. Minor Undine controlled the lakes and the ponds. Major Undine roamed the seas. Jumping Water did both. Of all the Undine, he could travel to any body of water at will. To him, they were all connected. This is why they called him Jumping Water. While he was not a king, he was first amongst the

Undine. They would listen, if not exactly obey. They all hated the gods and the Katar.

Jumping Water froze the water around the ship. Freezing caused the salt to leave the water. Ague would have no control over the ice. Jumping Water undulated with mirth. He willed himself to the rivers of the mountains. The mountains known as the Web of the Gods to the Old Ones. The Undine understood. The rivers between the planes were visible to them. They were almost water. Rivers of energy between the planes. Jumping Water flowed with the water that moved next to one of the rivers of the Web. If only he could control those rivers as he could water. If a Undine could smile, he would.

* * *

The dull moonlight of the overly long nights of this unknown plane reflected off the red skin of the banished Tarth. No breeze disturbed the depressed air, yet a sound insinuated itself across the washed out landscape. Thousands of Tarth felt the vibration within their souls. Within the mass of beings, a large circle formed. The old and decrepit stood, their humming moan like an organ running out of air. In the center stood Be Na Tarth, Lord of the Tarth. Tears streamed down his handsome red face, dropping to the ground in a slow steady drip, keeping time with the moaning of the circle. He bowed his head.

One hundred Tarth, the old, the crippled warriors, drew their knives. Their blood ran, the salty sweet red mixing with the tears. Their *ka* flowed, swirling unseen to those without the sight, around Be Na Tarth. His body shimmered, as if through a heat mirage. The moonlight seemed to brighten around him. He searched.

A tentative step in one direction, then another. His hands and arms moved, pulling aside a heavy tapestry. He must find the weakness between the planes quickly. The *ka* would run out all too soon. His people's lives wasted if he failed.

There.

He could feel the familiarity of his world, Nakana. Home. As the last of the sacrificial Tarth in the circle died, he pushed aside the barriers and stepped through.

He would be back to rescue his race.

Mankind, the Katar, and their gods would pay.

Nakana would be theirs again.

He fought the currents. It was so close, yet the forces pulled him in many directions. One was where he had just left. It pulled the hardest. He fought that pull fiercely. It was as if he were on the edge of a whirlpool. One of the streams joining the maelstrom was full of the sense of Hell. Hell, where the Tarth had been banished before. A weak stream, on the far side of the swirling tug of war, was Nakana. He could sense the complexity. The richness. It must be Nakana, the center of the planes. He swam toward it. His huge muscular body straining.

He knew it was a metaphorical swimming. It was not truly a stream or a river in the sense that his physical body thought of it, yet it felt like physical strain. Did he breath? It did not matter, he kicked, he moved his arms; he willed himself to make it to the weaker, complex stream.

Within the stream of Nakana he stood. He strode. He waded against the current. Suddenly, the resistance faded. He stepped out into the moonlight of three moons. He stumbled and sank to his knees, his face upturned and grinning.

Home.

Kneeling, he looked at his surroundings. Mountains. Fairly high up and near the pole from what he could gather of the stars. What year or season was this? It hardly mattered as the tilt of the planet made sure that this hemisphere was always warm. Up this high there was a chill, but the Tarth were largely immune to the vulgarities of temperature. Still, he was exhausted and this made the night cold.

Be Na Tarth was mildly surprised when the small stream next to him rose up into a pillar of water. Surprised not because he feared Undine, but rather because as far as he knew they had not been seen for thousands of years. From the time of the Tarth's first banishment. The Undine were neither friend nor foe, but they were of the old times.

"I know you Tarth. You are Sha Be Na Tarth. I felt a disturbance in the rivers between the planes, it was you."

"Be Na Tarth now, Undine. My father died in the banishment. I thought all of the Undine died also."

"We do not die, easily. The Katar have summoned us again, pulling us back from our own banishment. The foolish one known as Arlec has no idea of what he has done. He believes we are now here only to do his bidding. I warned him, as is required by the old compacts, but he fails to understand.

"Tarth, you are long lived, but mortal. Yet, after ten thousand years you are still alive?"

"To me it has been only a hundred years. We survived on Hell for one hundred years and then returned, only to be banished again by the traitor Talanas. He paid for his treachery. So did my mother, who died with him."

Be Na Tarth's voice broke at the end. It had been his own hand who had slain his mother. She had been foolish, throwing herself in front of his blade as he struck the traitor. She had taken the vows of marriage with the traitor too seriously. He was not Tarth. There was no need to follow the old ways with him. He pushed aside the guilt. If he did not, it would rot within and destroy him. He had too much to do. He had to save the rest of his race.

"Talanas. He is Death. It is good you have slain him. He was not as other mortals. There was something about him that caused some Undine to understand the concept of fear. The multiverse is better off without him."

"Which of the Undine are you? Are you of this river?"

"I am … *Gue Ta* in your tongue, Jumping Water in the common tongue.

First of the Undine. All water is my home. All water was my domain. All water will be my domain. Soon."

"Jumping Water. Yes, I remember you now. I remember, as a child, you came to my father's court. You were friends with the Tarth before the wars and the banishments. Are you still friends with the Tarth?"

"Perhaps." The watery loose shape paused, soundless for some time. Be Na Tarth waited patiently, as an ancient memory told him to do.

"Yes, I think that the Tarth and the Undine are still friends. We are both of this world. We have a common set of enemies: the gods of the humans and the Katar. The humans themselves, perhaps. Yes, let us talk of friendship. Let me tell you of my plans. Let me tell you of other Tarth and their plans. Where there is water, there can be Undine and we know much. You can then tell me of your plans and of that jade sphere hanging around your neck, so full of *ka.*"

Chapter 22

"What do we do now?" Tyna asked when she wakened, pulling Rosea close.

"Good question. The Tarth want you badly. They've done something to you which may explain our ... lack of inhibitions not so long ago." He glanced at their baby and his dark frown softened. "We can't return home."

Tyna nodded vehemently. Not only would that bring danger to her mother, but her mother would think of them both as monsters. Even now he still looked very much like her brother, albeit the way a distorted reflection in a mirror still looks like the viewer. If the overwhelming mating instinct that had overcome them both had not happened, she might have fought off her feelings for this man who inhabited a changed version of her brother's body. Maybe. Now, she felt bonded to him in a very unsisterly way. Was it her own feelings, or part of what the Tarth had forced her to drink? She admitted that she didn't care. She knew that Alan was now part of her and she loved him. And feared him. He had a dark power and memories that remained undiscovered. She felt it was better if some of those memories remained buried forever.

So what did that give them as options? Running. She hated the thought of running, but right now it was the only viable thing. She looked down at Rosea. Running was the best thing for her—get away from the Tarth. She looked at Alan. No, just running would never do. This man was not a runner.

"We find out what the Tarth did. We find a way to stop the Tarth from hunting us," she said.

Alan stood and nodded.

"Agreed. We get you to a town or even Zethicia itself. You take care of Rosea and I will deal with the Tarth."

"Not a chance."

She pulled herself up by the nearby tree. Rosea, slung on her neck and shoulders was awake, but quiet. She watched their every move. Tyna strode up to Alan and grabbed his shirt, leaning too heavily against it. Goddess of Mercy she was weak. She needed food. She continued.

"You are not doing this on your own."

"You need to protect Rosea."

At least he didn't focus on her current weakness. She could see in his eyes that he was more worried about her than the baby.

"I won't let you risk only yourself. I will not hide. Rosea is ours. I love her as any mother loves a child. Yet, we both know she is strange, because of the Tarth and what they did to me … and because of you. I love you and will not lose you. I will not die running, nor will let Rosea live through fear. Better we all die."

She gathered her strength and pulled him close. She kissed him, with strength, and then pushed him back a bit.

"We go to Zethicia and find some distant relatives of mine. We'll leave Rosea there and then the two of us will persuade the Tarth that it is in their interest to let all of this be."

Alan looked into her eyes. She saw his eyes flash with gold momentarily and then he smiled and kissed her in return. Zethicia was a long walk, it could wait until next morning.

* * *

Kulakoonstru stood up from his folded position. His bones, muscle, tendons, and joints all shifted automatically. One leg had been folded in a manner similar to a human, the other in reverse. He looked like a folding table being raised up until the legs snapped into their new position. The band of warriors rose with him. Forty. A large group for Yanín. Forty warriors once destroyed a town of one thousand humans. Back before the humans dominated the population of Nakana. Kula bared all his teeth and hissed. Only a fellow Yanín would recognize the chilling sound as a chuckle.

"It is agreed then. All new contracts with the Katar and humans are carefully defined. You include a statement that guarding anyone, anything, is only if it does not conflict with threats to the Yanín as a whole. This will include any agreements that the Yanín have made for our entire race. We have never done such an agreement, so the humans will not be worried."

The general hissing amongst them was acknowledgement and agreement. Kula continued.

"There is an offer of much wealth to any who find this human woman known by her kind as Tyna Valence. All in her company are fair game for killing, but she should be left alive for the Tarth. It is important that she is alive."

The latter was hard to comprehend for the Yanín. They did not take hostages. It was a terrible dishonor to be taken alive and they did not do such a dishonor to even their enemies.

"She was last seen with a man to the west of Tarin. To the west of the Tarth encampment. Deep in the Web of the Gods."

Silence. The Yanín did not fear anything, but there was a deep respect for the Web of the Gods among them. Their legends spoke of a trek by the Yanín from a distant land to Nakana through the Web of the Gods. They had almost immediately fought with the Hrýll and lost. The damned talismans of the Hrýll had been too powerful. It did not occur to the Yanín that since the Hrýll were already on Nakana that the Yanín were the interlopers. The Yanín were the Yanín. No one stood against the Yanín. Yet, the Hrýll had. This defeat, eons ago, was a continued source of hatred. The Web of the Gods was revered as the source of the Yanín. They would remove the humans from the Web and bring the woman to the Tarth; to do with what they wanted.

The forty Yanín dispersed, each to lead a small team. Kula felt confident that the human female would be found in a matter of weeks. He hoped they could restrain themselves from killing her. He had been careful in his promise to the Tarth. He said he would try to take her alive. It would be dishonorable to not try.

* * *

Larrina followed a trail that Tsom could not see. She warned him that they were near the Tarth encampment. Her concern was over not just the Tarth, but Hallam and her animal minions and she said there were Yanín tracks everywhere also. Yanín, as if the Tarth daemons were not bad enough. Tsom scowled to himself, two against a small army of beings strong enough individually to kill ten men. They should be mobilizing the revolution against the Tarth. Mobilizing Zethica. Now that the Tarth location was known, why bother with a fruitless search for a dead man. A traitor.

At least with all the riding he was becoming a fair horseman. The riding no longer caused his legs and back to ache so much that he stumbled as he dismounted. Larrina had brewed her healing teas that soothed the aches and allowed him to sleep, but she no longer slept with him. The healing of their love making was gone. With its absence he realized that she really had healed him deeply. He was no longer a young man trapped in an old and dying body. Now he looked middle aged, but healthy and strong. He was strong, he reminded himself. He occasionally manifested his hands to test the strength of his *ka*. It was not at the pre-war level, the level of his first discovery of his powers, but it was strong. His abilities with his hands were strong. And now his hands no longer required without massive draining of *ka*. This too made him strong. Almost like a living talisman.

Larrina had sensed his testing of his powers. She was constantly telling him some version of, "Tsom, you have mastered some of your powers. Mastery allows you to use them without self-destruction. Be careful. You are not a youth. Your *ka* is not infinite. If you try new powers it will be dangerous to your remaining life force. The temptation of trying new powers is a strong one. It has been the downfall of many Kinel. Perhaps the death of our race. Too much power without understanding the consequences. We fought too hard and too quickly against the Katar. We lost. Pure power does not always win the war, even if the battle is won."

Tsom didn't need to be lectured. He remembered his own past. As always, recall brought with it 'what if' thinking. He was only twenty, years old and look at him now. If he had a ring of the Katar again, like the one they had destroyed from the would-be-assassin, then perhaps it would be a different story. He chafed at the lack of progress the resistance was making. Oonie was right, Larrina should not be leading an army. She may be a good fighter, better than any he had seen except Lanos and Alanar, but she lacked the all-or-nothing instinct that Tsom knew was necessary. Her skill was one of age. How old was she? Four hundred, or five hundred years? He'd lost that all or nothing instinct for a while, but he felt it returning. The truth of war was that you had to win at all costs, or you lost.

Was that true in love also? Was he fighting hard enough for Larrina? Perhaps she would return to him once she found that Alanar was dead and she was chasing a dream. Or that Alanar no longer loved her. If he had, he would have searched her out. Then would she abandon Alanar and this woman? It probably wasn't even Alanar. How could it be? Tsom shook his head, knowing he was confusing himself. His horse turned its head in response.

True, the Tarth seemed to want those two, but that merely made them potential allies, nothing else. It hardly proved that it was Alanar. She would see this if they found the two before the Tarth. And the Yanín. Just two people who had annoyed the Tarth. She would see. Then they could focus on destroying the remaining Tarth and return to bringing down the Katar. Larrina would be reenergized when this dream had ended. She would return to him.

Larrina indicated that the trail ended along the ridge of a foothill from the mountains. Many ridges shot out from the mountains. Like giant fingers. Or like the arms of a spider web, or the spider itself.

Larrina cast about for signs of the trail. She dismounted the horse and searched on foot. Nothing. Tsom sat astride his own mount, too tired to get off and then back on. The horse lowered its head and grazed. The area was high plains. The trees were scattered, but large and old, providing enough shade for the grass to retain a lush green. After a long time Larrina sank to her knees on the grass. Her head bowed and her shoulders slumped. Suddenly she looked frail. Tsom had never thought of Larrina as frail. His heart ached for her.

Tsom eased himself off the horse. Both feet free of the stirrups he swung his right leg over and dropped down. Stumbling he threw out a hand, manifesting it instinctively, and caught himself. Walking with stiffness he rested a hand on her shoulder. His mechanical hand had no feeling, but he could touch her with his virtual hands.

"I'm sure it wasn't Alanar. You haven't lost him again."

"He is here. Somewhere. I sense his existence."

Tsom frowned. Would she not accept reality? He was about to say something biting, but saw the tear on her cheek. A wave of anger washed over him, followed by compassion.

"I have touched Alanar before. If he is anywhere within hundreds of marks, I will be able to touch him."

Before she could stop him he cast his hands outward. He sank to his knees for stability. Stretching them thinner and thinner he swept them throughout the surroundings. He stretched more. The Tarth, he brushed against them lightly. Fire. Their *ka* was like fire. He now knew where they were and how many. He felt the death cats, their strange *ka* and intelligence. Yanín, cool strong powerful. Vaguely like Alanar in that he felt death within them. No Hrýll nearby. He stretched further. At least three hundred marks out. He knew it was dangerous. It burned some of his *ka*. Still, he did it for Larrina. For himself. Fascinating creatures he touched. Some he did not know. Some he guessed at. He was about to give up when he touched ice. Burning cold. The very touch destroyed some of his *ka*. It was Alanar ... wasn't it? This was different from that touch over a year ago, when he had killed, or banished Alanar. It was like he touched two beings in one. A year ago the touch had seriously damaged him, burning his ka, sucking out his *ka*. This time it was muted. As if patches of this Alanar were missing, were burned out, or wiped out, or covered, or muted.

Tsom focused his attention on this life force. There were two other life forces nearby. Both were alien. At first he would have guessed human, but there were tinges of Tarth and something else. He felt a wave of lust as he brushed the one force. It almost overwhelmed him. He began to punch through the folds of space between them as he had over a year ago. Punch through and pull this female he sensed to him. He had to have her. He would have her. He could feel saliva dripping down his chin and felt blood rushing to his groin.

The slap almost knocked him out. He blinked to clear his eyes. Larrina stood before him. Sweet Larrina. She smelled good. He reached out and pulled her close. She struggled, but he wrapped his virtual hands around him. He pinned her arms. My Larrina.

"Tsom, stop. Snap out of it. You ..." She struggled he could feel her manifesting something. He didn't care. He wanted her. " ... cannot rape me Tsom. It will destroy you. Do not do this. It must not be rape. You don't understand. It will kill you if you rape me."

Rape? Rape? It was not rape to make love to Larrina. She was his love. He needed her. Rape?

The word sunk in. He remembered his 'sisters' at the brothel. They had killed a man once who had raped one of their circle. Yes, we sell sex. But we choose. We do it on our terms. Rape is inexcusable. It violates free will. It violates what little we have in this world. Sex given, or sold, is one thing. Taken is another. It burns to the very essence of our being. Her ka is damaged. She is scared forever.

Tsom stumbled back and let go of Larrina. He looked at her in shock.

"Oh Larrina, I did not mean ..."

Larrina stood shaking. A fear, of sorts, was in her eyes. Was it fear of him, or for him, or for herself? She stepped forward and caught him as he sank to the ground.

"It was not you Tsom. I felt it as you grabbed me. I saw it on your face as I slapped you. You were not in control."

He had almost hurt Larrina again. He had loved two women in his life. One was dead and he had almost raped the other. A year ago he had almost killed her in his desperation to save Shara and now this. What sort of a man was he?

She pulled him close and let him sob onto her breast. There was no lust now. No longing. Just shame and fear.

After a time, he could speak again.

"I think it was Alanar. Or part of him. It felt like a jigsaw puzzle with pieces missing and pieces of another put in their place. Yet, it felt like him. He is with two others. One caused the loss of control. The other I did not have a chance to 'touch.' He is far away, deep into the mountains."

Tsom pointed the direction. Even as he pointed, he felt regret. She must hate part of him now and he was pointing the way to someone she might love. Once, he had thought she had loved Lanos, the handsome soldier that had made up part of their team a year ago. Now, he was sure it had never been Lanos. It had always been Alanar. She had known Alanar for far longer than Lanos. There was some sort of bond between them. Something she had never told him about. A moment of rage and lust returned, but he pushed it down.

Larrina looked at him and looked at their horses. She hesitated a moment then unsaddled the horses.

"I will brew some tea. We will start in the morning."

Chapter 23

Rosea didn't act like any baby Alan had seen. She only cried occasionally and instantly stopped when fed or changed. The latter was a real problem. They tore up as much of their own clothes as they could. They followed streams to wash out the makeshift diapers. Rosea seemed to understand and her diapers were getting soiled at more and more predictable times. After a time, they would stop and she relieved herself without soiling anything.

Alan carried the baby half the time. He felt an attachment toward it, but he was not sure it was normal fatherly love. Most fathers have time to adjust to the idea. Twenty weeks at least. Even those two hundred days seemed like too short a time. One of his lost memories surfaced and said that women even secreted a chemical that helped the father bond to a baby. Rosea had been born much faster. Then there was the manner of the conception. He might have called it rape, except that Tyna had raped him as much as he her. That and he loved her with a passion that he found intoxicating. A vanishing part of his brain still screamed out that she was his step-sister, but he could feel that he was not Lerence. He could see it even in his hands. He had changed physically and his memories of Tyna as a sister and of his mother and his father were as if reading a book. It was as if he was referencing them, not as if he had ever experienced them.

He looked at Tyna walking strongly beside him. Her long exposed legs corded with muscle, yet so appealing. She had strength and he found that extremely attractive. Her dark skin had taken on a red tinge to it, which was oddly appealing with her red hair. He felt stirrings and a speeding of his heart just watching her, but this was not the urges of before. These were the normal lusty feelings of a man in love.

Tyna sensed his look and glanced at his groin. She flashed him a smile.

"Later, Love. Maybe at lunch."

He grinned back and glanced down at Rosea. Rosea was asleep. They kept up the pace until lunch, at which time Tyna was true to her word.

They had just finished making love, with Rosea sitting peacefully to the side, playing with the grass and flowers, when Alan felt the presence. He whipped out his sword. Alarmed, Tyna pulled out her sword and rushed toward Rosea. Suddenly, she stopped. Her back stiffened and her clothes and breasts flattened as if a giant hand were wrapped around her. She flushed a deep red and suddenly her scent filled the air. Alan felt the wave of lust wash over him. Rosea cried.

Within the fog of lust, unlike before, Alan was able to keep his sanity. The ground beneath his feet went black, the grass withering. The engorgement of his penis felt ludicrous with the rage he was feeling. Someone was hurting his woman. Rosea crawled over to Tyna and grabbed her leg as the circle of blackness grew. The grass under Tyna and Rosea remained green. The presence disappeared.

As Alan's rage faded he realized that he remembered what had just happened. This was different than the two previous times. He dropped his sword and ran to Tyna, who was clutching Rosea. She almost shrank away from him, but looking into his eyes she smiled.

"It's still you," she said.

He gathered her up into his arms, along with Rosea and squeezed them both.

"Rosea is immune to whatever it is I do. She knows it and knows you are not. I have to learn to control that killing rage that comes over me. I almost felt I had control this time. Almost," Alan said.

"What was that presence? It touched me and I felt … that madness again. Oh, my love, it was a terrible enough madness with you, but if it happens with anyone else, I could not bear it. I will not bear it."

Alan simply held on to her. He had no answers. Nothing to lash out at. Not yet. The Tarth, they were responsible. They had to fix this. Fix it or die. He felt his temper rising again. Rosea cried and he snapped out of it.

They continued in a more somber mood. They were a hundreds of marks from any town and the edge of the Muglanth Plains was closer, but hardly much better. On foot in the mountains that was a hundred days. A third of a year. He didn't fear any of the wild animals, nor getting lost. These were known quantities. It was the time. The Tarth could move. They could die. The strange presence could attack again. The unknown was bothering him. He licked his lips and wished for a glass of Hrýll brandy. A stiff one. A full bottle. The book he called memory reminded him that Lerence didn't drink.

After a few weeks they came across a small herd of horses. Alan signaled to Tyna to stop. She was about to say something, a look of disbelief on her face, then she nodded and slowly sat down with Rosea. Alan started circling.

He didn't try to hide his presence, but kept circling in an angle to the herd, an ellipse around them. Deep within him he felt this was the right thing to do. Finally the horses began to move away from him. He made sure they were able to see him and he went off in an angle away from them. This caused them to halt and they followed him for a while. Then he circled some more.

The entire process repeated itself many times. From atop the hill Tyna watched fascinated. This was further proof that Alan was not her brother Lerence. Lerence knew nothing of horses. Alan was almost one of them. He was now standing next to the stallion. The stallion's ears went from pinned back to rotating forward to pinned back, several times. Hours later he was petting the stallion and had his sword belt over its neck. He was blowing into the horse's mouth and she could hear a singing from down in the small valley, but could not make out the words. She was sure they were not any language she had heard before—except perhaps the day her brother died, for she accepted that is what happened the day the horse kicked him and this strange man had taken over his body.

The next day they were both riding. The horses were a bit hard to control, but her mare followed wherever Alan and the stallion went and he seemed to be training the horse by the minute. She asked him where the knowledge came from to catch the horses. What was the language? He had no real answer. When pressed his eyes rolled partially back into his head. His head tilted back and he began to speak in a half trance.

"I remember a vast plain. A fire rolled across the plain. A great fire. A huge herd of horses ran in fear. They ran straight toward a cliff. Somehow I saved them, but I have no idea how. It feels like a lifetime ago. I am not even sure it was my lifetime. A man, or something resembling a man, was grateful. He taught me what he called were 'songs of the horses' which I sang yesterday. Yet, I cannot remember what the songs say. I feel I know the meaning, but I cannot recall at this moment."

That night, Tyna stroked his head as he fell asleep. Rosea finished with her breast and crawled over to the meat bag. She pulled out the dried rabbit piece and began to chew. The teeth that Tyna had recently felt seemed to be up to the task. In two weeks, she had matured almost a year. Rosea crawled back and tucked herself in, between Alan and Tyna, then continued to chew. Both Tyna and Alan were asleep.

* * *

Kula let the eagle settle on his arm. His instincts rebelled. The eagles were predators. One fought with predators. The eagle landed, its sharp claws digging into the thick leathery skin of the Yanín. He almost felt pain. The eagle was strong and not holding back. Kula fished out the message tied to the left leg of the eagle. He signaled to one of the Yanín who brought a chunk of meat for the eagle as a reward. They tied it to a tree branch and let it eat.

The note was from one of the forty Yanín groups. They were deep within the mountains, further than they had orders to go. Of course orders to a Yanín were open to interpretation. Kula wasn't truly angry. An opportunity to travel toward Mount Silinare was hard to resist. It had been centuries since they had worshipped the Sun God, yet there was a nostalgic reverence to the tallest mountain on Nakana. The note spoke of a man who charmed horses. The man was with a woman and a child. This at first did not seem like their objective, but the description of the woman was compelling. Over six feet with red hair. It seemed worth investigating as there was no reason for two humans to be so deep within the mountains. Most humans avoided the Web of the Gods. He wrote a reply and tied it to the eagle. Issuing the return command that they had all been taught by the Tarth, he threw the eagle upward. Its ten-foot wingspan caught the air and in a few mighty beats it was flying upward.

* * *

Hallam lay on her couch. Two dui mar lay nearby, purring contentedly. She was tired. In her mind she was maintaining contact with over ten eagles simultaneously. One, or two, was her normal contact. The effort over the past weeks had been draining. Not of ka, she had plenty of that, but simple fatigue. Her head ached and she had a hard time concentrating. Soon, she would have to drop all contact and control and rest.

That bitch, Larrina, had killed one of her eagles while in contact. That had cost Hallam a day of rest. The shock had forced her to drop control as she fought to maintain consciousness. If she had not been controlling so many eagles she might have been able to avoid the arrow. As it was by the time it registered on her awareness, so many marks away, it was too late. There was a delay in her control and it was just enough to give that bitch the edge. When the time was right, she would kill her. For now, the revolutionaries were more important to her plan. No need to weaken them just yet.

Hallam was about to let contact drop for the day when the view from one of her minions caught her attention. She dropped focus on the other nine and concentrated on this view.

A man was circling horses. A strange sing-song was coming from his mouth. The eagle's ears picked it up, but either it was a language she did not know, or the wind was distorting it. The horses were not running, although they seemed alert. Hallam focused on the stallion and pushed her mind to enter it.

She almost had contact, but something was blocking it. The sing-song of the man was ringing in her ears and causing her focus to fade. Damn. She returned to the eagle.

The man eventually had the stallion. She admired how he handled the horse. He had a way with animals, something that she always found attractive in a man. In time he captured a mare also.

Over the course of the next several days Hallam watched the man, woman, and child. There could be no doubt that this woman was the woman See'arr had found and given the altered 'medication' to. The red tinge of her skin was too like a Tarth to be anything else. A baby. This was a surprise. It was too early for a baby. What was the gestation period of a Tarth? It had been so long since anyone had believed the Tarth even existed that most of the knowledge had died off. She had been young then, many eons ago. Then it came to her, it was over a year, the normal gestation. The man was human. Their gestation was twenty weeks. Two thirds of a year. Had she been pregnant before See'arr had captured her? Unlikely. See'arr would have known. No, this was an unintended consequence of the medication, or something else. Interesting.

She marveled at the bond that seemed to be developing between the stallion and the man. Stallions were notoriously hard to train from the wild. The man had skill and some sort of subtle power. Nothing like her own power over animals, but still it was impressive. He was muscular in a slim, wiry, manner. There was something vaguely familiar about him. Especially the eyes.

As the days wore on she ascertained that the Yanín were converging on the three. The Tarth had been notified also, but they were too far away. The Yanín would arrive first. Hallam considered. The woman had to survive or her plans would be set back by many a year. The meddling See'arr had somehow altered the medication in just the right way and now it was impossible to duplicate. At a minimum, it would take a very long time and many dead women.

Women were like any animal, they defended their young. This baby was going to be a problem. If the Yanín tried to capture the woman and the baby was in danger, she might destroy herself defending it. What if the baby was a girl? Yes, that would be interesting. Would she carry the traits of her mother—she should. That had been the intention. The baby might be her insurance policy.

She generally disliked controlling owls. Their brains were too primitive and small. So much space devoted to the eyes. However, for direct control, with no real thinking involved, an owl would be ideal. It took a day to find a Great Mountain Owl, the largest owl on Nakana. Wingspan was important. The opportunity she needed presented itself that very night.

* * *

They had abandoned efforts to keep watch during the night. Exhaustion had taken its toll. They slept the sleep of the near dead. Both Alan and Tyna had lost weight over the past four weeks. They ate large amounts of protein from Alan's hunting, but fruits and nuts were rare this deep into the mountains. Their horses were losing weight also. Grass was not providing enough calories and the grass had not yet gone to seed. Tyna's body was still producing milk, but less of it. Rosea now constantly chewed on the primitive jerky as they rode and often as they slept. She no longer needed diapers.

The owl landed on the branch above their camp with no noise. It's perfectly shaped feathers provided a noiseless flight. Patiently it waited. Rosea was tucked into Tyna's arms, but squirmed. She tried suckling on a breast, but finding not enough there for her voracious appetite, she crawled to the makeshift pack that the meat was stored in. The owl spread its wings and noiselessly dropped.

Rosea's cry brought instant results. Alan was running toward the cry with his sword drawn. Only one moon was out, a darker than normal night. His eyes fought to find focus. By then the owl was above the trees, skimming near the branches. Even if he had a bow, there was no shot. Tyna was running wildly beneath the trees calling Rosea's name. The baby cried out in response, but the cries were already distant.

Tyna slammed her fists onto Alan's chest.

"Why didn't you do something? Where was that damn power of yours? You should have killed it. Killed everything nearby. The baby is immune. Why didn't you kill it!?"

Alan held her hands as she still tried to hit him. He pulled her tight and let her hit his back. He didn't know how to control his dark power. She knew that. Something had to trigger it. Personal danger, or something similar. He didn't voice the other thought that he wouldn't have endangered Tyna. Without Rosea to protect her, Tyna would have died. He was thankful he hadn't even had the option.

He held her close and cried with her. For the first time since his 'awakening' after the horse's blow he felt totally helpless. He felt the beginnings of rage, but a corner of his brain felt something else. He was sure that Rosea was still alive. He sensed it.

"Tyna, stop. Hold still. Listen with your mind. Can you feel it? I feel that she is still alive."

Tyna's sobs and pounding subsided. She held still for a long moment. Shaking her head she sagged.

"I sense nothing. No, that is not true, I feel you. With my eyes closed I sense your presence."

"Focus on that. Do you feel something similar. A weak version of that? I sense her as a shadow of you. Can you feel it? The creature is doing someone's bidding. It is not killing for food. It would have broken Rosea's back if it was."

Long silence.

"It grows faint. The bird is taking it further and further away. I feel it now. Oh Alan, we must save our daughter. Even if she is some strange creation of the Tarth, she is ours."

Tyna could not see Alan's eyes with her face buried on his chest. They were gold within gold. No whites remained.

Chapter 24

Arlec surveyed his new manor. It did not escape him that almost all the rooms contained a water feature of some sort. Did the Undine think he was stupid? Obviously, they were planning something in the future. Their insurance. Well, he had been researching his father's library. Everyone had insurance.

He had sent for his sisters after the wedding. It was time to settle with them, one way or another. Piea and Larra were becoming a nuisance.

He was surprised when they refused to come. A colorful note from Argn, the color having some meaning he didn't bother to research, informed him that Argn was now neither fully Katar, nor in the hands of the rebels, but ruled by a bunch of arrogant females. What was Jern thinking, letting his daughters run wild like that? What was he thinking letting his sisters act against him? It was time to use the Undine again. He smiled. They were proving quite useful.

* * *

Flana reveled in her return to Argn. Despite the year of war, it was still a colorful city and the relative recent peace brought it back to life. A few of the shops were still being rebuilt, but the bright primary colors of most of the city distracted from any feeling of destruction. New bright yellow, red, and blue paint covered the multistoried buildings. Most of Argn was no taller than three or four stories, simultaneously, most were more than one story tall. Steel was too rare to waste on tall buildings and there was enough space to sprawl. Even the ruling center of the city was only five or six stories tall. This made the one or two buildings over eight stories stand out. Flana enjoyed the way that almost all the buildings, even those devoted to commerce and manufacturing, had decks and small alcoves to the outside. The Argn citizens enjoyed the outdoors. The houses looked like they had growths sprouting forth, yet there was a pattern to it all that Flana could not quite grasp. Regardless, it resonated with her. She loved that women were respected here. In fact they were now the de facto leaders of Argn. Even more surprising, the Katar were sharing power with others. Piea and Larra had been telling the truth. She almost twirled in the middle of a street as she thought of her freedom from Arlec and her father. She felt alive.

Her first meeting of citizens council had gone well. Almost too well, she thought, as she replayed the meeting.

Jern was away, negotiating a losing agreement with the other Katar families, as Crissa phrased it. He left the running of the city in the hands of his two daughters, Crissa and Mia. They had recently consolidated power with many of the discontented Katar women from all clans. The city, always favored by female Katar, had become a symbol and a gathering point. This prevented the Katar families from moving against Argn directly. The thought of killing one's own daughter, or sister, or even mother was too hard to take.

Additionally, they brought in the women of many rich noble families. Flana was from the richest and most powerful. She realized how important she was to the Katar women. Crissa, Mia, Piea, and Larra were the tetrarchy of Katar women leading Argn. By persuading Lana to join them they now had access to trade, or the potential of at least not getting blocked in trade. Her father and the Showa family would not turn against her immediately and the trade with Argn was profitable. Her father's network of ships would ensure that Arlec and his cadre could not stop them through economic means.

The rebels had negotiated a truce with Argn, although the main leader Larrina was not there to give final approval. The rebels also had a considerable number of women in their leadership and the Katar women of Argn had promised slow, but steady, change. The negotiations with the Hrýll were not going as well. The Katar had done too much against the Hrýll over the centuries. While they were no longer overtly attacking Argn, the Hrýll and the virtually extinct Srýll were no longer trading any talismans with any of The Cities. Flana suspected that if this continued for more than another year that all of The Cities would be in dire straits. Zethicia, far to the northeastern plains, would be less affected as they had never had as much access to modern conveniences as The Cities. Also, it wasn't clear if the Hrýll were trading with them. Still, the Katar controlled qenar. How would the Hrýll survive without qenar?

Flana sighed and not for the first time lamented that humans could not shape talismans, or bind them to qenar. Even the Kinel, legendary race that the Katar had destroyed, had been only able to shape *ka* for personal use, not to bind it to a talisman for continued use. Not even the gods seemed to be able to do that, beyond the primitive staffs that the priests carried. Those more like storage devices, or funnels. Not truly shaped.

Already some strange contrivances were cropping up to replace talismans. Lanterns were developed that threw off better light with whale oil that the Showa family controlled, making glow globes less important. A process for refining an oil found near the Slar Mar desert allowed for lanterns that could burn all night. Wagons were much better than even a year ago, with something called bearings ensuring that horses could haul larger loads. Flana had heard of other interesting devices that would never become practical as they required large amounts of steel, something Nakana had very little of. Still, they were intriguing. Maybe mankind would survive without talismans given enough time. Steel was one of the main issues. Almost all the steel was devoted to weapons, and small implements. Flana touched the small sword, almost a dagger, strapped to her side. What would be possible, she wondered, if steel was as plentiful as copper.

When she had free time, here or in Arbeneth, she would wander down to the docks. She supposed it was in her blood, the trading, the ships, the smell of fish. The Showa barges were large, powered by talismans and qenar. They were increasing in value already, these powered ships. She leaned on the railing and watched one of them unload. The extra security guarding the barge, not the cargo. She frowned. Things were changing and it was not all for the better.

The captain of the barge spotted her and smiled. Darne, was his name, she recalled. She had visited his wife and sick child last year, while he was away, and he remained grateful. She waved him up.

"Darne, it's a pleasure to see you," she held out her hands, which he grasped and bowed lightly over.

"Mistress Flana, Tarn and Talia ask after you all the time. They were saddened to hear you left Arbeneth and rumor has it you won't return?"

"Not while Arlec remains in control of the city, no. I won't marry that … man."

A look of fear flashed across Darne's face, but it was followed by sympathy.

"I understand, mistress. Yet, your father has not disowned you. That is good."

"No, he loves me in his own way. Plus, he is a trader. A pragmatist. My joining the emerging government here in Argn is advantageous to him and the Showa clan. He is angry, but will still use me," she laughed, trying her best to keep the bitterness out. Darne nodded.

"I must return to my ship, Mistress." He turned to leave, then turned back, slowly. "Mistress, if ever there is a split between you and the rest of the Showa, you know that many would flock to your side. Bringing their ships with them."

Flana kept her surprise hidden. Saying such a thing out loud was dangerous. He could be fired, or worse. She took his hands and drew him close, then whispered in his ear. "Thank you, Darne. I hope it doesn't come to that, but times are changing. If the Katar fall, it will be a new world in The Cities. That world needs people like you."

Darne looked embarrassed and pleased. He bowed lightly again and went back to his barge.

Yes, she thought, things were changing.

She used her network to put out the word that anyone finding a new source of jade laden with qenar would be richly rewarded. There had to be another source somewhere on Nakana. Even a small source could break the Katar and allow an alliance with the Hrýll. The Showa trading company had thousands of ships, either directly, or hired out. Nakana was huge and still not well explored, now she was providing some incentive for additional exploration. Father would not be pleased at the extra cost, but she hoped that during the exploration new goods would be obtained to mitigate the costs.

Within a month, Flana was included in the council of four Katar. They found her planning abilities invaluable and she had insights into the thinking of the populace that the Katar women simply did not have. She didn't feel they thought of her as an equal, but their respect for her grew and her power grew with it.

Flana never gave up her habit of wearing bright green, even after learning that it indicated that she was a woman not interested in men. She balanced that off with a sash around the waist that was bright yellow, indicating that she was not married, and boots that were black, indicating that she had a man. She smiled at the confusion her color choices caused.

During one meeting of the council of four, plus one, they were interrupted by a messenger. A young woman who glanced shyly at Flana as she told them that the High Lord Priest of Ague was there to see them. After a moment's hesitation, he was shown in.

Flana was shocked to see that it was not Marsan who entered. Her family was closely tied to the priesthood of Ague. What had happened?

The new Lord Priest of Ague, Triste, briefly bowed to them all. He gave a brief smile to Flana.

"Ladies, I bring sad tidings that the Lord Priest Marsan has died." He waited for the expected surprise and barrage of questions.

"We believe that the Undine are loose again upon Nakana."

Their silence illustrated their surprise. Undine? That was a tale sailors told. More legends from the past coming to life? First the Tarth, now Undine.

The high priest looked at Piea and Larra as he continued.

"It's believed that Arlec, of the Karn, has summoned them forth using old powers of the Karn clan. This is in deep violation of an old agreement between Ague and the Karn clan. Ague is angered that such a blatant breech of peace between the gods and the Katar has occurred."

Piea and Larra's mouths tightened, but they didn't say anything. The priest no doubt knew of the split within their family. Crissa and Mia looked slightly confused. Crissa spoke up.

"What are the Undine and what agreement are you speaking of?"

Triste did not seem surprised at the question.

"I have only learned recently some of the details. Ten thousand years ago, give or take, after the wars between the races and the banishment of the Tarth, the Karn clan built up their strength through the summoning of Undine, the water daemons. This is why Arbeneth has an island and lies on two sides of the river delta spilling into the Nylyr Sea. The old Karn stronghold was on the island with both salt water and fresh water surrounding it. The archives tell of Undine that are specific to each, by being on the island that spills into the ocean, both salt and fresh water Undine were accessible.

Arlec has restored the old Karn manor on the island, yet no workers were hired for the task. After the wedding between you ..." he stopped and nodded to Crissa "... and Garron, we suspected that something strange was happening. Marsan had ordered all records pertaining to the Undine to be sent to him. Not long afterwards he was assassinated by a creature that drained him of all *ka* and all water. He was *true deathed* in his own temple."

True Death. How horrible. Never to be reincarnated. To truly die. It was one of the punishments that Flana never agreed with the Katar on: the stealing of *ka* from criminals until they died. No crime deserved True Death, even murder. Murderers could be put to death, to go to the Sea of Souls and only to return when fate allowed them to, but wiping their existence out forever was horrible.

Flana had never used the now defunct gateway between The Cities and Zethicia for the very reason that thousands of lives had been sacrificed for its creation. Such talismans were horrific. Only a few Hrýll had been willing to participate in its creation. There was always someone willing to profit from death, no matter what race. She was one of the few who thought that the rebels had done a good thing by destroying the gateway. She hoped it was never re-opened. Not unless it was built without the *true death* of many a soul.

Triste continued his briefing of the council. Crissa interrupted him after a time.

"Lord Priest, while we appreciate the update, you would not have approached us in person simple to convey information. What else do you want?"

"Sar Tanec, you are a wise woman."

They waited. He licked his lips and his eyes were downcast. He took a chair and sank down. Very impolite in the presence of five noble women. He should have asked permission, but no one said anything.

"The gods are in trouble. Pé has all but abandoned his worshippers. Rumor is that he stays at the Rivers of Life and Death all the time, doing who knows what. The other gods are hording their power and not answering prayer. You ..." He looked at the Katar and avoided Flana's gaze, "... know that if prayer is not answered then people will stop praying. It has already begun. Without the *ka* that is given..." His eyes flicked at Flana then returned to look downward. "...the gods will begin to lose power. Ague has as much as said that only strong prayer will be answered. Strong and sacrificial prayer."

Larra pounded her fist onto the table at the latter statement.

"Sacrificial prayer? That hasn't been done for thousands of years. The people won't stand for it. The gods are foolish. You would bring back a Death

God? Gods that demand death and aging from their worshipers. No. The Katar would take up a unified battle against the gods at such an affront. The gods and the Katar bleed the people enough as it is. Something I am guilty enough, as is," she said, twisting her ring.

Triste looked guilty and would not meet Flana's gaze. She was aware of all this. Did he think that only the Katar knew the order of things? She spoke up.

"Triste, you know more. There's something going on with the other Katar families isn't there? I have heard rumors, Triste, tell us what you know."

Triste seemed to overlook the lack of 'Lord' in front of his name. Manners were falling by the wayside quickly. Now he would not look at Larra or Piea, but looked squarely at Flana.

"Arlec has persuaded all the families to ally formally with the gods. To go after the rebels and the remaining Tarth. To kill them all and sacrifice their *ka* to the gods and to the Katar. Of the gods all but Pé, and of course Hallam, have agreed."

Crissa, white with anger interjected.

"Father would never agree to such a thing."

"Your father is dead, Sar Tanec." The honorific indicating his acknowledgment that she was head of the family now. "Garron, your husband is claiming right to the family and has sworn allegiance to Arlec. It is this that I really came to tell you. That and that I do not agree with the gods on this and will aid you however I can. You see that I did not bring my staff of office in with me. My god, Ague, cannot eavesdrop without it."

The four Katar sat frozen. Flana rose and went to Crissa and Mia and enveloped them in her arms. This shattered their composure. For a time all that was heard was the soft sobbing of the Tanec women.

Visibly shaken, Larra took control of the meeting.

"The women of Tanec would never follow Garron. Most of the women of the other families who are in Argn will not follow such a path."

She whispered with her sister Piea and then continued.

"There are three thousand Katar alive today. I suspect two thousand will follow Arlec. Another five hundred will watch for the time being. That leaves five hundred, mostly women Katar in Argn. We can keep the main group of Katar out of Argn, but we cannot depose Arlec."

Triste nodded.

"I reached the same conclusion. I have no idea how many of the priests feel the same as me, but I doubt many do. They are too concerned with their source of power. However, I'm sure that Zethicia will oppose this. This means that the gods will abandon Zethicia. My thought is to let the rebels know this and perhaps they can move into Zethicia and keep it free of both the Katar and the Tarth. It would be advantageous to Argn to have an ally. Argn will no doubt be abandoned by the gods also, except for minor interventions when sacrifices are made against your wishes."

138

Flana muttered under her breath, as they continued to make plans.

"It would seem the gods are no longer the gods of the people, but the gods of the Katar."

Chapter 25

See'arr enjoyed the time alone. As one of the few female Tarth left alive she was almost always accompanied by one of the male Tarth. She was too valuable. Too rare.

It was not that she was all that modest, but it was such a good excuse. Bathing in solitude, in the hot spring near the camp, was her time. Things were not going as well as she would like, but they were progressing. So much to coordinate. Bal'alam was too primitive to handle all of this. He was primal and full of action. It made him hard to control. The one time he had been right in his life, concerning the Tarth alliance with Alanar, made him think he was always right.

The hot spring was surrounded by tall trees, the humid steam condensing on the leaves and dripping down back into the pool. The pool was fed through cracks in the rock that formed it. The overflow trickled out to be absorbed by the nearby soil. See'arr stripped quickly. Her reddish skin glistened from the humidity. Tarth were not slim; the way many humans were. She stretched her almost seven-foot frame to work the kinks out of her back. Her coal black hair spilled down below her shoulder blades. Normally, she kept her hair tied in warrior fashion, but this was her time. Muscles bulged as she lowered herself into the hot water. Her breasts were large, but so firm they almost did not bounce. Not useless flopping masses of fatty flesh that humans carried with them.

That woman, Tyna, had been strong and firm for a human. Hopefully, the Yanín would recover her. She lived, when no other had. She might be the one. Plus, she had some of See'arr's blood and *ka* within her now. It was not as if she was willing to do that experiment many times.

See'arr let her arms float on the water and tilted her head back. One knot at a time her muscles relaxed. Her breathing slowed. She was almost asleep.

The explosion of water in front of her caught her totally unawares. She tried to leap to her feet and slipped under water. Sputtering with water in her lungs she heaved herself out of the pool and rolled toward her clothes and sword.

"See'arr, you look as beautiful as ever."

She froze. She knew that voice. Her heart skipped a beat and she whirled around and stared. A pillar of water stood over ten feet tall within the hot pool. Heaving himself out of the water was Be Na Tarth. Turning toward the pillar of water he spoke again.

"Jumping Water, my friend, let us meet again in one week, after you accomplish what we discussed."

Words came out of the water, somewhat garbled but understandable.

"Old friend, we shall meet again."

The pillar dropped into the water and the pool became calm.

See'arr stood trembling. Be Na Tarth. Carnel to her. Alive. Here. On Nakana.

He strode up to her and pulled her close. Taller than she by only a few inches, she still tilted her head up slightly. It was so good to not have to tilt her head down. She parted her lips slightly and he did not disappoint her. Standing naked she ripped at his clothes until they were on equal footing. Her fingers dug into his back. Enough to shatter a human's bones he merely pulled her down onto the ground in response. He pulled off the chain from around his neck that had a jade sphere attached to it—to protect it from their mutual need. Even in her lust fogged madness she touched it reverently. The power to bring back the Tarth lay there, if anywhere.

With the sphere safely to the side their love making was desperate, near the edge of violence. Her screams as she orgasmed were so loud that soon Tarth and Kami guards were on the scene. They both recognized Be Na Tarth and had the self-preservation sense to back out of the clearing until both were clothed again.

* * *

Bal'alam was not the only Tarth who wasn't overjoyed to see Be Na Tarth. Once they found out that most of the band of Tarth were still alive, their stance softened. They all grieved over the loss of Be Na Tarth's mother and sympathized that he had been the cause of her death by killing Alanar. Be Na Tarth realized that he had to win back the hearts of these Tarth. Shear authority had not prevented them from deserting before and the fact that they had been right was not going to make it easier. See'arr wrapped her arm around his waist and whispered into his ear.

"You must admit wrong Carnel, or they will never follow you. Do not push the fact that they deserted you."

He nodded, putting his arm around her. He watched Bal'alam turn a darker shade of red. Time for him later.

"My fellow Tarth, I ask you to consider my plea."

He waited while the Tarth gathered closer. The word 'plea' was not often used in the Tarth vocabulary. The encampment grew quiet.

"I brought us close to victory slightly more than a year ago."

Grunts of affirmation and a few weak cheers. The Tarth here had all fought in battles with Be Na Tarth and recalled their many victories.

"I do not kill lightly. The words of my mother and her 'husband' – the human, or near human Alanar – swayed me that enough blood had been spilled."

A few heckles, but most respected his mother too much to voice strong disapproval.

"Bal'alam perceived the error of this crucial decision as did all of you who followed him. See'arr, my promised one, also saw the error of my decision. I do not shirk from admitting mistakes. However, I do not give up easily. The traitor Alanar and his allies banished the Tarth again and yet here I stand." His voice grew louder. He stood taller.

"What do you bring to the glory of the Tarth other than yourself. A killer of Nar Tarth, your own mother. A fool who allies with ancient enemies. It would have been better if you had sent a youngling through instead of you. You are not worthy to wear the Sphere of Souls around your neck. We need a leader who can produce results," Bal'alam shouted.

Bal'alam was standing in front of Be Na Tarth, forced to look up to him due to his diminutive height of just under six feet. There was affirmation in the crowd. Be Na Tarth was impressive as an individual, but he had failed at a crucial time. Bal'alam pressed his advantage.

"I, with my chosen See'arr, have allied with the Yanín and with the goddess Hallam. What need do we have of a failed leader who stands alone."

Be Na Tarth restrained See'arr. Most of those standing here would know it was her that had done all the negotiating, not Bal'alam. It was time to make his move.

"Bal'alam, I of course praise all that you have done to date. You have kept this band of Tarth alive until it could be rejoined with my main forces. A valiant effort for a few hundred Tarth. The allies you speak of will be helpful, but to defeat the humans, the Katar, and their gods, we need more. We need the full force of the Tarth. We need our allies from the past."

His voice boomed with the last statement and the river nearby erupted with a thirty foot tall by one hundred foot wide wall of water. Before anyone could recover their wits the Tarth began stepping through. Hundreds. Thousands. It was clear that Be Na Tarth had returned the full force of the Tarth. Fifty thousand or more cheering Tarth, chanting his name.

See'arr looked at him, a huge grin on her face.

"How?"

"The Undine that you met is not called Jumping Water for nothing."

* * *

Bal'alam was smart enough to not try another rebellion. The Tarth were united again and there was no traitorous human to point to. No huge major flaw that he could rally anyone around. Fifty Tarth remained loyal to him. Fifty who knew that with Be Na Tarth in power, they were nothing, but with Bal'alam in power they too had power. Bal'alam bid them to wait. Wait for the right opportunity. Until then they needed to improve their situation. Their standing within the Tarth community teetered.

The Yanín had no concept of politics, but they were used to dealing with males. While See'arr had worked on the negotiations with the Yanín, it was Bal'alam that they kept in touch with. When the woman that was so valuable to the goddess and to See'arr was found, Bal'alam did not pass on all the information. It would be good if he personally brought back the female.

The fool Be Na Tarth had kept him in a position of command. He was introduced to the Undine who were aiding them. Jumping Water saw no reason not to grant the request for Bal'alam and five others to be transported deep into the mountains, via a small mountain brook. The workings of the Tarth were too complex for him to care what particular mission they were on. Be Na Tarth had introduced him as a lieutenant to be trusted, that was all that mattered.

* * *

The villagers ran from him in terror. A woman dropped her baby as she ran and did not stop to retrieve it. He bent down to touch it and it died, withered and dry. Its mouth open to cry. Off in the distance a man fired a crossbow. The bolt hit him in the chest. He pulled it out, the wound closing behind the shaft. The man was reloading. He ran, impossibly fast. He grasped the man, who died the crossbow dropping out of lifeless fingers. Old before his time. A sack of bones. The energy felt good. He laughed. A voice behind him. Turning, his hand outstretched to grab, he stopped. The young woman looked familiar. Tall. Red hair. She touched him. Foolish. She did not die. Strange. They should always die. He was death.

Alan lay curled in Tyna's arms, shaking. She stroked his head and looked at his wide open unseeing golden eyes. What terrible nightmare was he having? The cries had awakened her from her own troubled sleep. They had both wanted to chase after the owl, but it was foolish. They needed sleep and daylight. Sleep had turned out to be wishful thinking.

She decided to try waking him again and grabbed his arms and shook. He awoke this time.

Alan stared up at Tyna. It took him a second to recognize her. He breathed in the fir filled air. No stench of death. Wet and fecund. Nakana. Of course Nakana, where else would he be? Why did Nakana not feel like home? He sat up. Tyna had a worried look on her face. She must be thinking of Rosea. Yes, their baby. Why did he have to think about that for a moment? He reached out and touched her hair, very gently. She spoke.

"Alan, is everything alright? You were having a terrible dream."

Alan. That sounded right. Almost right. He gently kissed Tyna. Yes, this was right. This was right.

"Everything is fine. A bit of a nightmare. I can't even remember what it was about."

Death.

She held him close for a moment.

"It's almost dawn, we might as well stay awake." She whispered. She looked up at the trees. Which branch had that owl been waiting on?

He nodded. Yes, falling asleep again was not an option. Rosea. Their daughter. They had to rescue their daughter. He was feeling more like himself now. Why did it seem impossible that he have a daughter? The dream part of his brain said that a daughter was impossible. Any child was impossible. He rubbed his face with an open hand.

"Are my eyes the same?"

Tyna stared at him long and hard. She pulled down his head and kissed each eyelid.

"They are still golden. On you it looks good."

Packing took almost no time. The advantage to having few possessions, other than what they had taken from those kidnappers only weeks ago.

"Tyna, have you ever seen me seriously injured?"

"Of course. The blow from the horse was serious."

"That was not me. I mean since then."

"There was those thieving kidnappers. You were injured then."

"Was I? Where?"

"Your … arm …" She grabbed his arm and pushed up the sleeve. She looked up at him with widened eyes.

"It was there yesterday. The still healing scar. I remember, when we made love, touching it and thinking how fast you healed, but this is beyond that. No scar."

She rubbed his arm again, looking closely.

He nodded. At least he had not dreamed that.

He pulled out his knife. Or rather the knife he had picked up from the kidnappers that lay dead on some other plane. Tyna watched and too late tried to stop him as he pulled the blade along the back of his left forearm. They both watched fascinated as only a few drops of blood escaped the rapidly closing wound. In a few minutes there was no wound. No scar. Rubbing off the blood, there was no trace.

"What does it mean Alan?"

"I am not sure."

Death. He should leave her now, or she would die. Everyone dies.

He grabbed her and pulled her close.

"Tyna, I have a feeling that I'm dangerous—to you. You need to promise me that if I change too much, you will leave me. You must be careful. I feel I am just awakening. I have the sensation that there are many memories that lie within me. Knowledge that I am old, not young as this body indicates."

She wrapped her arms around him and kept the embrace tight.

"Alan, I don't know truly who, or what you are. You're not my brother. You're obviously someone that came into my brother's body and changed it. You are the man I love. The man whose child I bore. The man who saved my life. The man who I cannot bear to live without. You will never change enough to harm me. Of that I am certain."

She let him go and mounted the mare. From atop the mare she grinned at him.

"We have a baby to rescue, old man."

He mounted in one fluid motion.

"We do. I still believe the Tarth are our best bet. They did something to you and I believe they are in league with Hallam. Only she could control animals in such a manner."

"Do you know how we will enter the camp and find Rosea?"

"Not yet. But this time I will not run away. The Tarth will do the running."

Alan's stallion's nose flared and it leapt forward. Tyna shivered as she looked at Alan's face. His own nostrils were flared, his brows deeply furrowed and his lips pulled back. His canines were slightly longer than the rest of his teeth and protruded a bit more.

* * *

Larrina fought the knot in her stomach. She had loved many men in her lifetime. Tsom had no idea and she saw no need to tell him. Oonie, the old Hrýll understood. Hrýll remembered the Kinel. Not all of her loves had been the same, but to truly heal a man, she had to love him. To make love to a man she had to love him in some way.

It was not as if she had never loved two people enough to heal them both. Not group sex, but alternating one month to the other. Or one week to the other. However, it had been rare. The older she got the rarer it had been. Now she found it unbearable to make love to Tsom with the memories of Alanar re-awakened. Tsom was not completely healed, but much better. He was as strong as a forty year old Kinel, now. Nowhere near his twenty years of chronological age, but better than a year ago. She wished she could help him more, but she could not. She was in need now. She needed Alanar.

Did he need her? As a woman, not as an old friend? Did he ever know how she felt? After the loss of his wife, she had been there. She had healed him then. But they had both moved on. She'd thought of it as her normal love that she gave any man that she healed. They had never become lovers again, but she had sensed a spark of jealousy in Alanar when she'd flirted with Lanos. Dear Lanos, his heart had been in the right place, but he could never understand Alanar. Very few could. Maybe no one.

From what the innkeeper told them, Alanar was in a new body. This confused her. He changed when the rage took over him, but it was always his body that he changed. Had he somehow inhabited this new body, or did he simply change to look like this young man that the innkeeper described. It was something unexpected. It created more variables.

She knew little of the banishment that had taken place. As a Kinel she knew something of the existence of other planes. Her conversations with Oonie had provided a little more knowledge, but not enough. Everyone had agreed that as Tsom had banished the Tarth and Alanar that Be Na Tarth had been in a rage. Lanos had died and Alanar would have been next. If Hell had been bad then it was agreed that four notches higher on the Sphere of Banishment would be worse. There was no higher setting.

She had tried to use the Sphere. Tsom had retrieved it before the Katar could get it. She had tried, knowing that it was most likely death. It refused to function. Oonie had been fascinated by it. He said it was not of Hrýll or Srýll origin, which seemed impossible. Who else made talismans? She told no one where she had hidden it. She had not destroyed it out of some hope that it could be made to work, but the demands of the revolution had taken her time and in her heart she had known Alanar was dead.

Now Alanar was back, in one form or another, and she was a thousand marks away. He was back and changed more than she had ever seen. He always suffered amnesia when he changed. Did he remember her? Part of her was sure he would. After all, she had healed him of his pain back then. He should always remember that. She prayed he did, which was funny as the Kinel didn't pray to anything.

She urged her horse on. Tsom struggled to keep up, looking tired and irritable.

"He married that old Tarth woman you know. Lanos told me before the end. He betrayed us."

"So you have said before Tsom. I explained to you that the plan made sense to me. Marriage of convenience is not new."

"Perhaps the presence of the woman I felt was his wife."

"Perhaps, but all indications point to his sister."

"His sister. See that is what is strange. It feels like Alanar, I admit, but not all of him. If the man the innkeeper described is this person, then it just doesn't make sense. Does Alanar now steal other people's bodies? Kill them and inhabit their body? If so, he has become more alien than before. More of a monster."

"You don't know him. We all can become monsters given enough reason.

146

Enough pushing. He would not intentionally do what you suggest. I admit I don't understand it all. I do know that he needs us."

"Us?"

Larrina was silent. Needs me? Or do I need him?

"No, the revolution needs him. If he has not come to us, then he has lost most of his memories. Both of us may be able to restore his memories. We all need each other."

Tsom snorted and looked angry. Then softened and turned to her.

"I can pull us there if you want."

He could. He was the only one she knew—living—that could do that trick. Pushing his 'hands' through the folds of space and pulling himself, or objects through. The last time he had done that, it had cost him dearly. No doubt he was better at it now. He had probably even practiced it despite her warning him not to, but it was too much to ask. She would not be able to heal him this time. No, it was not fair to him. She shook her head.

"It is sweet of you to offer Tsom. I know you have very mixed feelings about Alanar and you would do that only for me. I cannot ask it."

* * *

The movement through the water was disconcerting. Jumping Water enveloped them in a circular wall of water. The cylinder then shrank, enveloping them. They held their breath. The world became dark. Cold. The water was ice cold. How much time had passed? They were not gasping for air, but it seemed an eternity. Bal'alam kept his eyes open, but could not see anything. It was darker than the deepest cave. The lack of air was not what started the panic, it was the cold.

The spilling forth onto the stream bank was without warning. All the Tarth stumbled.

"Undine, you are sure this is the location I told you?"

"To the best of my understanding of your description. I do understand the concept of direction and distance as you perceive it. I have put you as close to the location you specified as possible."

With that the Undine sank into the water.

After some brief scouting Bal'alam found the small abandoned encampment, just as the message from Hallam had described. Only one day old. Two horses. This would not be a problem. Tarth on foot could easily catch up with horses. Tarth could run for days without stopping. Soon the woman would be his. He would be a hero again. The male human would be killed. If time permitted he would torture him. Be Na Tarth's prohibition on torture was foolish. These humans had to see that the Tarth were to be feared. Killing the male slowly in front of the woman would help tame her.

Bal'alam signaled his companions. The six of them set off. Bal'alam, already the shortest of the group, looked almost small as he stayed stooped to follow the horses traces. The ground shook lightly as the six Tarth ran, their combined weight more than several horses. All six had their teeth bared in smiles that would scare even another Tarth. Bal'alam ran his tongue over his upper lip and teeth.

Chapter 26

Time only made the anger worse. Alan felt the rage growing with each stride of the stallion beneath him. He did not see Tyna falling slowly behind as the mare struggled to maintain the pace. He did not consider that galloping was a waste of energy for such a long trek. The stallion felt his fury and responded. They were one. Alan had the mane wrapped in his left hand and his right hand was waving in the air where the stallion could see it and respond.

He was almost out of sight when he heard Tyna scream.

The stallion fell to one knee as they turned in mid gallop. Somehow Alan stayed on. He saw Tyna's horse rearing as six Tarth surrounded her and the horse. As he charged back the mare was already down, dying or dead. Tyna had her sword out, slashing wildly to keep the six at bay. No style, just desperation.

For a moment he had the image of a field of Tarth. Thousands of them. All dead with himself on a horse charging one remaining Tarth. The image disappeared in the next stride.

Alan did not attempt to slow the horse down. He felt a pang of sadness as it crashed into one of the Tarth, the largest, as he landed on his feet. He did not stop to see if either survived. Something in the back of his mind reminded him that the Tarth had exceptionally tough skin. Instead of slashing he thrust with the full force of his body at one of them.

The wound was not fatal, but slowed the Tarth down. Tyna was in the hold of one of the Tarth, but it was obviously not trying to kill her. Alan shifted his attack from the one holding Tyna to the smallest, less red, Tarth. This one was the leader, despite its size. The rage on the Tarth's face matched what Alan felt in his heart. The Tarth were the cause of all their problems. The Tarth had altered Tyna. Now they were back. No need to find the Tarth, the Tarth had found them. And now they would pay.

The more the rage flowed through him the slower the Tarth seemed to move.

He saw the two circling him and had time to carefully thrust his sword into the left eye of the one on his right and side stepped the blow of the one on his left. The short one had his mouth open as if frozen in mid yell.

As the Tarth on the end of his sword died Alan felt a surge of energy. Power. Strength. It was visible, as a small stream flowing to the ground and he instinctively reached out and the energy flowed to him instead of the ground. Part of him knew it was the very life force of the Tarth. Its *ka*. This Tarth would never make it to the Sea of Souls. He should feel repulsed at the idea of what he was doing, but instead he drank the energy hungrily.

The Tarth were still moving slowly. He slashed at the one on his left, who had stumbled after missing Alan a moment before. Part of him knew that slashing was the wrong thing to do with a Tarth's thick skin, but another part of him felt confident now. The blade bit deeply and he drank another stream of energy. He felt invincible. Drunk on the power, he danced toward the Tarth holding Tyna, who was now limp in the Tarth's grip. He ignored the short leader. He would get to him later.

Again the blade bit deeply into the surprised Tarth. He drank of his *ka* also, but felt no more boost to his energy. It was like eating on full stomach. Alan noted that both the horse and the Tarth that he had crashed into were dead. Two Tarth remained, the short leader and one other.

The larger of the two died quickly. Alan did not drink of his *ka*. *Let him die an honest death*, he thought. He concentrated on the short one, who was now running to Tyna, sword arcing toward her. This one should be left alive for questioning. He interposed his body and knocked the sword of the Tarth aside. With his fist he struck multiple times at the pink skinned Tarth's head. Each blow he felt as if he were dipping his hand into a pool of energy and scooping some out. The Tarth collapsed.

The adrenalin fading, everything seemed to move fast again. The Tarth collapsed at a normal rate. Alan rushed to Tyna. He lifted her head and felt her pulse on her neck. Strong. He briefly hugged her head to his side and then let her back down on the ground.

He slapped the face of the unconscious Tarth, multiple times. Finally the Tarth opened his eyes.

"Where is the child?" Alan said between additional slaps.

Bal'alam struggled to get up. Alan pushed him back down and standing put the point of his sword against the Tarth's neck.

The Tarth's face was twisted in rage and disbelief.

"I knew that Be Na Tarth was a liar. You are still alive Talanas. Kill me now and end it. I will not speak to you anymore."

Talanas. The name sounded familiar. It was an evil name. Did he remind the Tarth of someone? No matter.

"The child. Our child. Where is she?"

The Tarth snarled and before he could stop it grabbed the sword blade and thrust it into his own neck.

"At least I die a pure death, Talanas. You will not steal my *ka.* I will return someday from the Sea of Souls." With that the Tarth spit at Alan, a mix of blood and saliva, and died.

The clouds continued to gather. Rain was unusual this time of year, but up in the mountains it was not unheard off. They had searched the Tarth for supplies, clues, and anything that would be useful, but found nothing. Neither Tyna, nor Alan, felt it was worthwhile covering the bodies. Nature would clean up the mess.

Alan patted the stallion's corpse silently. Tyna, looked at Alan and shivered despite this act of kindness. His face was leaner, his cheekbones prominent, his eyes were slightly sunken. His yellow eyes, gold on gold with no whites, were narrowed. The muscles on his jaw and neck stood out.

Alan had thrown his sword away. It was badly damaged from the battle, the blade starting to separate from the hilt. Tyna marveled at the amount of force that must have been used to cause that. One of the Tarth blades was smaller than the rest, but still quite heavy. Alan took this and grimaced at its balance. He had the strength, but not the mass that this blade was forged for.

It began to rain. Slow, cold drizzle. No fast rainstorm, but the type of rain that promised to last a long time. They marched on as much to keep warm as to get to the Tarth encampment. Low rumbling of distant thunder sounded like groans and moans of warning. The rocky path that they were following became slick and dangerous.

"In the battle with the Tarth, you did not destroy everything around you. There was no circle of death as before."

"Yes, but I remember this battle, while I have no memory of the others."

"I wonder what was different about this one?"

Alan shrugged. There would be more battles.

The rain continued for several days. At night they huddled close to each other for warmth and comfort. It was too cold and miserable to make love. The morning of the fourth day Tyna was sneezing and shivering. She stood and staggered. Alan caught her before she fell. He took off his loose cape that they had fashioned from their scavenging and added it to Tyna's. Two wet layers did not seem to help. By the end of the day Tyna could not walk anymore.

Alan sat next to her and wrapped his arms around her. He rocked her back and forth and wished that he could help her somehow. Give her some of his warmth. He kept rocking her and staring off into space wondering if they would make it to the Tarth. He had no doubt before. Fending off thieves and

Tarth was something that his fury could latch on to, but how does one lash out at pneumonia? From the sound of Tyna's breathing that was what she had.

As his hands stroked her head he felt the small streams of energy. Similar to the battle with the Tarth, he saw the flow from his hands to her head as he stroked her. He focused on this flow, willing her to get better, to gain strength from him.

The clouds finally parted and he could see three of the five moons had risen. Rocking Tyna and stroking her hair he fell asleep.

* * *

Tyna awoke feeling strong. She sat up and looked down at Alan lying beside her. He looked tired. He was sound asleep. She shook him gently. Then more strongly. He slept on. She began to worry and shook him with vigor and finally slapped his face. No reaction. Suppressing her panic she got up and assessed their location.

They were in a widening of the trail that followed the mountain stream. A small valley that had been created by eons of rain and flooding of this smallish stream. The trees were ancient, untouched by man or fire. Tyna dragged the limp Alan to the shelter of a fallen giant, where the roots made a cave of sorts. She then got a fire started by fashioning a pointed stick and spinning it within the hole of a dry piece of wood filled with tiny slivers of wood.

Once the fire was going she went about finding food. She had a feeling that Alan was going to be out for a while. Somehow, her own feeling of strength and energy was related to his coma like sleep.

Alan slept for four days.

Chapter 27

Now that she had the child, what was she going to do with it?

Hallam held the quiet baby in her arms. No maternal instinct, just intellectual curiosity.

Her sanctuary was well hidden. None of the other gods knew of this location, away from the Valley of the Gods, where all the others were gathered. The fools had stormed her known domicile as if she would have been stupid enough to stay there after opening defying all of them during the Tarth war. Her only fear was Met. His abilities to control the weather may include some ability to see from within the clouds. He had never let on that he could do this, but she feared that he kept some of his powers secret. Her main hope was that Nakana was simply too huge for him to find her. Her sanctuary would look like any peaceful pastoral setting from above. No buildings were visible. The trees had grown through her guidance into a complex canopy. A multi-chambered canopy where rain did not penetrate.

The small swarms of fireflies provided a strange flickering light. The hot springs kept the chambers warm and Hallam enjoyed bathing in them each day to wash away her stress. She set the baby down, disrobed, and slid into the warm pool. She idly watched the baby where she had set it down. It must be about two or three weeks old. Yet, by her estimate it looked over a year. What does one do with such an infant? She knew about animals raising their young, but most of those were mobile almost at birth. As she recalled, humans were slow to gain mobility and other basic functions. It had been eons since she had been around human babies.

Hallam concentrated carefully as she bathed. One target. A focused call. Shortly a large female dui mar appeared. The large death cat was obviously laden with milk. Her tits hung low and her nipples were protruding. In her mouth was a single cub, perhaps a few days old. It squirmed and mewed for attention. Hallam stared into the mother cat's eyes and spoke to the cat's mind.

Of all the animals she controlled, only the cats were intelligent enough for true interactive communication. She still found it disconcerting how intelligent they were. Their thought processes were different from a human, or any other sentient race. The words were not really words, but concepts. However, she knew that most of the cats actually could understand spoken language. They simply had no ability to repeat the words, unless manipulated directly.

I want you to care for this human baby.

The cat dropped her cub gently and sniffed at the now squirming baby.

It is not human.

It is human for all intents and purposes.

Do you compel me to do so? The cat seemed to growl lightly.

I ask it of you.

The big cat dropped its head again and stared into the baby's eyes.

I see death. She will be dangerous.

Hallam smiled. *Yes, I know. But not to the Dui Mar. She will not harm you.*

The cat licked the baby, its tongue larger than the child's entire body. The baby squirmed and waved its arms as if trying to catch the tongue, but it did not cry. The cat lay next to the baby and with one of its giant paws, any one of its claws longer than the baby's legs, it pushed her against a nipple. The baby greedily drank, with its eyes open. The cub pushed its way next to her and drank from its own nipple. The large cat began to purr, the rumbling noise shaking both cub and baby. Hallam lay back in her pool and relaxed more.

You can hear me little one?

Yes.

She Who Compels does not know this, does she?

No.

This is good. Do not tell her.

You will care for me?

I will. So will your brother, Crooked Tail.

The small cub's bent tail flicked at the mention of his name.

I miss my mom.

I am your mother now.

What of my father?

You have no father now. You must adapt. Survive. The Dui Mar are your family now.

I am content. You are warm and have good food.

The big cat purred more loudly.

Chapter 28

Arlec cursed the fool Garron. He'd acted too quickly. Jern was not to be killed so soon. Now they had to deal with Argn again. He'd hoped to get Garron properly placed in Argn as the *recognized* next in line for the Tanec clan. Instead the whole damn city was united against the rest of the Katar; led by a group of women. That his sisters were involved just made it worse. He should have dealt with them as he had dealt with his father. His compassion was getting in the way of progress.

Arlec sat in the chair of his father's study, no his study, staring at the fireplace that burned eternal. It had been less than two years ago that he had removed his father's talisman and taken the box from the rear of the fireplace. His arrogant father, always giving him menial tasks and consulting his sisters in matters of state. If his father had only been more trusting with his power, maybe things would have turned out differently. It was all probably for the best. None of his sisters would ever rule the Karn clan now.

The library had been returned to an orderly state, now that the family diaries had been found and set aside. Arlec thought about gutting the entire library to locate any other hidden treasures, but thinking of the fireplace, decided that any such treasure might be protected against brute force intrusion. There would be time later.

A timid knock on the study door broke Arlec's revere.

"Enter."

A servant, he forgot his name, cautiously opened the door. He peered at Arlec and after a moment's hesitation entered.

"Well?" he growled.

"Sir, the Lord priests are here."

"Excellent. Show them into the sitting room. I will be down shortly. Offer them some Hrýll brandy."

At least this part of the plan was progressing nicely. The war with the Tarth and the war between Hallam and the other gods had proven an excellent opportunity. Rather than continue to contest power with the priesthoods, the Katar would assimilate their power by becoming the enforcement arm of the gods. Sacrificial worship. In exchange the gods and in particular the priests would provide services. With all the *ka* draining going on no one would notice Arlec's occasional sacrifice to the Undine. When the time was right, the priests would fall and with them the gods. Then there would be only Katar and Arlec at the head of the Katar.

For now he would have to deal with the priests. He hated their self-important titles of Lord Priests. They were not lord over the Katar. Let them keep their titles for now.

Arlec gathered his notes for the meeting. As he got up from his desk he cocked his head and listened. Beyond the sound of the fire he could hear the faint babbling of the small stream; a stream that he had diverted, so that it fed a fountain inside the manor. It was a mirror of the same fountain he'd built in the new manor on the island between the east and west shores of Arbeneth. The peaceful sounding stream, with his own Undine inhabiting it, reassured him and he strode out of the study.

* * *

Kaylee drank her tea and tried to stay calm. What she had seen both enraged her and turned her stomach. Her husband, Barin, was working on another of his contraptions. He set whatever it was down and listened to her attentively. Both of them were members of the revolution and chafed at this new wave of inactivity. Larrina had told them that they were more valuable here in Arbeneth as spies then as overt fighters. Kaylee suspected that it was their age that concerned Larrina. Larrina could be her great grandmother, but she was Kinel, so that didn't count. Still, Kaylee resented that anyone felt she was slowing down at sixty.

"Do you know that it is now mandatory for all of Arbeneth to worship Ague?" She didn't wait for an answer.

"Today I saw a shopkeeper dragged out by a mob, proclaiming that she was plotting against the Katar. They beat her with small 'prayer' sticks of Ague. I watched, helpless to interfere. Before my eyes she withered and died. The 'gods' are taking their *ka* now, not waiting for people to pray and sacrifice it. We cannot stand by and let this continue."

Barin's weathered face hardened as she spoke. His lips turned white and thin. Then his shoulders sagged and his head bowed.

"What can we do Kay? All of the resistance has fled to Argn. The other Cities are in a death grip of the Katar and the gods and their priests. What can we do? Nothing. We are two old revolutionaries with no one to back us up anymore. We should go to Argn with the others."

"Are you calling me old?" Kaylee attempted a smile. Unfortunately, the smile made her look old. It was the smile of a woman who had seen too much over too many years. Her handsome face showed fatigue, her graying black hair was more gray than black now. The crow's feet were heavy, as if the crow had been dirty and stepped around her eyes and the corners of her mouth. Despite these signs of age, she was slim, wiry and her breasts still stood up on their own without too much help. Barin smiled back at her.

"Ripe, but never old."

She sighed, reached over and held his hand.

"No, we must stay if Larrina thinks it's for the best. We'll wait until we hear from her. With so many having fled to Argn, we few spies need to stay."

"It'll be dangerous. Neighbor is turning on neighbor. They do it out of self-preservation, but we can trust no one." Barin said, squeezing her hand.

"Life is dangerous."

* * *

"Pé has deserted us."

Inlas, Goddess of Illusions, did not bother with making herself seem more beautiful and desirable. Without her powers manifested she was still attractive, a tall well build pale woman with dirty brown hair and green eyes. Ague had almost forgotten what she looked like without her 'makeup' as she called it. She must be truly upset if she didn't instinctively wear her illusionary guise.

Ague and Met, his oft companion, were the only other gods currently at the Castle of Hamesa, in the Valley of Dreams, north of The Cities. The Castle was showing signs of neglect as this neutral ground was impossible for any of the gods to shape as their own, so rarely used. The others were all cowering at their personal domains, hording their power and guarding against a potential attack from Hallam, the bitch animal lover. Well, Nu Arr may not be cowering, but he didn't bother showing up at the conclaves any more. He seemed to blame them all for letting that thief—Tsom—survive. Nu Arr seemed to think that all the events of the past year were brought into motion by the one young thief, simply by existing. Nu Arr was always a bit off. How can one be a god of luck and not think that strange things were possible?

Ague tried to calm Inlas down.

"What if he has? He never participated much in our dealings. He didn't care if he had worshippers or not. We need worshippers. We need their *ka*."

"Pé claims we are going too far with our sacrificial worshipping. He feels that the River of Life and the River of Death are being permanently affected. Too much *true death* is immoral he says. What if he is right? Have we become evil?"

"We are gods. There is no evil for us."

Yet, Ague had his doubts. But, what could they do? Immortality is a hard habit to give up. So was godhood. The damned humans had stopped worshipping voluntarily and had stopped giving up their *ka* through prayer. The revolutionaries had set that in motion and Argn made it worse. A few human lives couldn't make that big a difference in the grand scheme of things. After all, their population had been exploding over the past centuries, so what difference would perhaps a few million make over time.

Inlas was not assuaged.

"No evil? What about how we became gods?"

"That was a long time ago."

"Time does not heal all sins."

Met listened to the two of them, his brow looking stormy. Ague could swear he heard thunder in the distance.

"Enough. We are what we are. Pé is no longer with us. Hallam is trying to destroy us. Nu Arr is brooding and who knows what help he will be with his randomness. Be Na Tarth and the remaining Tarth have somehow found a way back to Nakana—again. We are allying ourselves with the Katar, our old enemies. Yet, here the three of us argue morality. We are fighting for survival. Fuck morality."

Inlas pouted, but kept silent. Ague nodded in agreement.

Met continued. The thunder in the background grew louder.

"My priests tell me that the Ne Na cult is growing stronger. More humans believe that they need not worship any god. The cult has changed its tactics and claims there is an 'Unknown God' that does not require worship and believing in him is better than believing in us. Our prayer *ka* is all dried up. To survive, we need to do this. We can deal with the Katar later."

"What does Juas think?" Inlas spoke softly.

"Why? Do you think that because she is 'Justice' that she knows what is moral? She is also known as Vengeance. She has ordered her priests to assist in vengeance killings if the worshipper pays and then she gets the *ka* of the deceased. She also has her priest court system working with the Katar. The number of drainings and true deaths meted out by the courts has quadrupled in a matter of weeks. That is what she thinks."

Inlas's color drained and for a moment Ague actually thought she might faint. But, she did not give up.

"De Nas?"

"Please. A war god could not be happier with the current state of affairs."

"Chne?"

This gave Met pause. What was the fire god up to? He had not been in contact with Chne since before the decision to ally with the Katar. Chne hated the Katar and had not even shown up to the conclave. He was not squeamish, nor did he hesitate in killing his worshipers. But, to some extent they expected it. He was sort of like Luck. His worshipers expected good and bad without blaming the god.

"I admit that I don't know what Chne thinks of this, other than he hates the Katar so much that it blinds him. I would not call that a moral decision, simply a personal one."

Met decided to move on. This topic was a dead subject.

"Inlas, what of the revolution and in particular the Hrýll? Your alter ego as the wife of that Hrýll—Oonie—has provided us with useful information in the past. What news?"

Inlas looked even more unhappy. Keeping her eyes downcast she spoke of her last time with her 'husband.'

Tiar—Inlas thought of herself as Tiar when she was in disguise with Oonie—smelled the mixed spices and knew that Oonie was behind her. She tried to replicate the odor of Hrýll as part of her illusion, but worried that she did not get it right. No one ever said anything, but she worried. Her control over any race other than human was weaker, so she kept her illusions to a minimum. The incredibly light hair that covered her body, almost a fuzz versus a fur, was hard enough an illusion to maintain. All the smells and even colors outside of the human eye spectrum were almost more than even she was capable of, even after all these years of practice. If she had not had the experience of mind linking with that female Hrýll, so many years ago, she would never have been able to pull this off. She put on a smile and turned to face her 'husband.'

"You are returned from the rebel camp."

Oonie nodded. He strode toward her and the stove. She anticipated him and put water for tea on and turned back to him and his silence.

"You are concerned about something."

"You know me well my mate."

"After fifty years one begins to know another."

"It has been said that one never truly knows another." Oonie stirred several herbs together for his tea.

Tiar averted her gaze, not looking at Oonie directly.

"Perhaps, but one can know ones partner well enough to say she knows him." Tiar now looked directly at Oonie, staring into his eyes.

"Certainly enough to love her." He smiled and kissed her lightly on the lips.

Tiar relaxed a bit and poured the now hot water into Oonie's cup.

"Civilization has not collapsed as quickly as all thought it would with the withdrawal of Hyrll talismans. Are we to continue our fight against the Katar, mankind, and their gods?" She rested a hand on the back of Oonie's neck and massaged it while he sipped his tea.

"The gods and the Katar have allied. Sacrificial worship. Too much *ka* is being destroyed. Too many are dying the true death. I fear the long term consequences," he said.

Tiar tried to hide her trembling. She had similar fears and doubts. She kept massaging Oonie's neck.

"At least the Tarth will be dealt with. I never liked the alliance we had made with them in the beginning. I never trusted Alanar," she resisted using his old name, Talanas.

Oonie sipped his tea, inhaling the thick vapor drifting out of the cup. Tiar sniffed herself and felt light headed. What combination of herbs had Oonie concocted this time? She had tried them herself, but never was able to replicate his brews.

"Change is still in the air," Oonie paused, his eyes disappearing into his head. Tiar had once thought that this was some sort of convulsion, but no longer. He continued after a long moment, as Tiar continued her massage.

"The remaining races are doomed if the gods and Katar win," he finally finished.

"Even the Hrýll? Don't you think they will want our skills and talismans once it is over?"

"Mankind will be the victor, but enslaved by the Katar and gods. A dark age will take over. Only when mankind gains the skill of manipulating *ka* directly, or manufacturing their own talismans, will they emerge from the dark age."

Tiar wiped a tear from her eye before Oonie could see it.

"Is this inevitable?"

"Nothing is inevitable. This is only what I see if the gods and Katar succeed."

"So what do we do?"

"We stay allied with the rebels. Argn is once again in the hands of forces opposed to the Katar and the gods. Larrina is negotiating with Zethicia."

Tiar momentarily gripped Oonie's neck too hard. He flinched and turned toward her.

"You are jealous for no reason. She is Kinel. Kinel and Hrýll cannot mate."

"Cannot reproduce."

"Her heart is with another and mine is with you."

"Tsom, that thief that all thought was a catalyst."

"Perhaps"

She cursed within her head. Sometimes she wished the gods had a better repertoire of curses. Most humans used some god or banishment in their curses, but the gods had no such myth to draw on. The Hrýll curses were all around *ka* and true death, which were as big a curse to a god, but seemed so unlikely that they never used such curses. Despite all her years with the Hrýll, she never really picked up their cursing. Instead she simply screamed inside her head. Oonie was so frustrating sometimes. No question was answered directly.

She pulled him toward the bedroom and changed the subject.

"You are in love with a Hrýll." Nu Arr said from the side.

The gods turned toward him. No one had heard him enter the chamber. He looked somewhat disdainfully at Inlas, but all noticed the flash of jealousy.

160

Inlas looked at them. Did they believe that? Was it true? No, it could not be. She enjoyed Oonie, but he was a mortal. All of the gods took lovers amongst the mortals, occasionally they had even kept them alive longer than their normal lifespan, but the mortals always died. Occasionally, before the love died. But the gods were more like humans than any race. This is why they could capture human energy. *ka.* Was it obscene to have a Hrýll as a lover? She couldn't even prolong his lifespan the way she could a human.

"What if Oonie is right and we are agents of destruction of all the races?" she asked of all of them. Nu Arr was the one who answered.

"So? We have no need of them. The Hrýll were convenient for their talismans, but those talismans were for our priests, not personal use."

"Do we have the right to destroy entire races?"

"We are gods, we have whatever rights we determine."

"What of the worries Pé has? What if we permanently disrupt the balances between the rivers of Life and Death and the Sea of Souls? We don't really know how they work. We are not gods in that sense, are we?"

They looked uncomfortable. Nu Arr continued to push back.

"Granted we don't know the workings of the multiverse. We do know that we have the power here, on Nakana. We need to protect that power. You argue for the right of the Hrýll to self-preservation—we have that same right. If the Hrýll and other races die, that is simply the natural process of survival."

"Do we need to survive as gods?"

"We don't reproduce. You know that. How many of us have died in ten thousand years? Almost all. We once numbered almost one hundred. No reincarnation has occurred. Pé looked for their *ka* in the River of Death and found nothing. The price we pay as gods is never to be reincarnated. If we do not get *ka* from worshippers we will fade. We will die our own true death."

Inlas shuddered. That was what they all feared. Oblivion. Surely they had a right to fight off that? Yet the extinction of a race seemed to mean that all of their 'souls' were lost forever too. Reincarnation was always within the same race. Always. She cried silently, hiding the tears with an illusion that she draped around herself quickly.

Chapter 29

He opened his eyes and met Tyna's gaze. She is beautiful, he thought. And exhausted, was his second thought. He sat up, immediately feeling light headed.

"Careful, you're weak." Tyna brushed his cheek with her hand.

The sun was out and warm. He must have been out for some time.

"How long?"

"Four days."

Four days? Four days that they could have been pursuing Rosea. Anticipating him, Tyna forced him to stay sitting. He sniffed the air and again anticipating him she handed him a piece of cold rabbit, slightly burned on the outside. He missed the salt, but only slightly as he felt he needed the energy, fast. She handed him the water bag and helped him drink.

The cheerful sounds of birds were annoying. He thought about how tasty one of them would be right now. Despite his ravenous hunger and feeling weak, he also thought of how enjoyable it would be to make love to Tyna right now. He grinned a little, thinking that he must be generally well enough to travel if he was thinking thoughts like those. Again Tyna seemed to read his mind. Pushing him down, she undressed him and alleviated that hunger too.

Alan missed having a horse underneath, not just because he was weak, but it felt natural. By the fifth day of walking, his energy returned to normal. He kept an eye on Tyna, but she remained healthy, strong, and focused on getting to Rosea, which for now was getting to the Tarth encampment.

Despite all the time they had to think, they could not come up with a plan on how to find and rescue Rosea, beyond their initial thoughts of finding the Tarth woman and getting the information from her. The thought of a Tarth female conjured up images of an old, once beautiful, still handsome Nar Tarth. Somehow he knew that 'Nar' was the proper honorific for a female Tarth. He felt sadness at those images. Who was she?

The beauty of the mountains was lost on both Tyna and Alan. The tall trees were spaced after centuries of uninterrupted growth, creating a park-like setting underneath them. They were still at a high enough elevation that the warmth and constant sun was tempered and the shadows cast by the surrounding peaks. To the east they could now see the Muglanth plains stretching out and disappearing at the horizon. To the northeast the plains merged with the forest. This was their destination. There was no beauty in the view, only wearying marks of travel still to come.

"Should we go to Tarin first? We need better clothes and equipment. It's probably only a few days detour from where the Tarth encampment is." Tyna was rubbing a sore foot where the ill-fitting boots they had taken off the dead were chafing.

Alan considered. He was surprised Tyna was willing to detour at all. He had always thought that a woman's love of a child was so strong that it drove her to haste. Yet, he also knew that Tyna was strong and level headed. Success was what they were after, not blind lashing out.

"It might be worthwhile. Will we be able to get credit in town for purchases?" He could not remember, within the memories of his other self, whether their family had a good credit line.

Tyna looked at him strangely and then understanding came to her.

"You are losing your old memories. We have enough sintar at the bank for our needs. The family is not rich, but it will be enough."

"Yes, yes, I remember now."

"I will probably have to sign for it. You look almost nothing like Lerence now. Like his older brother perhaps. Older and handsomer," she grinned, rubbing his butt.

They agreed on the slight change of plans and altered their course subtly.

The next few days lulled them into a false sense of security. They were peaceful sunny days. While both of them never forgot their goal and their loss of Rosea, they enjoyed their lovemaking, their solitude with each other and the chance to heal. Hunting was easy and water was plentiful, since they stayed near the various mountain streams.

Tyna felt more and more drawn toward Alan. He was so sure of himself in some ways and so vulnerable in others. His dreams, both waking and sleeping, troubled him and she wished she could help. Who was he in the past? Had Pé sent him back in the River of Life before his time? She understood among the Hrýll it was not unheard of for some to remember parts of their past lives, but she was sure this was not Lerence who suddenly had his past lives awakened, but more a rebirth of some sort.

It was not that she didn't long for her daughter. She did. But the daughter was born out of something the Tarth had done. She had only had a few weeks to adjust to the concept of being pregnant and only a few days with the child.

The bond was there, but it was not what she knew some mothers had with their daughters. It was both love and duty. She would rescue her child, but she would lay down her life for Alan even faster. She put her arm around his waist and squeezed him tightly.

Rounding a curve in the rough trail they were following they were almost run over by two horses and the man and woman astride.

Alan's sword was drawn before the horses had fully recovered and before Tyna had drawn her blade.

"Alanar!" The woman spoke. She was a beautiful woman just entering middle age. She wore her sword in the same manner as Alan did and momentarily Tyna thought she was Katar. She had almost a Katar look about her. 'Alanar' was the name she had called out. Too close to 'Alan' to be a coincidence. Tyna drew closer to Alan, her own sword drawn.

"The woman knows you," she said in a low voice, to be heard only by Alan.

"So it would seem. She is no woman though. She is Kinel."

"How can you tell?"

"You don't see the 'mask'? The skin color differences around the face. They are both Kinel. Look, look closely."

As he spoke she stared at both of them and indeed their coloring seemed to be different than it was at first glance. The darker, normal, skin color came up from the neck but narrowed to a point on the forehead, making a mask of light and dark skin. The eyes and cheeks were lighter skinned, the mouth and chin darker skinned. It was only visible when she looked for it.

The woman was dismounting and walking toward them, her arms outstretched. She slowed and focused on how Tyna and Alan where touching each other. She stared carefully at Alan and her arms dropped to her side. She spoke again.

"You do not remember." She sounded hopeful, as if she wanted to be wrong, but the statement was not a question.

Alan opened his mouth, said nothing, and shut it. Tyna felt him stiffen. He was looking not only at the woman, but at the man still astride the horse. There was something strange about his hands. The slim middle aged man looked like he was wearing gauntlets, but there were straps and cables running up the forearm and a band below and above the elbow. The man was frowning, almost scowling. She felt something brush her; it was cold as if something had touched her from within. The man spoke.

"Larrina, be careful. The woman is not human. She is the woman I sensed earlier," said the man with the strange gauntlets.

Tyna stiffened. What was he talking about? She spoke.

"Who are you two? What do you know of us? What are you doing here?"

Larrina stepped back a bit. Tyna could swear the woman looked jealous.

"We have been searching for Alanar," Larrina said, gesturing toward Alan. "He has changed, but it is him." She looked toward the man on horseback

164

with a 'I told you so' look on her face. The man nodded reluctantly. "Everyone thought you were dead."

Alan looked confused, struggling to put things together, as if he almost remembered something that was eluding his grasp.

Tyna did not wait.

"What is your relationship with this Alanar?" She asked.

Larrina's eyes narrowed and she looked at Tyna with a raised eyebrow. The effect was interesting with the mask look of skin color.

"We are … old friends." The last was with a bit of a sigh.

Tyna did not believe just friends for a second, but was not going to push the matter. These people had some knowledge of Alan's true identity. Part of her was relieved at further proof that she really was sleeping with a man other than her brother. Most of her was afraid.

The woman was obviously interested in Alan's welfare. The man she had mixed feelings about. He seemed hostile.

The woman gestured to the man.

"This is Tsom, I'm Larrina. We're part of the revolutionary movement with Alanar; not long ago we thought he'd died." She kept her eyes on Alan, looking for some sign of recognition.

Tyna relaxed a bit. The revolution. They were no friends of the Katar. Not necessarily to be trusted; revolutionaries had their own agenda. Her father had been sympathetic to their cause, but hadn't actively supported it. The Tarth had been too big a threat. There had even been rumors that the revolutionaries had allied with the Tarth, but no hard evidence.

"If you knew this Alanar from the revolution then how could he be the same man as Alan? Alan has been … with me … for much longer than a few months."

"He is Alanar. Both Tsom and I can tell in our own way." Larrina turned to Alan.

"You've undergone recent changes, haven't you?"

Alan seemed in a daze, one hand was rubbing his temples, his head dropped forward. His other hand used the oversized Tarth sword for a prop as he almost swayed.

"He has," Tyna answered for him. She trusted the woman, at least her intention to help Alan. "When in battle, he was wounded, and a change came over him. One could see that he was draining the very *ka* out of everything nearby. I could feel it."

"You were there?" Larrina looked amazed. "Nearby?"

"Next to him."

"Impossible. How did you survive?"

"I think our unborn baby protected me."

The look on Larrina's face confirmed Tyna's suspicions. This woman was either a past lover of Alan's or was in love with him now. She would have to be careful. Larrina was silent for a period of time.

"Where is the baby, you are obviously not pregnant now."

Alan sheathed his sword and spoke up.

"Hallam, or the Tarth with Hallam's aid, has kidnapped her."

"We should talk. Perhaps even if you do not remember us, or fully trust us, you will accept our aid." Larrina looked at Tsom. He sighed and nodded his head. As he was dismounting, Tyna noticed that it seemed as if he were momentarily suspended in the air above the horse. As if he was supporting himself with invisible hands.

Larrina struggled to compose herself. A baby? It was impossible. He was sterile. He'd always been sterile. Of all those she had healed, only with Alanar had she opened up that avenue and then failed. Kinel were famously infertile, yet Larrina knew that was not the case with her. She had control over that part of her body beyond what human mother's taught their daughters. Alanar was not fertile, or not enough like a Kinel or human to breed. She suspected the former, had been sure of it.

As Tyna told part of the story she acknowledged to herself that it might true. Somehow as Tyna's brother had been struck in the head Alanar had come to inhabit his body. It was the only explanation. Was it because the body was human and had not changed enough into Alanar? Obviously the body was changing every time Alanar utilized his powers. He resembled the Alanar of old. A very long ago. Was he still fertile? She glanced at him and then glanced away, flushing lightly.

The woman was another matter. Tyna exuded sexuality that was partially chemical. Larrina saw that even Tsom was affected. This was what had made him go crazy before, when he had reached out with his mind hands. The effect had been strong then too, so it must be beyond chemical. She knew that Tsom was still in love with her, so the effect was at a pure physical level. The woman was a walking aphrodisiac. Something that the Tarth had done to her had altered her. It obviously affected men, not women, or at least not Kinel women. She could sense Tsom's change, but felt none within herself.

Larrina sketched out Alanar's role in the revolution, without going into any detail beyond a few years ago.

"You were the financier of the revolution. You had vast wealth at your disposal and over a long period of time built up a network of spies and underground revolutionaries. Your wealth gave you power and few, if anyone, suspected your careful plotting over ... a very long period."

Why did she hesitate in giving away how very old Alanar was? She admitted to herself that it was partially because her knowledge of his past was something she had that this woman Tyna did not. Stupid to be feeling jealousy at her age.

"Tsom arrived on the scene rather unexpectedly, after stealing a Katar ring and fleeing their wrath. He didn't know of his Kinel heritage, nor his potential powers as a Kinel. Nor, of course, the dangers of using those powers. Tsom is younger than you are Tyna."

Tyna looked shocked, but stayed quiet. Larrina suspected that so many unbelievable things had happened to the woman recently than anything was believable.

Larrina left out the fact that Alanar had been negotiating with the Tarth and that Tsom was responsible for the banishment of Alanar. She shot Tsom a look to keep silent on this point. She did tell of Tsom's banishment of the Tarth and both Alanar--or should she call him Alan for now--and Tyna looked at Tsom with new respect. This was good, as Tsom needed a bit of an ego boost. He had been feeling slightly useless of late.

While Alan did not seem to remember anything she said, he did warm to them as she relayed their history together as revolutionaries. As she finished, he spoke.

"If we are such good friends then I will presume upon both of you. Will you help us rescue our daughter? If you'll do so, perhaps there is something we can do to aid the revolution."

Larrina smiled and looked at both of them squarely in the eye.

"Of course. You do not have to promise anything in return. If the Tarth, or Hallam, find your baby valuable, then it is in our best interest to rescue her."

"We were headed to Tarin for supplies. It's still worthwhile for us to do that. While you both look well supplied, you are equipped for two, not four."

They alternated riding and walking. Tyna noticed that whenever Alan finished riding the horse seemed more refreshed than when he had first alighted its back. Alan, on the other hand, seemed to be more tired and gain back his strength after walking. Tyna also noticed that Larrina took note of the same thing and that she shook her head but seemed to smile at it.

Meals always included a wonderful tea that Larrina would brew. They all gained energy from the tea. Their first tea together Tyna had a visionary flash of the Tarth forcing her to drink the concoction with Tarth blood and she waited while the others drank their tea. After a moment of slowing her breathing down, Tyna drank also and immediately felt calmer and slowly more rested.

Although they would sleep away from Larrina and Tsom, neither Tyna nor Alan felt comfortable making love near their companions. Tyna could tell that Alan was struggling with this and desperately wanted to. It was a bit of a thrill knowing she had such an effect on him, but truthfully, she shared the frustration.

On the occasions that Tyna glanced at Larrina she was sure that she was just catching Larrina averting her gaze. That's right, he is mine now, she thought. Hands off.

Neither Tsom, nor Alan seemed to notice this interplay between Larrina and Tyna. Tyna wondered if they were both just blind to it. She did notice Tsom staring at her quite often and he flushed if she caught him looking at her.

The remaining days to Tarin were uneventful, but tiring.

Tarin had changed in just the few months since they had last been there. At the outskirts of town there was a renewed tension in the air, similar to the days of the war. They soon found out that the Tarth encampment had been discovered. It had been impossible to hide the now huge force that had replaced the small band previously hiding in the woods.

As they approached the city gates the large bearded guard approached them. "Those are two fine animals you have there. The guard is in serious need of good horses for scouting. The council has authorized the guard to 'buy' animals as necessary. How much do you want for the two horses?"

Tsom growled that they were not for sale, but Alan, who was riding Larrina's stallion Lani, smiled and slid off the stallion. Tyna caught a glimpse of him poking the stallion with two of his fingers as he was dismounting. Alan spoke to the guard.

"If you really want these beat up old horses, you are welcome to them. The stallion here has a bad front leg that gives out all the time."

He led the horse to the large bearded man and sure enough the horse was limping badly, favoring his front inside leg. Leaving the reins in the guard's hands Alan walked over to the mare that Tsom was on. He patted the horse on the neck and whispered into its ear. Then he rubbed the neck again with a quick motion. Taking the reins he led the mare over to the guard also.

"Poor old lady, she stumbles so much it is a miracle my friend stays on her at all."

As if on cue the mare stumbled and went down to one knee and then rapidly struggled back to her feet. Tsom struggled to stay on and looked ungraceful.

The guard narrowed his eyes and led the stallion limping around. He tried rubbing the stallion's leg, but the horse pinned back its ears, raised up onto its rear legs and almost smacked into the guard. Cursing he handed back the reins and waved them into the town.

Tyna hesitated on where they should spend the night, but decided on the Ne Mar as the place to stay. She wanted to see if Gar recognized Alan as Lerence.

Gar was standing in the doorway as they approached.

"Tyna, my friend welcome, welcome. Ah and the two strangers from earlier. Indeed, indeed. How could I forget such a pretty face?" He beamed at Larrina. "And who is this? You look familiar sir, have we met?"

Tyna smiled. "Perhaps you have met his father, Narlan Orsin? This is Alan, my husband."

"Husband? Indeed, indeed. What a surprise. So sudden. Congratulations. Congratulations. You are staying of course. The best room for you. Indeed."

They set out, leaving their horses with Gar. No need to tempt other guardsmen.

Tyna was set on pulling money out from the bank that their family did business at, but Larrina waved her aside.

"Nonsense. I have enough and it is all Alana—Alan's." Larrina smiled sweetly and Tyna did not know how to gracefully refuse. Alan had no problem accepting the money.

Weapons and supplies were not an issue, although weapons were double the price of just a couple of months ago, when Larrina and Tsom had been there.

Horses were another story. Alan was the one who solved that problem. They went to the city stables on the edge of town. Military were more frequent here, many on horseback. The famous Tarin riders stood out among the others on horseback. Their horses were the cream of the herd and they road with quiet superiority. They were one with their mount. Most, but not all were men. All the men who came within ten feet of Tyna had a tangible change wash over them. Their attention would focus fully on her and several actually licked their lips. Tyna scowled at them, but this had no effect. Alan slowly became agitated, while Larrina watched with a morbid curiosity.

Twice a fight actually broke out between the men who Tyna passed. Alan kept them moving toward the stables.

The stables covered a huge area, with several hundred horses outside grazing and at least that many stabled within. Tyna suggested that she talk to the stable master if he was a man. Why not use this affect she was having over men to her advantage? Even Larrina thought this was a bad idea.

"Your affect is not to your advantage. Men normally lusting after a woman might be willing to do things for them in the even faint hope of gaining favor, but you are causing a blind lust. Standing next to you for too long and the stable master is as likely to rape you as help you."

Both Tyna and Alan blushed at that, but Alan nodded his agreement.

"I'll go in alone."

"I'll go with you," Tsom said. He had a guilty look on his face. Larrina's words seemed to have hit too close to home.

The stable master looked dubious.

"The horses we could sell would not be of much use to you, better off sold as meat."

"Yes, however I am a fair hand at nursing horses back to health. If you can provide me with a bill of sale that guarantees I don't lose the horse back to the guard, I am prepared to pay twice the meat cost." Alan smiled a winning smile that Tsom found just a bit disconcerting. The Alanar he knew would have never been able to pull off such sincerity.

The stable master thought for just a moment then smiled. He was no doubt going to keep the difference. Tsom's thief instincts kicked in. His ability to read a person had saved him in the past. This person reeked of avarice. If the stable master could, he would sell them out also.

Alan inspected the thirty or so horses slated for destruction. He patted each and every one of them and looked genuinely sad that he was only picking three. The three he picked were the skinniest creatures Tsom had ever seen. Skin and bones was being generous. They had tired, resigned looks in their eyes and initially did not even turn their head to Alan as he approached. He whispered in their ears and the three that he chose swiveled their ears toward him and managed to lift their head up a little and look at him.

The stable master shook his head at the poor choice, but willingly accepted the sintars that Alan passed to him. Tsom knew that Alanar had a gift in picking horses, but these seemed beyond hope. Maybe after a year of good feed and light work, but they didn't have time to waste.

Leading the three horses back to the women, Tsom took one and Alan two.

When they reached the women, Tyna just stared with her mouth open, almost laughing.

"That was the best you could get?"

Larrina did not look so shocked. She watched the horses carefully as they walked up. When they stopped she walked around each of the horses, touching them occasionally.

"Don't drain yourself too much healing them. I will make a 'soup' for them that will help."

Alan smiled appreciatively at her. Tyna's open mouth turned to a scowl.

Chapter 30

Tsom would not have believed it if he had not seen the change happen before his eyes. By the third day all three horses were trotting for over an hour each day. Each had gained at least a hundred pounds, although they still were underweight. Already they had to show proof of purchase to two guards interested in confiscating the horses. Soon, this proof would not hold as no one would believe that these horses were sick.

On the fourth day Larrina, Tyna, and Alan returned from riding. Tyna refused to let Larrina and Alan ride alone and she was a much better rider than Tsom. When Tyna was gone he missed Larrina. When she was back he forgot all about Larrina and had eyes only for Tyna. If not for the knowledge that this was due to some artificial enhancement and the effects of a tea that Larrina brewed to counter the lust, he would have acted on his urges. He could feel that he barely had himself in control. Worse the intensity of her effect seemed to increase with time, not decrease. Larrina commented on this.

"I think as her body adjusts to the loss of the baby that she is becoming fertile again. Once completely fertile, I don't think you, or any man, will be able to control themselves. It is an evil and cruel curse upon her. She can never know if someone truly loves her."

Tsom saw Tyna look up sharply at Larrina's words. Was she sensing the hope Tsom heard in Larrina's voice? Tyna bit her tongue. Tsom could almost hear her thoughts. Tyna knew that Alan loved her. He had stayed with her after the baby. He had been drawn to her before the Tarth woman had done this to her. Tsom pushed the feelings of glee at the silent interchange he played out in his head. Maybe Larrina would see that Alanar was lost to her.

At the inn they ate up in their rooms after the first night. Three fights had broken out over Tyna that first night and Gar's wife had almost killed her husband as he kept fawning over Tyna.

The fourth day, the three dismounted at the inn where Tsom was waiting at an outside table.

"Gather the other two horses and our supplies," Larrina called out as she checked her horse, "we leave right away."

"What happened?" Tsom asked.

"A small incident," muttered Alan.

Tyna scowled.

"Alan beat three Tarin riders almost to death." Tyna said.

Tsom noted the combination of anger and pride in her voice.

"One of them made the mistake of beating his horse in front of Alana – Alan. The second mistake was not stopping when he told him to. Perhaps the third mistake was ganging up on him," Larrina said, looking as if she were really mad that it hadn't been her that Alan had defended.

Tsom scowled and shook his head in disgust, then went off to saddle the two horses.

They told Gar they were headed back to Zethicia. Hopefully, he would not try too hard to protect them and tell the Tarin guard this quickly.

They left the gates and headed east, in the direction of Zethicia. After an hour they turned north and headed toward the Tarth encampment. Tsom, the worst rider fell behind the other three by a few paces; ahead, Alan rode with one woman on each side.

* * *

The Argn council of women was divided. They had not originally limited the council to women, but it had rapidly evolved to that. The core of the council consisted of Piea, Larra, Crissa and Mia—representing the Katar women who had come to Argn—Flana—representing the noble women as a whole—and five commoners from Argn. As each new woman had been added to the council it became inevitable that their next choice would be a woman. The percentage of men remaining in Argn was shrinking. Flana insisted that they needed men represented also.

"We need to represent all of Argn, not just women," she had insisted.

"We let the commoners vote for their representatives, the voted for women," Crissa shot back.

"The tyranny of the majority. We have to be as careful of that as much as the tyranny of the few, such as the Katar," Flana said and to her surprise Piea and Larra agreed. The council grudgingly took on five men as advisors, not full council members.

The division in the council was not just the elite and the common, but a division between those who wanted to ally with the rebels to the north and those who felt it was too dangerous.

Women were the best at communicating in the language of colors that was unique to Argn. This proved an invaluable skill in ferreting out spies from the other cities, and sometimes even from within Argn. As Flana prepared to go

172

out for the day she would stop by Crissa's quarters and verify that her colors were correct.

"The yellow should be worn on the left wrist. Not that you would be mistaken for a spy, but you might get some interesting offers for money that could be embarrassing."

Flana grinned.

"Well given my love life recently, that might not be all bad."

The colors of the city itself were subtly different. Flana notices a subdued quality to them and many of the colors on the houses indicated that only a woman lived there. The red between two pale blues indicated that there was a husband, but that he was no longer there. Sort of a missing in action, although she knew it was more likely that the husband had gone over to the cities controlled by the Katar and their gods.

The priesthoods had also fled Argn. The temples all stood empty, not yet looted but looking lonely and powerless.

The council set up permanent living quarters in Mia and Crissa's family compound. Not quite a castle, the compound of ten buildings covered twenty acres. It was filled with former Katar women, still wearing their Katar rings, but also wearing a color combination that would be hard to imitate by an outsider. Flana was not sure she would get the combination of colors, worn in the right order and on the proper garment correctly. It was something that a lifetime of living with made instinctive for the natives of Argn.

Crissa was divided against her sister Mia on the matter of negotiating with the rebels. Flana agreed with Crissa, the rebels were good fighters, well organized, and from what they had heard they were headed by a woman, Larrina. Rumor had it that she was Kinel and the other Katar women could not get over their prejudices. Piea was currently arguing against an alliance.

"The Kinel almost destroyed mankind in the past, we cannot trust even one of them."

"Come now Piea, we both know that the Katar have Kinel blood in their veins. Father showed us the ancient manuscripts. The only threat the Kinel posed was that they were against the Katar becoming a permanent ruling class. We are the sinners, or our ancestors, not the Kinel and certainly not this one woman." Crissa was standing as they sat, to emphasize her points.

"I don't deny that, but what of the rumor that the rebels had allied with the Tarth. Those daemons were what the Katar were formed to fight ten thousand years ago and allying with them is treason against mankind itself." Larra stayed sitting, emphasizing her point by the calmness of her manner.

"Rumors are not truth. Wasn't that thief, Tsom, that your brother had tortured and who had escaped, wasn't he the one who had ultimately banished the Tarth again?" Flana was surprised at her own boldness. Criticizing a Katar openly would have been unheard of months ago. Even with her family's power she would have feared to do such a thing. Now, within the council, they were almost equals. Katar, nobles, commoners. They were citizens of Argn.

Piea and Larra looked ashamed for their brother. Larra maintained her reasonable, calm voice.

"Perhaps, but it is more than rumor that the small band of Tarth to the northwest of Tarin is no longer a small band. They have all somehow returned. Not much of a banishment. When we banished them it lasted for ten thousand years."

"Legend has it that the Katar had help with that," Siacca, one of the newer members of the council spoke up, "A daemon of a man that helped create the Katar."

"To the matter at hand. Shouldn't we invite the rebels into the city? We are fighting for the same cause," Crissa was looking angry.

"Will they ally with us given that so many Katar are part of the group?" said Siacca. She was part of the group wanting to ally with the rebels.

"The only way to know is to ask," Crissa said and sat down, now looking tired.

They argued for hours, but finally decided that it was worth negotiating with the rebels to find out what their terms would be to ally with Argn. After more debate it was decided that a single negotiator would be the best route. Less conspicuous to the forces patrolling the outside, and a show of trust to the rebels. Crissa was finally allowed to volunteer, despite Flana pushing that it should be someone who was not a Katar, such as herself.

Crissa rode almost straight north for ten days. She kept a grueling pace, pausing only for the health of her horse. Her legs and back ached. She hadn't ridden so long since her training days, more years ago that she would like to admit. Like most Katar she did not show her age. The Kinel blood in their veins made them longer lived, although some said it was also the rings they wore, which drew upon the *ka* of those around the wearer. Crissa was dreading the day that the Katar would have to give up their rings. For now the Katar women of Argn wore them out of self-defense. If they were attacked by other Katar, they would need the rings to remain on equal footing. The other cities knew this and that was what had kept a full scale attack from occurring. For now the cities were content to try the leverage of an embargo.

Embargos only worked if there was no cheating. Zethicia was sympathetic to Argn and while they did not openly defy the cities, they did nothing to prevent the caravans of trade to and from Argn. That and the Showa family allowed some smuggling, with Flana's help. No embargo would crush Argn. It was too large, too self-sufficient. Except for qenar. The ore that fueled all the talismans. Civilization. That would eventually hurt.

Crissa had heard of attempts to create devices that did not require *ka* and qenar. The problem was most of them required steel. Steel was too rare to be used for large devices. Only the rich could afford more than a few knives and sometimes a steel or iron pot. Copper was the favored metal. Her crossbow quarrels were tipped with copper.

Crissa liked to plan, to ruminate. These details and others ran through her head. She knew the rebels had the Hrýll as allies. If they could get the Hrýll to make them talismans in exchange for protection, then it would be the cities that would be suffering, not Argn. There was enough qenar laden jade to last a few years, to fuel the existing talismans and possibly even new ones.

The forest she was now within was dark. The large trees had survived fires and were too far from the cities to have been logged. She was no nature lover and had no idea what species of tree they were. Some sort of fir.

Argn's spies had indicated that the rebels were near here. The encampment itself had not been penetrated, but the movements of people to and fro and been observed. She slowed her tired horse down to a walk, feeling a twinge in her tired back that was more than fatigue. Instinctively she started to reach for her sword, strapped to her back in Katar style.

"Don't move. You have six crossbows aimed at your chest. While one of us might miss, not all of us will."

Crissa halted her horse and waited.

"Take off your weapons and drop them to the ground."

She did so.

"Take off that ring. Don't try and use it, even with Katar speed you cannot outrun a crossbow."

Crissa hesitated. Katar never took off their rings, once they reached the age of maturity and had undergone their training. That fool Arlec had taken off his ring and look at the mess it had created. Yet, she was supposed to be showing goodwill and trust.

She took off the ring, pulled out her small purse and with show put it into the purse and threw the small pouch to the ground with her weapons.

"Alright, I am unarmed. I assume if you wanted to kill me, you already would have. I want to meet with your commander and discuss an alliance."

A lithe young woman stepped out, crossbow in hand. She gathered the weapons together and signaled for Crissa to get off the horse. Once she did, the woman smoothly mounted.

"Alright Sar Tanec, you walk in front of me."

So the woman knew who she was and was willing to use an honorific address. Was she being sarcastic? Hard to tell. Crissa began walking.

"What about the others, will they come with us, or stay guarding this area."

The woman laughed.

"Oh, I lied. There's only me."

The woman's name was Beena. She was from Argn, which was not surprising as the rebels had held Argn for several months after the defeat of the Tarth in Zethicia and before the Katar could mobilize their forces back in The Cities. With Argn no longer united with the other five, Crissa no longer thought of The Cities as a single entity. In her mind they had simply become 'the cities,' small letters. Someday, perhaps with the aid of these revolutionaries, the cities would unite again, only without the gods and their draining of ka, and yes, without the Katar. The Katar too might lose their identity and over time meld with mankind. Crissa didn't fear it, well, maybe she was a bit nervous, but she welcomed the possibility, the concept.

The encampment was really a small city. She marveled that its exact location had not been discovered yet. Ten days out of Argn was not really that far, but the wilderness of Nakana was extensive and civilization did tend to disappear suddenly. Except for the large training arena, most of the trees had been left intact. The buildings were nestled in amongst the giant trees. From any distance they were invisible.

People bustled with energy and focus. Most paid them little heed, or called out to Beena.

"Hey Been, what did you catch in the woods?" The call came from no particular direction and Beena waved without looking.

While there were plenty of men amongst the rebels, the ratio of women to men must have been still been close to two to one. Crissa wondered if the encampment was having some of the same issues as Argn. Behavioral issues due to so many women focused on too few men. Even Crissa, busy as she was, had begun to feel the strangeness of not having men around.

Beena stopped to let the horse off at a corral. There was a young man working on the horses that smiled and offered to unsaddle the horse for her so that she would not have to spend the time. He looked interestedly over at Crissa and sized her up. He smiled at her too and led the horse off.

"Boyfriend?" Crissa asked.

Beena laughed. Her laugh was quick and came easily. Crissa found herself liking her 'captor' more with each laugh.

"No, I suppose he wishes I was, but being a man with so many women he should be content with others. He is not my type. Nice guy though. Maybe just too nice." She shrugged and motioned the direction that they should walk.

Off the horse Beena had a smooth flowing walk. No spring in her step, but a glide. She seemed to just suddenly be further along than she was moments before and your eye almost didn't catch how she'd done it. They approached one of the buildings and Beena gave a perfunctory knock and then opened the door, signaling Crissa to enter.

Crissa blinked in the lantern lit room. No glow globes out here. There were open windows, but the day was nearing its end and the forest was dark enough to filter most of the light. When she could see again, she was standing in a large room with scattered chairs and a large desk or table. Behind it was an older woman. Crissa blinked to focus in the dim light and before she could say anything the woman spoke.

"Crissa. What a pleasant surprise. I am so sorry to hear about you father. He was a good man."

It was Sundra, her old fighting instructor from the Katar academy.

Chapter 31

The gentle, yet loud, splash of water from the inner courtyard fountain was only one reason for Garron and Arlec's raised voices.

"She's my wife. We can't simply have her assassinated," Garron said, as paced back and forth, his head down, not meeting Arlec's gaze.

"It's exactly because she is your wife that she must die. What did you think this was all about? Did you think that a woman of Argn would simply roll over and obey your every command? Did you think you, we, had Jern killed just so she could head the Tanec clan?"

"What use is it now, with Argn split off from The Cities and their talk of an egalitarian government?"

"The use is that with Crissa out of the way, you are the legitimate heir to the clan. The rest of the Katar will be more strongly united against Argn. Some of the Katar in Argn will return to our cause. Don't be a fool, Garron. She will never love you. After she is out of the way, you can have any woman you want, even a Katar woman."

Garron scowled and kept pacing. Arlec wondered at how long Garron was going to be useful. He needed him until Argn was back under his control.

The Katar council was now firmly under his command. Telem Sho, ruler of both Qenaril and Vranin had been the hardest to persuade. At first Arlec considered simply eliminating him, or threatening members of his family, but in the end Telem's love for his wife had been his downfall. That and yet more discoveries in his father's library. Old Devon had a wealth of tricks hidden within those books. The poison was one with no antidote and, even more surprising, it worked against Katar. However, the right formula would hold the effects a bay, if given every day. Telem knew that he could not even strike against Arlec, for if Arlec died, so did the secret of keeping his wife alive. He kept his smile to himself, not wanting Garron to think that he was smiling about the current conversation.

Eventually, Garron came around to his way of thinking. There were minor members of the Tanec clan that were now loyal to Garron and felt that Crissa was a traitor. They would be useful in the execution.

Arlec went to the newly built library. He felt safe on this newly built manor on the island of Old Arbeneth. He felt a sense of history. Of destiny. His family had once ruled from this island and had wielded great power. Once again the Karn family would be rulers of all of mankind.

The other families suspected his summoning of the Undine. Too many deaths near water. Too many glimpses of watery creatures crushing ships attempting to trade with Argn. There was no longer a need to keep it a secret. With the Sho family under his control, they would not try anything.

He augmented the books in his library with those of the other families. He had moved swiftly to confiscate them, before they could hide the crucial volumes. Most were useless notebooks kept by weak old fools. Yet, occasionally a gem would be found. Devon would have been surprised that his son had become a bookworm. All those years of pushing him to study and to emulate his sister's habits and now here he was enthusiastically pouring through volumes of books.

The sound of the omnipresent water fountains was soothing. No one would ever survive stealing a book from this library. The small fountain, connected by pipes to all the other fountains, held surprises that no thief would ever suspect. Arlec had never forgotten the insult of having his ring stolen by that wharf rat, Tsom. Still alive, if his spies were accurate. Someday that score would be settled. Too bad he had no family left to destroy.

The book he currently found interesting was very old. It was from the Terrel family, in Bronin. Bronin was on the border with Argn, thus strategically crucial, but other than that the city-state was weak. The craftsmen were fairly good with steel and made the best swords. They also had a fair agricultural base, filling in the gaps made by Argn and the long distance from Zethicia. Without the gateway between Zethicia and the cities, Arlec was unable to deal effectively with Zethicia. He knew their sympathies lay with Argn, but they would not openly oppose him. Not when he had the gods on his side also.

The priesthoods had been more than happy to throw their support behind a single leader. The gods found his methods effective, at least the gods that mattered. The minor gods didn't matter. The gods were fading as fast as his own power was growing.

This volume from Bronin spoke of the time before gods. According to the book there was a migration to Nakana from some other plane. The gods were human, if the book was to be trusted. Or almost human. The gods, before they were gods, interbred with several races. Distasteful as it seemed, there was even a trace of Tarth in mankind. While this was all interesting, it was the discussion of the other planes that was the most interesting. At one time, it would seem, there was easy passage between multiple planes. They were all connected by the Web of the Gods. His research was now extensive enough that he knew this was really the translation of Hrýll term for the mountains to the far north, the complex mountain range that covered so much of the northern hemisphere. The small cities on the edge of the Muglanth Plains still referred to the mountains as Ron D'Olanth. He would have to question the Hrýll someday as to the accuracy of the translation.

The most fascinating were references to the gods gaining their powers. They were not always immortal. They had not always had power over mankind. If they could do it and mankind was related to the gods, then perhaps there was a way for him to do the same. Immortality and power. A god. Wasn't his power of the Undine already something special? The Undine had recognized him as being from the Karn family. There must be something closer to godhood in the Katar bloodlines than in an average human. And something special in the Karn bloodline. He would find a way.

Word of the enlarged Tarth encampment reached Arlec mere days after the Be Na Tarth returned. A servant entered the study timidly and ran out the moment Arlec let him.

Despite the distances, the use of birds brought news faster than human travel and Hallam couldn't control all of them. Somehow the Tarth had returned from the banishment. So he'd given up his sphere to Lanos for nothing, a year ago. Simply a respite from the Tarth. Arlec suspected the thief had somehow interfered. His spies told him he'd been spotted in Zethicia. He and that Kinel woman, Larrina. He understood why the Katar wanted all Kinel dead. They were too dangerous. It was good to have some Kinel blood flowing in Katar veins, but only some. These purebreds were too strong. Too much of a threat to Katar power. His power. Mankind would never follow Kinel, they looked different—when their camouflage was down. The Katar looked like the rest of mankind.

The good news was that the Tarth forces were so far to the north. This time the Katar would not aid Zethicia. Let them weaken the Tarth. By the time the Tarth were a threat, he would have all of The Cities reunited. Argn would be his and he would use the Undine to destroy the Tarth. The Katar, combined with the gods and the Undine, would wipe out the Tarth once and for all. No mere banishment this time.

There was a gentle tap on the door. Arlec was about to get angry, when he realized how late it was. Probably dinner. He rose from his desk and stretched his cramped muscles. The glow globes had brightened, as the sun set, automatically. Arlec realized he was famished. Who would have thought that research and planning could work up an appetite?

* * *

The loss of Bal'alam was probably for the best. See'arr called it a blessing in disguise. Be Na Tarth was worried that the others would think that he had killed Bal'alam out of spite, but if that were true the Tarth did not seem to show any resentment. With his mother, Venicia, dead and See'ar, a Tarth woman of high birth now firmly back in his camp, his power was once again consolidated.

Humans had a love of water. Wherever there was a human settlement, there was fresh water. Water meant access through Jumping Water's unique ability. The Undine was proving invaluable.

They started their raids cautiously at first. Small isolated ranches. Be Na Tarth went on all the raids. He had to, as he would not give his jade sphere to anyone else. The jade sphere that sucked the *ka* of the dead, killing them forever. No reincarnation. He would destroy mankind permanently. No mercy this time. No hesitation. No compromise. No alliance with old enemies. The Tarth would not tolerate mercy this time and he was in no mood to even try and persuade them differently.

Their first ranch was at the end of the road from Tarin. No real roads beyond this location, so no fear of any resistance from the north suddenly appearing. Jumping Water opened the gateway from the stream flowing near the main ranch house. Surprisingly fast a man with an arm in a sling came charging out of one of the out buildings, a sword in his good hand. He was yelling for someone named Sera to run.

As Be Na Tarth killed him the window to the main building opened and a middle aged woman, reddish hair, with a crossbow was framed within the window. She managed one shot before the well-aimed rocks thrown by the other Tarth shattered her skull and the crossbow itself. The quarrel bounced harmlessly off Be Na Tarth's chest, but he admired the aim. As the rest of the Tarth were searching the buildings for anything useful, See'arr bent close to the woman, turning her head from side to side.

"This one looks familiar," she said, frowning.

"All humans look alike," he said after tucking the jade sphere away. A twinge of guilt and destroying this woman's *ka* flashed through him, but he brushed it aside.

See'arr nodded and joined the rest in their search. A ranch this large would have a wealth of supplies that would be useful.

The next few ranches proved as easy as the first. The horses were used as mounts for the Kami. No horse was strong enough to carry even a small Tarth for any length. Everything else was burned. Be Na Tarth felt the energy within the jade sphere grow slightly with the *ka* of each of the dead.

The Kami's ability to move silently in the dark proved useful when it came time to attack Tarin. The movements of the Tarin riders were relayed back to the camp and the Tarth struck when most of them were out on patrol. They never expected an attack from within the city itself.

Jumping Water's largest opening allowed twenty Tarth at a time to move through. At full charge, through water, that was almost one hundred in less than a minute. The Tarin stables, with the stream running through it and the garrison of military fell within the first five minutes. It took hours to kill the entire town, as they had to be killed within range of the jade sphere.

Even some of the Tarth were sickened at the carnage. The burning of the town was almost a cleansing. They took the time to pile the bodies upon the flames, so that they were incinerated. Casualties were so minimal among the Tarth that Be Na Tarth felt a rapid series of attacks from now on was in order. To the outside, it would appear as if they were simultaneous. The apparent size of the Tarth forces would be multiplied and put everyone on edge.

Over the next ten days nineteen small towns were destroyed. Be Na Tarth finally called for a rest, not because of injuries, but sheer exhaustion of movement. Jumping Water was feeling the effects of so many jumps. He needed to feed within the oceans for a time, to recharge on the *ka* of millions of small organisms. It had been agreed that he would not use the *ka* of the humans.

Be Na Tarth and See'arr plotted their attack on Zethicia. Despite their ease of destruction upon the smaller towns and cities across the plains of Muglanth, they knew that Zethicia was simply too large to simply take in a single strike. It was a sprawling city state of nearly a million and a half of mostly humans. The Yanin provided intelligence on the city, as they were not yet known to have allied with the Tarth as a race. It never occurred to anyone that the Yanín would use nuances in their mercenary agreements to their advantage and ally with the Tarth and still hire out in small bands to Zethicia. Once Jumping Water was fully recovered, they would strike and Be Na Tarth's conscious might finally be free of the guilt of his mother's alliance with Alanar and her death.

Chapter 32

As Alan and is companions moved toward the Tarth encampment they soon realized that it would be impossible to approach without being spotted. Twice they managed to avoid patrols of Kami. It soon became apparent that the dui mar, the large death cats, were also still part of the Tarth. Traces of their recent scat were all over.

Alan was sorely tempted to ride into the encampment alone and trust that his dark destructive power would take over. Larrina, who seemed to know more about his power than he did, warned him that would be suicide.

"Haven't you noticed that there is a ring of destruction around you, from you recent events? Your ability to drain all *ka* is localized. The Tarth would simply throw large boulders upon you from a distance, once they discovered what was happening."

"I could move, charge them."

"True, and you might get a few more that way, but they will not panic. The Tarth will simply take their losses and destroy you. Even drunk with power from their dead, you cannot move as fast as a Tarth indefinitely."

Some deep part of him knew this to be true. Yet he raged at his inability to get back at the Tarth for at least being partially responsible for kidnapping his daughter. He could not get at Hallam directly. Her domain was unknown, but the Tarth must have some inkling as to her whereabouts. Some method of contacting her.

It was Larrina and Tyna who came up with an alternative plan, one that both Tsom and Alan hated.

It became apparent that the will of two men were no match for the will of two women.

Tyna rode openly toward the two Tarth males. The three of them stayed hidden, watching. Alan was trembling as he stood with his sword drawn. They had left the horses some distance back as one could not depend on a horse not spooking at the wrong time and giving them away. Especially since Tyna was riding. The possibility of one horse calling out to another was too great, even with Alan's control.

Larrina gently laid a hand on Alan's shoulder and he felt calmer. He looked over to her and nodded thanks for her support. He didn't catch the look of anger on Tsom's face.

Alan could feel Tsom had manifested his hands. Larrina and Tsom had told them of Tsom's abilities and Tsom had even demonstrated a bit. It was Tsom's ability that made this slightly less risky. Their bows would be useless against a Tarth. The story of how Tsom had squeezed the hearts of the guards within Arlec's prison illustrated the true power of hands that could reach long distances and through solid matter. Both Tyna and Alan had rubbed their chests in discomfort during the story. Tsom seemed to take a little glee in Alan's discomfort, although that might have been Alan's imagination.

The two Tarth jumped slightly when they first saw Tyna, but as she was obviously approaching with the intent of coming to them, they waited for her. What could one human woman do to two Tarth?

As she got within twenty feet the effect that they anticipated took hold. Their jaws slackened slightly and their nostrils flared. One of them licked his lips. By the time she actually reached them they were fighting. Two males in rut.

Two Tarth fighting hand to hand was something few have ever seen. Several small trees were destroyed. Tyna had her hands full keeping the horse under control. She was making sure that she stayed near them, near enough that they could keep smelling her. They seemed more sensitive than the men within Tarin. Either Tarth had better sense of smell, or Tyna's effect was more pronounced on Tarth.

The Tarth were evenly matched and it was almost twenty minutes before one was victorious. Larrina said the noise would be recognized as two Tarth and most likely no one would investigate. They were too slow in preventing him from killing his companion. Tyna maneuvered the horse back toward her waiting companions and the tired and injured Tarth followed blindly. Between the four of them they were able to knock him unconscious.

They had to keep Tyna away from the Tarth while interrogating him. Whenever she approached too closely he went mad with lust and struggled to reach her. Surprisingly the interrogation, once Tyna was a fair distance away, went well.

Larrina did most of the talking. She felt speaking in Tarth was the best method and she had expected Alan to do the interrogation. When he assured her that he did not speak any Tarth she turned to the Tarth spoke. She was rusty, but knew enough from the written form of the language.

"What sort of woman is that?" demanded the Tarth. He was indicating Tyna off in the distance.

"You should know, her affect over you is because of the Tarth.'

"Ah, the female that See'arr is searching for. I see. Then she was successful, or at least partially successful. We have all been told to look for her."

"What did See'arr do to her?"

"I do not know the details, but all the Tarth know of her attempts. She is trying to find a way to increase the fertility of the Tarth, even if it means diluting the race with the blood of a human. It was the combined idea of See'arr and Hallam, your Goddess of Nature."

"Not my goddess. Nor, I suspect, any human now."

The Tarth laughed. Larrina continued.

"What of her baby, what have the Tarth done with her baby."

The Tarth looked surprised. He did not try and disguise anything.

"I know nothing of any baby. Has she given birth to a Tarth half breed?"

"No, it would be a … human baby."

"Then what good would it do to us? No, I do not know of any child."

Further questioning revealed nothing new on the child. However, they were all shocked to hear of the destruction of Tarin. They had been there only a short time ago and it was hard to process that it no longer existed. As the details of the other destruction were revealed Tyna understood that it was her own ranch and her mother that had been the first to die in the Tarth raids. Larrina did her best to ignore the comfort that Alan was giving her.

The captured Tarth didn't know what the plans were for Zethicia. Those plans were secret. He did seem to be hiding something about how they had entered so many towns in so short a period. Alan and Tsom were both ready to torture the Tarth for information, but Larrina didn't like the idea. Torture was neither led to accurate information, nor ethical in her mind. Death was acceptable. Defending yourself was acceptable. It was, again, Tyna who came up with a compromise form of torture.

They tied the Tarth securely to a massive tree. Larrina seemed confident that the ropes they used would hold. Then Tyna approached the Tarth. He went into a frenzy, trying to get to her. She stroked his face and exhaled on him. While he was in this frenzy Larrina again questioned him. In gasps, without really knowing what he was saying, he told them about the return of Undine and some ability to move large distances in an instant. Be Na Tarth had returned and could now transport himself to almost anywhere. The half insane Tarth did not seem to know the details of how Be Na Tarth was jumping from location to location, but no simple banishment would work on him and the Undine were now loose upon the world again.

"What do we do with him now?" Asked Tyna.

"Kill him," replied Alan. Tsom nodded agreement.

"That seems so … unfair," Tyna said. She looked to Larrina for support. She hated the Tarth for what they had done to her mother and the ranch, but it felt so wrong to kill someone bound up.

Larrina shook her head, not supporting Tyna.

"What choice do we have? It's admirable that you do not crave revenge for what they did to your family, but what would you have us do? We can't take him with us. We can't let him go. The Tarth will be after you if they know you are so close. The Tarth don't have your child, nor do they know where it is, nor even that it exists. Hallam has her somewhere. She has some plot of her own. Regardless, we have no use for the Tarth alive. Kill him and he goes to the Sea of Souls and some day will be reborn."

"Do we know that? What of the extinct races? What of the Kinel, Larrina? If you die are you reborn? There are no more Kinel for you to be reborn to. Are you reborn as a Katar, who has only some Kinel blood? Or are all races doomed to die, except mankind?" Tyna was voicing something Larrina had considered before. It hurt hearing it out loud.

"You may be right. Yet, the alternatives are worse. What if by letting this Tarth go we doom all of mankind to extinction. If mankind is destroyed, then those souls are never reborn. Indeed, if Be Na Tarth is capturing their *ka* as they are destroyed they have no chance to be reborn. He did that to your mother. *True deathed* her. He is but one individual you may say. We know that each individual can be a tipping point in great events. Tsom was, and still may be, a catalyst. The people we encounter when he is near are pivot points. We make the decisions, but he draws us to the pivot points. This Tarth might be a pivot point. I agree with the men, he must be killed."

"Who kills him?" Tyna asked backing away from the group.

"I will do it, I can make it quick and relatively painless. I know enough about Tarth physiology to do so." Larriana pulled out a long knife.

"No. Oonie once said it was bad for a healer to be doing so much killing. I think he is right. You're a healer, who happens to be an excellent fighter. I will do it." Tsom gestured with his hand to the Tarth.

Before Larrina could react she felt the *ka* flowing from Tsom. The Tarth convulsed briefly and was dead. There was blood dripping from the Tarth's ears and eyes. He has become very efficient at killing with his mind hands, she thought. I hope it's not from practice.

"We must postpone the search for your child. This information is too important to Zethicia and The Cities. I must return to the rebel camp and we must prepare to help against the Tarth. There is no reasoning with them this time. I am afraid it is war to the end."

Tyna grabbed Alan's arm and looked at him pleadingly.

Alan looked into Tyna's eyes and then looked at Larrina and finally at Tsom. He pulled Tyna close to him.

"I don't see what value we can be to the war against the Tarth. Even if I am who you say I am, I have no real control over my power of death and ultimately it is, as you already pointed out, a vulnerable power from any sort of distance. I have no memories that will be useful to you. You have your army. You have what was Alanar's wealth, or as much as I certainly could get my hands on. Tyna would be more of a hindrance to you than help, with her strange effect over men. No, we part ways. You must do what you can, but I must help my wife rescue our child."

Larrina wanted to scream at him that she loved him and he should be with her, not this human who would grow old before his eyes. Yet, she felt Tyna's pain. She had never born a child, but had yearned for one before. Even a child born of such strange circumstances was part of her mother. How could she ask the two of them to sacrifice their child for the good of the war? Without Alanar's memories, what could he really do? Nothing, except to be with her, which she did not want if he loved this woman. Over the past days she had become convinced that his love was genuine and not part of the effect Tyna had over other men. Alan, or Alanar, seemed to be partially immune to the effects. At least now. From what she had gathered, he had been fully susceptible to the effects before.

"I think this warrants true speed," Tsom grabbed Larrina, but she pulled down his arm even as she felt him manifest his hands.

"Wait." She looked him deeply in the eyes, knowing that it was unfair to play on their recent love, yet doing it.

"I want you to search with your hands for the child. Cast out as you did when you first pulled yourself to Zethicia. As when you located Alanar." She did not bother correcting the name to Alan. You know what they both 'feel' like, cast out and see if there is someone like both of them out there."

Tsom scowled and looked at Tyna and Alan. There was a pleading look on both of their faces. Larrina didn't ever recall Alanar with a pleading look and she felt jealous that it was not for her, but for Tyna and this child. Tsom looked back at Larrina and she put her hand to his face.

"Please Tsom. I ask this for me."

She felt the *ka* flow and a brush of something as his hands grew thin and tenuous. Invisible, yet she vaguely sensed them. He closed his eyes and moved his arms around him as if he were blind and feeling his way around. Occasionally he would flinch and she could see him getting tired, yet he continued. Once his eyebrows shot up and he almost opened his eyes, moments later he smiled and opened his eyes.

"There is a girl perhaps a thousand marks to the northwest in a valley. I know it's a valley from the feel of it. I am sure it is Hallam's domain. The trees and plants all felt shaped somehow. I could feel warm, so the valley must be deep, not simply a dip in the mountains. The valley has no entrance, nor exit, yet is not filled with water, very strange."

Tyna ran forward and gave him a kiss. Alan nodded his thanks.

Tsom was sweating from the touch of Tyna and turned to Larrina. In a hoarse voice he said, "I think we had best go quickly now."

When he grabbed her this time she did not struggle. She knew what he was going to do and the cost it would incur. What choice did they have? We all have so few choices.

Tsom manifested his hands and reached. He reached for Zethicia. He brushed against small towns and felt the people of Zethicia. The teaming millions. He reached for a familiar presence. Barnus, who they had talked to not long ago. He spread his hand wide and swept the city. There, there he was. He imagined the distance between Zethicia and here as being simply the other side of a folded paper. Punch a hole in the paper and you do not have to travel the length of the surface. He punched and then he pulled.

Larrina had traveled with Tsom this way once before. It didn't make it any easier the second time. She caught Tsom as he sagged from the effort. Barnus, who was alone, was already lowering his raised sword.

"You certainly make a dramatic entrance," Barnus said, as he added his aid to Larrina's and helped Tsom to a chair.

Chapter 33

Rotating between the four horses they made good time. Tyna was not sure where they were making good time to, but from what Tsom had told them this was the direction. In that direction laid Mount Raisnor, the core of the mountain range, the Web of the Gods. The king of the mountains, it had never been climbed. It was too hard and pointless. Thousands of marks of mountain range surrounded it. A vast wilderness that none of the races had ever penetrated. This valley that Tsom had described would be well before Mount Raisnor, but in the same direction. A thousand marks. How long would it take in these mountains?

With two sets of extra supplies they were in no immediate danger of needing anything. As before, whichever horse Alan rode, that horse was the freshest. Alan refused to stop whatever it was that he was doing. "Right now their energy and health is more important than mine."

During the evenings Alan worked with Tyna on swordsmanship. Tyna marveled at the man who one time had resembled her brother. He seemed to know her every move before she did it. She had some training with a sword. Her father felt that she was better than Lerence, but this wasn't Lerence. Occasionally, she still had to remind herself of that.

While Alan had an enormous amount of strength, she noticed that part of his skill was similar to her father's—albeit amplified. It was the skill of someone older. No wasted motions. No needless flourishes. No useless expenditure of energy. She had watched the arms master of Tarin training her troops once. She had been fascinated that a woman could be an arms master. Her father had told her most women could not.

"Women have the skill, but not the strength, nor the stamina. There are exceptions of course, as with Tiran here, but she is not using strength. Look at how she conserves her strength. She lets her opponent waste his strength. She is over fifty years old, yet can take any of these men, even after an hour. Age is not only a disadvantage for her, she has learned over the years and it is also her advantage."

This was what she noticed about Alan. He was incredibly fast when necessary, but it was almost never necessary. How old was he? That Kinel woman spoke as if he was old, and rumor had it that Kinel lived centuries.

Her thoughts were interrupted by a smack on her butt.

"Pay attention, wench." A grinning Alan flicked his sword at her as she was about to protest. She felt a light tug at her waist. She looked down as her pants slid down to her ankles. The swordplay degenerated into play of a different nature.

It never occurred to either of them to worry about an attack from the front. Their destination was weeks away.

The Yanín struck almost before Alan could react. Almost. The horses had not heard or smelled them, but some instinct within Alan had gone off. Luckily, Yanín almost never used bows. It was too removed from real battle. There was no sport in fighting with bows. What Tyna saw was a blur. Her brain did not really process all of it. Alan had pulled the crossbow from the back of his horse, shot one Yanín, re-cocked the bow by hand instead of the crank, shot a second, and smashed the crossbow into the face of a third, while pulling his sword free of its scabbard and wheeling his horse around. Slapping the rear of the two unridden horses he grabbed the reins of her horse and rode toward a nearby rocky hill with two huge boulders at the top.

Glancing back Tyna blinked several times at the Yanín. It was hard to process their movements. They ran so strangely. The rear leg looked like it was bent the wrong way, as if someone had taken a human leg and broken it at the knee so it bent backwards. Instead of a human gait--where the rear leg is straight and pushing so the runner is in the air momentarily--the Yanín's leg would bend backwards and the Yanín was almost never in the air. It made for an incredibly stable run and it was at least as fast a human, if not faster. It reminded Tyna of a two legged insect. The boney plate on the top of their heads heightened that feeling. Their battle cry was not insectoid. It was somehow a scream of joy. Battle lust. The joy of killing.

They made it to the top of the hill before the Yanín. To fit between the two boulders they had to dismount. One facing in each direction, the boulders protected their sides. The horses tried to run, but the Yanín cut them down mercilessly. Tyna could feel the anger radiating from Alan as he watched them kill the horses. At least they were quick.

The first two Yanín attacked without thinking. Neither Alan, nor Tyna had any real problem killing them. Tyna used the moment's respite to call out to them.

"Who hired you? What honor is there in killing two humans? So many

190

Yanín against just the two of us."

"Their honor does not work that way," muttered Alan.

"We kill only the man." This was from a Yanín in the back. Although he was speaking in common tongue, for their benefit, it was as if he were reminding all the Yanín there also.

"The must work for the Tarth," Alan said, between clenched teeth. "Use it to your advantage. They will try not to kill you. But, don't trust it. The Yanín have a hard time with the concept of stunning someone, or attacking to wound only."

The boulders partially protected them. They came in waves of four, two for each of them. On the second wave Tyna killed one, but her sword stuck in its skull plate. She was wrestling with the second one who was trying to hit her over the head. Alan pieced it through the eye, reached over to pull the sword free just as the third wave hit them.

Tyna soon lost count of the waves of Yanín. Each one was harder to take. She marveled at the stupidity of the Yanín who still attacked hand to hand and waited to see if the wave in front of them was successful. When she had enough breath to speak, she asked Alan about this.

"Pride. They want to be the ones who succeed, to brag to the others. By now we have killed more than they expect. We are now worthy opponents. It would dishonor them to attack en masse, or from a distance. Their pride is always their downfall."

He sounded like he had seen the Yanín in battle many times. Again Tyna wondered at how old Alan's memories were. Did he even really remember, or did her question simply trigger access to some limited memory? Some filed away bit of information?

The next wave hit.

The warmth of her back was comforting. It radiated love and security. As long as he felt it he knew that he safe from behind. As long as he felt it he knew she lived. That was all that was important.

There was a lull in the waves of Yanín. Time to breath. Bodies of Yanín were strewn around them. Up on the top of the rocky hill the sun beat down on the still warm bodies. Their joints looked like someone had broken all of their bones and bent the limbs the wrong way, but that was simply the Yanín physiology, even in death they looked like badly drawn human. He pushed the nearest one away so that he would not trip over it.

The last wave had been the tenth. They were discussing tactics below. Not frightened. Yanín were never frightened. Still, forty Yanín dead against two was unheard of. They were probably swallowing their pride and honor. No need to waste more lives immediately. Their objective, he thought grimly, was not going anywhere.

There was only twenty left. Only. If they swallowed their pride more and rifled through the packs on the dead horses, they would have bows. Something within his head told him he might be able to knock one or two arrows aside, but not a continuous stream. Hopefully, they really did want Tyna alive. It was probably what had saved her so far.

He drew a deep breath, savoring the ability to breathe slowly after the last intense battle. He reached back with his right hand—the empty one—and touched her. She reached back also. Their hands intertwined. Both gripped tightly. He loosened his grip and caressed her hair and brushed her ear, then her neck.

"No time for that, old man. We make it through this and you'll have plenty of time."

"By then we'll both be too tired."

"I've never known you to be too tired."

He reached back and squeezed her firm butt. She giggled for his benefit. It sounded a bit forced.

The next wave hit.

This time the Yanín were cooperating with each other. Normally solo fighters, they were coordinating their attacks. One engaged while the other probed for weaknesses as he parried. His small dark steel blade moved faster than any Yanín had seen. It seemed that any strike was dangerous. Small wounds would cause the injured to fall in pain almost screaming. He could feel strange energies swirling around him. Each dead Yanín seemed to give him more strength. He didn't notice that the scraggly grass at his feet had turned black. Part of his mind enjoyed hearing the Yanín scream. Another part wondered. It was unheard of, a Yanín screaming.

The one coordinating the attack looked familiar. It was almost as if he were seeing two Yanín, one superimposed on the other. One of them was talking.

"Talanas. You have brought these beings here. Why? Why have you done this to us? You must die Talanas."

The image resolved itself to a single Yanín. Who was Talanas?

Suddenly the warmth was gone. He flicked a glance behind.

She was down. A Yanín stood over her looking surprised.

His mind screamed and broke.

He was in a field of dead. Tyna/Tyra/Tula lay dead. Her red/blond/black hair surrounded by a pool of blood. Killed by her own kind ... no wait these were Yanín.

Three more Yanín perished, screaming. The circle of black started to grow at his feet.

She was down.

The Tarth begged him to stop. It had been an accident. Was one woman worth an entire race, they begged?

He barely parried. He absently struck and killed the Yanín attacking. It took

192

no effort. Did he die before the sword hit?

She was down.

They had killed her. The Stinking Katar. Half breeds. They killed their own kind. He had saved them and this was their thanks? The families begged him to stop. Their children were all dead. It was not enough. They must pay.

Two more Yanín died. He was not thinking anymore. He strode out between the boulders. The charging Yanín withered and died before reaching him. Their eyes grew wide as they realized their fate. True Death. Their *ka* flowed to him and he drank. He drank and he changed. His eyes were gold on gold. No visible iris. There were tears in his eyes, but he did not need to see. He grew leaner still, his muscles stronger. He drank of their life force and remembered.

She was down. He loved her and she was down. He did not have to touch her to know she was dead. The smallest, still sane part of his mind, noted that the blackness at his feet had not touched her. At least she had died a clean death.

The jewels on the sword handle dug into his hand. The blade was a black metal that seemed to not reflect light. The jewels were black and white diamonds. It swallowed light. Its touch was death. Tyna/Tyra/Tula/Tss'ra/Tarni/Thryl was dead. She was down and he had caused her death. They must die. They must all die. They always died. Those he loved always died. Those who killed them always died. It was the way.

The remaining Yanín felt fear. It was a new emotion for them. The emotion was short lived.

Chapter 34

Met soared above the mountains. He was within a massive storm front. At any moment he could manifest a tornado from the built up energies. He felt the power, the electricity of the lightning he could summon, the force of the winds. When he was part of a storm he knew he was a god. A very small part of him remembered his body, lying on its bed in his domain. Vulnerable, if another god might enter. No other god would dare enter, except that bitch Hallam. Hallam. That was why he was here, within the storm, searching. Wasting energy that was so hard to replenish now. Not enough worshipers, not enough sacrifices.

Hallam's domain had to be somewhere in the mountains. The plains were too exposed, the forests of the flatlands were a possibility, but Met's spies told him that all the signs pointed to the mountains. A tornado would be hard to manifest here. She knew that. Concentrating a storm would be hard. The peaks and temperature differences would be battling his will. She knew that.

Ague was sure she was in the northern continent. She would never dare to cross the seas. Ague would find her and destroy her. No, she had to be in the mountains.

He sent gusts of wind and the edge of his essence down to ground occasionally. It was like touching and smelling with the same sense.

Pain. Burning. Cold fire. Weakness. He pulled back. What could be doing this to him? He focused on the area and rained lightning upon it. After a time he reached out and touched the area tentatively. The pain from the first touch remained, but no new one entered. Nothing lived below. He felt the energy of his lightning strikes still echoing, but nothing else.

What had that been? Something of Hallam's? No, it was something else. No matter. Nothing could have survived that lashing of lightning he'd given, even most of the other gods. Still, he could search for Hallam tomorrow, it was best that he return to his body. He felt weakened and with the dearth of worshippers it would be some time before his *ka* was restored.

The storm dissipated rapidly, as a balloon untied and let go. The sun returned to the mountains, brightening everything except for the perfect circle of black below.

* * *

Alan. Alanar. Arcoth. Talanas.

He was Talanas now. The Old Ones had called him that. Not the Hrýll. Humans referred to them as the old ones, but they were not old. Not as he counted years. No, from before. Before the Web had been opened. The Old Ones had called him Talanas. The Hrýll had called him Arcoth, which meant death in their language. Talanas was a consuming rage. Destructive. Uncontrollable. The storm touched the periphery of his consciousness. The wind whipped his clothes and face, the darkness of the clouds obscuring his face, but not his eyes. His eyes were gold on gold. No iris. No whites. Even the center was a shade of gold. From a distance he was a wraith, two floating gold eyes and bared teeth.

The lightning strikes nearby did not cause him to flinch, but he did turn his face upward. Curses in a language no one on Nakana would recognize streamed out of his mouth and he shook his fist in the air waving his sword wildly in the other. One bolt found his sword.

His clothes burst into flames and Talanas momentarily stumbled. He screamed in pain in rage. His skin blistered and then healed. A wave of death radiated out from him incredibly fast. Thirsty death, searching for more fuel. A deer in mid-leap, over a mark away, stumbled and died of old age. Trees blackened, cracked, and fell down. A low flying bird plummeted, dead before it hit the ground.

He remembered. Everything. And went insane with grief, guilt, and rage.

Talanas felt the Web pulsating with his insanity. He reached and strummed the strands. It vibrated in resonance to his being. He felt the power flowing through him and he channeled it to the web of rivers. He fed it the energy of the dead, of the lightning. He channeled to the Web and it came alive. Long dormant, it wakened slowly. He was the nexus and the strands tugged at him. He tugged back. The rivers between the planes that were the Web of the Gods flowed free again, dams broken, riverbeds long dry. The world blurred. Images from other worlds flickered into sight and disappeared. He weakened the barriers in his insanity, not knowing what he was doing, not caring.

A herd of horses, galloping a full speed, nostrils flared and eyes rolled in the back of their heads, burst out of one of the blurred spokes radiating from Talanas. The stallion leading the herd was eighteen hands tall and black. It charged Talanas and at the last second reared. On two legs it raked the air in front of Talanas wildly, screaming, its ears pinned and its teeth bared. Just as it was about come down on Talanas it landed to the side. Its wild eyes rolled back and focused on Talanas. Its pinned ears rotated forward and its head dipped. Talanas spoke. Not the same language as the curses, yet no language of Nakana. Grabbing the stallion's mane he pulled and lifted himself on the horse, which reared, but did not throw him off. Talanas whispered into the horse's ear and the stallion's ears went back again and it galloped off.

As the energy diminished, the rage subsided. Slumping forward, spent, vulnerable, barely conscious, his body instinctively stayed on the horse. The herd of twenty horses followed behind the stallion.

As the dust settled behind the horses, the once blackened ground of the Yanín battle was now a deep green. A jungle green. Large plants, large leaves, and moisture. Further back there was a blurring. A fog as the moisture of the hot jungle mixed with the cooler mountain air. A large humanoid stepped out of the fog. He was covered in a thick bright yellow fur. A small cloth wrapped around his genitals was the only clothing he wore. A sword was strapped to his back. He looked around, flexing his hands in and out of a fist. The ends of his fingers were tipped with short sharp claws. He sniffed the air. He grinned. A set of pointed sharp teeth, made for ripping, were bared. He called out, sounding something like a growl and speech. He strode forward.

Behind him, out of the fog, more Zintu emerged. Soon the mountain valley turned yellow, a river of fur. The river flowed east, downhill, toward the plains, toward Zethicia.

* * *

While exhausting, the effort of moving through the folds of space did not cause as much damage to Tsom and his *ka* as it had in the past. Each time he used his 'hands' in any way, he became more efficient. Of course, he might die from the effort before he became truly good at it. This happened to many Kinel, Larrina constantly warned him.

He sipped an invigorating tea that Larrina had prepared. She and Barnus had been speaking for hours. Much of what they were discussing was already tactics and strategy. Large maps of Nakana, or what was known Nakana, were out on the big table in Barnus's room.

"Even at full march the Tarth would not get here for weeks." Barnus was pointing to a potential route from Tarin to Zethicia.

"Possibly, but I would be prepared for something faster. The Tarth destroyed several major towns simultaneously. I don't think it was separate groups. Be Na Tarth is back and he will be draining the *ka* of those killed—as he did before. They have some method of transport. Something similar to Tsom's ability." Larrina nodded in Tsom's direction as he sipped and listened.

"I am only able to pull through people I am holding on to. This must be something more like the gateway that once existed between The Cities and Zethicia."

Tsom refrained from saying it was his doing that destroyed the gateway.

Now they could use the help of The Cities and there was no fast way to get that help. The breaking of the gateway had prevented fast movement of the Katar to and from Zethicia, which aided the rebels at the time, but now it seemed that this might have backfired.

Larrina nodded in agreement. "Yes, the principle is the same, only the execution is different. They are aided by an Undine that allows them to open temporary gateways."

"Water daemons? Have all our legends come back to haunt us? As if the fact that the Tarth are many times stronger than a man, move quickly, and have the aid of Hallam and a device which causes *true death* as one is killed were not enough." Barnus slumped in his chair, looking defeated already.

"I lost one son to the Tarth already. Another to thieves. I don't know if I can bear the loss of another," he continued. "What of your rebels, Larrina? Will they come to our aid? Do you think you can persuade your Hrýll allies to create some new talisman to help us?"

"The rebels will help, but I cannot speak for the Hrýll. They join us against the Katar, not against the Tarth. The Tarth are one of the original races, just as the Hrýll. They may feel a certain empathy for them. We know the Hrýll know how to make a gateway, they made one for the Katar, but that gateway took years to build and cost the lives of many to fuel it. The Hrýll considered it an abomination, but were forced to build it."

Larrina looked as if she agreed with the last sentiment, Tsom certainly did. He had known many petty criminals who had their *ka* drained as punishment. *ka* that had gone to fueling the creation of talismans. Many of the conveniences of civilization were built upon the shriveled bodies of the prematurely old.

"Please try." Barnus looked over to Tsom. "I know you have paid a lot just to get here, but I beg you to go to your rebel groups and ask them to join us. We will ask the Katar for help, but I doubt any will be forthcoming. With the breakaway of Argn from the rest of the cities the Katar have been focused on self-preservation and retaking Argn. Zethicia will not seem important."

Tsom finished his tea and with some effort stood up. Larrina was at his side quickly. Before she could protest he had manifested his hands and felt to the southwest for their encampment. It was something very familiar and he found it quickly. Not wasting any energy on speech, he pulled them through.

* * *

Inlas, in the guise of Tiar, sat in the simple home of Oonie, her mortal mate who did not know who she really was. Oonie was due soon. The goddess of illusions was having a hard time maintaining her appearance as a Hrýll. She kept crying and the accompanying waves of emotion caused a loss of control. Her appearance flowed from a good looking human woman to that of a Hrýll woman, covered in light fur, almost a fuzz. She heard Oonie approaching and pulled herself together. The handsome Hrýll woman solidified. No tears were visible, although they were still there. She simply created the illusion that they were gone.

Oonie came in and let his eyes adjust to the lower light. He then sat at the central table, on the ground cushions as was Hrýll custom. Inlas/Tiar sat across from him and waited. Shortly, Oonie spoke.

"The gods and the Katar are committing evil."

Inlas/Tiar nodded, without speaking.

"The Hrýll are prepared to die, as a race, to defeat them. The time of mankind's, of the Katar's gods, needs to end."

Again, Inlas/Tiar nodded. He had heard, as she had known he would, of the latest atrocities. She had suspected that the Hrýll would finally unite in battle. She had lived amongst them for too long, pretending to be one of them, to not know.

"Which side will you fight on, my woman?" Oonie looked at her, his eyes seemed to see into her soul.

Her heart leapt. There was only one reason he would ask such a question. She felt her illusion wavering.

"You know?"

"Of course."

"How long?"

"Always."

Inlas, no longer Tiar, burst into tears. Her true appearance revealed and she made no effort to manifest the visage of Tiar.

"Why? Why did you not say anything? Were you using me?"

"No more than you were using me."

The balance of the betrayal didn't make her feel better, less betrayed. She looked at her husband, or rather the Hrýll she had pretended was her husband all these years. She knew where her heart was, but where was his? He'd known all this time. What was his game?

"I become mortal if I join you. If I no longer accept the *ka* of worshippers. I may even die before you. The Hrýll are a long lived race."

"This is true."

"You would still have me? Looking as a human? I would not waste energy every day looking like a Hrýll. I would look like I do now."

"You look as you always have. Your illusions do not work on Hrýll."

How could this be? All these years all the other Hrýll had always treated her as one of their own. They were all in on it?

Understanding some of her expression, Oonie continued.

"Oh, we see the illusion you are throwing, but only as a weak image. It is too similar to what the Kinel have always done. We existed with the Kinel for eons before the arrival of man and their gods."

Tiar, for she was thinking of herself as Tiar, stammered, "But, why?" She hugged herself, the tears falling freely. She had been used, which was ironic because this had all started as a way to spy on the Hrýll. What was more devastating was the thought of losing Oonie.

Oonie smiled, and shrugged. "To us, to me, you are simply Tiar. Your charade hurt no one."

"But, what of your charade? You pretended to love me," she whispered. It wasn't fair, but it was the way she felt.

"I participated in no charade. I love the woman you are, not the woman you pretend to be. But, your charade must now end. The Hrýll, after all this time, will take a stand."

"The gods will be angry with me. If they get a chance they will punish me."

Oonie nodded, but now he was silent.

"I am your woman?"

"You are my woman."

"Then, I am no longer a goddess."

"That is good," he went to brew them some tea.

* * *

Sundra was perhaps the best female warrior Crissa had ever known. She was both skilled in hand to hand combat and a brilliant tactician. She had taught at the academy for decades as one of the very few non-Katar instructors there. Most of the Katar women were in awe of her and really thought of her as a Katar.

"I should have known you would join the rebels. You always taught us the importance of honor and the obligation of our station. The Katar have failed that obligation for too many years."

"It was not an easy decision," Sundra leaned forward in her chair and poured Crissa some more Hrýll brandy. One of the advantages of being allies with the Hrýll, thought Crissa, access to the best brandy and whiskey on Nakana.

"I like the direction you and the others are taking Argn. I always thought that if the Katar could learn to share their power and let people rule themselves, that ultimately mankind would grow stronger. The corruption within the Katar families would have a check. The gods and their priesthoods would no longer be the only other force that man would turn to."

Sundra's face revealed that something was troubling her, despite her words of encouragement.

"But, there is something else, isn't there Sundra? You know something I do not."

"Yes, the breakup of the Katar and of The Cities could not have come at a worse time. Be Na Tarth and the full force of Tarth have returned once again. It would seem their banishment this time was very temporary indeed. They have more powers than before, some method of transporting forces great distances, and the Katar will not come to the aid of Zethicia this time. Mankind is divided and we will fall divided. Yet, I don't know how we can unite. We will not go back under the ring laden fist of the Katar."

Crissa took a moment. Sundra always said to process information and not let it force one into hasty decisions. Sundra waited.

"We could try and aid Zethicia, but we would never arrive in time. Even with the gateway open, we probably could not get forces through the gateway fast enough, with the gateway gone it is many weeks for a large force to get to Zethicia."

Sundra nodded acknowledgement. She signaled for her former student to continue.

"I assume you're still allied with the Hrýll and exploring any talismans they might have, or could create, that would help. The rebels and Argn united are a formidable force, able to withstand the Katar and the rest of The Cities, but not enough to overwhelm them. They must know this and might be willing to form a truce, possibly an alliance, against the Tarth. We could let Zethicia fall and concentrate all our efforts on preparing for the inevitable attack by the Tarth. Possibly the Yanín could be persuaded, or bribed, to join forces. To them a battle is a game, they care little which side they fight on."

"Your thinking is similar to my own. The gods have abandoned Zethicia. They're now so intertwined with the Katar that they're powerless without the sacrificial worshiping instituted by the Katar. However, they need mankind to survive and one assumes that they will aid us as much as possible against the Tarth—although they may not be able to directly affect Be Na Tarth with his device that consumes human *ka*." Sundra paused, heaved a sigh, then continued.

"I rail at the thought of abandoning Zethicia. Millions of innocent people will die the *true death* at the hands of the Tarth. They're bent on total annihilation. They want no human to be reborn on Nakana ever again. My conscience doesn't let me accept sacrificing them." Sundra looked angry.

"Atem's luck. We have no choice. Zethicia will have to fall while we prepare. We'll have to negotiate with Arlec and The Cities. We must present a unified front to the Tarth."

Crissa downed the last of her brandy. "What of the Hrýll?"

"Larrina and Tsom are in Farnlaran talking with the Hrýll and Oonie, their leader—for want of a better term. I don't claim to understand how the Hrýll make their decisions as a group."

"Larrina, she's the Kinel woman? I thought she was in Zethicia."

"She was. Tsom has his own ability to move quickly from one point to another." Sundra raised her hand to stop the hopeful look on Crissa's face. "No, only one or two people at a time can go with him and it drains both his physical energy and his *ka*. He will kill himself if he keeps it up."

Somewhat reluctantly the two of them started making plans to unite Argn and the rebels and created negotiating points for talks with Arlec and the Katar. The future of Zethicia weighed heavily on both of them.

Chapter 35

The raids on Zethicia began a few days after Larrina left. They never lasted long, but were devastating. The Tarth appeared out of nowhere and killed hundreds each time, with little to no casualties on their part. It was not until the second attack that the exact mode of entering the main city was perceived. Water itself was the gateway. The connection to the Undine that Larrina had warned them of.

The news of how the Undine was using water as a means of transportation caused widespread panic. The city had rivers and wells and streams running throughout. There was no way to protect themselves from the watery gateways, but they tried. The military garrisons were moved away from the water, with barrels being brought daily to and from the river. Citizens did their best to stay away from any fresh source of water.

Barnus sent a number of carrier birds to warn Larrina and the rebels of this tactic. She had warned him that Hallam was active in the skies, so he sent his messages with several birds released simultaneously from different parts of the city. He sent the same warnings to The Cities, not caring that the Katar were not coming to their aid. He knew that the end of Zethicia was inevitable without aid, but would not withhold this vital information from the others.

The mass exodus of citizenry stayed away from all sources of water and headed toward The Cities in clumps of a few thousand each. Many starved. Some were killed by Tarth. Some were killed by large roving marauders. Barnus listened to the reports with a leaden heart. Those fleeing had done what they thought was best; he would stay with the remnants of the city and fight. They who stayed knew their fate at the hands of the Tarth, who simply killed any messenger they sent to sue for peace.

The Tarth, in between their watery attacks, moved their main force within sight of the Zethician watch towers. The afternoon of the final attack Barnus went to the graves of his wife and two sons. The first son had died only a year ago, against the Tarth also. It seemed an eternity, with the hope of peace after the Tarth banishment. Ten thousand years the first banishment had lasted. Who would have thought the second time the Tarth had been defeated that it would last only one year.

His first son had died the true death. No Sea of Souls. No reincarnation. His second son's death had been cleaner. He had defended the city against a small band of thugs in the aftermath of the second Tarth war. After Dalin's death Marsa, his wife, had lost the will to live. She too had died a cleaner death, at her own hands.

Barnus was not religious. He knew the truth of the gods, confirmed by Larrina and Tsom. He grieved for his third son, who stood within the group nearby.

"Pé, guardian of the rivers of Life and Death, guide my loved ones to the Sea of Souls to be reborn. Do not drain their *ka* for your own use. Enough have died for the gods, let those two souls drift by your nets."

He bowed his head, knowing that he would not be joining them. The Undine and the Tarth left no souls to travel the rivers. Standing, he looked to the West where the Tarth and Undine had massed. No stealth this time. They knew the city was theirs. He unbuckled his sword and pulled his sword free of the scabbard. Tossing the scabbard aside he strode west, sword in hand. As he left the cemetery the remaining members of his guard fell in behind him. Three thousand men and women. They knew their fate. Their last fight was not pointless. The better they fought, the more would escape the city.

They died the true death.

Barnus was the first to fall.

When Zethicia fell, only a hundred thousand remained within the city that had once contained over a million. Although the Tarth celebrated their victory, burning and looting the town, Be Na Tarth did not take part. Despite his hatred of all mankind, the carnage sickened him. The pulsing of energy from the jade sphere around his neck felt like the heartbeat of some giant beast whose appetite would never be satiated. It fed on the *ka* of mankind and would be his key to victory against the Katar and their gods, but he did not enjoy its burden. For the first time he felt a certain sympathy for Alanar, once called Talanas. A bitter understanding.

* * *

Talanas failed to contain the explosions in his head whenever he regained consciousness. As he rode furiously on the back of the giant stallion, he was on countless battlefields of the past. Always the same, the masses of people turned to masses of dead. If he killed enough, no injury to himself was too great. All he had to do was kill more. And he did. He always did. He remembered now. For the first time he remembered it all, no partial amnesia to save his sanity. Eons of memories long suppressed. He was never able to stop killing. Something always triggered his rage, his fear, his need for revenge. He remembered and did not care. He felt the craving to kill the Tarth. They would all die this time. They had killed his love too many times, they deserved to die. He screamed in rage and stroking the horse under him, it leapt forward with more speed, leaving the herd behind. No matter, he would keep this horse alive. He stroked the horse and called forth the *ka* from within. The vitality flowed forth. The horse moved faster, with incredible strength and speed. Its muscles near their ripping point. It was not lack of energy, but the frailties of flesh and blood that was keeping the horse from going faster still.

Talanas, once known as Alan, once as Alanar, many times known simply as Death, burst upon the Tarth encampment. The dui mar, the death cat, that had been patrolling the periphery died quickly. Its feline face showing a strangely human look of horror as it realized that it was dying a true death, its very soul being drained to fuel Talanas' fury.

The encampment had only few hundred wounded Tarth and Kami. His timing had been off. The main encampment had moved and was destroying Zethicia. A few hundred would not satiate his thirst for revenge.

After the first dozen Tarth died, the rest realized that hand to hand combat was ill advised. The huge spears that they flung took down the horse, but missed Talanas. This only seemed to enrage him more. He flung several of the spears back at the crowd of Tarth. He needed no real skill to hit them, but the aim was true enough and his strength equaled that of any Tarth.

The remaining Tarth fought with the desperation of all creatures that are cornered and know they will die.

His wounds were becoming an increasing hindrance. Talanas couldn't spend the time to heal himself and give the Tarth an opportunity to finish the job, nor was he able to tap into the energy of the dying. They were staying too far away, throwing spears and shooting arrows. His charges worked, but only served to kill one of them, while the others would use the opportunity to fire more distance weapons at him, even rocks.

He tried to tap into his rage, his anger, but it was finally exhausted, burned out after the ride and the fighting of the past hour. No lightning bolt to recharge him. Too much energy was being spent on healing each successive wound. In his anger and rage he had not really thought through his wild attack. This was not some battlefield of thousands who had nowhere to run. The smaller group was actually working against him.

In the end it was fear that saved him. Too many Tarth fled the thought of true death, rather than sacrifice themselves to kill him. They didn't notice that most of their fellow comrades were now simply dying a natural death. Talanas was once again simply Alan. He dealt death, but was too tired to maintain the rage. He was able to think again and thinking made him vulnerable.

It took him another half hour, but those who had not run now lay dead. The ground near him was blackened with *true death* and his clothing was in tatters. His many wounds were slowly closing as he poured the last of his stolen life force into healing.

The need for healing battled with fatigue. Even Death needed time to rest. Finally, he lie atop of the dead horse and fell into a sleeplike coma. The last major wound stopped healing in a preternatural way and his blood mixed with that of the stallion and several dozen Tarth. He didn't hear the thunder within the rapidly forming clouds overhead.

Chapter 36

Arlec called upon his Undine. The fall of Zethicia had shocked even him. The summaries of the Tarth tactics had arrived, followed a few days later with the word that Zethicia was no more. If the Tarth could move huge distances now, how much time did they have. Arlec called the Katar council. It was time to reveal his power over the Undine. Time to crush the Tarth. Time to show the Katar families that he was the right leader. Without him, they were doomed.

Jumping Water appeared within the bubbling fountain that Arlec had installed in the council chamber months before. To Arlec's eyes there was something different about the Undine. He, it, seemed more solid, if that could be said about a creature made of water. The stunned silence of the Katar family heads was broken by Telem.

"Arlec, do you know what you have done?"

Arlec turned to Telem, angry at the tone of his voice. Instead of awe and gratitude, he heard something else. Didn't Telem see that the Undine would be their salvation against the Tarth?

"What have I done, other than come up with a way of saving us from the Tarth?"

"Fool, you never learned your history did you? You never listened to your father. If he had not been … murdered before his time you would have learned something of the history of your own family."

Jumping Water had grown to ten feet and was now no longer part of the fountain.

Telem had stood up as he spoke and pulled a pouch from his shirt. Quickly, he poured a circle of jade powder around himself. Jade meant qenar. Touching a hidden device the qenar laden jade flared into a wall of yellow fire.

The Undine laughed. The room began to fill with water. The other Katar ran for the doors, but there were now more Undine within the room. The doors were sealed. The sounds of hungry Undine filled the room. The rings on all of the Katar flared. They moved quickly, but were hindered by the water. Within the water the Undine were still faster. The Undine felt the movement of *ka* as the rings went to work. The Katar would be strengthened and faster, but not fast enough in water. The rings had no real effect on the Undine. They were not designed for Undine, but more humans.

"Stop. Stop. I command it. I command you to stop!"

"Do not worry, son, of the son, of the son, of many sons, of Karn. You will live."

"I command you to stop this. Do not kill them."

More laughter. Steam began to fill the room as the wall of fire around Telem continued to boil off water. The water was over four feet now. The steam was hot and made it hard to breathe.

"Why?" demanded Arlec.

"The man with the fire can tell you," laughed Jumping Water.

"You have doomed us, Arlec. The Undine were not truly enslaved by your family, only partially. The Karn family learned the truth of this much later. They were immune to the Undine and the Undine could not kill them, but they did not obey your family unless it served their purposes. The Karn control was strictly defensive charade by the Undine. Self-preservation. The Undine were banished, just as the Tarth were. Banished until you brought them back. They are from before all the races on Nakana. They are primordial. They feed off of all life that they can envelope. The Karn family used its strange power over the Undine to trick them into banishment. Using the same sphere that was used to banish the Tarth." Telem was pouring more of his jade dust onto the floor, futile as it seemed to be. The flames from his first wall were starting to sputter.

Jumping Water, standing tall within the water, the top five feet of his form towering above it, howled with remembered rage.

"Yes, Karn. Your family banished us. Your ancestor had to come with us as part of the activation of the sphere. We kept him alive for two hundred of your years. He was conscious that entire time."

Telem's fire held out for almost an hour. The rest of the Katar in the council room died during the first fifteen minutes. All but Arlec, whom the Undine kept alive. He was forced to watch as the Undine consumed the bodies. All the liquid was drained from the dead. Skin sacks of bones remained, bereft of water and *ka*.

Chapter 37

Alan awoke in pain. The rage was gone, but not the grief. He grieved for Tyna; he was Alan again. Pain. He opened his eyes and looked down. Down? He was sitting against something hard. His arms were restrained behind his back. It was unclear what the restraints were, but they hurt. His muscles protested their position and the pain told him they had been in their unnatural position too long. He focused his vision with difficulty. He was in a room. Sitting in a comfortable looking chair, looking at him intently was a man. Something familiar about that man.

"Death awakes," the man chuckled. Alan failed to see the humor. Maybe it was the headache and the feeling that he had not eaten in weeks.

"My name is Alan."

"Death by any other name … is still Death. You will always be Talanas."

The man knew his old name. He dipped into his memories. It had been so long. So many of them were memories he had tried to destroy over the centuries. Each time he killed he had lost some of them, but losing Tyna had awakened them all. Yes, it had been centuries. Longer.

"Nerman. The weather boy. I remember. Calling yourself a god now, aren't you? Mit, Mat, Mut?"

"Met," growled Nerman

"Ah yes. Met. God of Weather. Savior of Zethicia and keeper of its crops. Oh, wait. You abandoned them when the Tarth last attacked, didn't you. And now you are no doubt not helping with the latest Tarth attack."

"Zethicia is no more, Talanas. The Tarth have destroyed it completely. The Tarth and the Undine."

No more? So quickly? Undine. Yes, the Undine. They were from the forty eighth plane, or was it fiftieth: Darna. The water worlds. Once full of life, but the Undine had sucked them dry. They had not thought of the future, they had simply consumed all the *ka* of all the life on Darna. They had been destroying

Nakana when Karn had helped in banishing them back to their own world/ plane. It had taken years to push them back. Karn. Only a Karn could have let them back. It must have been that fool Arlec, the murdering bastard who had killed his own father. He must have let them through again.

"Call me Alan."

Met smiled, which made Alan slightly ill, and nodded.

"Alan. You are chained to a post which even with your full strength you could not break. Do not try and enter a rage and drain my *ka*. If you kill me, you die of starvation here. My life force will make that a long process, but you would die nonetheless."

Met knew nothing of how his rage worked. Well, realistically, neither did he, even after all these centuries. He knew he could not simply turn it on and off. Something always triggered it. He thought of Tyna and the rage and despair swirled. Met rose hastily and backed further away. The rage dissipated and left only the despair.

"We are far from the mountains. Far from the Web of the Gods, or whatever you might call the weakness between the planes that you have some sort of control over. You will not be able to move yourself from here, or call upon something." Met looked more hopeful than certain at this last statement. Alan smiled silently at him.

"What do you want of me Met?"

"We have similar goals. You have reason to hate the Tarth, again. You also don't want mankind destroyed."

Alan nodded, knowing the direction this was leading.

"I also have no love of the Katar and their gods." Alan emphasized the word their in such a way that it sounded like the Katar owned the gods. As if they were pets.

Met glowered and the sounds of thunder outside were audible.

"In fact the gods have no fondness of the Katar either, but they are necessary for now. We have three groups in common."

"Perhaps, but what could I do? I am but one simple man, you are gods," Alan chuckled, although it hurt.

Lightning struck outside as Met glared at him. The rain was now falling hard. It sounded as if the room was really just a small one room hut. Well lit though. No glow globes visible. Maybe the walls themselves.

"Enough, Talanas. You could have been a god too. Death, you could have been the God of Death. You spurned our offer."

"And you thought I died in the battle with the Tarth."

"You should have. After arming the Katar with those rings, you deserved to die. They have been a thorn in our side ever since. We know you regret it. You were the leader of the rebellion. Always leading one rebellion or another, aren't you? Not that thief that everyone thought was a catalyst. That Luck was so afraid of. No you and that bitch Kinel are the cause of all this."

Larrina! He remembered now. Larrina. Was she alright? She was going to warn Zethicia. Did she get caught up in the battle? He abruptly stood, summoning strength that he did not know he had. The muscles in his arms screamed and the pain almost sent him back to the floor. Met jumped back, a look of panic in his eyes.

"I told you what happens if I die."

Alan grinned at him viciously. Let him worry a bit. He was unable to summon his life draining rage on command. But, he felt the potential of it with the thought of Larrina in peril. She had loved him once and he could feel the memories of his own love for her. They were memories of love, not the same as the boiling surface of his emotions still alive for Tyna. Tyna was now, the memories fresh. The others were memories that were returning to life and with their resurrection came his concern for Larrina. He'd treated her badly, not just recently, but over the centuries. Had simply accepted her love that she gave unconditionally. He had been healed by her once, when he should have died.

Centuries. That still felt strange. Had he been alive that long, or were his memories of many lives simply blurred together. No, Larrina was a constant for many of those years. She was Kinel and lived a very long time and he knew that he was older, much older.

How could he have not remembered her before? There were so many things he had not remembered, for many, many years. From before this body. This body was not his own. It was becoming his own and the more it changed, the more he was remembering. It still had traces of Lerence, just as he still remembered being Lerence. Or dreams of being Lerence. Fading dreams.

"You have changed Talanas. I see it in your expression. You have become soft. You care too much. You want to live and you want those close to you to live also."

Met leaned closer, no longer afraid.

"You could banish them again, the Tarth."

"To Hell? It was wrong to have done that before. That plane is evil. It is death to the Tarth, simply slow death."

"Then kill them outright. Lead the Katar to victory. You did it once."

Had he? It sounded right, but he could not access the memory just now. It felt right. It felt as if he didn't want to remember. Too many memories was a return to insanity. He needed the amnesia. He stopped trying.

"Then I made a mistake. The Katar are as bad as the Tarth. Worse. They suck the life out of their own, while the Tarth attack mankind because we invaded their lands."

Met laughed.

"We? Well, you always cared more for your slaves than you did your own kind."

Own kind? He could not remember. Something was wrong with the statement, but his memories were blank and he was afraid to call them up. The insanity was bubbling close to the surface. With the insanity was power though. He could taste it. Trade a little of his sanity for freedom and power?

"I will not help the gods, nor the Katar. Even if I said I would, you would not believe me."

"Probably not."

Met rose and went to the doorway. The storm outside increased intensity, the wind howled with anger and the one room dwelling shook with a death palsy. Met turned back to Alan.

"I will not kill you outright, Talanas. I don't mean to be cruel in letting you simply rot here, but killing you outright might trigger that nasty self-preservation habit of yours. Pé himself thought you dead and yet here you are. No, best you starve to death slowly, no rage left for you to tap into, nothing living nearby for you to kill."

With that he opened the door and the storm absorbed him. A gust of wind slammed the door shut, leaving Alan alone within the fading storm.

Chapter 38

Larrina sat at the Argn council, not bothering to use her Kinel chameleon effect to hide her two toned skin. Several of the newer council women were openly hostile to men, making a point of ignoring the male advisory group. These were mainly Katar women who saw men—Katar or not—as untrustworthy and the cause of all the troubles Nakana was in. Sharalaca was one of these.

"I say we form a band of women who can fight and retreat to the desert. The Undine won't be able to get us there. I've traveled the Slar Mar desert, there are ways to survive there and even get water in ways that this Undine cannot utilize."

"So you would abandon all those who cannot fight and who are male? The children too?" asked Flana.

Sharalaca scowled. Larrina could see that she was smart enough to realize that agreeing to this would sound too extreme to most of the council.

"No. Of course not. The children would come too. But no men. This entire war is the cause of men, not women. No men and no gods. We don't worship anyone. The boys would be raised with proper values. This travesty won't happen again."

There was murmurs of agreement from many. Crissa was in agreement. She had lost her father and been forced to marry a traitor. Her father was the last man she loved. He always told his daughters that women were better rulers than men. She could see letting some men join, if they understood there place. But only a few. Others spoke out in rapid succession; Larrina couldn't remember all their names.

"We can't just abandon Argn to the Tarth and the Undine. The combined forces of the Katar and the gods should be enough to turn them back."

"Zethicia fell in a matter of days. You heard the reports. The Tarth take no prisoners. Total destruction. True death. The gods are powerless against their leader, Be Na Tarth, and his artifact. Larrina tells me that it's impossible to banish them as was done before. This Undine called Jumping Water can simply bring them back."

"Then we destroy the Undine."

"How? Even the Sea God has been unable to kill them. Our gods are simply weak parasites that can affect only us."

"Don't forget Hallam is with the Tarth now."

"I heard rumors the Yanín were also."

"If we save a core group of ourselves in the desert, at least mankind survives."

"What of the Kinel, Larrina? What can she do? Maybe she has some racial power we don't know about?"

They all turned to Larrina.

She smiled. It held neither warmth nor hope. They were concerned only about their own survival. Their own race. She was a tool to them.

"I have no skill that can save us."

"What of the extraordinary powers that Kinel were said to have? The Katar feared your race as they did no other."

Many of the Katar in the room, especially those from the five families, averted their gaze. Larra spoke for them.

"Katar are part Kinel. We destroyed the Kinel out of fear. Fear because they did not need rings—" she held up her left hand "—and anger that the Kinel felt the rings should be destroyed. Fear that the Kinel and mankind would learn to exist without the Katar, that was what drove us to destroy the Kinel. It was not any power they had. Yes, some Kinel can wield great power for short periods of time, but doing so ultimately kills them."

There was shocked silence from the rest of the room. Larrina broke it.

"Larra is partially right. Of course she knows only what she can glean from family histories and books old enough to mention the Kinel. Each Kinel is born with the ability to use *ka* directly. We need no talisman, nor qenar. The price is that the stronger the power, the harder it is to control. To learn control uses huge amounts of personal *ka*. The greatest among us died in their twenties, while the less spectacular of us live for many centuries. I am very old, which should tell you about my powers. They are weak and subtle."

"Centuries?"

"To live so long and stay so beautiful, that is a power."

"What of the thief? He's half Kinel."

"I heard he was born on the night of the five moons."

"Yes, Larrina, what of Tsom?" Lanna asked, interrupting the cacophony of the others all speaking at once. She remembered the young thief who had stolen the ring from Arlec.

"Tsom has great power and has indeed mastered it without dying, but I do not know how his power can save us." She went on to explain Tsom's hands and traveling.

The meeting went on for hours and Larrina listened with only half an ear. She had been in too many meetings over centuries to expect this one to be more efficient. They were afraid and would act partially out of fear. She had no solution for them. No talisman, or stronger artifact, that would solve all their problems. She wished Alanar were here with her. He would not have any solution to this, she was sure, but it would be nice to have his forceful presence near. It would give her comfort. A kindred spirit. They both were alone and had had only their friendship for each other for so long.

Would he be happy with Tyna? She hoped so. He could always flee with Tyna to another plane, if he remembered how. How long would his happiness last? It did not matter. She had never seen him truly happy. He deserved some short period of happiness.

* * *

Stop, hairless one. You are consuming more than my milk. I feel you draining my life energy. The big cat swatted Rosea to get her attention. The tap sent her flying across the shelter comprised of trees that had interwoven their branches at Hallam's prodding.

I'm sorry second mother. How do I stop?

I don't know, but you must. You are like She. *You drain us.*

I don't want to be like her. I will learn.

This is good. I will teach you things that She does not know.

More milk.

Rosea latched back onto the huge cat's teat.

You see the rivers, don't you hairless one.

Of course. Doesn't everyone?

No, I see them only in your mind. Your father saw the rivers and used them. I will teach you of them.

More milk, Rosea demanded.

I have no more. You drink more than a dui mar. For a hairless one you grow very fast. You must eat something else. I will bring you something.

The big cat disappeared for a time and returned with a struggling rabbit which it tossed in front of the baby girl.

You must kill what you eat.

The baby girl looked at the rabbit and at the big cat.

No more milk?

No.

Rosea crawled over to the wounded rabbit. It tried to run away but the big cat nudged it back to the baby. In desperation it bit Rosea, trying to get past. She jerked her hand back and screamed in surprise. The rabbit twitched and died. The grass under it turned black.

Rosea ate.

The big dui mar lay down next to the baby. Its eight foot body curled in a half moon around Rosea. It looked at the dead rabbit and the blacked grass, then raised its head and looked toward the compound where Hallam was. She purred.

Chapter 39

Oonie sat at the low wooden table, his lightly furry hands resting upon the wood worn smooth by centuries. He sat at the head of the round table. First among Equals. He was not their leader, but he was their guide. They could ignore him or override his decisions. It had never happened to a First, but it was allowed.

"You have heard Larrina speak. She is Kinel. Perhaps the last full blood. She throws in her lot with the humans, against the Tarth."

Silence from the twenty Hrýll. They waited.

Oonie would not be rushed. He sipped from his cup of hot tea. The others followed suit. Inlas/Tiar, standing behind Oonie, shook her head in frustration. She knew Hrýll customs, but still could not accept their calm when their entire race was at stake. Oonie reached back and patted her hand.

"We have suffered a great deal from mankind over the centuries." He paused, but the rest remained quiet. He sensed their agreement and anger, as much as Hrýll displayed anger. "Most of that suffering was at the hands of the Katar, but mankind as a whole were willing servants to the Katar mastery over the Hrýll." He sipped his tea. He was really buying time. The Equals knew the situation as well as he did, except for a few key points. He was waiting for confirmation on those points.

Salamn interrupted the silence.

"First, we know all this. Even for a Hrýll, you are studiously avoiding getting to the point."

The sudden surge of *ka* in the room saved him from replying. Tiar/Inlas jumped and made a small squeak as Tsom and Larrina appeared in the chamber. Not instantaneously, but as if rapidly pulled from a tear in a curtain. Tsom first with Larrina following on his right arm. Tsom sagged momentarily and then stood straight.

The Hrýll were startled, with a few holding talismans at the ready.

"Thank you for coming," said Oonie, with a slight smile.

Before either could answer there was a rap on the door, followed by the door opening. In stepped a Riconé. He towered above all in the room by a full head. Unlike most races in the north, the Riconé were pale skinned with pale hair. Not albino, but stark contrast to the dark skins of Tsom and Larrina and the dark skin and fur of the Hrýll. The Riconé glanced around the room and ignoring Oonie and the others turned to Larrina.

"Sar Larrina Sur Grena." The Riconé bowed deeply, his thin angular frame looking like it might snap. His narrow face resembling a human face made of wax that had sagged in the midday sun.

Larrina raised an eyebrow and stepped forward.

"No one has called me that in years. Many years. Do I know you?"

"Alas, no we have not met Sar Grena. My great-great-grandfather was Flarngth. You saved his life. I am Flarqgth Ron Toran."

"Flarn. Of course. I see the resemblance. Your great-great-grandfather? Has it been so long?" She smiled a smile that held sorrow and longing. Her eyes lost focus momentarily.

"I fear that Oonie has set us up Flarqgth. He must have known of our connection." Larrina looked to Oonie who remained impassive. He hadn't known of the connection, but he often found it useful to simply be silent rather than explain too much. Did Tsom still have some influence over events and people? Was he still inadvertently acting as a catalyst? Perhaps. Or perhaps it was simply that someone who lived as long as Larrina knew a great number of people.

"Sar Grena, I of course remain faithful to the bonds that my ancestor has put upon us."

"That was too long ago. You are not bound by the promises of those who no longer exist. I release you of any bonds you may think exist." She held out her hand, palm up and bent backward.

Flarqgth blinked. Then he bent and bared his teeth. Two fangs sprang forth and he plunged them into Larrina's wrist and just as quickly withdrew them. A small drop of blood on each fang was briefly visible.

"You are now bonded to me. Our bonds are even. We are both free," Flarqgth spoke in a ceremonial tone.

"We are both free." Larrina agreed.

"What just happened?" whispered Tsom to Oonie.

"The Riconé are controllers. In the past they drank the blood, and the ka, of their enemies without killing them. This bonded the victim to them and put them under their control. Larrina offered her blood to remove the bond that Flarqgth perceived existed due to something Larrina did for his great-great-grandfather. It is ceremonial only. She is not under his control," he assured Tsom seeing the look on his face.

Oonie chided himself for again forgetting that Tsom was not as old as he seemed and did not know much of the world. He might have the power of a master weaver Kinel, but he was still in many ways a young human. He regretted having to pull Tsom and Larrina into his plans, but it was time for the Hrýll to act to save themselves—before it was too late

"It is kind of you all to come." He did not wait for a reply, knowing none was coming. "Recently, the Hrýll have allied with the rebels against the Katar. We have cut off the supply of talismans to The Cities and supplied the rebels with as many military talismans as possible. Still, the rebels lost Qenaril and Argn after holding them briefly. The Tarth and Undine now control much of Qenaril and its crucial qenar, but the Katar are fighting well, if desperately. The Katar have recently approached us with a deal, hoping to get talismans to use against the Tarth and Undine. They are desperate now that the heads of the families have been killed by Arlec's foolishness."

Oonie nodded to Tsom.

"Yes, my young friend, your enemy is dead."

He couldn't tell if Tsom was relieved, or angry that he could not wreak revenge himself. Probably both. He paused to sip his tea. The Hrýll were impassive, Flarqgth, Larrina, and Tsom looked expectantly at him, waiting for the surprise. They knew something was on his mind. He set his tea down.

"We cannot wait for the rebels to try and retake Qenaril and negotiate with the Katar. Even if by miracle they managed to, it will be too late. The Tarth and Undine are already destroying The Cities." He looked to Larrina for confirmation. Tight lipped she nodded.

"We plan on offering the Katar an artifact, known as the Umei Saigo." Several of the Hrýll Equals looked startled, but said nothing.

"We have already let the Tarth know that the Katar have this device, and other artifacts, and are planning to hold out in Qenaril. This will force Be Na Tarth to attack himself, with his jade artifact that steals *ka* and protects those near him. He will use the Undine to transport himself there. I believe that the Umei Saigo, used near the qenar mines will be powerful enough to overcome Be Na Tarth and the Undine."

He hoped that no one would ask the right questions, but knew that was a foolish dream. Larrina spoke first.

"What does the device do that it can be effective against Be Na Tarth and his own artifact, which effectively neutralizes all *woven ka* – be it in the form of a talisman or directly woven?" She nodded toward Tsom, to emphasize the latter. "And what do you need from us?" She indicated the Riconé, Tsom, and herself.

Oonie hated to lie, even if it was by omission, but he could not tell them everything.

"The artifact will channel all the energy from the nearby qenar into every talisman and artifact within a large radius. It should overload all of them."

Larrina pursed her lips and was silent. It was Tsom who saw the next piece.

"You aren't going to tell the Katar that are you?" he asked.

"No."

"They will all be wearing their rings."

"Yes."

The room was silent as they absorbed the thought of the treachery they were proposing.

Oonie waited and then continued.

"You cannot warn the few Katar that are allied with Argn. It is too risky. If possible, persuade them to flee for other reasons, as many of The Cities are already doing. Larrina, you must make sure that the rebels do not ally with the Katar. This will ensure that the Katar accept our offer and follow our plan."

"It will affect even Argn?" Tiar asked.

"It will affect all of The Cities, even the rebel encampment to the north. The qenar mines are massive."

"Every talisman?"

"Yes, my wife, thousands of years of work destroyed," Oonie replied. "The end of civilization, but perhaps the saving of our race and the destruction of the Katar and gods."

"What of the Riconé, we are few and have no real power?"

"You have one power that is very important. One that is not just for ceremonial symbolism."

Oonie sipped his tea again, emptying the cup. He then tapped the cup with his spoon three times.

The door to the chamber opened and two Hrýll entered with a weakly struggling Tarth between them.

"This is See'ar, lover to Be Na Tarth. We have her drugged for now, but you must use your powers of old. Control her. She is our insurance that Be Na Tarth will be at the main battle. We will fill her mind with the appropriate thoughts once you have her under your control."

See'arr looked at the Riconé with fear and hatred. The Riconé had controlled and destroyed cousins to the Tarth millennia ago. She summoned her strength and shook off one of the Hrýll, her red skin glowing with the effort of fighting the drugs.

Flarqgth acted. His fangs sprang forth and he leapt on See'ar's back. She threw herself backwards, but it was too late. Flarqgth's fangs found her neck and penetrated the thick skin of the Tarth. The room felt the surge of *ka* and the flow from See'arr to the Riconé. He drank deeply of the blood and the *ka* until she stopped struggling.

Flarqgth stood, blood dripping from his mouth onto his chin and shirt. His eyes were unseeing and he bellowed a curdling cry of victory and satisfaction. Several of the Hrýll had talismans in their hands and Tsom had manifested his mind hands. Flarqgth 's body seemed to swell with energy and his color turned a light pink. Then Flarqgth blinked and looked down at the Tarth. His look turned to sadness.

"We are reverting to our old ways Unchya," he said, using Oonie's formal name.

"We are, my old friend, and we will all pay for it."

They discussed the plan in more detail. Time was of essence and Oonie felt that Larrina should be the courier, with Tsom's help, to bring the Umei Saigo to the Katar. Two weeks was the timetable they set. In that time those that would flee with the talismans had to be over one hundred marks from Qenaril.

Oonie gave her what looked like an oversized bracelet, with one side of the band very wide and the other narrow, with a hand grip molded into it. He warned her not to try using it and to emphasize to the Katar not to use it until the Tarth were in full attack and they could see Be Na Tarth.

"I cannot stress enough that you should not use this. The Katar should. You should deliver this to the Katar and then Tsom should take you to the refugees, far away. You will be needed as a leader for the refugees. Away from The Cities. Take as many talismans as you can with you. You need to be hundreds of marks away from Qenaril."

Larrina looked at him as if she were going to ask something more, but nodded, her eyes slightly narrowed and her lips pursed. Holding onto Tsom, they disappeared much as they had arrived; through an invisible tear in space.

After they left Tiar spoke.

"You're holding something back Oonie."

Oonie nodded. Tiar may not be Hrýll, but she had been masquerading as his wife for decades. She knew him better than Larrina or the others.

"Well?"

One of the other Hrýll of the Equals spoke, as the rest all bowed their heads in shame.

"All intelligent living things can be thought of as living talismans. Umei Saigo is a suicide device. In battle, or worse simply among civilians, it would destroy all those within a hundred feet or so, until all the qenar nearby was used up. Near the qenar mines…it's a doomsday device. Every living thing within the power of the device and the power of all that qenar will be burned out. It is limited only by the amount of qenar."

Chapter 40

Be Na Tarth did not need the map in front of him to plan his next attack. With the aid of the Undine and the gateway that Jumping Water provided they had been able to take hold of Old Arbeneth and from there all of Arbeneth. The fool Arlec had made it all so easy with his faith in the Karn family control over the Undine. In one fell swoop they eliminated the heads of the Katar families, with the exception of the Tanec family with the two females leading Argn. Arbeneth was the center of The Cities, with all port traffic under its control. The rest would be easy.

The destruction of the family heads had not destroyed the Katar. They were too well trained for that. His spies indicated that they were focusing on Qenaril as their stronghold, taking back most of the city. The source of qenar would keep their talismans and artifacts fueled, making it hard to break the city through blockades and direct attack. He was immune to their direct attack. He rubbed the jade spherical cage hanging from his neck appreciatively, the *ka* of hundreds of thousands radiating from it with raw power. The guilt of killing so many was fading as his goal became more attainable. Soon mankind would no longer plague Nakana. Immune yes, but he could not be everywhere. Each attack took time and the Katar had learned their lesson. They no longer depended on direct talisman and artifact weavings. The last probe into Qenaril had been disastrous, relatively speaking:

Jumping Water opened the gateway within Qeneril, upon a small stream flowing through a residential neighborhood. Tarth began to pour through, ten abreast, rushing to make room for those behind them. Suddenly, there was a flare in the sky, with the trail of fire pointing to their gateway. Lightning lashed out at the group, absorbed by Be Na Tarth's pendent. The lightning was followed by a rain of huge boulders from all sides. Many missed their mark, but sheer quantity ensured that some inflicted damage. The Tarth were many times stronger than a human and their skin as tough as armor, but that did not make them immune to boulders the size of wagons crashing down. The few Kami that came through on the first wave were all killed.

Jumping Water yelled, if the voice of an Undine could be said to yell.

"The water from the stream is drying up, the fire hurts even me. I must leave soon. Reluctantly, Be Na Tarth called his first retreat.

"We have to take Qenaril in the traditional manner," Be Na Tarth grudgingly admitted out loud as See'arr entered his tent room. He was using the elaborate manor that Arlec had constructed on Old Arbeneth as his headquarters. He had grudgingly acquiesced to the demands of the Undine that Arlec Karn be left in their care. He shuddered at the meaning of that. Better to die than live in perpetual torture by the Undine. Even *true death* was preferable to an eternity of torture. At least he had the rings of the fallen Katar leaders. He had crushed the rings, setting the *ka* of his ancestors free.

"I concur, Carnel," See'arr said, standing behind him rubbing his shoulders. "We must take Qenaril by standard military procedures, but we must take it. I have word that the Hrýll have created an artifact that will be dangerous if they have time to fuel it in the qenar mines. Remember their gateway? We must take Qenaril soon, or risk losing, when we are so close."

Only See'arr called Be Na Tarth by his given name. He twisted in his chair, the wood groaning with his force and weight. See'arr was in charge of the spy network, which included the animals that Hallam had under her control.

"What have you learned, my Mar'in?" The other Tarth in the room pretended not to hear the pet name for See'ar. If any of them had called her a puppy to her face, they would get themselves killed.

"The Hrýll, after all these millennia, are acting."

"The Hrýll? They're craftsmen, not fighters. What can they do, or give to the humans, that they have not already given up?"

Be Na Tarth waved his hand in a dismissive manner. The Hrýll were weak. They let themselves be servants of the Katar and man. They did not fight. They were a dying race already ten thousand years ago, simply refusing to acknowledge it.

See'arr shook her head and shook Be Na Tarth by the shoulders.

"No. They are a patient race. They are simply moving now. They are more devious than you might imagine …" She tensed, squeezing his shoulders so that it hurt.

"What is it Mar'in?"

"Nothing," her voice sounded strained. "My network indicates that the Hrýll have developed a way to weave without the use of *ka*. To manipulate qenar directly. What then, my love? Your pretty cage will be useless. It destroys ka, not qenar. It works because *ka* is the catalyst of every talisman, artifact, or even the weaves of the gods. Destroy the *ka* and the weave unravels, but what if there is no ka, but only qenar?"

The other Tarth in the room grunted with shock as the full impact of her statement sank in and penetrated their egos. They weren't stupid. Humans had numbers on their side and if they could weave qenar energy directly the Tarth lost the advantage.

"How long before they can effectively build weapons in Qenaril with this new method of the Hrýll?" Be Na Tarth's shoulders had sagged imperceptibly as See'arr spoke. It seemed impossible, everything needed ka, but the Hrýll were masters of talismans. If anyone could do it....

"In two weeks the Hrýll will deliver the means for direct weaving of qenar to the forces in Qenaril."

"Can we intercept them?"

"It's doubtful. We don't have any spies within Farnlaran. We've persuaded a few humans to join our side, but no Hrýll. We never really considered the Hrýll a threat. However, it's our understanding that the way the knowledge is trained, or passed on, to others is through an artifact that is one of a kind. The Hrýll haven't been able to replicate it, yet. If we attack Qenaril as soon as we hear that it's delivered, we can destroy it, the city, and the backbone of the Katar all at the same time."

"Two weeks. We will succeed. The future of our race depends on it." Be Na Tarth gripped the edge of the table to keep his hands steady. The wood groaned. When he let go the impressions of his hand were visible in the wood.

* * *

"You lose very little *ka* when you pull us through. You have mastered yet another aspect of you power." Larrina put her hand on Tsom's upper arm, still flesh, knowing he hated to be touched on his wooden lower arms.

"Yes, I've noticed that I don't feel very tired afterwards and it is a physical exhaustion, not an inner tiring."

They strode the path from Larrina's tent to the council tent of the rebel encampment. There was a nervous energy in the air as the encampment prepared to move to Argn and join forces in mutual defense against the Tarth.

"The council will wonder why you have changed your mind about fleeing." Larrina nodded.

"I do not lie well," she said.

"Nor betray your friends. I'm better at that."

She touched his cheek briefly.

"Lanos was dead already and you felt Alanar had betrayed you. I do not blame you, nor does he."

"He doesn't even remember who he is," muttered Tsom.

Larrina felt a pang of jealousy and sorrow. It's probably best that he never remember. Perhaps he was not fully Alanar now, but really more human. He had fathered a child after all. A child. What would his child grow up to be? If the Tarth won their war, what would anyone grow up to be? Nomads fleeing the Tarth in hopes of survival? Was the potential loss of some lives and all of the Katar worth the survival of mankind? Mankind had not treated her own race all that well, why did she care?

Because Kinel and human must ultimately be from the same stock. We can interbreed. We must all be human, or some other name. People. Katar were half breed Kinel, yet they were the ones who had ultimately destroyed the Kinel. Was it the human part of the Katar or the Kinel part of the Katar that had committed genocide?

Entering the council tent she noticed that the others were already assembled. News of their traveling to and from Farnalarn, via Tsom's mind hands, had spread faster than even his powers to transport. Good. She started right in.

"After conferring with the Hrýll I find that I must align with Sharalaca, or at least with her basic concept of fleeing. If some of you want to form a group led only by women, so be it, but all of those who can flee should. We should flee in multiple directions, without telling the others where we will go to protect them. We should scatter across Nakana, instead of concentrating all of mankind in one set of easily destroyed cities. But, we must flee The Cities."

The cries of protest from the rebel camp, and many of the Katar and leaders from Argn, rose quickly in answer to her speech. They would fight and not run, they protested; as she knew they would.

"Those of you that would stay and fight, you must consider that your skills are best utilized with the refugees. Nakana is vast, with perils that are poorly understood. We have inhabited only one small part of this vast world and no doubt dangers other than the Tarth exist. Put aside your desire for revenge and flee. I recommend that all the talismans of Argn and those cities remaining unconquered be given to the refugees. It will help them start anew. Talismans are of little use against the Tarth, only brute force and the small aid that the gods give will help."

Chaos reigned for the better part of an hour, but her basic plan was finally adopted. They knew something was up, but since she remained in the dark, so did they. They would break into thousands of smaller refugee groups. One, led by Sharalaca was all women and young children – boys and girls. The others would probably split along family, or trade, or city of origin. The intent was to keep the bands to no more than a hundred or two hundred people.

"Which band will you lead Larrina?" Crissa asked, hinting that she join the band of women.

"I am the last of my kind. I will stay and fight, to delay the Tarth while you flee."

She felt a sharp pressure on her arm and glanced at Tsom across the room. He was wide eyed and for the first time in two years she saw fear there.

"You just told us how important it was for leaders and fighters to go with the refugees," Crissa said with a scowl. Others murmured their assent, although many were silent.

"I have been a revolutionary for more years than anyone here has been alive. I am no good as a refugee. I have no other purpose in life. I propose that Tsom lead one of your bands. His ability to move from place to place and his mind hands will prove invaluable. Through him a small band's survival is ensured. In fact he can keep several bands in contact with each other."

The pain in her arm made her jump and she motioned for Tsom to stop. He glared at her, but the grip on her arm disappeared. She was going to have to persuade him later.

The rest of the day was spent in small groups hashing out the beginnings of plans. Larrina was surprised at how easy it had been, ultimately, to persuade most of the council to her plan. She'd expected days of debate, not hours. The news of Zethicia and the fall of Arbeneth had their effect. The confirmation that the Yanín had truly joined forces and were on the march to The Cities provided the last impetus needed.

Tsom found her that night as she sat on the edge of her bed contemplating her meager possessions. Two piles: One meager mound of herbs, teas, and medicinal supplies sat intimidated by the dangerous grouping of weapons in the second pile. Her short sword, with its jewel encrusted handle and dark black blade, a short bow that looked stocky enough for a Tarth to string, a small quiver of arrows, a small throwing knife, a small stack of tiny sharpened spikes in the shape of a cross. With the weapons was the misshapen bracelet. The Umei Saigo.

Tsom walked over to her and she watched him, feeling tired. *Tsom needs to get away from conflict and recover more.* He frowned over her weapons and reached out to examine the spikes. She grabbed his hand without thinking and then smiled a dry bitter smile.

"I was going to warn you that those were poisonous."

Tsom smiled back a reflection of her own, tapping his two wooden prosthetics together and raising an eyebrow.

"Poison. I didn't think you used poison."

She shivered inside. No, she didn't. It was an abomination, using her herbs to kill.

"Times change," she whispered.

"You know I won't leave you," Tsom said.

He sat next to her and manifested his mind hands, taking her left hand in his two invisible hands. She could feel them as if they were flesh, except there was no warmth, and knew he could feel her hand this way. She did not chide him. He was so good at it now that it used only an imperceptible amount of his *ka*.

"You will because I need you to. You can help them."

"No more than you. You're a healer." He gestured with his wooden left hand at the pile on the bed, which was disconcerting as she could feel his other left hand still holding hers.

"You know that my healing arts are not well suited for mass groups."

Tsom blushed slightly.

"Your skills extend to more traditional means, such as your teas, or binding wounds."

Larrina laughed at his blush and kissed him on the cheek. He really was young. It was so hard to remember in his aged body. But, his body would recover some more, now that he was not wasting *ka*. Let him discover that on his own, when he was far away from her.

"Tsom, I do love you, but cannot love you again. Now that I know Alanar is alive, again, I cannot."

"Despite the fact that he loves another and does not really remember you," Tsom did not phrase it as a question. She nodded nonetheless.

"I will help the Hrýll and mankind by joining the forces in Qenaril. I can perhaps increase the odds."

She reached over and hefted the short sword. Tsom winced. That sword had injured his mind hand, not so long ago. Permanently injured it.

"You cannot use that, it is a talisman of some sort."

"I don't think so. Do you feel any *ka*? Don't touch it, but feel for the *ka* that you sense with any talisman, or artifact. There is none."

Tsom nodded in agreement.

"You never told me where it came from." He said.

"You never asked. Alanar gave this to me. He said he made it just for me and no other should ever use it."

"I thought only Hrýll could bind a weaving to an object."

"So it is said. Why would only one race have such an ability? We all have ka, all races. The Tarth are strong with *ka* and can crudely weave it in the manner of Kinel, but when they do successfully weave it's as if they forget how they have done it. It's like the Tarth themselves, a thing of brute force. As a race they almost never manipulated ka, but Be Na Tarth must have some ability in this regard. With an unlimited power source to experiment with he must have found a way to return from where you banished him."

"Oonie speculated along the same lines," Tsom said.

Larrina set the sword aside.

"Yet, this has no *ka*. No weave is present."

She took Tsom's face between her hands.

"Tsom, you're half human. You must preserve your race. You must help them survive. I have considered your power and what I know of how the Hrýll shape talismans."

Larrina stood and went to the glow globe hanging from her ceiling. Taking it down she placed it in Tsom's wooden hands.

"You remember how you picked the lock of your cell, when you escaped from Arlec?"

It was not a pleasant memory, she knew. Arlec had cost Tsom his second hand. Punishing him for daring to wear a Katar ring and for being a thief. He'd manifested his mind hands and felt inside the lock. Felt how the mechanism worked and manipulated the mechanism from within. His fingers pushing only where he wanted and passing through where needed. He nodded.

"Manifest your hands and feel the *ka* of this glow globe. Pick it apart like a lock."

He raised an eyebrow, but she could feel him manifest his hands. His brow furrowed and then his eyes closed. She watched him intently. Would it work? Could he injure himself somehow? His eyes flew open and he had a huge boyish grin on his face. She hadn't seen that on his face since the first week she had met him, when he was falling in love with Shara.

"I understand how it was done," he exclaimed.

A cup from her table floated over, carried by his mind hand. It settled in Larrina's lap. She felt his mind hands on the cup and in her lap. He closed his eyes and concentrated. She felt a small surge of ka, nothing to worry about, flow from Tsom to the cup. He then took the small piece of qenar laden jade out of the glow globe and dropped it in the cup. It leapt to life giving off a brilliant light, far stronger than the glow globe.

"I noticed a mistake in the glow globe. At least I thought it was a mistake. I tried correcting it and it worked." His grin grew, then suddenly vanished.

"I *might* be able to teach others, human, how I did that. Guide them with my hands."

She nodded, a sad smile on her face.

"Hrýll aren't the only ones who can weave *ka* to objects."

She nodded again, letting him think it through.

"But qenar is the key. The fuel. We are fleeing and destroying the source of power."

"No. Qenaril is the main source of qenar. The only known reliable source, but even the Hrýll know that occasionally jade is found elsewhere, in minute quantities. Never much and the Katar always confiscated any that they heard about, but there must be other sources. You, with your mind hands, could find more. You could lead one or more of the bands of refugees there. If we win against the Tarth, you can return. If we fail, you must hide and fight on for your race, the human half. Survive and teach."

"But, you ..." he pleaded, holding her face in his mind hands. Tears were streaming down his face. She knew he'd made the right decision.

"I'm tired. I will fight this last battle."

"You sound as if you know you will die."

"No, but win or lose, I lose. I go to full battle. I go as a Kinel warrior, not as a healer. I will be using the powers of our race in battle. I have never done that. The toll will be enormous and I do not have the reserves of *ka* that you had when you learned."

Tsom held her and cried and she held him back. She didn't let herself cry.

She was a warrior now, she told herself. The last of Kinel. In two weeks she would fight her last fight. She hoped her blaze of fire would be as spectacular as the legends of her race spoke of. She had lived long enough; the only person longer lived was safe with his new bride.

Chapter 41

Garron ignored the knock on his door. He was half asleep, slumped over his desk, exhausted from the past week of constant fighting. He had left orders to not be disturbed. The knock was insistent, insinuating itself through the fog of semi-consciousness.

"Enter," he croaked and reached for a glass of water. He glanced at the pitcher on the table. Too small for an Undine to travel through, but everyone looked at water differently. Anything larger than a barrel was suspect. Even barrels were now two chambered, to ensure that the size of any single water source was small.

Ekron, of the Maycon family entered. He looked paler than usual and didn't even bother to salute. What were the Katar coming to, thought Garron. I'm now the leader of all the remaining Katar and I don't even get a salute.

"What is it?"

"There is a woman to see you sir."

"I have no time to see anyone. Why do you think I would want to see her."

"She is Kinel. Larrina Shur Grena, leader of the rebels –"

"Former leader of the rebels, Garron," Larrina strode in. "I'm sorry, your two guards will recover soon," she glanced back at the doorway. Ekron blanched even more and exited.

Instinctively Garron activated his ring.

"Turn off that abomination, or I'll cut your hand off before you can blink."

He did blink and briefly considered ignoring her threat. He was Katar. Head of the Katar now. No one gave Katar orders. But, she was Kinel. He hadn't believed the stories that there was a Kinel left alive and leading the rebels, but here stood a beautiful, slightly past her prime woman, with the two toned skin mask of a Kinel. The Kinel were rumored to be able to weave *ka* without binding it to a talisman. To directly manipulate *ka*. With his ring activated he should be able to withstand almost any human attack. His movements were

228

sped up. His senses were enhanced. His strength increased. He would heal faster. He hesitated too long.

He never really saw her move. There was a blur and then there was the tip of a short sword made of some blackened metal against his throat.

"I said turn the ring off," she said through clenched teeth. The tip of the blade she held pierced his skin and pain shot into his neck and radiated like a noose of fire. His ring flared as it tried to heal him and to his astonishment the pain did not go away. With an effort he forced his right hand to his left and pulled the ring off.

Larrina was sitting down across from him, her sword sheathed, before he could draw a breath. The breath he drew was painful and the hot coal of fire on his throat still burned.

"What have you done?" He croaked.

"You stole some of my *ka* with your cursed ring, you will now have a reminder not to do that again."

There was a pounding on the door accompanied by shouts asking if he was ok. The other Katar in the building must have felt his ring drawing power, their rings flaring in response. He yelled for them to leave.

The fire on his throat was not getting better.

"If you kill me you will not get far. There are over a hundred Katar in this building."

He rubbed his throat gently. Only a small drop of blood smeared his finger. Was it poisoned? His ring would protect him against poison, even the strongest poison. Maybe he should put it back on. He rubbed his left hand ring finger.

Larrina smiled and he felt fear.

"If I am forced to kill you, you will die the true death. But, you won't die from that neck wound. The pain will never go away, but you'll live. The ring protected you that much, as I knew it would."

True death. Garron swallowed, and then regretted the action as his throat burned hotter.

"What do you want, Larrina, former leader of the rebels?"

"I am here to offer my services, just mine and a small band of followers. The rebels and all those that can fight in Argn have fled, leaving you to battle the Tarth alone. They felt that their best chance of survival was in scattering, trusting neither you, nor the Tarth."

By the Sea of Souls, that was bad news. He had been hoping for an alliance with Argn and the rebels. The Yanín were a month away, destroying any small community in their path. The gods were close to no help. They bolstered the defenses and helped with intelligence on the Tarth movements, but the high priests as much as admitted that the gods were so weak and frightened that if the tide turned against them, they would abandon mankind. The Katar could not keep sacrificing innocent people to fuel the gods hunger for *ka* and no one willingly prayed to them anymore. Their source of power had dried up.

"That is … unfortunate. How many in your band that will stay and fight?"

"Just over one hundred. Ten of those are Katar."

One hundred? That was nothing. Qenaril had sixty thousand trained soldiers and another two hundred thousand badly trained, but able bodied men and women who would fight. One hundred. He slumped in his chair, the fire in his throat momentarily forgotten.

"In the next week the Tarth will attack in full force. You have to hold them for at least that long. In one week the Hrýll will deliver an artifact--they call it the Umei Saigo--that could turn the tide."

"Not another banishment? The last so called banishment lasted only a year."

"No, this will destroy the artifact that Be Na Tarth wields."

Garron leaned back in his chair, rubbing his throat. The pain was distracting. He glanced at his ring, then shifted his gaze to Larrina. He wished command had not been thrust upon him. He hadn't done all that well at the academy. Worse, the wars they trained for were conventional wars. No artifacts. No Undine allowing for the transport of groups to any spot with water. The rules were not those he had learned and he was not adapting well.

"Will that be enough? The Tarth now have strong allies."

"The Undine. Released, by your former leader, Arlec," she reminded him. "If the Undine are near Be Na Tarth when the Umei Saigo is used, I have reason to believe that it will destroy the Undine also."

"Alright, tell me what we must do to use this Umei Saigo."

Chapter 42

Tsom kept himself from wallowing in his lake of grief by staying busy. He examined as many talismans as he could get his hands on. Floaters, lenses, fire-starters, heaters, ship propulsion units, water purification, weapons, healing. So many talismans were used in everyday life. How did they survive before them? Where would they find qenar to fuel these and any that they could manufacture in the future? He memorized the weave of all of them. Some were complex, hard to imitate, some were so easy that he was sure anyone could make one if they knew how. So much to learn and so little time. Could he really memorize them long term? He tried writing down notes on the weave, but it was impossible. Like trying to tell a master painter how to create with words. He tried sketching, but the weaves were not something you saw with your eyes.

Hundreds of marks from Qenaril. That had taken them almost a week on horseback and wagon. They didn't have enough floaters to go faster and even with his ability to pull himself through folds in space he could only take one or two others with him. With supplies and so many people they had to travel slowly.

Of all things, the group that he was part of voted him their leader. Had Larrina planted that seed? He was no leader. He was a thief. He was young and inexperienced. Young, he mused, rubbing his rough face. Young in years only. His body and his soul were old. Old enough to lead a group of over five hundred, one of the largest of the diaspora? He hoped their faith in him was not misplaced.

Lassa, a young girl whose father had died in battle not long ago, pulled on his hand. He gazed down at the dark haired fawn whose huge eyes searched his face for comfort and when she smiled at him he was forced to return the smile.

"What is it, Lassa?"

"Will you be my daddy, Tsom?"

What could he say to this? He didn't even know Lassa's mother. A minor noble who was under Flana's wing. Flana, who remembered him from the day he had stolen Arlec's Katar ring, over two years ago. Flana and a group of her followers had joined his party that was headed southwest to the ocean and from there they hoped to make it to a chain of islands that she knew of. Flana had been the one to first nominate him as leader.

"I cannot be your father, Lassa. I'm not married to your mother."

Lassa pouted and looked ready to cry.

"You could marry her."

"But I love another. You would not want me to marry someone I don't love, would you?"

She didn't seem so sure.

"You love Flana, don't you?"

He laughed. Flana. A noble.

"No, no. Larrina. I love Larrina."

"Does she love you?"

Tsom tried to hide his discomfort.

"She did."

"How do you know if you love someone, Tsom?"

"You love someone when you will do anything for them, even when it hurts you. You do what is best for them, no matter what the cost."

"Love is hard," Lassa said. She held on to Tsom's hand.

"Will you be my friend, Tsom? Friends don't have to work so hard, do they?"

"I'll be your friend, Lassa. Now you go find your mommy and make sure you are ready. We reach the ocean tomorrow, you know."

"I know." She pulled on his hand and he leaned down. She gave him a fast kiss on the cheek and then solemnly walked away.

Tsom returned to his tent and sat on his cot, unmoving, for an hour. He sighed and manifested his mind hands. He concentrated on his recollection of Alanar. The cold flame of his *ka*. He stretched his hands out. To the north and the mountains where he had found him before. Nothing. He brushed tens of thousands of beings, but didn't concentrate on any of them. The touch was as if he were running his hand through sand. Each grain a being. A soul. Without knowing where Alanar was, even with his distinct presence, would he be able to feel him? He stretched. Thinner and further. The strain was building. Nakana was huge. Larger than he had conceived. He was beyond the equator. Still he stretched and sifted the grains. Time lost meaning. He could feel the strain on his *ka*. This was not something he had perfected. This was going to cost him, but one does what one does for love. He sifted and stretched.

There.

Pain.

Cold fire. Death.

He punched a hole and pulled himself through.

"Tsom, my young thief. You look like dui mar crap. I don't suppose you brought any Hrýll brandy with you?"

Chapter 43

Tsom looked at Alanar, sitting tied up to a chair and a post running from roof to floor. They were in a small room, probably a one room structure from the sounds of the storm outside. No window. The light came from a single dim glow globe on the ceiling. Tsom reached with his mind hands and fixed the weave. The globe brightened.

Alanar looked at Tsom and raised an eyebrow. He was different from when Tsom had last seen him. Closer to what he remembered from when they had been allies over a year ago. He was no longer 'Alan,' but back to Alanar. Maybe even leaner and more muscular at the same time. His eyes were bright. Yellow and glowing. Not the glow that one read about in bad books. The glow was visible to those familiar with *ka*. They glowed with power.

"Your skills have increased. Where's Larrina?" Alanar said, glancing at the glow globe.

"Why do you care? You're in love with another."

Tsom felt a grip of death upon his soul and saw the look of rage on Alanar's face. His eyes burned cold fire.

"She is dead. Tyna has been murdered. I will avenge her death."

Tsom staggered at the rage and the very real pain it caused.

"Not if you kill me. You're tied up. How will you avenge anyone."

There was a madness in Alanar's eyes. Had his words penetrated that rage? Or was the madness more than simple rage? The Alanar from before had seemed saner than this man.

Suddenly the strain upon his *ka* was released and the fires subsided. Alanar sagged.

"You didn't answer my question on Larrina. She lives, I think. I believe we are linked, just as you and she are linked. She has loved you and healed you."

"How can you know that?"

"You're not as damaged as you were when you betrayed me. Your *ka* has actually recovered a bit of its strength. Only Larrina has that healing skill and she can only heal in one way."

"So that is how she knew you were alive … again."

Alanar didn't answer.

"I didn't betray you. You betrayed us. Mankind. You brought all the Tarth to Nakana from Hell. They hate mankind and were going to destroy us all. Lanos told me what you'd done."

"Lanos was a fool. He believed what only his prejudices led him to believe. The Tarth, or most of them, would have honored the agreement I'd crafted. This war could have been avoided. Tyna could have lived. Now I must destroy them all."

The madness was back. Tsom kept his mind hands manifested and punched a hole between space. If Alanar went into another rage, he might be able to pull himself out in time.

"Larrina said something similar. She believed in you. I'm not sure I do."

"Free me and bring me to her."

"I can't do that. She is in Qenaril, working with the Katar to defeat Be Na Tarth and his allies."

"She would never work with the Katar."

"To save mankind and the other races, she would."

Alanar was silent. After a time he nodded.

"What's her plan?"

"It is actually the Hrýll's plan. They have an artifact that they think will counter Be Na Tarth's. The call it the Umei Saigo."

"Umei Saigo …." Alanar closed his eyes and muttered the name several times.

"Doom," he said. "It means doom."

"The artifact?"

"The name. It is ancient Hrýll. Not modern usage. What is this device supposed to do?" He leaned forward the rope obviously cutting deeply into his arms and wrists, yet he seemed to feel no pain, or ignored it well.

"It overloads all talismans in the area, drawing upon the Qenar to do so."

The chair creaked and then shattered. Alanar fell forward, blood dripping from his wrists and his arms near the elbows. Tsom started to pull himself through the folds in space.

"No. Wait. Larrina must not be there when it is used. She'll die."

Tsom hesitated. He did not feel the icy rage around his soul. Alanar sounded in control, not in a rage. He sounded more in a panic.

"What do you mean?"

"We're all talismans. Anything that shapes *ka* is a talisman. All intelligent beings shape *ka*. She'll overload. She'll die. Everyone nearby will die. This is something I would have done. It's evil, or amoral. I would have never dreamed that the Hrýll would do such a thing. It is against their nature. When. When is this to be used."

"Today or tomorrow. When the Tarth attack in full force."

"Take me with you. Take me to Qenaril."

Tsom hesitated only a moment. It took that long to find the right fold in space and punch through.

Into the maelstrom.

Tsom easily located Larrina. They were linked, as Alanar had known. He couldn't sense what was happening around her through that link.

She stood alone.

Against a dozen Tarth.

Her Kinel two-toned skin was plainly visible, no chameleon effect. She wore no armor. Simple tight leather on both chest and legs. The short jeweled sword was up to its hilt in the chest of the nearest Tarth. The shocked look on his face turned to terror as he felt the sword do more than kill him. As his last act of defiance he grabbed the sword and held on as he fell back, the last of his *ka* destroyed.

She held on to the hilt and kicked the nearest Tarth in the nose as the dying Tarth pulled her down. The bones entered the brain, killing him instantly.

Tsom had pulled them through approximately one hundred feet from Larrina. He could not react as a Tarth charged them. It took Tsom a few seconds to recover whenever he pulled through space. A snarl behind him and to his astonishment Alanar was between him and the Tarth. The Tarth grappled with Alanar, or tried to. Alanar leveraged the huge being's momentum and used it against him. The Tarth was up on his feet almost as soon as he hit the ground, like a ball striking the ground and rebounding with the same force as used on it.

"Get to Larrina and pull her through to safety. The Umei Saigo could go off at any moment."

"I can only pull one with me at a time, especially after having done this twice already today."

"Do it. We both love her. Save her."

The last was said through clenched teeth as Alanar pulled an arrow out from his side, just below the ribs. Taking the blood drenched arrow he plunged it into the eye of the Tarth that had bounced back from his last attack. Alanar's eyes were glowing with the madness that Tsom knew was dangerous. He ran toward Larrina.

Larrina had dispatched two more Tarth with that sword that cut Tarth skin and drained their *ka*. He could feel that some of the *ka* was flowing to Larrina. Her eyes were taking on the insane look he'd seen in Alanar. He made sure she could see him, but did nothing to distract her as there were still several Tarth surrounding her cautiously looking for an opening. A fourth focused on Tsom.

He manifested his mind hands and reached into the chest of the one shifting his attention, and sword, toward Tsom. Squeezing tight he knew the Tarth was dead, but the Tarth refused to acknowledge it right away and slammed into Tsom with eyes already glazed. Tsom felt ribs break and felt a stab of pain in his thigh.

No time to do this right.

He reached with his left mind hand and grasped Larrina, hoping she would realize what he was doing. If she used that sword of hers on his mind hand, as she had over a year ago, then they were both dead. With his right mind hand he reached for the encampment, over a week's journey away, and punched a hole through space.

He heard Larrina scream in rage, but she didn't use the sword on him. He pulled them through as he felt the twin spears of destruction: Alanar's killing rage from one side and the Umei Saigo from the other.

Larrina started to scream at him as the wave of energy hit them both, knocking them both unconscious.

Tsom awoke to two faces. Larrina on the left, Flana on the right.

"He'll live." Larrina laid a hand on Flana's shoulder. "He'll even keep the leg. Any more limbs lost and he'd be more wood than flesh."

He tried to take a breath to speak, but the pain caused him cough which caused more pain.

"I didn't focus much on the ribs. Those hurt, but will heal on their own," Larrina said, addressing him this time.

"The Umei Saigo? Qenaril?"

Flana and Larrina exchanged looks. Flana spoke.

"The Cities are gone. Everyone is dead. It is a dead area. There is no re-building. No one would go back, even if they could."

"All the Tarth and Undine?"

"Some were not in the area, but only a few. Be Na Tarth is dead as is the Undine Jumping Water. The Yanín were untouched. They weren't close enough."

"Alanar?" Tsom looked at Larrina. How was she taking his death?

"He … lives."

"How?" By the Sea, was he indestructible? Millions dead and Alanar was alive?

"No one was there to see. The Hrýll went to the epicenter with artifacts that protected them and returned with his body. At first they thought he was dead, but Oonie felt the *ka* still flowing through him. He gave him drugs to stay unconscious. Something about his mind being stuck in a killing rage."

"You are going to him?" He didn't need to ask. She nodded slightly.

Tsom stared at her and then looked at Flana. She had a tight lipped expression and her features were held in a frozen mask.

The image of Lassa, the little girl holding his hand, tipped the balance.

"I will stay with the colony," he said.

Flana seemed to relax and Tsom thought he saw a smile, but he couldn't be sure.

Colony. That was what all the diaspora were now. Colonies. Mankind was devastated, but not completely destroyed. Only a few Tarth remained. And Yanín. And probably some of the gods—although both Oonie and Larrina said that many had been near The Cities when the Umei Saigo was triggered. Tsom no longer thought of them as all powerful. Perhaps some of the gods had died. Hopefully, Hallam had been helping the Tarth and perished also.

He would always love Larrina, but he no longer needed her as much as before and others needed him. They needed him not for destruction, but for building and teaching. For fashioning talismans. They would need to find a source of qenar. Then they could rebuild. Without Katar and without gods.

Larrina smiled, looking genuinely pleased.

"Have lots of children, Tsom. It will benefit the colony."

She laughed again at his blush and at Flana's smile. She turned and lifted the tent flap to exit. Tsom noticed the sword strapped to her back. She was no longer the healer he knew.

* * *

Oonie walked in behind her. She knew it was him. His *ka* felt different from a human's. She didn't sense *ka* from a great distance, but this close she could feel his life force; that and the slight smell of cinnamon that all Hrýll had. They used many of the same spices she did. She didn't turn. There was no need. She kept her eyes on Alanar, his face twitching even in the drug induced coma.

"He's insane. If we let him awaken he will destroy either himself, or us. Or both." Oonie said quietly.

He laid a hand on her shoulder. She felt another presence. Massive *ka*. It must be his wife, Tiar. No longer a goddess she still reeked of power. Larrina didn't trust her, not fully. Tiar wanted Alanar dead. Larrina knew there was some ancient animosity between them. Still, she didn't turn. Tiara would do nothing without implicit agreement from Oonie.

"He is wracked with guilt. Too many of his past sins are remembered," Larrina brushed a non-existent hair from Alanar's forehead.

"I'm a healer and I can do nothing. Not when it's his mind. Not when he is unconscious. Yet, if we let him awaken …." The vision of the recent carnage was fresh in both of their minds. "My abilities are too … subtle."

Larrina didn't bother hiding her tears. She didn't need to be strong in front of Oonie and the damn woman/goddess could drown in the Sea for all she cared.

Oonie leaned forward and lay two bands of steel inlaid with jade on Alanar's chest. They had identical patterns and were large enough to wear on one's head. Garlands of cold metal and qenar laden jade. Larrina recoiled from them, turning to look at Oonie.

"Those are mind links." The revulsion in her voice was mixed with curiosity. All her years and she had never actually seen them before. Only the Katar had used them, or had someone use them for Katar purposes. No Katar would risk their life using one. Two linked minds was not an accurate description. One was the master band and the other the slave. The technique was generally referred to as 'mind rape.' The victim often didn't live. Occasionally, the person using the master band did not survive either.

Oonie nodded, but didn't say anything. Larrina glanced at Tiar. Was this her idea? No, she looked as surprised as Larrina felt.

"I thought all of these were in the hands of the Katar or destroyed?" Larriana leaned forward, almost touching the bands.

"We gave up many of our talismans and artifacts, but not all. Even some of our old and evil ones remain."

She wondered what other items of power the Hrýll had hidden. She touched the bands and withdrew her hand immediately. Just touching them she felt the minds of all in the room. The hatred from Tiar. The hatred of a jilted lover, she realized with shock. That was the past sin of Alanar's? Oonie was a pool of calm, but she sensed its depth and hidden emotions within the pool. Alanar was chaos. A dangerous swirl of incomprehensible chaos. The expressions on Tiar and Oonie showed that they had felt it also.

"You are one with the 'gift' for using these," Oonie said. "Many healers are. Their empathy is stronger than they often realize. We leave now."

"You and Tiar?"

"The Hrýll. We are leaving to where mankind will not find us for a very long time."

Larrina did not probe. Oonie had said as much as he wanted. She glanced at Tiar and Tiar smiled at her. She looked content.

"If I fail?" She touched the bands again.

"I will mourn both of you." He placed a hand on her shoulder again and squeezed lightly.

"The drugs will keep him in a semi-coma until the antidote is administered, or until you wake him with those." He let go and held out his hand to Tiar, who took it. They both turned and did not look back.

The slave band was easily identified by touch. Touching the master band gave her the ability to feel his mind with, or without the slave band. The outer layer of his mind. It was a thunderstorm of self-loathing, anger, hatred, and sorrow. It threatened to engulf her. She wept and pounded his chest without knowing what she was doing. Gathering herself she pushed away the storm as if closing a door against a fierce wind.

With the storm raging outside the mental door she placed the band over her head. The chaos roared and pushed against her door, but the mental image of a door held. She breathed as she noticed that she hadn't for some time.

Alanar moaned and writhed in the bed. A nearby bird went silent. Dead.

Larrina leaned over Alanar and kissed him gently on the lips. She then placed the slave band over his head.

The door exploded and she was swept away and merged with Alanar.

They became one.

His/her memories crashed over them, one destructive wave after another.

S/he was standing in a field of dead, holding her/his wife in her/his arms. The field was strange, only a single moon overhead and it was cold. This was not Nakana. The dead were his doing. Had s/he killed her/his own wife? Or was it revenge?

S/he was on a huge horse with a herd of thousands, tens of thousands behind her/him. The enemy was ahead. No, wait it was a village. Women and children ran screaming from the small houses. The herd never slowed down, their hooves struck deliberately and s/he laughed swinging her/his huge sword overhead. A young man ran out with a pitchfork, s/he charged and swung the sword and ...

The Tarth lay dead. Hundreds of them. Thousands were executed, s/he held up a ring with white and black diamonds and the ka of the Tarth flowed to the ring. The rings. Thousands of them. No chance of rebirth. The Tarth souls were not completely destroyed yet not set free to the Sea of Souls for rebirth. Enslaved. S/he laughed and ordered the next execution.

So it continued. Lifetimes. Many lifetimes. Death. Destruction. Revenge. No end. Evil. I/he is evil. Let me die. Leave me. I deserve to die.

She recoiled and lashed out at the evil. Yes, yes you must die.

No. No, you are not only this. There is more. She pushed against the winds of death. Up ahead. There, there was a calm spot.

A hundred. Maybe more, maybe less. We flee the destruction of our world. I have found an opening between the planes. We can start a new life. Rebuild our civilization.

Yes, agreed Pé. A second chance. We will do better this time.

Yes, said Inlas, putting her arm around his/her waist. You feel the rivers between the planes. You guide us and we will follow.

Here. Here is a world that is warm. Green. There are other races here, but we can live in harmony with them.

Harmony.

S/he was content. Almost happy. Until the others grew jealous of the other races. The Hrýll. The Srýll. The Riconé. The Enclar. The Zintu. The Tarth. The Hlorenka. The Kinel. The parade of races flashed in front of his/her eyes. Races that once roamed Nakana. Once. Before mankind.

The races taught them about ka. Soon, some realized that they had abilities they could use, much as the Kinel. Their abilities were weak. They helped the rest prosper. Their population grew, but those with abilities did not reproduce.

The price of power was infertility. The more the population grew, the stronger the core group became. Eventually they were worshipped as gods by many, but not all. They fought amongst themselves for worshipers. More worshippers meant more power.

Power.

The gods led their armies against the other races. Their worshippers wanted their own power. The races were a threat. The races fought back. Mankind and their gods underestimated the power of millennia practice using ka. The Kinel fought back.

'Help us, Talanas. Save us. We are doomed.'

S/he cried with anger. 'We fled our past sins and now look what you have wrought.'

'You are the greatest general that ever lived. You have powers we do not understand. You can save us. Do not desert us in out our of need.'

S/he refused at first. The races broke the armies of man and their gods. Broke them and punished mankind. They killed his/her lover. Killed her and violated her.

Rage.

Blackness.

Power.

S/he led the newly formed armies in a swath of death. No prisoners. No mercy. Death. Women/children/old/crippled/men they all died. All fueled his rage, his power, his insanity

Peace returned. History repeated itself. Over and over. Races died. Mankind prospered. S/he fled. Hid. Disappeared.

Time scarred his/her mind. Alcohol dimmed her/his memories. S/he took lovers and grieved when they grew old and died. Then s/he found Carml. A princess Kinel. A beautiful woman who would live perhaps as long as s/he. S/he knew happiness.

The Tarth had been driven back, but were too proud to be beaten. They plotted. They waited. An artifact was created. Many artifacts. They drew upon the ka of their own race. They sacrificed thousands for the chance to win the war. They persuaded the Kinel to join them. The Kinel who had not mixed with mankind, but roamed Nakana as they had in the past. The Kinel who could wield great power, at great cost.

History repeated itself.

Carml loved mankind. She could not stay apart from the war. S/he begged her to let mankind and the races settle this once and for all. 'Leave them be. Stay with me and be happy,' s/he replied to the pleading.

'Join us, Talanas, and become a god,' begged the gods. 'Leave the mortal woman behind she is one of them. Kinel. Kill her and join us.'

S/he refused to fight, but stayed with Carml. To protect her.

And failed.

The Kinel and the Tarth killed her.

History repeated.

Death. S/he was at the center of death. The gods were more powerful, but the races were more united. The Kinel and the Tarth were willing to die to the last person. The Hrýll created talismans that rivaled the power of the gods. Talismans and artifacts that boosted their power with the discovery of qenar. Even with the leadership and the power of Talanas they were losing. The Tarth massed for one final death blow to the armies of man.

'We are doomed,' cried the gods and man.

'I have been doomed for a long time,' replied Talanas.

S/he understood how the weapons of the Tarth were made. It was evil. The ka of the living was completely consumed. More evil than the gods, who stole but a little. The Kinel knew how to make these, but used only themselves as weapons.

Vengeance is mine, said Talanas, as yet another lover died.

And they died. The prisoners died. The innocent died. Talanas felt the Rivers within the Web of the Gods. The Rivers between the planes and he captured them within the sphere. The sphere mirrored the Web of the Gods. All it needed was ka. The living provided the ka. So many living.

S/he rode into the encampment under a flag of truce. They let him in. S/he was Talanas the general out of legend. The Tarth knew no fear. He was but one, even a single god was no match in the middle of their encampment. They would listen. Then they would send him back with demands for total surrender.

Amongst the Tarth he revealed the sphere. Choosing the River that led to the most terrible of planes he opened the sphere. It expanded, thirstily finding the ka of the living and pulling them into the River. They fought back, wading against the current, reaching for him. S/he laughed and killed those nearby. The Tarth were no more. Not dead, but banished to another plane. One Talanas called Hell.

S/he disappeared. Five thousand of his elite troops remained. Five thousand of the Kinel/man half-breeds armed with the rings s/he had made them. Let them guard mankind. Let them save them next time. S/he wanted nothing more to do with war.

History.

Repeats.

S/he was near the epicenter when the Umei Saigo went off. Cold rage was already coursing through his/her veins s/he was at the center of his/her own destructive sphere. Draining off the ka those around, s/he was already full of power. The Tarth were massive storehouses of ka. S/he had killed over twenty. The wave of Qenar energy hit. S/he laughed at the sense of ultimate power flooding into him/her. S/he was used to absorbing power. S/he drank and moved forward.

Still the energy flowed into her/him. It was becoming uncomfortable. The rage swallowed much of the energy, channeling it to more death. But, they were already dead. Overfilled with qenar they were all dead. S/he tried to channel the energy. Use it up, but still it came. S/he looked up. The storm clouds were bright with continuous lightning. Met. Nerman as s/he remembered him, was there. He too was struggling to channel all the energy away. He was failing. More lightning. The smell of ozone made breathing hard. The buildings were all aflame. S/he did not hear the scream so much as feel it. Nerman was no more. At least one god was dead.

Still the power came on. S/he would suffer the same fate at Nerman if s/he did not find a way out. So much power. S/he looked to the north. The mountains. The Web of the Gods. Ron D'Olanth. One of the rivers between planes was near. S/he could sense it with his/her enhanced power. The rivers were his/hers. Come. Come to me.

The river changed course. So much power. S/he could not move anymore, but the river came to him/her. As s/he felt that s/he could hold no more, the river flowed over him/her and s/he was no longer here. S/he was within the river and on another plane while still here on Nakana. S/he felt the power of the qenar, but could now channel it to the river itself. It flowed to the other plane. It took whatever was thrown at it. S/he did not know where the river led. Perhaps those on the other side would all be dead. More dead on his/her soul.

On his/her knees s/he fell as the river washed over him/her and the qenar was finally all gone. The Cities were no more. Tidal waves and lightning had destroyed all of it, which hardly mattered as they were all dead.

Larrina found herself. She was no longer part of the s/he and somehow separated from him. They were Alanar and Larrina. She had to pull out, or become insane herself. So much death. So many innocents destroyed. She pushed the memories of death aside. She knew what she had to do. If Alanar was to retain sanity he had to never again become Talanas. Never again wield such power. She felt a small piece of him agree. 'Kill me Larrina.' A small sane voice begged. 'I am evil and will destroy again. Kill me.'

She embraced his mind. Enveloped it. Loved it. Made love to him, inside his head, as they had centuries ago when she was young. It was the only way she knew how to heal. They made love and she wiped his mind. No suppression, she wiped it clean. He did not struggle as they were enveloped within each other. She swallowed his memories and made them no more.

They made love and he gave himself to her and she took. There could be no sifting, no discrimination. All must go. All went. In a sense she was killing him and she wept.

She wept for the loss of her love, the loss of being a healer. She was now a destroyer, just as Alanar was.

Larrina and her husband Balcom rode the last wagon. There were one hundred wagons, each with a family. They were well east of Zethicia, or the remains of that city state. At first the leaders of the group were against letting two strangers join, but Larrina demonstrated her healing powers on one of the children and they welcomed them in.

"What does your husband do?"

"He was injured during the war and suffers amnesia, but his skill as a brew master was unparalleled. I am sure that his skill will return."

They were sympathetic to his wounds and the ability to brew alcohol at the colony they would establish was welcome.

Larrina sighed as Balcom slid his arm around her and drew her close. He sneezed. He had been fighting a cold for the past week. This was yet another sign that her 'healing' had done more than wipe his memory. It had made him mortal. Maybe it was the body of Lerence he had taken over that had been the catalyst, or maybe without the knowledge of his power he was mortal. She rubbed her stomach, which was starting to show. That was another sign that Balcom was simply a man now. She had thought she was too old for childbearing, but she welcomed this new life. The Kinel were not totally extinct with this baby. Perhaps one of the diaspora of refugees would form a city that would know peace. Her child would know nothing of the Katar, nor the gods.

Balcom sneezed again and she laughed with contentment. He looked at her crossly.

"You find my cold amusing?"

She laughed and kissed him.

"I find your love comforting."

He squeezed her and rubbed her bulging belly.

Epilogue

"Kill me," begged Arlec.

The words sounded strange within the water. His skin was shriveled and painful. His eyes hurt. He had tried to kill himself, but there were no sharp instruments in the room. He could not drown, that much was clear. Would he live to a full Katar age before dying? He looked at his ring and tried to pull it off, but it seemed to have become part of his finger.

"We cannot. You are Karn. The Undine cannot kill the Karn. It is part of our ancient pact." The shadowy water within water form was hard for his pain-filled eyes to focus on.

"Yet you torture me and keep me alive against my will."

Laughter, under water, was multiple short ripples that irritated his raw skin. "That is not against the pact."

"Where is Jumping Water? Perhaps I can persuade him."

"He is no more."

"Then why keep me?"

"It amuses us. There are so few of you humans left. You are perhaps the last of the Karn. We keep you out of nostalgia." More ripples. More pain.

Arlec screamed, but under water it served only to cause a few more ripples.

* * *

She is angry little one. Be careful. The big cat got up to leave. You can come with me. I am leaving. We are leaving.

She will find you and be even more angry. Rosea stood. A young girl, almost a woman. She stretched like her adopted mother, the big cat. Her slim muscles rippled.

Perhaps. We understand her power now, because of you. She will not be able to control us all. This will make her cautious in controlling any of us.

Or she will kill you all.

Perhaps. Freedom has its price.

I will stay. I want to know her plans for me. To understand them. I am safer here than fleeing her.

To her we are all tools. If you no longer serve a purpose, then you may be discarded. The big cat was already loping away from the valley. Her voice was becoming faint. Distinct, but faint.

Perhaps, Rosea laughed.

* * *

Glarin'th wiped his dripping mouth with the back of a furry yellow hand, streaking it with blood. Talan'th had fought well. It did him honor to be eaten by the entire clan. He should have waited another year or two before challenging me.

Slloom'pth, one of his females waddled up to him. She would give birth soon.

"We are trapped on this world Glarn'th. We must not kill each other so frequently, or we will die off."

Glarin'th backhanded her, keeping his claws retracted. She rolled with the slap and bared her teeth. She knew that she was his favorite, so she did not strike back. Also, being so close to birth she was mellowed. She would not endanger the unborn with a fight.

She was right. He hated to admit it, a female with wisdom. It was why she was his favorite. Slloom'pth had given him sage advice in the past. She was a bit too soft with the offspring, protecting them far longer than most women, but she saw the consequences of actions.

"Would you have me let a challenge go with no response? Soon everyone would challenge me."

"We must teach the others to challenge in such a way that death is not the end result. Perhaps forming a group of power sharing so that others have a vested interest in your retaining power." She steeled herself for another blow and he thought about it, but there was no need to strike her. No one else was watching.

"There is some value in what you say," he growled. "We must grow strong before we conquer this new world. The Tarth were worthy opponents. If they are vanquished as the human we captured told us, then there is more to these humans than meets the teeth."

"We might have found out more if you had not killed her so fast."

"Who knew that they were so fragile? Yet, they vanquished the Tarth. Next time I will hold off eating our captive long enough to learn more."

"There is plenty of other food on this world, we need not hunt humans." She placated him with a scratch on the back with her claws distended slightly.

His stomach growled in response.

"Maybe we can breed them as we did the Kami."

246

"That way we can study them." She scratched him some more. "It is important to know ones prey."

Glossary

Arbeneth – One of the six city states known as The Cities. The main port city, with an island in the center of the river it controls both riverbanks and the sea.

Arcoth – Ancient Hrýll word for Death. One of the many names for Alanar.

Argn – One of The Cities, the training center for female Katar and the only city where women were considered full equals to men.

Ague – God of Seas

Alam – As in Festival of Alam. Alam is simply one of the seasons in Northern Nakana, which is a permanent sub tropical area due to the tilt of the planet's axis. The southern portion of the planet is much colder.

Alanar – Pseudonym for Arcoth, Inlas, Alan, Lerence and other names.

Arlec – Katar guard, member of the Karn family

Argn – Northwest city, partially agricultural, of the five cities it gives the most equal rights to women. Known for its colors and meaning behind every color scheme.

Atem's luck – An expression of being fooled into thinking something is good when it is not. Atem is a person from legend whose good luck always turned into something bad.

Bal'alam – leader of the smaller band of Tarth. Lighter pink skin and shorter than most Tarth, but enormously strong.

Barnus – Head of the guard/army of Zethicia

Beena – Young rebel woman who befriends Crissa.

Be Na Tarth – Literally King of Tarth. An honorific name/title. Carnel is Be Na Tarth's given name. See'arr calls him Carn.

Barin – Husband of Kaylee. A craftsman.

Cappa – A cadet or young untrained person.

Carnel – Be Na Tarth's given name. See'arr calls him Carn.

248

Cities, The – The Cities were six cities so close to each other that most people referred to them as a single unit. Arbeneth the southern most was the main port city spanning both sides of the Darnen river as it spilled into the Nýlyr sea. Just North, on the Western shore, was Slurne. Across from it lay Vranin. East of Vranin lay Qenaril, so named because of its proximity to the Qenar mines to the North. West of Slurne lay both Bronin and Argn, the agricultural cities. Generally, the six cities were referred to as The Cities. The total population of The Cities is nearly 20 million, accounting for over 80% of the human population on Nakana.

Crooked Tail – A male death cat (cub in this book) who is the "brother" to Rosea and was raised with her.

Darnen river – Major river of Arbeneth

Darna – forty eighth plane. Home to the Undine.

De Nas – God of War

Djarn – Lord Priest of Nu Arr, God of Luck

Devon – Head of the Karn clan

Dui Mar – Death cat. Extremely intelligent, they are long lived and breed rarely.

Farnlaran – The largest city of the Hrýll. While large, still under 100,000.

Flana – Young noblewoman who has a relationship with Arlec. Her father is Pentar Showa. The Showa family controls most of the shipping industry and the docks.

Flarqgth Ron Toran – Riconé. Grandson of Flarngth, whom Larrina once saved.

Garron – Of the Trias clan, one of the minor clans affiliated with the Karn clan. Later marries Crissa.

Governor Courie – Governor of the Zethicia region, including the main city. A lifelong appointment, but not hereditary.

Hallam, Lady – Goddess of nature.

Hrýll and Srýll – Two of the old races: They were humanoid, but covered in a fine light fur, or hair. Not heavy, or shaggy, but still enough to protect the skin somewhat. Most had brownish hair, but there was a variety of colors was analogous to hair color of humans.

Inlas – Goddess of illusions

Juas – Goddess of Justice (and Vengeance).

Jern – Head of the Tanec family

Jumping Water – One of the Undine that Arlec summoned. Gue Ta in the language of the Tarth.

Kami – The companion race to the daemons. Short fur, more dog like than the Hrýll, with very human faces. A dog's face had been compressed by a frying pan. Sharp pointed teeth were visible. Their sweat has a vaguely horse-like smell.

Karn family – One of the five families forming the Katar. Arlec and Shara are Karn.

Katar – Katar are human with traces of Kinel blood. They have ruled mankind for ten thousand years, with most of their power and abuse taking place in the past five thousand.

Katar ring – a ring with five small white diamonds set in a pentagram, with a small black diamond in the center. The *ka* from one Tarth was used/captured in each of the white diamonds, with the black diamond serving as the control mechanism.

Katar Families, by family head and city they rule:
- Jern [Argn - Tanec Family: Crissa and Mia daughters],
- Devon later Arlec [Arbeneth - Karn Family],
- Telem [Qenaril and Vranin – Sho family (second most powerful of the families)],
- Wara [Bronin – Terrel family]
- Jahone [Slurne - Katir family]

Kaylee – wife of Barin – human – member of the resistance.

Kinel – An old race that was long lived when they did not abuse their use of *ka*. While they were not one of the "old ones" they were one of the earliest races to arrive in Nakana, according to their own legends. They were hunted to extinction by the Katar.

Kula, or Kulakoonstru – Yanín leader.

Lani – Larrina's stallion. She named it after Lanos.

Larra and Piea – older sisters of Arlec

Larrina – Last of the Kinel. Old ally of Alanar, perhaps one time lover. Age unknown. Larrina Shur Grena.

Maite dogs – Daemon-Tarth-war dogs. Size of horses.

Mark – a mark is a unit of distance. Based on a theoretical horse running a full speed, each mark is a minute of local time (100 seconds). One mark = 6600 feet (a little over a mile). No horse known has ever sustained this speed, yet it is rumored that when the measurement was created it was from a real horse.

Marsan – Lord Priest of Ague.

Met – god of weather

Mount Raisnor – tallest of a huge mountain range. Called Silinare by the Yanín.

Muglanth Plains – vast plains near Zethicia. Very fertile.

Nakana – The world, or planet, that most of the story takes place in. Also the plane of existence.

250

Nart – a mildly intoxicating leaf, rolled and smoked. The rolled version also called a nart.

Nar Tarth – female daemon. An honorific address.

Ne Na – cult that does not believe that the gods are gods.

Nerman – name Alanar uses for Met, god of weather.

Nu Arr – God of Luck

Oonie – 'Unchya' translated to common tongue as 'First of the Tea Family'

Pentar Showa – Father to Flana. Head of the Showa family which controls Arbeneth's shipping industry: both the ships and the docks.

Pé – "soul" god. Guardian of the rivers of life and death.

Piea and Larra – Arlec's two older living sisters.

Ptroni – a black metal, extremely rare. It reacts with ka, draining it. When killed by a ptroni weapon, the victim is thought to be *true deathed*," or never to be reincarnated.

Qenar – generally found in jade, qcnar is an inanimate form of *ka*. It can fuel many talismans, but cannot be used to create a talisman, which requires *ka*. It is the fuel of 'technology' on Nakana and only one source is known, in the city state of Qenaril.

Qenaril – the city that controls the qenar mines.

Riconé – one of the old races – banished the daemons with the Kinel.

Rosea – Tyna and Alan's baby girl.

Saman – another human population center. Smaller than Zethicia.

Sar – honorific used for both male and female. Acknowledges high birth.

See'arr – Female Tarth who is an alchemist for want of a better term. Lover to Be Na Tarth, who calls her Mar'in.

Shara – younger sister of Arlec, deceased. Lover of Tsom.

Sheelem – leech that is known for secreting a narcotic into its victims while living off of their blood for years, slowly killing them.

Shenar – "judge"

Sintar – Unit of currency

Slurne – one of the major cities

Srýll – one of the old races, almost extinct. Can interbreed with the Hryll.

Synr – one eyed Kami under Bal'alam's command, who led the kidnapping of Tyna.

Talanas – another of the names for Alanar. An ancient name.

Tanec – family – Katar of Argn

Tarin – Elite portion of the Zethician army/guard. A cavalry unit of only 100 that was famous in both Zethicia and The Cities. Also the name of the town where they came from, on the edge of the Muglanth plains, near the forest and the mountains.

Tarth – Hrýll name for the old daemons.

Tarth River – river of Argn, flows into the Darnen

Tiar – Oonie's wife. A Hrýll. Possibly Inlas in disguise.

Triansriat – A semi religious sect that does not pay homage to the known gods, but worships the purity of music. Comprised primarily of women this sect originated in Argn. The women were highly educated and sympathetic to the Na Ne sect.

Triste – New Lord Priest of Ague.

Tsom – When not using his chameleon effect his description is: Gold eyes both the iris and pupil. His skin dark, except for parts of his face. The dark skin covered his neck, all of his jaw, but narrowed to a point at the top of his forehead. His hair was white blond.

Umei Saigo – a doomsday device.

Undine – A water sprite, daemon, or similar elemental being. The Undine are not from Nakana, but in the past were summoned to Nakana by the Katar, the Karn clan.

Valence – family name of Lerence and Tyna. An old ranching family near Tarin. Well respected in the area. The matriarch is Sera. The dead father is Cram.

Venicia – mother to Be Na Tarth. Oldest of the Tarth. Former queen of the Tarth. Died at the hand of Be Na Tarth as she defended Alanar.

Vranin – one of the five cities.

Web of the Gods – the translated name for the giant mountain range cutting across the northern continent. (Ron D'Olanth).

Yanín – warrior race. Reduced to mercenaries for centuries. Their joints are all double jointed and they have a partial exoskeleton which acts as an armor. Their one weakness is a tendency to drink too much and to reproduce three of them must mate together—which is a rare occurance, but their population is stable at a small number. Like the Tarth and the Hrýll, they cannot interbreed with humans.

Yarm – Dead mentor of Tsom's

Zethicia – large geographically, sparse population (relative to The Cities), mostly agricultural. One of the several other major human population centers. Linked by gates and roads. On main continent.

Zintu – the dominant race on the plane referred to as "Hell." Humanoid, also covered in fur as the Kami, but the fur is a bright yellow and thick. They have a doubled rib cage, one inside the other and two hearts. They are strictly meat eaters. They form clans and fight ritual battles. The winners often ate the losers. They know no fear and fight to the death. They are extremely prolific and the females give multiple births, often every year. They use a naming convention where *'th* indicates a male and *'pth* indicates a female.

.

www.ingramcontent.com/pod-product-compliance
Lightning Source LLC
Chambersburg PA
CBHW060314260626
47160CB00007B/2600